The Liverpool Rose

Katie Flynn has lived for many years in the North-west. A compulsive writer, she started with short stories and articles and many of her early stories were broadcast on Radio Mersey. She decided to write her Liverpool series after hearing the reminiscences of family members about life in the city in the early years of the century. She also writes as Judith Saxton.

Also by Katie Flynn

A Liverpool Lass
The Girl from Penny Lane
Liverpool Taffy
The Mersey Girls
Strawberry Fields
Rainbow's End
Rose of Tralee
No Silver Spoon
Polly's Angel
The Girl From Seaforth Sands

The Liverpool Rose

KATIE FLYNN

ARROW

Published by Arrow Books in 2001

1 3 5 7 9 10 8 6 4 2

Copyright © Katie Flynn 2001

Katie Flynn has asserted her right under the Copyright, Designs and
Patents Act, 1988 to be identified as the author of this work

First published in the United Kingdom in 2001 by William Heinemann

Arrow Books Limited
20 Vauxhall Bridge Road, London, SW1V 2SA

Random House Australia (Pty) Limited
20 Alfred Street, Milsons Point, Sydney,
New South Wales 2061, Australia

Random House New Zealand Limited
18 Poland Road, Glenfield
Auckland 10, New Zealand

Random House (Pty) Limited
Endulini, 5a Jubilee Road, Parktown 2193, South Africa

The Random House Group Limited Reg. No. 954009

www.randomhouse.co.uk

A CIP catalogue record for this book
is available from the British Library

Papers used by Random House are natural, recyclable products made
from wood grown in sustainable forests. The manufacturing processes
conform to the environmental regulations of the country of origin

ISBN 0 09 942926 8

Typeset by SX Composing DTP, Rayleigh, Essex
Printed and bound in Germany by
Elsnerdruck, Berlin

For Jim and Eileen Greenwood, who introduced me to the delights of the canal and tried not to laugh when I steered us into the bank!

Acknowledgements

I am greatly indebted to the staff at the Ellesmere Port Boat Museum who provided me with a great many books dealing with the Leeds and Liverpool Canal, showed me round their excellent collection of canal boats and explained how everything worked. It is a truly fascinating museum. Anyone with a bit of time to spare and an interest in both the present day canal boats and those which travelled the canals in the past cannot do better than pay a visit.

I am also indebted to Deb and Graham McCleod who lent me an out-of-print book on the canal, and to Jim and Eileen Greenwood, who pointed me in the right direction for finding out some of the more obscure details I needed, and as usual, my thanks go to the Liverpool Local History library and to the Wrexham branch library for their never-failing help.

Chapter One

JUNE 1923

'Lizzie! Lizzie Devlin! Our mam says you're to go indoors at once or she'll scalp the ears off your perishin' head! She says she told you afore breakfast that she's gorra load o' messages for you, only you slipped out on the quiet when she weren't lookin', and now, when she needs stuff, it ain't there!'

Lizzie, about to throw her lucky piece of slate into the last-but-one hopscotch square, glared at the speaker, a pale, discontented-looking boy with spectacles perpetually askew on his puddingy, spot-speckled face. Of all the cousins, she told herself, wondering whether she could pretend deafness just until her slate had reached its mark, she disliked Herbie the most. He was a tale-clat, a cheat and a bully – but he was also nearly fourteen, two whole years older than she, and a great deal larger and stronger. It would not do to ignore him, she supposed crossly. But that did not mean to say she had to scurry to do his bidding. She turned to her friend Sally, throwing her bit of slate at the same time, seeing with some satisfaction that her friend's had slithered sideways and missed its mark; with a bit of luck she might yet win the game! 'Oh . . . I'll just finish this game, Herbie,' Lizzie said with pretended non-chalance, beginning to hop forward, her bare toes stirring up the dust every time she landed. 'It won't take but a minute, and me aunt won't mind . . . besides, why couldn't you go?'

1

She glanced at her cousin's face as she spoke, turning neatly to pick up her slate and hop back again, and saw from the way his eyes slid about that he had probably been told to run the messages but had passed the job on to her. As usual. Aunt Annie was not a bad kind of woman. She had taken Lizzie in when her parents had died, after all, though she had four boys of her own to bring up. That had been five years ago, mind you, and since then both Henry and Ned had got work and were no longer a charge on their parents, though Herbie and Denis were still at home. And it's only natural, Lizzie mused to herself, making her way back to number nine Cranberry Court, that Aunt Annie expects more help from a girl than she would from a boy: boys is pretty useless when all's said and done.

The house in the court was a back-to-back, like all the others, which meant that the only means of entry was through the front door, so Lizzie skipped up the three filthy steps which her aunt was always meaning to scrub and whiten, pushed open the rickety wooden door and turned left into the kitchen. Aunt Annie was sitting in a creaking basketwork chair with a saucepan on her lap, rather inexpertly hacking a carrot into sections and dropping them into the pan. There were obvious signs that she had already butchered a large turnip and some potatoes – and also an onion, to judge from her streaming eyes – before she began on the carrot. Blind scouse, Lizzie told herself, mentally licking her lips. Aunt Annie, perhaps because she enjoyed her food, was a first-rate cook and could make even a blind scouse enjoyable.

Her aunt looked up and grinned, displaying a number of gaps between her large teeth as her niece entered the room. 'Lizzie, love, I'm meking blind

2

scouse for us suppers, but I thought if you could run down to the Scottie, you'd mebbe manage to get hold of a bone for stock and some bacon ends to cheer up the scouse a bit, like.' She plunged her hand into her apron pocket and held out a damp and grimy paw with some coppers nestling on the palm. 'I'm near on out of spuds, so get me tuppence worth, and if you manage to get some bones, better pick up some veggies for the stock pot – onions is nice, and I could do with a few more carrots, and peas are good at this time of year.'

'If I get bacon bits, it won't be blind scouse no more,' Lizzie observed, taking the money from her aunt's hand and pushing it into her skirt pocket. 'The cheapest stuff is at the market so I'll go there for the veggies, but I'll shop around for bones and bacon bits, see what's going cheap. And if I can't get bones, you'll not want the extra veggies for the stock, will you?'

'You've gorra head on your shoulders, chuck,' Aunt Annie wheezed, smiling broadly. 'That's why I'd rather you did me messages, 'cos it'd take me a month of Sundays to get Herbie to understand that there ain't no stock without bones. But you'll get bones, queen. You're like meself,' she gave another wheezy laugh, 'all charm and beauty, the sort no feller can resist. You'll charm some nice marrer bones out of some butcher, I don't doubt it for a moment.' She put the saucepan down on the floor, heaved herself to her feet and gave Lizzie's cheek an encouraging pat, handing her the large canvas bag which she always used for bringing home a quantity of vegetables. 'Off you go now, queen, and don't be too long or you'll get no scouse till tomorrer breakfast.'

Lizzie, grinning, let herself out of the house,

3

skipped down the dirty steps and stood for a moment, contemplating the game of hopscotch which her friends were doggedly playing, despite her absence. Sally glanced up. 'Where's you going, Lizzie? Shall I come along wi' you?'

'No, you stay here and finish the game,' Lizzie said grandly. She glanced around the court with its blackened walls and high, narrow houses, so tall that the sunshine never penetrated the place. At the end where the houses finished were the lavatories, and beside them the one water tap which served all twelve houses in the court. Above the lavatories reared a blackened brick wall, all of twenty foot high, which did its own share of preventing the sunshine from ever making an appearance in the court. But by tipping her head right back, Lizzie could see the hazy blue of the sky and guessed that it must be a nice sunny day. So though under other circumstances she would have enjoyed Sally's company, she thought that today she would be better off by herself. Aunt Annie had given her no extra money to buy buns or a toffee apple for running the messages and Sally, who was an only child and whose father worked on the docks, would not have dreamed of going a message without some reward. Lizzie knew her aunt was not mean and would have given her the odd ha'penny had she been able to do so, and had no desire for Sally to spread the news around that Mrs Grey was a miser, who wouldn't even part with a ha'penny for messages.

'Why don't you stop and finish the game, queen?' Sally asked plaintively. She would probably have enjoyed getting out of the court for a bit, but clearly did not like to do so once her offer had been rejected. 'Surely your aunt can't want her messages that quick?'

Lizzie hesitated, but only for a moment. It was not as though hopscotch was a game in which you won anything or even gained any particular kudos; if it had been ollies or cherry pobs she would have had difficulty in tearing herself away, especially had she been on a winning streak, but she could play hopscotch any old day and besides, if she did not get a move on, the scouse would not have time to become impregnated with the delicious taste of bacon – if she got the bacon bits, that was. So she looked around her and saw a small urchin, filthier than any of the others, hanging around looking wistfully towards the hopscotch squares. Lizzie indicated the child. 'She'll take over for me, Sal,' she said grandly, then turned and addressed the younger girl. 'You're dyin' for a game, ain't you, queen?'

The small girl said that she was and Sally sighed and waved a hand to Lizzie, who hurried out of the court and into the sunshine of Burlington Street with a clear conscience. At least she had not spoiled Sally's game, she thought, turning right towards the Scottie. As she had guessed from that glimpse of the sky overhead, it was a lovely sunny day and she trotted happily along the pavement, eyeing the shops as she passed them. When she reached Lime Kiln Lane she turned right again and presently emerged on to the main road, opposite Paddy's Market, deciding she would try Staunton's first, since it was the nearest butcher's shop. Before reaching the butcher's, however, she glanced into a nearby shop window, not to examine the goods on display but to check her appearance. Looking critically at her reflection, she pulled a face at her skimpy grey cotton dress – it had once been blue but had lost its colour and gained its greyness from rare and unenthusiastic washings –

and at her bare and dirty feet. However there was nothing she could do about either dress or feet so she turned her attention to her hair and face. Earlier that day, she had pulled back her thick, fair locks and plaited them into a pigtail, securing the end with a frayed and elderly boot lace. Now, she untied the boot lace and let her hair fall free. Then she licked the hem of her skirt, wiped it briskly round her face and, having checked as well as she could that she was reasonably clean, she abandoned her reflection and walked along to Staunton's Family Butcher's shop. She glanced in through the open doorway and saw that Mrs Staunton herself was serving customers along with Joe Lydd who lived in the next court to Cranberry, off Burlington Street.

Lizzie sidled in through the door, scuffing her feet in the thick sawdust and wrinkling her nose at the smell of blood. It would have been easier to have obtained some bones, she knew, had she been buying meat of some sort as well, but it was clear from the small amount in her pocket that Aunt Annie was a trifle short this week. However, if she could just make sure it was Joe who served her and not Mrs Staunton, she might be lucky.

The fat shawl-clad woman in front of her took a newspaper-wrapped parcel of chops off the battered wooden counter and turned to leave and Lizzie allowed another woman to take her place, pretending she had dropped a coin into the sawdust at her feet, until Mrs Staunton was safely engaged with the new customer. Then she gave Joe her most engaging grin. 'Gorrany bacon bits, Joe? Six penn'orth would be grand,' she hissed, pulling her money out of her skirt pocket. 'And – and a marrer bone or two, for stock?'

Joe turned away, saying over his shoulder: 'I'll pick

you out some nice ones, chuck,' as he made his way into the back, presently returning with an untidy parcel which clearly contained more than six penn'orth of bacon bits. Neither Lizzie nor Joe made any comment, however, she merely giving him a grateful smile as she handed over the cash.

Leaving the shop with the canvas bag a good deal heavier than it had been, Lizzie felt well satisfied with her first purchase. She did not know what proportion of the parcel was bacon bits and what marrow bones, but knew that Joe would not cheat her. The parcel would probably prove to contain a good deal more than six penn'orth, however it was made up.

Humming a tune beneath her breath, Lizzie sauntered along Juvenal Street, turning left when she reached Cazneau. She kept to the left-hand pavement for the right-hand one was bounded by the back of the market and offered no diversion in the way of shop windows. Presently she crossed the road and dived down Great Nelson Street, turning into the market and beginning to examine the fruit and vegetables displayed on the stalls on either hand.

Lizzie, along with most other Liverpool children, loved the market. The delicious smell of fruit and vegetables and the rich repartee in which the stallholders indulged were enough to keep her happy for a whole morning, but since she had sensibly bought the two penn'orth of potatoes and carrots first, she decided that she would have to get a move on or by the time she reached home her arms would have stretched until her fingers grazed her ankles. Chuckling at the thought of how absurd she would look with arms like a chimpanzee's, she bought a couple of pounds of peas and some onions from a fresh-faced country woman, graciously accepted a

7

bruised but perfectly eatable orange from the stall-holder and set off for home. When she reached Scotland Road, she stood her canvas bag down for a moment and squatted on the pavement beside it, peeling and eating her orange. She half wished she had let Sally come along, since they could have shared the orange, but on the other hand, the delights of a whole fruit rarely came her way and Sally, she knew, had oranges whenever she fancied them. The joys of being an only child were considerable, Lizzie thought, remembering the first seven years of her own life when her mam and dad had spoiled and petted their little daughter. Still, Lizzie knew she was lucky to have Aunt Annie; but for her mother's sister taking her in, she would have ended up in one of the many orphans' homes in Liverpool, just a number amongst other numbers, kept from the streets and the warm and bustling life which she so loved, confined to an ugly uniform, short walks through the streets in a supervised crocodile, and with no choice but to obey the adults who had her in charge.

Lizzie finished the orange, spitting the pips into the palm of her hand and shoving them into the stained pocket of her skirt. Once, long ago, her father's family had farmed on the Wirral in Cheshire and her mother had often teased her for her love of growing things. There was little enough soil to be found in the courts off Burlington Street, but whenever Lizzie could scrape together enough to fill an empty conny-onny tin, she would plant something in it. As a result, Aunt Annie's front parlour had a window sill crowded with strange plants, of which her aunt was rather proud, though it was Lizzie who watered them, turned them daily so that they grew straight and did not lean towards the light, and generally fussed over them. If I could grow an orange tree, Lizzie thought longingly, perhaps I could be like Sally and have an orange whenever I fancied one. She fingered the orange pips; there were five. Imagine five orange trees flourishing in Aunt Annie's front parlour, their fruit as brightly glowing as any sun!

Smiling at her own fancies, Lizzie got to her feet and heaved at the canvas bag once more. It was dreadfully heavy, and dreadfully awkward too so that when she tried to take two hands to it, it made walking forward impossible, banging into her legs and forcing her to change its weight from hand to hand and even, at one point, to tow it along the pavement like a recalcitrant dog which simply sits down whilst its owner heaves on its lead.

She was engaged in this undignified pastime when she noticed the boys. By now she had reached Burlington Street, and ahead of her three husky boys were kicking a round stone or ball of some kind along the pavement, passing it from one to the other and considerably inconveniencing the passers-by. Lizzie hesitated; she had no particular desire to get her ankles or her canvas bag kicked, either by mistake or on purpose, and she knew a good deal more than she liked about the horseplay indulged in by her cousins. From the look of them, the boys ahead were in the sort of mood to enjoy either teasing her or, should she get in their way, simply trampling her underfoot. What was more, despite the fact that they were nearing Cranberry Court, she did not think that the boys came from this neighbourhood. Certainly she had no recollection of ever having seen them before. So she loitered, continuing to pull the heavy bag along the pavement, albeit slowly.

All might have been well had not one of the boys

got a little ahead of the other two, dribbling the ball, which he then kicked hard in the direction of his companions. Too hard, as it turned out. Both boys dodged the missile and it shot past them and landed, with a painful crack, on Lizzie's bare ankle.

Lizzie promptly forgot caution, her hard-earned knowledge of boys, and her desire to stay out of trouble. For a moment, she simply squeaked and tried to nurse her ankle, dropping the bag as she did so, but then a flood of invective rose to her lips and she told the boys what she thought of them, saying things which would have whitened her mother's hair, had she been alive to hear them.

Oddly enough, this masterly reading of their characters did not seem to infuriate two of the three boys, but filled them with what looked rather like admiration. The tallest of them, a fair-haired boy, in ragged kecks and shirt, whistled. He wore a checked cap on the back of his head and boots which appeared to be several sizes too large for him. Lizzie saw that, despite his size, he was no more than fifteen or sixteen and his two companions probably a year or so younger. The boy nearest her, however, was scowling. He was dark and stocky, with eyebrows that met in the middle and a square, pugnacious chin. He came towards her, bending to pick up the ball and examining it as though he feared Lizzie's ankle had done it no good. 'What was you doing, acting as goalie, when no one so much as asked you to join in the game?' he said aggressively, glaring at her. 'You'd got no call to interfere with us, lerralone giving us a mouthful and using language a docker wouldn't stoop to. Just who do you think you are?'

'I were attacked, that's who I am,' Lizzie said ungrammatically. She glanced down at the vegetables rolling around the pavement. 'Look what you've done with your bleedin' ball! Them's me aunt's veggies and that, what she's been waiting for half the morning. You slowed me up anyway, 'cos I dare not try and pass you – you were taking up the whole perishin' pavement between the three of you and now me aunt will think I've nicked a few fades from the vegetable market instead of buying good fresh stuff.' She picked up a sorry-looking turnip, which had gathered a good deal of dust before coming to a halt in the gutter, and displayed its bruised and battered complexion to the scowling boy. 'Look at that! No one would take that for a fresh turnip, not now.'

'Well, you can't have done them messages much good yourself, dragging that bag along the pavement as though there were coals in it,' the scowling one remarked. 'Why didn't you carry the bag like a Christian? You ain't done that much good, either,' he finished, eyeing the dirty canvas bag disparagingly.

'Oh, leave off, Geoff,' the fair-haired boy said amicably. 'Them's a lot of messages for a bit of a girl to carry and that bleedin' cricket ball is hard as a stone – you can still see the mark on her leg, so it must have hurt.' He bent down and began to scoop vegetables back into the bag, and after a moment's hesitation both his companions began to do likewise, although the scowling one did so with a bad grace. Lizzie, meanwhile, sat herself down on the dusty pavement to examine her wound and saw that it was already turning blue and puffy and hurt horribly when she touched it.

When all the vegetables were back in the bag, she struggled to her feet, giving a gasp of pain as she put her weight on her right leg. She looked pathetically up at the tallest of the boys, saying tremulously: 'I

11

think me leg must be broke. It hurts something terrible when I try to walk. Oh, oh, what'll I do? Me Aunt Annie will tear the hair from me head if I don't get these veggies home soon.'

The middle-sized boy, the one who had not yet spoken, bent and seized the canvas bag. 'Where d'you live, queen?' he asked gruffly. 'I'll carry your messages home for you, seeing as it was me what dodged out of the way of the ball. I should of stopped it, but it were coming so bleedin' fast . . .'

The tall boy gave an exaggerated sigh but shook his head. 'No, Tom, let our Geoff carry the bag, then you and me, being almost of a height, can make a chair and get the young 'un indoors.'

This was going a good deal further than Lizzie thought desirable, for though her leg certainly did hurt, she was well aware that it was merely bruised and not broken in the slightest. Besides, she had no desire for the boys to walk into the house and tell Aunt Annie how she had been dragging the messages along the pavement. What was more, if Uncle Perce were home, there would almost certainly be trouble. Her uncle was a strange man, pleasant enough when sober, but a raging devil when he had drink in him. Many a time Lizzie had hidden beneath the blankets on her little truckle bed while, in the room below, her aunt and uncle shrieked and fought until one or other of them triumphed.

Accordingly, as the boys bore down upon her, she said, affecting an air of wonder: 'Well now, if that ain't the strangest thing! The pain's ebbing fast – I do declare, I believe I *can* walk after all.'

All three boys grinned, Geoff with the infuriating air of one who'd known she was lying all along. 'Well, if you ain't going to carry the girl, Sid, then I'm damned if I'll lug her bleedin' bag all the way to – to wherever she lives,' he said truculently. Lizzie thought, balefully, that Geoff would probably grow up to be like her Uncle Perce, or possibly worse, since the feller seemed to be in a perpetual bad temper, even when sober as a judge.

Geoff dumped the bag on the pavement but it appeared that Sid, as the eldest of the three, held considerable sway over them, for without losing his smile he said in a quiet but dangerous voice: 'You'll do as I say, young 'un. You'll tek the lady's bag wherever she wants you to tek it, do you hear me? Sid Ryder's the boss and what I says goes, remember?'

Lizzie waited for Geoff to object, or even to storm off in a temper, but instead he bent and hefted her bag once more, though she distinctly heard him mutter as he did so: 'Lady? I don't see no lady, only a bleedin' little kid what hasn't had a wash for a week by the looks of her.'

Lizzie considered replying sharply, but decided against it. The bag was heavy and although her leg was only bruised it would not be improved by having to bear the weight of her shopping as well as that of her own small person. So she pretended she had not heard the remark and limped ahead of Geoff while the two older boys disappeared out of sight amongst the hurrying Saturday crowds.

Although Lizzie had not noticed her, Chinky, as she was always known, had been an interested observer of the whole scene from her position ten yards behind the boys. She often followed them around though they seemed totally unaware of her, as indeed she meant them to be. She followed them for a good reason: when he was in the money, Sid occasionally handed out the odd ha'penny to any child who was down on their luck and by a dint of crossing his path every now and then, she had managed to become the temporary owner of several ha'pennies.

Chinky was a pathetic scrap of humanity, the unlovely result of a brief union between a Chinese seaman and what the more respectable women of the courts called 'a part-time prozzie'. Chinky's mam, whom she scarcely remembered, had gone off with some feller when she had been no more than four, leaving her little daughter to the untender mercies of a neighbour, already cursed with eleven kids of her own and neither time nor patience for an extra mouth to feed. When she was seven, Chinky had heard Aunt Lily, as she had been taught to call her foster mother, telling a friend that she meant to dump Chinky in one of the orphan asylums which abounded in the city. She knew little enough about orphanages, but had a shrewd idea that she would not enjoy such a restricted life. Accordingly, she had taken herself off very early each morning, never going home – if you could call it home – until late at night when the reluctant foster mother and her family were already in bed. She lived on any scraps she could pick up from Aunt Lily's pantry, but mostly she fed herself, wheedling bits of food from stallholders and shopkeepers, good-hearted publicans, or the men who always saved some of their carry-out for the street kids who clustered around them when the factory gates opened to spew them into the street at the end of their working day.

That had been in the early days, of course. Now, at the age of around ten, for Chinky had no idea even of the year in which she had been born, she managed a good deal better. Because she had never attended school – no school would accept a child who was always barefoot, filthy, and in rags – she had to be careful to avoid the truant officers on the lookout for kids sagging off school, but such persons were easily identifiable and she steered clear of them.

Being unable to read was a real disadvantage, she knew that. But she was becoming quick and clever in other ways. She knew that Sid stole, and admired him for it because he never got caught, and though she was careful never to intrude upon him and his friends, she wondered sometimes if Sid were aware of her; if so, it was possible that the ha'pennies which came her way were a form of hush money: 'Don't tell,' Sid was saying as he slipped her a coin. 'Keep your mouth shut and your eyes open and mebbe there'll be another ha'penny in it for you.'

However, when she really put her mind to it, she could not believe that he would put up with her following him around if he had actually noticed. Someone like Sid, who lived on his wits, would be careful not to attract unwanted attention by allowing a scruffy kid like herself to follow him about. He was old enough to escape the notice of such persons as schools' inspectors and would not want to be involved with a kid who was plainly not only sagging off school but probably up to no good as well. So Chinky continued to follow Sid around, more careful than ever to remain unnoticed.

With considerable astonishment she had become aware of the addition of Geoff to the little gang who thieved so expertly. He did not look the type – *was* not the type – to go thieving up and down the Scottie, but she very soon appreciated Sid's cleverness in involving the younger boy. Geoff was so neat, so well brushed and well fed, that no one would ever dream he was keeping douse for Sid and his gang, let alone conniving at their carryings-on. So this afternoon she had watched with great interest as the cricket ball first knocked Lizzie's basket on to the floor, and secondly brought the four of them into what appeared to be lively conversation. Had Sid not been involved, Chinky would have streaked forward to grab as many of the rolling vegetables as she could hold, but since he was, in a sense, a friend, she let the opportunity pass by, though her mouth watered at the sight of the bright green pea pods. She was too far away to catch what anyone was saying so was considerably surprised when the group split up, Sid and Tom continuing to walk swiftly along the pavement while Geoff, leaning sideways with the weight of the girl's canvas bag, headed for the courts.

After only the slightest hesitation, Chinky began to pad along behind Geoff and the girl. What were they up to? Why had Sid not gone along as well? And who *was* this girl? Chinky admired the long hay-coloured mass of hair which rippled almost down to the girl's waist and envied her the faded cotton dress and her air of independence; she was clearly someone to be reckoned with, otherwise Sid would not have made Geoff carry her bag. Chinky had been too far away to hear what Sid had said, but only an idiot would have been unable to interpret his look of command, and Chinky was no idiot. It occurred to her now, following well behind them into Cranberry Court, that so far as she knew, neither Sid, Tom nor Geoff had any time for girls. She would never have dreamed of suggesting to Sid, even had she known him sufficiently well, that she herself might be useful to him. So surely he would not be interested in adding this girl to his gang, no matter how clean and bright she might seem in comparison to Chinky herself. Probably, she decided, Sid had wanted to get rid of Geoff for some reason and had sent him off with the girl simply to get him out of the way.

Geoff and the girl turned towards one of the houses and Chinky sauntered past, not wanting to be seen following them, but she need not have worried. There was a brief exchange of remarks between the girl and Geoff, then she pushed open the front door and the two of them disappeared inside.

There was a game of run-in skipping going on in the centre of the court and Chinky, who despite her lack of practice was a good skipper, jumped into the rope. The two girls on either end continued to revolve it smoothly, accepting her presence without comment. Indeed, Chinky, who rarely played any sort of game because life was too serious for such amusements when you had only yourself to rely on, proved to be so good that she was last one in and therefore was invited to take a turn at holding the rope. Feeling rather pleased with herself, she was taking the rope when the door of number nine opened again and Geoff and the girl came out.

'Want to have a go, Lizzie?' the biggest of the girls shouted across. 'We're just startin' again.'

So the girl's name was Lizzie, Chinky thought as Lizzie smiled but shook her head. Chinky handed her end of the rope to the girl nearest her, muttering an excuse that it was time for her tea, and made off in Geoff and Lizzie's wake, keeping well back. On former occasions she had always followed Sid home, since he lived in the same court as she did, so she had no idea where Geoff lived, though she knew he and Sid had been at St Mark's school together. Now she would discover where Geoff hung out, and perhaps she would also find out why a respectable boy like him should take up with the likes of Sid. Smiling gleefully to herself, Chinky slipped out of the court and turned right along the dusty pavement, keeping her eye on Lizzie's fair hair as it bobbed along ahead of her.

When Lizzie and Geoff had reached Cranberry Court, Lizzie unbent enough to turn and give her companion a smile. Not that he noticed because he was staring straight ahead, his scowl, if anything, deeper and more ferocious than before. 'I live at number nine, the one with the red curtains,' Lizzie said briefly, pointing. The curtains had been red once, she realised belatedly, but were now more of a dirty brown. 'If you dump the messages at the top of the steps, I'll bring 'em right inside.' As they wended their way through the groups of children playing on the filthy paving stones, she wondered whether she should thank him and decided to do so since boys were strange and awkward creatures and you never knew what they would do if they felt themselves slighted. Many a clout round the ear had been delivered by Henry, Ned, Denis and Herbie when she had, in some way, either transgressed against the mysterious male code or annoyed them in some other fashion.

As they crossed the court, heading for the door of number nine, Lizzie glanced at Geoff and saw that he was eyeing his surroundings with considerable interest. She thought this odd, assuming that the boys were local and would know the courts as well as she did, but this one, judging by his intent appraisal, was astonished to find himself in such a place. Indeed, when they reached the steps which led up to her door, he put the shopping bag down and turned to her. 'Ain't it dark, though?' he said. 'After all that sunshine, coming in here was like descending into the pit. Lived here long, have you?'

'Since me mam and dad died,' Lizzie said briefly, 'before then I lived in Bootle. Bootle's grand, it's only a step away from Seaforth Sands.' She sighed reminiscently. 'Me dad were a seaman,' she ended rather lamely, realising that she had been going to tell Geoff a good deal more than he could possibly want to know.

She was about to take the bag and thank him for his help when he swung it up once more and clumped up the steps ahead of her; clearly he meant to take a look inside the house while he had the chance, and Lizzie did not know that she blamed him. She supposed vaguely that he probably lived somewhere a good deal smarter, and knew that, given the opportunity, she would have liked to have a nose around his home, wherever it might be. Accordingly, she slipped passed him at the top of the steps and pushed open the door, then led the way in, saying cheerfully: 'We'll go in the kitchen; the other room's the parlour, only we're not in there much, 'cept on summer evenings and at Christmas, 'cos the fire's hardly ever lit in there – can't afford coal for two. I live with me Aunt Annie and Uncle Perce Grey.' She opened the kitchen door and entered the room, smiling at her aunt who was stirring a pan over the fire. One good thing about Aunt Annie was that she never minded you bringing your friends, so long as you didn't offer them a meal. 'I'm back wi' the veggies, Aunt,' she said cheerfully. 'This is me pal Geoff. He carried the bag for me 'cos it's awful heavy.'

Aunt Annie smiled at Geoff and waved a spoon in greeting but said anxiously, 'Wharrabout the marrer bones, queen? And the bacon bits?'

'Oh, I gorrem all right,' Lizzie said. She took the bag from Geoff and emptied it out on to the large kitchen table, then had to field a sliding mountain of vegetables to prevent them cascading all over the floor. Rather to her surprise, Geoff jumped forward to assist her, even pursuing a round, brown onion across the kitchen floor and recapturing it on the very hearth. The butcher's parcel, being at the bottom of the bag, was now on top of the pile; Lizzie picked it off and began to unwrap the newspaper, revealing an enormous marrow bone, chopped into four, and a quantity of excellent bacon bits.

Aunt Annie, with an exclamation of pleasure, seized the bacon bits and waddled across to the fire, tipping them into her big, blackened stewpot. 'Good gal! By the time this has simmered for a few hours, you'll not find a better scouse in the whole of Liverpool. Will you give me a hand to chop the veggies for the stockpot, queen? Or do you and your pal have other plans?'

'I'll give you a hand . . .' Lizzie was beginning, when Geoff chimed in, 'I'm OK with a kitchen knife and I've nowt else on, so I might as well give a hand, too. I haven't got no plans . . . not now Sid and Tom have buggered off,' he added gruffly, in a voice so low that Lizzie only just caught it. She was about to tell him – and pretty sharply – that she could manage perfectly well without him and that it was not *her* fault that his pals had deserted him, when she looked at his face. He seemed eager, as though the prospect of chopping vegetables was a pleasant one, and she realised, that far from blaming her, he was simply stating a fact: his pals had gone on without him, so he was at a loose end.

Accordingly, the two of them settled down at the

kitchen table and began to peel and chop the vegetables, talking in low tones while Aunt Annie sat in the creaking basket chair with a broken pair of spectacles perched on her nose, and read last night's copy of the *Echo*.

In point of fact, with both of them working on the vegetables, Aunt Annie's big, black stockpot was soon brimming and, without even being asked, Geoff went to the buckets of water which stood under the table where Aunt Annie's washing-up bowl was perched, and filled the pot to within an inch of its rim. Then he turned to his hostess and asked her politely whether there were any more tasks which he and Lizzie could help her with.

Aunt Annie slid her spectacles down her nose and looked at the two children over the top of them. 'The two of you can heft me stockpot on to the fire – the scouse can pull over a bit – and refill me water buckets and then your time's your own,' she said generously. 'Lizzie, there's a batch of soda bread in the bin and a jar of jam on the shelf. Make yourselves some butties and take them with you.'

'Thanks, Aunt Annie,' Lizzie said, grabbing a couple of the galvanised buckets from beneath the sink and handing one to Geoff. He, however, firmly took the second bucket as well, advising her to: 'Make them butties while I fetches the water,' in a low but firm tone.

For a moment, Lizzie wondered whether he intended to steal the buckets and run off with them before he was missed, then decided that this was too ridiculous for words. Besides, even if he gained two buckets, he would lose his jam butties, and what boy would risk that? So she went over to the cupboard where Aunt Annie kept the food, hacked four hefty slices off the loaf and spread them with Aunt Annie's delicious strawberry jam. Then she wrapped them in a piece of greaseproof paper and was crossing the kitchen when Geoff reappeared in the doorway, a full bucket in either hand. 'Here you are, Missus,' he said breezily, thumping the buckets on to the floor. 'You ready for the off then, queen?' he asked Lizzie.

She shoved the greaseproof-wrapped parcel into her pocket and nodded vigorously. She was more puzzled by Geoff than ever, and suspected that as soon as they left the court, he might abandon her, but that worried her not at all. If she wanted companionship, she could call for Sally, or Bet, or one of her other friends. But on such a warm and sunny day there were a variety of attractions which could be enjoyed by a solitary child and even as they left the house, Lizzie was mulling over which she would prefer. She had no money, so the picture house and the swimming baths were both out, but she could skip a leckie and go off to the Pier Head, or even to Seaforth Sands, without having to part with cash. If the tide was out, she could go down to the Landing Stage, slide down the chains on to the mud, and have a delicious, dirty time, seeing what treasures had been left by the outgoing tide, or she could go to Sefton Park and see the birds in the aviary, or to Princes Park to feed the ducks with a portion of her bread and jam . . . on a sunny Saturday there were a heap of things to do!

'Want to have a go, Lizzie? We're just starting a game,' one of a group of girls skipping called out. But though Lizzie smiled, she shook her head. There were better things to do on such a day than skipping rope, and as she turned away she saw that she was not the only one to think so. A small and grubby girl with the long eyes and black hair of the Chinese quietly passed her end of the rope to someone else and came scuffling out of the court behind them.

Geoff fell into step beside her as they left the court. He's sticking to his bread and jam, Lizzie thought, grinning to herself. But whatever the reason, she suddenly realised that she would enjoy his companionship. After all, he wasn't one of her wretched cousins, he had no reason to be jealous of the attention Aunt Annie meted out to her, so no reason either to bully or tease her. As the two of them turned into Burlington Street, she glanced questioningly up at the boy beside her. 'Well? Are you going to tell me a bit about yourself?' she enquired. 'What's your other name? Where do you live? What were you doing with them boys? And where's we going now?' she finished, grinning up at him for he was half a head taller than she.

For a moment she thought he was not going to answer her but he drew a long breath and said, ticking the answers off on his fingers as he gave them: 'Me name's Geoff Gardiner. I live in Shaw Street and me and the lads were – were just sort of seeing what we could pick up. As for what we'll do next, that's up to you.'

'Shaw Street! That's a real posh street. I went to a Bring and Buy Sale at St Augustine's church a year or so back, with me Aunt Annie, and we walked along and looked at the houses – they're grand. Which one is yours, then?'

Geoff gave her a look in which contempt and amusement were nicely blended. 'What does it matter?' he said baldly. 'I could say I lived at number nine or number ninety-three and you wouldn't be no wiser. What say we go along to the Scottie, see if we can skip a leckie going out to the sands? Why, it's that warm I reckon we could bathe. And we gorra picnic – we should have asked your aunt for a bottle of water, I daresay she'd not have grudged it.'

'There's a drinking fountain in Princes Park,' Lizzie said dreamily as they walked along. 'There's probably another in Seaforth, somewhere.' She turned to him suddenly, her eyes bright. 'Tell you what, Geoff, we might go along to the market and see if anyone wants messages running or an odd job doing. If we earn some pennies we could buy a couple of bottles of ginger beer.'

Geoff vetoed this suggestion, however, on the grounds that it would waste a good chunk of the sunny afternoon, so the two of them strolled down to the Pier Head and sat on the edge of the Landing Stage, with their legs hanging over the water, talking idly and hoping that the tide, which lapped only feet beneath them, would presently begin to ebb so that they might drop down on to the mud and begin searching for treasures.

After a while, however, Geoff remarked that the tide, far from obliging them, seemed to have come a little higher up the wall since their arrival and suggested that they might stroll along by the water until they reached Princes Dock, where they could take a look at the shipping.

But this sounded pretty dull work to Lizzie and the name 'Princes Dock' made her think of the park and the delights to be found there by someone like herself who was interested in growing things. It was the wrong time of year for nicking seed heads, of course, but very much the right time of year for looking at the flowers and trees and deciding which seed pods to nick when autumn came. What was more, the June evenings were long and the pair of them could walk to Princes Park, even if they couldn't skip a leckie. Accordingly, she told Geoff, in no uncertain terms, that staring at shipping when you could be floating paper boats on the lake up at the park, or even having a crafty swim if the park attendant was looking the other way, seemed a good deal more fun.

'Ye–es,' he said doubtfully. 'But – but me time's not me own . . . that's to say, I've gorra be in for me tea come five o'clock. If we go to the dock to look at shipping, we can cut back to Burlington Street for you to get home for your aunt's scouse and then I'll go on to Shaw Street for me own tea.'

'But we've got jam butties!' Lizzie exclaimed, dismayed by this faint-hearted attitude. 'Besides, me aunt will save me a bowl of scouse – bound to, since it were me what got the bacon bits. Won't your mam save your tea, seeing as how it's a lovely day and she'd probably sooner you were out in the sunshine than cooped up indoors?'

There was a short silence, during which Geoff studied his boots with what appeared to be rapt attention. They were strolling along beside the river, in the direction of the docks, but now he pulled her to a stop and swung her round to face him. 'Lizzie, do you want to be me pal?' he asked earnestly. 'Because if so, there's a thing or two you ought to know. It wasn't no lie that I live on Shaw Street, because I've lived there as long as I can remember, but – but I live in Father Brannigan's Orphan Asylum.'

Lizzie stared at him. Then, very carefully, she looked at him properly for the first time, from the top of his head to his shining boots. His thick, dark hair was cut cruelly short and his face, now that she came to look at it with more attention, was far too pale –

and clean – to be the face of a normal Liverpool lad who, at this time of year, would have been roaming the streets from dawn to dusk, except for the hours which he spent in school. She also noticed for the first time that his clothing was more like a uniform than the odds and ends and ragged garments worn by ordinary kids. Despite the warmth of the day, he was wearing a grey flannel shirt and trousers and his boots had plainly been bought to fit him and not passed on by an elder brother or sister. Besides, Lizzie thought, looking down at her own bare feet, most kids chose not to wear boots in the summer.

'Know me again?' Geoff said sarcastically, though he gave her a grin as he spoke. 'Orphans don't have two heads, you know – nor do foundlings, which is what I am. The only difference between me and you, chuck, is that no one'll save me tea for me, nor yet me supper neither, because that isn't how institutions work. We're just bleedin' numbers to the staff.'

'What's a foundling?' Lizzie asked, hastily turning her eyes from Geoff's sturdy figure and looking out across the River Mersey. 'I know what an orphan is, 'cos I'm one meself, but I haven't even heard of a foundling.'

'It's just what it sounds like – I were found, not handed over by me parents,' Geoff said briefly. 'Me mam dumped me at Waterloo Station and a scuffer found me and took me round to the Branny – that's what we call the Home – and Father Brannigan took me in.'

'Oh,' Lizzie said, inadequately. She thanked her lucky stars that she had been seven when her parents had died; how awful not to know who you were or where you'd come from, even. Then it occurred to her that Geoff Gardiner wasn't just any old name, and her new friend must have come by it somehow or other. Having given the matter a moment's thought, she worded her next question carefully. 'If you are a foundling, then how do you know your name? Were you a little baby when the scuffer took you to the Home?' She bethought herself of one of her favourite romantic tales which involved a baby left on a doorstep with a note pinned to its shawl. 'Was your name written on a bit of paper and pinned to your clothes, then?'

Geoff rolled his eyes at yet another list of questions, but answered them patiently. 'Yes, I were two or three days old when I were found, so far as anyone could guess. As for me name, the scuffer was called PC Gardiner and Father Brannigan chose "Geoffrey" because there wasn't anyone else called that in the Home. Now are you satisfied?'

'Not really,' Lizzie said frankly. 'Only I can't think of any more questions now – oh, yes I can. Those other boys, Sid and Tom, are they orphans an' all?'

'What, those scruffy buggers? No, they're a couple of lads from school what I palled up with, so when I can get away, the three of us go about in a sort of gang, seeing what we . . .' He paused and shot an odd look at Lizzie.

'The three of you was out on a nickin' spree, I reckon,' she said wisely. 'I *thought* it were too good to be true when the tall lad was so nice to me. Most fellers would have just laughed and done nothing to help, but he didn't want to draw attention, did he? Where were you bound, then? Paddy's Market? Or the fruit and veg market? Or were you going to kick that ball into a shop window, grab what you could, and run for it?'

'You aren't far out, queen,' Geoff said, grinning

sheepishly at her. 'They're always on the nick – Tom and Sid, I mean – but usually I'm just the look-out or I case the joint for them because I don't look like a street urchin.' He plunged a hand into his pocket and brought out a dark blue neck-tie, decorated with thin, silver stripes. 'When I've got me tie on, I look real respectable; I could be a young gent from one of the posh schools, for all they know.'

'Well, now you've got me for a pal, you'd better stop that lark or you won't see me for dust,' Lizzie said belligerently. 'It's easy enough to get into trouble round here without stealing, because that's what it is – stealing. Everyone nicks a few fades from the market or the odd gob-stopper from old Ma Kettle down the Scottie, but thievin' will get you into *really* hot water.'

'I know it,' Geoff assured her, neatly re-rolling his tie and replacing it in his pocket. 'To tell you the truth, I'm a bit scared of Sid. He's a wild 'un, he's not afraid of anyone and he'll do anything – I've seen him snatch a bracelet off a jewellery stand, right in front of the assistant's eyes, with a shop full of people all grabbing for him, and him in and out before you could say knife, slippery as any eel.' There was enough admiration in his voice to worry Lizzie and this time it was she who caught hold of his arm, stopping him in his tracks.

'There's nothing clever in stealing, chuck,' she said fiercely. 'Besides, if that Sid is slippery as an eel, you can be sure it'll be you what ends up in trouble and not him. Fellers like him don't have a conscience, 'cos they don't know right from wrong. If he were caught, he'd slap the blame on someone else, quick as a wink. But he's no end older 'an you, so you can't be in the same class; where'd you meet him?'

'Oh, Sid left school more'n a year back, but he still hangs around the place 'cos he's not gorra job yet,' Geoff explained. 'But don't worry, Lizzie, I won't be seeing him again because I'd rather hang around with someone like yourself. Not that I get away all that often, what with the senior boys watching us like hawks and the staff always on the look-out for any feller trying to slip past them,' he concluded bitterly.

Lizzie, nodding her head grimly, decided to say no more, and presently the two of them dodged in through the dock gates when no one was looking in their direction and began to stroll past the ships moored to the quayside, bobbing placidly on the water like a line of ducks on a pond. The two children found a couple of iron stanchions, sat themselves down, and shared out the jam butties. They ate contentedly, watching the hustle and bustle on the quayside as some ships were unloaded while others prepared to depart. Presently Geoff glanced up at the clock tower and remarked that it was time he wasn't here. 'Brother Mark is on dining-room duty today and he just about hates the sight of me so it wouldn't do to be late.'

'I'll walk you home, if you've got to go now,' Lizzie offered. She had enjoyed examining the big houses on Shaw Street and imagining what went on behind their impressive front doors. It would be interesting, furthermore, to see for herself the Father Brannigan Orphan Asylum for Boys since she did not recall seeing it the last time she had visited the area. 'But if you can't get out official-like, Geoff, how are you and I going to meet up again? Any chance of getting away on a Sunday, or do they watch you closer than ever at weekends?'

'I'm a chorister,' he told her, 'so I'm kept pretty

busy on a Sunday. Until after Sunday dinner, that is. There's generally a couple of hours in the afternoon when I can slip away if I can get someone else to cover for me. If you were to come up Shaw Street and just keep walking up and down outside the Home, I could probably get away for a bit.'

This waste of a Sunday afternoon, however, did not appeal to Lizzie at all and she said vaguely that she herself might be busy then. 'We has our dinner midday on a Sunday, 'cos Uncle Perce and the boys is home,' she explained. 'Tell you what, Geoff, if you *can* get away, come round to the Court. There's always something going on round there.'

'Right,' he said, though he looked a little disconsolate. 'And if I can't get away, we'll manage something one evening next week. This here's the Home, the big house with the iron railings and the brass door knocker. You'd best make yourself scarce now or I'll be in trouble.' He grinned impishly down at her. 'Father Brannigan don't approve of fellers meeting girls.'

Geoff headed for the back door of the Home, slipping his tie round his neck and knotting it with quick, experienced hands as he went. Haircuts had been handed out the previous Saturday, but he spat on his hands and slicked down what was left of his with both palms. Once inside the house, he slid unobtrusively into the mass of boys already queuing to go into the dining room. In their uniform, with their hair cut short, it was easy to remain anonymous in such a crowd and presently Roy, who sat next to Geoff in class, turned round and spotted him in the throng. 'Where have you been?' he enquired, though without much interest. 'There were a game of footy in the backyard and I made sure you'd be out there, but you weren't 'cos I checked.' He lowered his voice. 'You weren't with that Sid, were you?'

''Course not,' Geoff said righteously. 'It's against the rules, isn't it?' He winked at Roy, who laughed. 'Actually, I've gorra new pal. The family live in Cranberry Court, off the Burly, so we went down to the dock to take a look at the shipping – took a picnic with us.'

'Cor!' Roy said reverently, gazing at him round-eyed. 'You have all the luck! Still an' all, I've got a heap of cousins living in the Courts who like me to visit a couple of times a month. You've got no one.'

Geoff flushed angrily. He knew that Roy did not mean to make him feel bad about his lonely and somewhat friendless state, but that was what such remarks did. Sometimes it seemed to Geoff that everyone in the Branny had dozens of relatives willing to take them out for an hour or even the odd week end, except himself. However, he did not intend to let Roy – or anyone else for that matter – guess at his sensitivity over such things. Instead, struck by a bright idea, he turned impulsively to his friend. 'I know what you mean,' he said. 'But these people are really friendly. They asked me into their house – no one's ever done that before. It's only a little house, but it was kind of nice. I helped Mrs Grey to chop vegetables and carried in buckets of water . . . it's all very well for the rest of you fellers, but unless I seize an opportunity like this, I'll never get to see how ordinary folk live.'

'That's true,' Roy said, looking puzzled. Clearly he did not see where this conversation was leading. 'Are you going back again, then? I know you slip out from time to time after school. There's often an hour or two free when we're playing footy or doing homework or just waiting for our teas, but . . .'

'Well, that's where you come in,' Geoff said quickly, eager to make his point before they all began to shuffle into the dining room. When Brother Mark was in charge, there was no knowing how he might rearrange the seating, deliberately parting friend from friend on the grounds that this would mean less chattering and fooling about at table. 'Suppose you say, next time you're visiting on a Saturday, that your gran's asked you to bring a friend along? That would mean we could leave here together and arrange to meet somewhere at around eight o'clock – if you are out for tea that is. Then I could nip along to Cranberry Court and see me pals and come back in with you, no harm done. What do you think?'

'Seems all right to me,' Roy said, but he sounded doubtful. 'What about your tea though, our Geoff? You can't rely on this Grey family wanting an extra mouth to feed.'

'Oh, I reckon they're the sort of family who wouldn't grudge me a plate of scouse, seeing as how Mrs Grey handed out butties this afternoon,' Geoff said airily. He felt that to get away from the Branny now and again, particularly on what appeared to be legitimate business, would be worth any number of missed teas. What was more if he got away for a whole day, he and Lizzie could earn themselves a few pence in the morning and spend the afternoon in some pleasant manner with some coppers in their pocket for a drink and a bun. 'Don't you worry about me, old feller. When are you going out next?'

Roy was about to reply when the double doors leading into the dining room were opened from the inside by one of the boys on monitor duty. Despite the fact that they had been formed into a queue, the boys promptly broke ranks and surged forward. Considering the type of tea which awaited them Geoff thought ruefully, this wasn't a particularly sensible way to behave. There would be large jugs of tepid tea, platters of bread and margarine, and presently the monitors on duty would come round with tureens of stew, usually as tepid as the tea and with a thick skimming of fat on the surface of the dish. This would be doled out sparingly to each boy and would be followed by a dish of rice pudding, semolina, spotted dick or stewed apple, depending on the cook's fancy. But even this repast would be denied them until they had reformed their queue and entered the dining room in a suitably chastened fashion.

Brother Mark, standing just inside the door, yelled at the boys and drove them back into the hall. Geoff, seeing the brother punching and shoving at the boys who had broken ranks, hoped devoutly that Brother Mark's feet were getting as trampled as his own.

Presently, with order restored, the boys at last gained their places. Geoff, as he had feared, had been separated from his friends and was seated at a table with much older boys, but at least this enabled him to think. He had a good deal to think about, what was more.

The day had been a surprise right from the start, he told himself as the monitor poured tea into his tin mug. He had slipped out with every intention of meeting up with Sid and Tom, because they were the nearest he ever got to finding out how normal boys, not those who lived in orphanages, managed their lives. Accordingly, he had hung around on the corner of Netherfield Road and Prince Edwin Lane and sure enough, after about twenty minutes or so, the boys came slouching round the corner, quickening their pace as they reached the main road.

Sid and Tom looked a bit alike but in fact were not brothers, as Geoff had first supposed. They were bezzies, however, and it is never easy for a third person to become accepted by two best friends. Geoff realised, almost from the first day they had allowed him to go along with them, that this was for convenience – theirs – rather than friendship. They were a wild couple, up to all sorts of mischief, and only allowed him to go along as look-out, if they needed one, or for some other purpose which suited their plans. That very morning they had given him an empty jam jar and sent him into the Gaiety Cinema on the Scottie, in order that he might hold open one of the fire doors for Sid, Tom and several others to enter without paying. It was odd, Geoff reflected now, how extremely difficult it was for a boy who lived in an orphanage to pal up with boys who did not. There could be no reciprocal visits should you be lucky enough to be asked into someone's home, and anyway most kids lived in crowded little streets where everyone knew everyone else; thus it was not necessary for such children to look for friends amongst the boys in the Branny. Furthermore, most of the boys in the Home had no desire to make friends out of it. They had relatives so that they knew considerably more about the life lived by ordinary people than Geoff did. It would have struck them as peculiar in the extreme had they realised how desperately he longed to see ordinary homes.

So he had made friends with Sid and Tom, hoping that one of these days they would unbend towards him and ask him to visit them. He knew that they lived somewhere in the rabbit warren of tiny houses in the mean little streets, alleys and courts which surrounded Prince Edwin Lane, but he did not know exactly where. He had never dared to suggest that he might go home with them – indeed, they seldom seemed to go home, preferring the life of the streets to whatever domestic delights awaited them – but he waited in vain for a casual invitation from one or other of the boys. He had hinted, of course, offering to carry a nicked roll of lino back to Sid's place for him, suggesting that he might run back for something forgotten if they would tell him where their homes were, but this had always been either ignored or brushed aside; there was obviously going to be little chance there.

Accordingly, when the three of them had met up earlier in the day, Geoff had had very little expectation of attaining his goal. Indeed, as Lizzie had predicted, he felt there was more chance of seeing the inside of a police station when in Sid's company than the inside of an ordinary home. So when the boys had run off, leaving him to lug Lizzie's messages, he had not really regretted their loss. They were dangerous company and though he would have stuck by them had he thought that there was the remotest chance of a really close friendship developing, he had begun to realise he was wasting his time.

In all his dreams of acquiring a friend from an ordinary household, however, Geoff had never considered meeting or befriending a girl. Girls, so far as he was concerned, were a completely alien race, as foreign to him as though they spoke a different language and came from a different world. The only female members of staff at the Branny were Cook, who weighed twenty stone and hated boys; Mrs Fletcher, the housekeeper, who was thin and sour, had a flourishing moustache and seldom mixed with the children; and Ethel and Ellen, the elderly charwomen whose combined age, Geoff thought, probably rivalled Methuselah's.

There were no girls at St Mark's school, of course, nor were there any female teachers. In fact the only other women with whom Geoff came into contact were the shrill-voiced usherettes at the Saturday picture show and one or two shop assistants, who might smile as they handed over a purchase he had made.

He rarely thought of girls, therefore, except as persons to be avoided. He saw them as he walked along the street: giggling little groups of them perched on a wall, or crouching over one of their weird pavement games. They would look up at him, give what he assumed was a knowing smirk, and then the heads would draw close and stifled giggles would break out once more. Convinced that they were laughing at him, Geoff positively disliked the local girls and would never, for one moment, have dreamed of getting to know one.

Yet that very day, and by the merest mischance, he had fallen in with Lizzie. He had glanced disparagingly at her: a thin waif of a child with fair hair, large blue eyes which had flickered over him scornfully, and a small, jutting chin which should have warned him of her determination, he thought now, if nothing else. She had been wearing a ragged cotton dress whose colour had faded from what had once been blue to a dreary grey, and she could not by any stretch of the imagination have been called pretty. Yet Geoff acknowledged that she had an appealing face, particularly when she smiled and her entire countenance lit up and softened. He had not wanted to carry her wretched messages, nor to go with her to her home, because if there was one thing he was convinced of, it was that no girl would ever invite an unknown boy to accompany her indoors. Which just proved, he thought now, spooning the thin gravy into his mouth, that no one ever knows what is in store for them. He had gone into Lizzie's home, met her aunt, helped to chop vegetables and to carry water the way ordinary boys must do daily, and had then walked through the streets with her, chatting idly as though they had been friends for years. In other words, the breakthrough for which he had always longed had come out of the blue, without any real effort on his part. Now that he came to think about it, he had been so blind to the opportunity he had nearly mucked it up by being extremely rude to Lizzie. He shuddered inwardly to think how easily he might have stalked off in high dudgeon, letting Tom pick up the canvas bag.

However, this had not happened and he had made a new friend and enjoyed a thoroughly interesting day. In all his wanderings, he had never actually entered a court before, being wary of the gangs of kids to be found playing there and of the dark dinginess of the surroundings. Courts were tiny closed communities in which they all knew one another. He had always assumed that a stranger entering one would be immediately mobbed and possibly thrown out on his ear.

'Finished, have ya?' The dining-room monitor's voice in his ear made Geoff jump and clutch the edge of his plate protectively.

'Hang on a second,' he protested, realising that he had still some stew on his plate. He leaned forward and took a slice of bread, swiped it round the plate, collecting the rest of the stew on it, folded it over and thrust it into his mouth. Speaking thickly, he said:

'You can have the bleedin' plate now, la'. There's not enough left for a cat's lick so you might as well take it back to the kitchen. What's for puddin'?'

'Murder on the Alps,' the monitor said, smacking his lips. 'Since you was last to finish, young feller, we'll start serving up now.' He whisked Geoff's plate away but left his spoon and fork – it was generally understood that one set of what Father Brannigan called 'eating irons' should last the whole repast.

Presently, with a bowl of semolina decorated with a daub of jam, Geoff began dreamily mixing the pudding into a pink mush while he contemplated the home he had visited that afternoon. Lizzie's Aunt Annie was a large woman, but surely it could not be just this fact which had made the room seem so small? Despite the heat of the June day, there had been a big fire in the kitchen grate and he realised that Aunt Annie would have to put up with the heat in order that her family might have a cooked meal. What was more, apart from the creaking basketwork chair and the large, scrubbed wooden table, there had been very little furniture in the room. He had tried to take everything in without appearing unduly nosy, and it had not been difficult. He recalled a stained calendar hanging on one wall, a battered tin clock on the mantelpiece above the fire, and two rough, and obviously home-made, wooden benches. He wished he had thought to ask Lizzie if he might take a peep into the parlour, since that was where the family would be sitting this evening. He was pretty sure she would have unquestioningly opened the door for him. But he had not thought of it, so now he could only imagine what the Greys' other room was like. Geoff did not repine, however. Having at last discovered that girls were every bit as nice as boys –

probably nicer than most – he was savouring the warm and pleasant feeling that he now had a friend he could visit whenever he was able to do so. Next time he would ask to see the parlour, might even go upstairs, take a look at the bedrooms.

His spoon, squeakily scraping up the last smear of Murder on the Alps, reminded him that the meal would soon be finishing with yet another grace. Father O'Malley, who was Father Brannigan's deputy, was hurrying up the monitors, eager that the bowls might be collected and carried through to the kitchen for the staff to deal with. Once that was done the boys would be at liberty for a couple of hours before bedtime. There would be organised activities in the back yard, if you could call it that, for it was large enough for the playing of energetic games, and one of the masters would probably accompany the older boys to the Whitley Gardens where they might amuse themselves for an hour or so. Geoff enjoyed the impromptu games of football, cricket and various other past-times, but tonight he thought he would go with the older boys. Despite having spent the whole of supper time thinking about his afternoon, he still had to make up his mind whether this new friendship would fit into his Plan.

For ever since Geoff had been five years old, he had been working on his Plan. Even at five, he had realised that those who are clever, determined and somewhat ruthless are the ones who end up at the top of the heap, and despite the disadvantages of being a foundling and living in an orphanage, Geoff was determined that he would do well for himself one day. Because of this, he had always worked extremely hard at school and had done more than his share of homework when lessons finished for the day. A teacher had realised early that Geoff was a natural mathematician and had encouraged him, in every way possible, to pursue his understanding and love of figures. Because he worked hard, he was popular with all the teachers and with most boys in his class as well, since he was never averse to helping anyone who asked for assistance, even doing the work for them if they proved too stupid to understand it. After all, it did not matter to Geoff if the whole class got good marks; he did not intend to compete with his fellow orphans for the sort of jobs the Branny thought suitable for their station. Railway porters, deckhands, street cleaners and gardeners were the usual occupations offered to Branny boys, with the occasional clerk's or shop assistant's, if a past boy proved to have the mental capacity for such work.

Geoff, however, intended to aim higher than that. He was a member of the free library and spent some of his spare time there, studying the newspapers which were set out on big stands for anyone to read. He always turned to the Situations Vacant column and was learning what a multitude of different jobs existed, though it appeared that one had to start at the bottom first in order to do well.

'Where's you goin', Gardiner?' Roy's voice cut across Geoff's thoughts as he came sauntering out of the dining room. 'Want a game of footie?'

Geoff was about to refuse, to say loftily that he would rather go over to the Gardens, when he remembered that he must keep in with Roy if he wanted to get away from the Home for a whole day without any fuss. Besides, all work and no play make Jack a dull boy, Geoff told himself virtuously. He grinned at Roy. 'Why not?' he said cheerfully, turning towards the back door. 'Who's picking sides then?'

Chapter Two

It was dark in the narrow passageway along which Clem Gilligan and his pit pony were making their way, the darkness only dimly illuminated by the miner's lamp on Clem's head. Ahead of him, he could see the lights of the main tunnel which would lead him to the dropping off point for the coal in the trucks clattering along behind him.

Clem sighed. By his calculation, this should be his last drop off before the change of shift which meant that he could return to the outer world once more, after he had fed and watered the pony.

The thought of the June evening waiting above ground was as good as a long, refreshing drink of cold water – which was something that Clem could have done with right now. It was always hot in the pit of course – the deeper you went, the hotter it grew – but there was no satisfaction in the stuffy, dusty heat down here. Above ground, he would be glad of the sunshine – if it was still sunny, that was. Trapped below, you simply could not tell. It had been fine when he came to work that morning, but by now the blue skies might have clouded over and rain might be pattering on the slate roofs and cobbled streets of the village.

Clem brought his line of trucks to a rattling halt at the collection point and unbuckled the pony's harness. He led the small creature to the underground stable block, rubbed him down with a handful of hay, fed and watered him and then, with a valedictory slap on the pony's neck, he turned away and began to walk back towards the cage. As he walked, with his empty bottle and food tin banging against his side, he wondered how his mam was today. She had been ill for a long time, though no one seemed to know what was the matter with her. She was rarely up when he left for the early shift but by the time he got home he would find her moving about the tiny kitchen, preparing the evening meal.

Clem swung into the cage with a great many other men whose shift ended at this time and waited while the last workers pushed into the already crowded space, eager to get back to the surface. Through the throng, Clem saw Billy Evans and grinned at him; he and Billy lived quite near each other and often walked back together after the day's work was done. Billy, however, came from a mining family and had lived in the village all his life, unlike Clem and his mother. They had moved to the pit village when Clem's father had found that he was no longer capable of doing the heavy work which navvying entailed. He had got a surface job at the pit but the consumption, which had already begun to attack his lungs, increased inexorably month after month until, towards the end, he was just a frail little figure, sitting at home in the chimney corner while his wife and son worked at any job which would bring in a few shillings. Cleaning in the big houses and taking in washing, sorting coal and running errands, were just some of the ways in which mother and son attempted to keep body and soul together.

Sean Gilligan had died two years ago and, almost as though his wife had been keeping her own illness a secret for his sake, it soon became apparent – to Clem at any rate – that Bridget Gilligan was very ill indeed. She had struggled on for almost a year, doing any work she could manage, but as soon as Clem was sixteen and had got himself a proper job in the pit, with a regular wage, she had stopped even pretending that she could work outside the home. When you considered that they were newcomers to the village, the neighbours had been wonderful, Clem thought now as the gates clanged shut behind the last man to board. Because he had not worked in the pit for long enough even to be considered for a pension, and because his illness had been upon him when they first moved to the village, Sean's death would have been a mortal blow to the family finances had the neighbours not rallied round. But rally round they had, even the mine owner conceding that Clem should start work down the pit a full year before he would normally have been allowed to do so. The villagers had had a whip round to pay for the funeral, and Bridget Gilligan was constantly astonished and touched by the generosity of people she knew to be by no means rich.

The tiny cottage, little more than a lean-to on the end of a row of sturdy two up and two down dwellings, had been cheap to rent. But Clem thought now that the draughts which whistled under the ill-fitting door and around the window frames could not have helped his mother's condition. For the hundredth time he told himself that now he was a man – or at least almost so – he should do his best to block up the draughts and make the house more habitable. The trouble was, he was always busy. When his mother had been fit he had only been responsible for bringing in the water from the well, the fuel for the fire and other such chores. Now that he saw her so weak, however, he did everything he could to help. He had grown expert at cooking vegetables, washing the clothes and cleaning the house, and never grudged time so spent, though in summer he often longed for the freedom to play football or cricket with lads his own age, to explore the countryside, perhaps even to work for a bit of extra money on one of the surrounding farms.

The cage clanged to a stop by the winding house and the men filed out to pick up their tallies and hand in their lamps and shout greetings to friends as they left the yard. Billy fell into step beside Clem and the two of them wrestled amicably for a moment before Billy apparently recalled that he was no longer a carefree lad and began to talk about the day's work.

'Comin' out this evening?' he said presently, though without much hope. He must have realised, from past experience, that Clem rarely joined the others once his shift was over. 'There's strawberries just about ripe at Tatlock's place,' he said. 'He'll pay a penny a basket to pickers and no one notices if you eat the odd one or two.'

Clem swallowed; the thought of strawberries was delicious to one who usually ate mainly bread and potatoes, but nevertheless he shook his head. 'You know I'd come with you if I could, la',' he said rue-fully. 'But by the time I've had me dinner and seen to whatever me mam needs doing, I'm that tired, it's all I can do to get up the stairs and climb into me bed. You on earlies again tomorrow?'

They had reached the little end cottage and Billy stayed his step for a moment, staring at the open door. 'Your mam's got visitors by the looks of it,' he said. 'Were you expecting company?'

Clem stared at the half-open door, a frown creasing

his brow, and was about to answer that so far as he knew no one was calling on them, when the door swung right open and two men came out, halting in the doorway when they saw Clem. One was Dr Dickinson; the other, a smartly dressed, middle-aged man with a small case in one hand and a black Homburg hat in the other, was a stranger. Clem opened his mouth to ask what was happening but the doctor stepped forward and took hold of his shoulders, giving them a slight squeeze as he did so.

'Clem, my lad, you've known for a while that your mam was a very sick woman. Earlier today she was taken bad – so bad that Mrs Wetherspoon sent for me to do what I could.' He paused, clearly reluctant to go on, and Clem gently disengaged the older man's hands and went past him into the low-ceilinged, dark little kitchen. He did not know quite what he expected to find there but he knew, with every fibre of his being, that something terrible had happened – something so terrible that not even kind Dr Dickinson could bring himself to speak of it. He looked across to the shabby little sofa where his mother had so often lain, but found it empty. His eyes took in the rest of the room: deserted. He made for the stairs, taking them two at a time, the dread in his heart increasing until it seemed to fill his whole body. He told himself that Mam must be really ill, that there would be no one in the bedroom because she would have been taken to the nearest hospital, there to be made better at last. He entered his mam's bedroom, which was separated from his own by a thin, wooden partition, and saw that she lay on the bed, very small and very still. Her hands were crossed upon her thin breast and her eyes were closed, yet even while one part of his brain accepted that she was gone, that this was just the shell of his mam, all that was left of her mortal frame, another part insisted that such a terrible thing could not have happened so quickly. What would he do without her? His life had revolved round her for so long now that he could not envisage going on alone.

A hand touched his shoulder, making him jump. The doctor had followed him up the stairs and now turned him away from the still figure on the bed and propelled him gently out of the room. 'She's been in constant pain, lad, for longer than she's let any of us see,' the doctor said gently. 'It's a merciful release to go quietly as she did. She was sitting by the window peeling potatoes when the breath just slipped from her. Mrs Wetherspoon came in to ask if she'd like a few turnips and found her gone.'

Clem stared bleakly up into the doctor's strong, understanding face. He wanted to protest, to explain that without his mam his life would not be worth living, but found he could not do so. All he could manage was a small tight smile as he turned away.

The day after his mother's funeral which had been paid for by a whip round amongst the members of the small mining community, Clem Gilligan packed his few belongings into the old ditty bag which his father had brought back from the war and set off along the road which led eventually to the nearest city. He had cried over his mother's loss until no more tears had come and had then decided that there was no point in remaining in the village any longer. He hated working underground, but coming back to a cold and empty house was more than he could face. Every stone of that place made him think of his parents, and though he could not pretend that he had known much happiness while living there, he could not bear the sad memories which assailed him every time he went in through the door.

Besides, it was high summer, a good time to go on the tramp and start a new life. The weather was fine and he could sleep in haystacks, earning a few coppers on the way by working for farmers or small tradesmen who might need a husky lad.

He had no idea where he was heading, save for the nearest big city, and no idea how he intended to earn his living when he got there. At the moment, he felt so bereft and alone that he could not imagine any future, let alone a happy and successful one, but he had enough common sense to realise that this feeling would pass.

'Time is a great healer,' the rector who had presided at his mother's funeral service had told him, his watery blue eyes behind his spectacles full of sympathetic understanding. 'I know that right now all you can feel is sadness and loss, and you're thinking you'll never feel any different. But if you think your mam – or your dad for that matter – would have wanted their boy to go through life mourning for them, you couldn't be more mistaken. They'll expect you to miss them, of course they will, and to think of them often as you go through life. But you've a great many years ahead of you, God willing, and you'll find comfort all around you. Folk will want to help you and it's your duty to let them do so, to appreciate such help and to reward the givers of it by showing a cheerful face and spirit. Are you staying in the village? I know you've no relatives here, but your parents were well liked and respected and a mining community looks after its own. You could do a great deal worse than to take a room in the house of a kindly local body. There's old Mrs Pratt, she'd see you were well fed and looked after for a few shillings a week, if you'd a mind to stay on.'

Clem had murmured something appropriate, had said he would think things over, but even then he had known he would not stay. And now that he was actually on the road, with the sun burning hotly on his shoulders and a light breeze stirring his dark locks, he was already aware of a lightening of the burden he had carried for so long. Besides, he had not burned his boats; the pit would be waiting for him should he change his mind, as would a room in the house of kindly Mrs Pratt. He could count this as a sort of holiday, a time for deciding what the future should hold for him.

Half smiling at his thoughts, he continued to tramp along the dusty road.

Within three days of setting out from the village, Clem knew he had done the right thing. On the first and second day, the weather had been pure summer, with sunshine from dawn to dusk and the wild flowers on the wayside verges breathing out their sweetness as he brushed against them. There were dog roses, white as snow, pink as a seashell and a dark, dramatic cerise colour in the hedges, fighting for supremacy with the coral and gold of honeysuckle. The air was heavy with scent, and bees, drunk with honey, seemed to accompany him along each winding lane. After almost two years in the pit, Clem felt that this was some sort of fairyland and also felt almost guilty for enjoying it when his mother could not.

But on the third day it rained, slanting, silver rain which came down steadily from the lowering clouds overhead. Rather than get soaked to the skin, Clem took shelter in the hollow of a huge oak tree and sat there perfectly content for several hours, so still and quiet that the little animals of the countryside never even noticed him and went about their business, unaware of the watching eyes.

That night a haystack would have been a wet bed indeed so Clem stayed in the hollow oak, using his spare clothing to wrap himself in, though in truth, despite the rain, the night was mild enough to make coverings largely unnecessary. And for the first time since leaving the village, he dreamed.

He was sitting by a river bank – he thought it was a river – with a sloping meadow behind him and the water softly lapping below. It was a warm and somehow dreamy summer's day and he was not at all surprised, upon looking sideways, to see that his mother sat beside him. She looked young and happy, very different from the way she had looked since his father's death, and when she saw his eyes on her she turned to face him, smiling at him, her expression full of love.

'This is a change from the village, eh, Mam?' Clem said, indicating the beautiful rural scene around them. 'I wish we could be here always, don't you?'

'It's the sort of place where I was brought up back in Ireland,' his mother agreed. 'The sort of place I'd have brought you up, Clem, if I'd had any choice in the matter. Your daddy always talked about renting a little farm in Connemara when the money was right, only it never seemed to be right enough and your daddy had the two of us dependent on him.' She looked around her, contentment obvious in every line of her body, her mouth still gently smiling. 'But there's nothing to stop you changing your way of life, son, because the countryside is in your blood, both on your daddy's side and on mine. So just you forget coal mines and industry and all, and go for fresh air and a decent life.'

As she said the last words, she got to her feet and Clem suddenly knew that she was about to go, that perhaps he might never see her again. He reached out to clutch her skirt but she was fading and his hand went straight through the material as though it were no more than mist. 'But, Mam, what sort of work can I do what'll give me enough money to live on?' he asked wildly, suddenly afraid of the hugeness of the world in which he must begin to make his own way. 'I'm all by meself now, without even a roof over me head, and the only thing I know is mining – and the pit ponies, of course – and mining won't keep me above ground and in the fresh air.'

His mother was yards away from him now, but she paused and turned back, smiling at him. 'Your gran'daddy dug canals when he were a young man and later he took a job aboard a barge and travelled the country. Why, your own daddy helped to dig the Manchester Ship Canal and you're young and strong . . . you'll find your path, same as they did.'

Clem was beginning to say that he knew nothing about canals and that he doubted very much whether a boy of his age could possibly get employment where the main need was for enormous physical strength when the dream twisted, wriggled and changed completely and, even as he realised that his mother and the country scene were gone, he was seeing once more the blackness of the pit and the shaggy head and pricked ears of his favourite pit pony. He grabbed at the pony's forelock to guide it into the mine and, at the same moment, the oppressive warmth and the smell of coal dust hit him, causing him to recoil so violently that he woke himself up. To his infinite relief, he found he was curled up inside the hollow oak, with sunshine streaming through the branches and falling across his unprotected face.

Struggling to his knees, he peered out into the brilliant morning. The rain had cleared while he slept and a strong breeze was already drying the twigs and leaf mould underfoot. Heaving an enormous yawn, he gathered up his possessions, shoved everything into his ditty bag and set off to find himself some breakfast. He remembered, vaguely, that he had dreamed and that in his dream his mother had been advising him, but he could not for the life of him remember more than that. The river, the countryside and the conversation which they had held on the river bank had gone completely from his memory. But with his awakening on this fourth day of his adventure, he was aware, more strongly than ever, of the *rightness* of what he had done. Suddenly self-confident, he knew that he would find work which he could both do and enjoy, and that his future would be neither dark nor lonely.

Tremendously elated by the thought of the adventures he was sure would lie ahead, Clem whistled as he walked along, heading for the farm-house on the brow of the hill where he would try to get some work and also some breakfast.

It was some weeks later that Clem came across the canal. He knew that if he followed it, it would take him to the great city of Leeds where everyone seemed to think he would find permanent work. He hated the thought of working in a factory or mill, but had common sense enough to realise that when the summer was over, there would be little or no work on the land, particularly for a wanderer with no home of his own.

Winters, furthermore, were hard in this area and Clem had no desire to be found stiff and stark, dead under a hedge when the snows came. Neither did he intend to go back to working underground and he had a strong suspicion that if he left if too long, he would not be the only person seeking work in the city. Therefore it behoved him to follow the canal and try to get work either along the way or in Leeds itself when he reached it.

Accordingly, he took to the towpath and rapidly became fascinated both by the little villages clustered alongside the water, and by the canal barges themselves. What was more, many of the barges still used horses to tow them and it was not long before Clem's natural love of the animals led him to gather handfuls of dandelion leaves, cow parsley and other such dainties from the verges as he passed, so that he might slip the fresh greenery to any horse he happened to meet.

He guessed that as he got nearer the city the canal would become less attractive. Already, he thought, there were more mills and warehouses alongside the banks than fields, woods and meadows. He decided that if he could get work near the canal he would do so, and one day, while sitting on the bank eating the bread and cheese with which a farmer's wife had paid him for his help in cleaning out and repainting her milking parlour, it occurred to him that it would be grand to work on the canal itself. Astonishingly, as though the thought had been a key turning in a lock, he remembered the dream he had had after he had left the village. Everything came back to him all in an instant: his mother's face, her gentle loving look, and the advice she had given him. His father and grand-father had helped to dig canals and his grandfather had actually worked on a barge. Surely he could do the same? He had always loved horses and knew himself to have a way with them, so that they would obey his commands with alacrity where other people had to threaten and scold to get the same results.

He had no idea how canal folk lived, but guessed it was a hard life as well as a rewarding one. They could, to an extent, live off the land, he imagined, since there were plenty of fish in the canal, and the banks and meadows through which it passed abounded with rabbits. Furthermore, surely no one would object if a boatman helped himself to a few turnips or a nice cabbage? If he did so when the boat was tied up for the night, it seemed highly unlikely anyone would notice the loss.

Finishing his bread and cheese, Clem got up and began to move along the towpath once more. The next time he came to a lock, he would stay by it for a while, giving a hand with the lock gates and asking about the possibility of work. If he had still had no luck in a day or so, he would begin to offer his services at the mills and warehouses along the bank. But the memory of his dream was still green in his mind and filled him with hope. It was as though his mother had been advising him, wanting him to have the sort of life his forbears had enjoyed. Whistling a catchy tune beneath his breath, Clem began to walk along the towpath once more, breaking off a hazel switch and planning to try his luck at fishing when the cool of evening arrived.

It was only a day or so later that his luck changed. He was sitting in the long grass, munching a carrot from the bunch he had pulled in a nearby field and cleaned rather doubtfully in the canal which was getting dirtier as they neared the city. He had been idly watching the approach of a sturdy canal barge, towing another boat behind it and hauled by a Clydesdale horse with a white star on its forehead and magnificent white feathering around its huge hooves. An elderly man, brown as well-tanned leather, was sauntering along beside the horse, one hand on its bridle.

As Clem watched, a figure jumped off the second boat and ran alongside the barge, coming to the other side of the horse's head, and dragging the animal to a halt.

'I tell you, I isn't goin' a foot furder,' shouted a youth, hauling on the horse's bridle. 'I never said I'd stay forever, good though you've been to me, and now I want out. I've been sayin' so for two weeks or more, and what notice have you took? Why, none, because it don't suit your book to have no one you can put all the work on.'

The old man began to reply but he had barely got two words out when an old woman, who had been hidden from Clem's view by a line of bushy plants ranged along the decking, appeared above them. 'What's up?' she said sharply. 'I heared you yellin' your head off, young Bert, but I don't recall as you've ever told us before that you wanted out. Norrin' so many words, at any rate.'

The old man glanced at the woman, then turned towards the youth once more. 'It's your right to go if you've a mind, Bert,' he said heavily. 'But you must know your Aunt Priddy and meself can't manage *The Liverpool Rose* and the butty boat without you to give us a hand through the locks. If you'll just wait 'til we can get someone else . . .'

54

'I ain't waitin',' the youth shouted angrily. His face, already red with temper, became dangerously empurpled, and Clem thought for one awful moment that he was going to strike the older man. 'I told you a week gone, Jake, that I was sick of the bleedin' canal and the bleedin' boat and the locks and the water and the bleedin' horse an' all.' Here he aimed a spiteful kick at one of the horse's enormous fetlocks and Clem, who could never bear to see an animal ill treated, jumped up from his nest in the grass and hurried forward, determined to interfere should it become necessary.

However, the horse tossed its head and rolled one pained eye in the youth's direction, before shifting his hoof and bringing it down upon Bert's foot. Clem saw with pleasure that the horse had no idea why the youth suddenly gave an agonised scream but continued to stand patiently upon the foot while its owner shrieked imprecations and tugged futilely at the bridle. The horse continued placidly swishing its tail and staring mildly ahead. 'Ow! Ow! Gerroff me foot, you ugly bastard!' shrieked Bert, trying in vain to extricate himself. 'Oh, I'll bleedin' beat you to a pulp when I get free! Jake, make the swine move or I swear I'll scupper the barge and butty boat, an' you along with 'em!'

The older man gave a grim smile but obligingly backed up the horse and watched, with what seemed like cynical amusement, as Bert sank on to the towpath, wrenching off his boot and examining the split and purpled flesh beneath. 'You asked for that, young Bert,' he said dryly as the lad began to swear once more. 'Well, you're no use to me now wi' a broken foot so you might as well go back to the mill and see how keen they'll be to employ a one-legged man.' He saw Clem standing watching and laughed aloud as Bert began to shriek and swear once more, his rage encompassing the boats, their owners and the horse. 'You look a likely lad,' the old man said amiably to Clem. 'We'll be needin' someone to help with the butty boat, because it takes Priddy and me all our time to manage *The Liverpool Rose* as well as loading and unloading, seeing to the horse of a night, and so on aboard both boats.' He chuckled. 'How do you fancy a life on the ocean wave? It's all found and a few pence over, mebbe, at each end of the voyage. D'you like horses?'

For answer, Clem walked over to the horse, carefully skirting the hunched figure of the unfortunate Bert, and held out the last of his carrots. While the horse munched with drooling enthusiasm, Clem rubbed the satiny head beneath the forelock, smiling into the kind eyes well above his own. 'I worked with ponies for years down the pit and liked them a good deal better than many a miner,' he said. 'This chap's just like a pony only about four times the size, so I reckon we'd get along fine. What's more, me grandfather worked on a canal boat when he were a young man, and years back his father helped to *dig* this canal. I'm strong and keen, but you'd have to explain what I'd need to do, 'cos though I've been opening and closing the locks for any boat which could use a hand, I've not worked aboard one afore. D'you mean it, Mister? Can I really work for you?'

The old man grinned at him. 'You can call me Jake and me lady wife Priddy. Our name's Pridmore but us boat people are an easygoin' lot and don't go in for titles nor stand on ceremony,' he said, then turned back towards the barge. 'Priddy!' he roared, and immediately the woman, who had gone below while the argument took place, reappeared.

'Yes?' she said baldly. 'I ain't *that* deaf. You bellow like a fog 'orn, old Jake.'

While he explained to his wife that he had offered 'this young feller-me-lad' a job, Clem was taking covert stock of Bert, who was still sitting on the towpath, nursing his foot and eyeing the barge, occupants and even the horse, with considerable venom. He was a big chap, probably six inches taller than Clem himself, and at least two years older. He wore a chequered open-necked shirt and moleskin breeches, and his hair, which stuck up like a gorse bush, looked as though it had not been combed for a week. His face was broad, his brow low and his eyes small and furtive. Clem decided that no matter how strong he might be, he was somewhat lacking in intelligence. I'll do as well as him aboard the boat even if I'm not as strong because I'll work out ways of doing the job which won't need so much muscle, he decided. Yes, if they're willing to take me, I'll give it a go.

He had not been attending closely to the conversation taking place between the two old people, but guessed from their broad smiles that they had decided, as he had, to give it a go. Priddy disappeared into the bowels of the boat once more and Jake turned back to Clem, repeating his earlier invitation to join the crew of *The Liverpool Rose*. Clem was beginning to thank him and to shoulder his ditty bag before climbing aboard when Bert lurched to his feet, his face beginning to redden once more.

'Don't you dare set foot aboard that bleedin' boat or I'll perishin' flatten you!' he said threateningly, limping over to the boat and raising one meaty fist. 'I know I said I were leavin', and so I were 'til that evil, misbegotten bugger crippled me like he done. Now I

57

ain't got no choice, I'll have to stay aboard 'til me foot heals. They won't take me in the mill whiles I'm lame as a butcher's dog.'

Clem had wondered what Priddy was doing when she went below but as Bert finished his speech all became clear. The old woman bent and picked up a meal sack which she flung on to the towpath, giving a cackle of laughter as she did so. 'You told us you were leavin', and glad I was to be rid of you, you idle, greedy young blighter,' she said roundly. 'Never a day has passed since you joined us but I've had to clear up after you because you've not even tried to learn how things should be done. You're sent off to put Hal into a stable, to rub him down, pick out his hooves and see he's snug for the night, and all you ever do is drag the harness off the poor critter and leave him all of a muck sweat and without so much as a mouthful of hay or water, come to that. Oh, Jake's a big softie, and he were mortal fond of your mother and felt he had a duty to see you right, but all that went overboard when you said you was goin', no matter how much we begged.' She pointed to the sack which had tipped over as it hit the towpath, spilling out its unlovely contents of worn clothing, split boots and remnants of food. 'There's your stuff, young Bert. Now just you clear orf 'cos I don't never want to see your spiteful face agin, d'you hear me?' She turned to Clem. 'Don't you take no notice of him, young 'un, just you hop aboard and I'll show you where you can stow your bag. Then Jake will get aboard the butty boat – that's the boat we're towing – while you lead the horse. He's a grand feller, is Hal, he'll do most of the leading to tell the truth, but as it's a warm day you may have to give a good tug on the bridle when we reaches a dogwash.'

'Dogwash?' Clem said interrogatively, taking the bridle from Jake's hand and slinging his ditty bag on to the deck of the boat.

'That's right, dogwash,' Jake confirmed. 'Ain't you never noticed them sort of ramps leading from the towpath into deep water? Them's been 'specially built so's horses what fall into the 'oggin can swim along until they reach the nearest ramp, then they can scramble out wi' no harm done.'

'I didn't know horses fell into the canal,' Clem shouted above the roars and shrieks Bert was giving as the older boy tried to clamber back aboard the boat, only to be fended off by Priddy, vigorously wielding a bass broom. 'Hal's a big feller, is it deep enough for him to swim?'

'I told you to make yourself scarce and if you don't go I'll come ashore meself and tell old Hal to roll on ye,' Priddy shouted, catching Bert a thump over the ear with the broom, which made him roar louder than ever. She glanced behind her as another boat appeared, heading fast towards them, with steam billowing from its short smoke stack. 'Ah, here come the Hortons. They've never forgiven you for pushing little Elsie into the water just because she reached the lock gates first. When I tells 'em we want rid o' you, they'll give a hand to chuck you right into the middle of the water at the first lock we reach.'

Bert appeared to take this threat seriously for grumbling mightily, he began to jam his possessions back into the meal sack and presently set off along the towpath in the direction from which they had come.

'Ho! I see you've forgot your limp – left it on *The Liverpool Rose*, I daresay,' Priddy shrieked after him. For an old lady without a tooth in her head she certainly made up for it by the strength and shrillness of her voice, Clem considered. He had noticed her bare pink gums the first time she had smiled at him and thought her face as engaging as a baby's; could even discern signs of the prettiness which had once been hers in her large, long-lashed brown eyes and short, straight little nose.

Having seen Bert off, Priddy took the rudder and Clem began to lead Hal along the bank. He guessed from the delicious smell of food which wafted to him every now and then on the summery breeze that a meal was cooking.

They had not gone far before he noticed that Hal's head was constantly trying to turn towards the canal, and guessed that the heat, and the attention of the many flies which buzzed around the horse's body, were making him think wistfully of the joys of a nice swim. Despite having a certain sympathy, for he would not have minded a dip himself, Clem kept a tight hold on Hal's bridle and presently was able to reward the big horse for his good behaviour by snatching up a large clump of dandelion leaves and feeding them, a few at a time, between the animal's long, soft lips. And when Priddy shouted that the meal was ready, he was only too happy to tie Hal to a handy stanchion – for they were now awaiting their turn to enter a lock – adjust the horse's nosebag, and join the two old people in the quaint little cabin of *The Liverpool Rose*.

During the course of the next few days, Clem not only proved himself a worthy member of the crew of three who ran the barge and the butty boat, but also became very fond of Jake and Priddy, to say nothing of Hal. Right from the start, the big horse had made it plain, in ways only a horse lover could understand, that he both liked and respected Clem and was eager to do everything he could to please him. Consequently he no longer tried to slip into the water when passing a dogwash, although there were occasions when he must have longed to rid himself of the dust and sweat of his working day.

The barge had been heading away from Leeds and towards its eventual destination, Liverpool, when he had come aboard, so Clem found, to his intense pleasure, that the canal was making its way through increasingly wild and beautiful country. The great shoulders of the Pennines rose on either side of the canal and when Jake tied up for the night, Clem was able to explore a good deal of the surrounding countryside. He found tiny streams which had carved themselves rocky ravines over the centuries and now tumbled recklessly downward, heading for the nearest lake, river or reservoir. In the folds of the hills, rowan, hazel and hawthorn trees flourished, bent and twisted by the bitter gales of winter but at this time of year gaily caparisoned with bright summer foliage. If they moored alongside a village then there was stabling for horses in winter time, but in the summer Hal had the freedom of the nearest meadow or common land, where Clem would tether him on a long rope and leave him to graze contentedly most of the night. Sometimes, as he walked back towards the canal in the velvety dark, he would see a badger, black and white face clear in the moonlight, waddling back towards its sett. Other times he would see foxes, the vixen teaching her cubs the ways of the world they would soon have to learn as they matured, and always there were rabbits, stoats, fieldmice and voles, going about their business as soon as dusk fell.

Clem also discovered that Jake was a keen

naturalist and knew more about the countryside through which they passed, and the creatures which lived there, than did many a local farmer. And if Jake was the authority on wild animals, Priddy was the one who could tell Clem everything he wanted to know about the flowers and plants which grew along the entire length of the canal. Not only did she know about such things, she also used them, for she was a noted wise woman and called upon whenever the work horses of the canal – or indeed the boat people themselves – needed any sort of doctoring. In the tiny cabin of *The Liverpool Rose* hung bunches of drying herbs, and the cupboard beneath the folding bed contained a variety of bottles and jars and a large tin of the goose grease which was the basis for most of Priddy's ointments.

Discovering Clem's own love for the countryside, she soon began to make use of him in the gathering of herbs and other wild plants, which she used in her medicines. Naturally, this meant that in order to bring back the right plants Clem had to be told what they looked like, how they smelt and where they were mainly to be found. In the long summer evenings, when Hal was grazing in the meadow and Jake sat on the bank, puffing at his pipe with a fishing rod dangling in the water, Priddy and Clem put their heads together over a small notebook in which she had drawn, with delicate precision, the flowers and leaves of the plants she most wanted. What was more, she told Clem as the boat began to make its way through the industrialised countryside surrounding Wigan and Liverpool, that presently she would show him wonders of plant life which he would see nowhere else in England.

'For as we run into Liverpool, you'll see growing

on the banks and in the verges, plants you've never clapped eyes on before,' she told him impressively. 'They say it is from seeds caught up in the hemp of sacks brought in from furrin parts, but I dunno about that. All I knows is that there's rare and beautiful stuff growin' in the city limits what you'll find nowhere else. Sometimes I thinks mebbe sailors bring 'em in on their clothing. Sometimes I think mebbe the sacks of cane what Tate's have delivered, or the sacks of tea from India and China, may have something to do with it. But wharrever it is, it's God's gift for my remedies and I'm duly grateful.'

By the time August came, *The Liverpool Rose* had traversed the whole length of the canal, had returned to Leeds and was approaching the great city of Liverpool once more. On Clem's first visit to Liverpool they had had a quick change-round, since they had entered the city unladen and had only to load up with the sugar from Tate's, which they would be delivering to various destinations en route. On this second occasion, however, they would be in the city for a day or two, since Priddy intended to stock up with food for the voyage back to Leeds and also to visit her Aunt Bertha, who was almost a hundred years old and lived, Priddy said, in poor circumstances in a tiny, dark little room, not far from the canal.

'She were a canal woman all her life but she's outlived all of her fambly and when she couldn't manage the boat no more, she sold it to a strapping young feller from over Wigan way, stuck her money in a sock and moved into her little room. She must ha' bin ninety by then and never figured on living more'n a year of two longer, so I reckon her stock o' money must be runnin' low. Me and the other boat people take it in turns to pop in with a basket of groceries whenever we're in the 'Pool . But it ain't the groceries she loves so much as the talk of the canal, and that's easy to pass on.'

The three of them were in the cabin of *The Liverpool Rose*, eating an excellent rabbit stew. They had passed the Coxhead's Swing Bridge and had moored on the left-hand bank before Jackson's Bridge, since there was grazing for Hal alongside the canal at this point. When his wife had finished speaking, Jake looked up and grinned his toothy grin at Clem. 'I reckon Bertha's good for a few years yet,' he observed. 'But when she feels the end's near, someone will take her aboard their boat for a last cruise down the canal, so she can join her old man in Burscough churchyard. It's wrong for a canal woman to die alone in a stinkin' city.'

Clem, though he had only worked the canal a few weeks, felt that he thoroughly understood what Jake meant. He knew that this was the life he most wanted, and that Jake and Priddy were the two people whose company he most enjoyed. The thought of someone like Priddy having to eke out a lonely existence ashore, cut off from the countryside she loved and the canal she knew so well, horrified him. He had never met Aunt Bertha but felt he would willingly have her aboard for her last voyage if *The Liverpool Rose* was around when she needed a berth.

He said as much to Jake, who patted his shoulder kindly. 'She's nobbut a step from the canal, though,' he said comfortingly. 'Fine days, you'll find her a-settin' on a bench near the water, smoking her old clay pipe and callin' out to any boatman who happens by. You'll mebbe see her when we gets near to Houghton Bridge.'

'You can come visitin' wi' me, if you like,' Priddy volunteered, but Clem thought he would rather explore the city itself. He had accumulated a small store of pennies from helping at the locks and running errands, and thought he would like to buy some small treats for the crew to enjoy as they made their way back to Leeds. Both Jake and Priddy had a sweet tooth, and though he was sure they were far too honourable to use more than the minimum from the sugar sacks which would presently be aboard, they dearly loved toffees, boiled sweets and even the odd bar of Nestle's milk chocolate. His pennies could buy a quantity of these things if he took Jake's advice and went along the Scotland Road.

'You could try Kettle's confectionery, only watch the old biddy, 'cos she's a tendency to weigh her thumbs along wi' her sweeties,' Jake advised. 'Still an' all, we reckon she makes the best sweets in Liverpool, don't we, old gal?'

'I used to be a dab hand at toffee,' Priddy said reminiscently, cleaning her plate of gravy with a wedge of bread and speaking rather thickly through her mouthful. 'Trouble is, since I took to doctorin', I don't have much time left over for fancy cooking.' She glanced from one to the other. 'Whose goin' to give a hand with the washing-up? And you'll want to bed the butty boat down for the night and get off to sleep yourself 'cos we'll be off at dawn,' she added, addressing Clem.

'I suppose that's another way of telling me I'm on the washin' up,' Jake grumbled, gathering up the tin plates and shuffling over to the bowl which Priddy used in place of a sink. 'Off wi' you then, lad. We ain't in open country now so we'll batten down the hatches, as they say – there's folk who'd steal the parings off our nails if they thought they could get away with it, and I don't mean to lose what's left of the cargo before we docks agin the wharf.' Clem already knew that his mere presence aboard the butty boat at night probably saved the old people from suffering considerable losses. They were safe enough in the countryside, and even the villages through which they passed, but once they reached the industrial area, it was every man for himself. Jake had told Clem that they had owned a dog, a leggy hearth-rug of a creature called Zip who had been a great deterrent to thieves, but he had died of old age shortly after Bert had joined the boat and they had not yet replaced him.

Leaving Jake clattering dishes in the cabin, Clem swung on to the bank and walked along until he reached the second craft. Boarding the butty boat, he began to check the canvas covers and the ropes which fastened them to the deck, tightening some where they had already dropped off the cargo the canvas had sheltered. Having made sure that the cargo was securely stowed, he jumped ashore again, loosened the mooring ropes, fore and aft, by a foot or two and jumped back on board, pushing his craft further from the bank as he did so. Now no one would be able to step aboard without his noticing. Having taken these precautions, Clem checked that Hal was still securely tethered and that *The Liverpool Rose* was also snug for the night. Then, comfortably aware that he had finished his tasks, he climbed into the bed roll in the tiny cockpit, where he had slept ever since he began work on the canal, and was very soon asleep.

Over the weeks which followed their first meeting, Lizzie and Geoff got to know one another a good deal better. Lizzie was quite astonished at how alike they were, despite the difference in age and sex, and was delighted to have a companion who enjoyed every new experience so very much. She knew that one reason for Geoff's enjoyment of even simple things was because living in the Branny cut him off from the everyday events she took for granted. However, with Roy's help, Geoff was now managing to get away from the orphanage on a fairly regular basis. He had told Lizzie that he suspected Brother Laurence, who was also one of the senior masters at St Mark's, knew that he was getting out to meet a friend rather than staying with Roy's family. Since Brother Laurence clearly approved, though Geoff had not yet worked out why, it made meeting Lizzie easier rather than harder and he did not worry so much in case he was seen with her.

Lizzie thought she knew why Brother Laurence approved. Geoff's ignorance of ordinary life – particularly street life – would certainly not help him when it came to finding a job. She had only seen Brother Laurence once, a middle-aged man with a ginger beard and shrewd grey eyes, but she thoroughly approved of his attitude to Geoff. 'I'm a bit of a favourite with him,' Geoff had confessed, 'because I'm a hard worker and good at maths, which is his subject of course. When we go on a trip – and we do that sometimes – I always try to get next to Brother Laurence because he knows an awful lot and enjoys passing it on.'

So by now Lizzie and Geoff had established a firm friendship and she had quite a job to find new entertainments for her friend. They went to the Saturday matinees at one of the picture houses whenever they had either sufficient money or empty jam jars with which to pay their admittance, but Saturday afternoons were usually free for a more relaxed form of entertainment. On this particular Saturday Lizzie had decided that they would go down to the Scaldy, where she intended to give Geoff his first swimming lesson. She had been astonished to discover that the Brannigan boys were not taught to swim, though the city was full of good swimming baths. What was more, living in a busy port where the majority of young men became seamen at some time in their lives, she thought it a dangerous practice to keep young boys from water.

When she had first suggested it to Geoff, however, he had not been at all keen. 'Swimming in the *canal*?' he had said incredulously. 'But it'll be filthy, won't it? And what about them barge things? I don't want to be cut down in me prime, young Lizzie, nor drownded for that matter.'

'You're more likely to be drownded if you don't learn to swim,' she had said briskly. July had turned chilly and rather wet, almost as though it knew the school holidays would soon be upon them, so she would not have suggested swimming had she not remembered the Scaldy. It was close up against the Tate & Lyle sugar factory, where the outflow from the works belched hotly into the canal, so since the water there was always lovely and warm, it was a great favourite with local kids. Lizzie had not actually told Geoff this, thinking to give him a pleasant surprise, but she began to wonder if she should have done so when ten o'clock arrived and he did not.

Lizzie helped Aunt Annie with the washing, although her aunt did less than usual because it was so hard to get a line full dry when the weather was overcast and drizzly. Then Lizzie brushed through, prepared the spuds for the evening meal and cut herself, at her aunt's suggestion, a carry-out of bread and cheese.

'There's a couple of them big pickled onions in a jar on the bottom shelf,' her aunt had advised her, when Lizzie was packing the bread and cheese into an old string bag. 'You might as well take 'em – one for you and one for young Geoff. It gives bread and cheese more of a bite, somehow.'

Uncle Perce had actually worked for the past ten days and, since a number of ships had come into the docks needing unloading, Lizzie assumed that he must have handed over at least some of his wages to Aunt Annie, for she did not normally buy such a large wedge of cheese, nor hand out her home-pickled onions. She was glad, for Aunt Annie's sake, that her uncle was behaving himself, but knew from past bitter experience that this state of affairs was likely to end suddenly, and probably violently. Weird though it seemed, Uncle Perce would behave like an angel for a few days, keeping well away from the pubs and doing no more than share a jug of porter with his wife of an evening. Then, as though all this goodness was secretly offensive to him, he would go to the pub, drink until he had no more money left and come home evil as a devil, to beat up anyone who crossed his path – provided they were smaller and weaker than he – and make his wife's life a misery once more.

Thanking Aunt Annie for the pickles, Lizzie made up a bottle of cold tea from the remains of their breakfast drink and was wondering whether to shame Geoff by going up to the Home and demanding a word with him, when there was a rattle on the outside door. She flew across the kitchen just as Geoff, who had become at ease with the whole family, pushed the door open and stepped into the hall, grinning broadly. 'Sorry I'm late,' he said breezily. 'But I had to tidy the dormitory 'cos it were young Paul's turn and his gran came calling to take him to his cousin's wedding. It were just my luck that old Brother Mark was on dormitory duty today, otherwise I might have got away with it. Still an' all, he didn't stay to watch me do the work, so I got a shift on and here I am,' he ended triumphantly.

Lizzie, who had been cursing his late arrival, promptly forgave him and went back into the kitchen to remind Aunt Annie that she would be gone 'til dark and would like some supper saved, please. Aunt Annie, who seemed to have grown quite fond of Geoff, said she would save them both a helping and actually waddled to the door to wave them off. 'As though we were family – both of us I mean,' Geoff said rapturously. 'Your aunt's all right, Liz.'

'She were really fond of my mam,' Lizzie admitted as they emerged on to Burlington Street. The cobbles were wet with rain but a glance at the sky above told her that the heavy clouds scudding across it were now more white than grey; it might turn out to be a nice day after all. 'I think Aunt Annie's quite fond of me, too, though the boys don't like me much and Uncle Perce positively hates me. Mind you, he hates everyone just about, even Aunt Annie. Me mam once said that Uncle Perce was crazy because he'd be lost without me aunt, but that's fellers for you.'

Geoff laughed and punched her lightly on the shoulder. 'I'm a feller meself,' he reminded her. 'Not that I fancy having to drink all that bitter old stuff that your uncle downs whenever he's in the money. Someone gave me a sip of Guinness . . . yuk!'

'Yes, I know what you mean,' Lizzie said, dancing

along beside him, with the string bag banging against one skinny calf. 'I think you have to be quite old before you like the taste because Herbie thinks it's foul, same as we do. But the big boys – Henry and Ned – are getting to like it. At least, they go down to the pub a couple of times a week and come back talking rather loud, so I suppose they're drinking the stuff.'

They were crossing Vauxhall Road when Geoff grabbed Lizzie's arm. 'Oh, damn and blast,' he said in a furious undertone. 'There's bleedin' Sid – I hope he doesn't recognise me. I've kept well out of his way ever since you and I met up and I certainly don't want him tagging along with us now.' He had lowered his head and turned towards Lizzie but now he risked a quick peek to his right and groaned aloud. 'Tom's with him! Keep walking, Lizzie, don't run or they'll spot us.'

'It doesn't matter if they do,' Lizzie said briskly, continuing to hurry across the wide road, though they both had to pause to allow a tram to rush past. 'If they come up to us, I'll say we're off to me grandmother's funeral – that'll put them off.'

Geoff chuckled but kept his head bent and hurried with her across the road, not pausing until they were halfway to Houghton Bridge. Only then did he pull Lizzie to a stop while he scanned the scurrying people behind him, before giving vent to a long whistle of relief. 'They're not in sight,' he reported, rather breathlessly. 'Thank the Lord for that! I wonder where they were off to, though? Saturdays were always a favourite with Sid, 'cos he said the more people there were about, the easier it were to dip a pocket or prig a shop.'

'Let 'em gerron with it, I say,' Lizzie said, also

scanning the crowd. She realised that she was no keener than Geoff to meet up with his former companions. All the boys she knew could swim and most of them favoured the Scaldy as a bathing place and she had no desire to find herself sharing the water with Sid and Tom. But it would, she considered, be carrying coincidence rather far if the older boys intended to bathe at the Scaldy on the one day of the year that she and Geoff meant to do the same.

Heartened by this thought, she continued to hurry along the pavement beside him, chattering away as she did so and telling her companion that Aunt Annie meant to save him some supper. 'And she's give us each one of her big pickled onions to eat with our bread and cheese,' she ended triumphantly. 'Before you know it, you'll be calling yourself Geoffrey Grey. She's taken to you so well you're as good as one of the family.' She grinned at her companion, knowing that the remark would please him.

They reached the Houghton Bridge and slid down the steepish bank on to the towpath. The canal was wide here and when Lizzie looked ahead of them to where the great bulk of Tate's loomed, she saw that already several of the local urchins were frolicking in the water, jumping in as hard as they could in order to splash one another. Lizzie knew most of them by sight and called out a greeting as she and Geoff hurried along the canal bank and settled on a good spot where they could eat their food and dump their clothing when they went in for their swim. The grass was meagre here, but perhaps because of the heat from the factory there were foreign-looking flowers in bloom and Lizzie admired them while making a sort of nest for herself and her companion. Geoff, wide-eyed, stared at the steam rising from the water and asked Lizzie, almost timidly, what had caused it.

'It's Tate's,' she said, accepting a peppermint ball from the bag which he held out. The Branny boys were given two ounces of sweets each Saturday morning, through the goodwill of some long-forgotten benefactor. 'It's the overflow from the factory – something to do with making the sugar clean, I guess. At any rate they make hot water and then belch it out into the canal when they've done with it. Look, I think we'd best have our swimming lesson before we eat our snap, 'cos then our bellies won't go getting cramps.'

Geoff looked at her doubtfully. 'But will our stuff be safe, just sitting on the bank like this?' he enquired. 'Learning to swim is going to make me awful hungry. I don't want to come back and find me dinner has gone down some other feller's throat.'

'There's not many about. Everyone's going home for their dinners soon and it's a drizzly sort of day,' Lizzie pointed out. 'We'll wrap our snap in our clothes, so's no one can see it, have our swim and then eat. Honest, Geoff, you can get cramp, belly-ache, all sorts if you swim on a full stomach. Or so they say,' she added.

The children removed their outer clothing but the sun still stayed behind the clouds, making swimming seem far from attractive. However, Geoff and Lizzie were soon in the water and after the initial shock he allowed Lizzie first to show him how she swam herself and then to hold up his chin while he had a go. Because the water was so warm, they soon began to enjoy themselves wholeheartedly and Lizzie actually voiced the opinion that it would not be long before: 'Geoff was froggin' it as well as any kid in the neighbourhood.'

Their snap, sitting on the bank well hidden by their clothes, was forgotten. Learning to swim occupied them both.

Sid and Tom had been mooching along the road, wondering what to do with themselves, when Sid spotted Geoff and Lizzie dodging amongst the crowd ahead of them. He grabbed Tom's arm, drawing his friend to a halt. 'The little bleeder!' he said viciously, indicating Geoff. 'He's been avoidin' us for weeks, tellin' everyone he can't get out no more, lyin' his bleedin' head off in fact, an' all the time he's been playin' around with that scruffy kid – the one we hit with a cricket ball – and norra thought for his old pals what were good to him in times past.'

Tom squinted up his eyes and peered ahead. 'Are you sure it's Geoff?' he asked doubtfully. 'As for the gel, she might be anyone. What makes you think it's the one who stopped our cricket ball?'

Sid snorted. 'Who else could it be?' he said derisively. 'Them holy brothers keep the fellers at the Branny on such a short rein they don't never get to speak to a gal, lerralone walk through the streets wi' one. Besides, there can't be two mucky grey dresses like that, and that yaller hair. A proper little gutter-snipe, that's what she is. Why, now I come to think of it, it's downright insultin' if he prefers her company to ours. What's more, he were useful in his way.'

'Yes, he was,' Tom admitted. 'It were that innocent, clean sort o' look that the Branny boys have – it gorrim into places what would have slung us out after one glance. Still an' all, our Sid, you kept him at arm's length, never really lettin' 'im join in. I weren't that surprised when he stopped comin' out wi' us on a Saturday, to tell you the truth.'

'He's nowt but a bleedin' orphan,' Sid said obstinately. 'He don't have no rights, 'specially when he could be useful to fellers like us.' He frowned and began to whistle beneath his breath then broke off to remark: 'Where's they goin', d'you reckon? They're off on the spree, there's no doubt about that, and they ain't half gerrin' a wriggle on!'

'They could be goin' anywhere,' Tom observed, but quickened his pace to keep up with Sid who was beginning to hurry forward. 'What's it matter where they're goin', our Sid? You ain't goin' to persuade him to join up wi' us again, are you? 'Cos if he'd wanted to, he could have made contact in the old way.'

'I ain't goin' to persuade him to do what he ought to want to, I'm goin' to teach him the error of his ways,' Sid said grimly. 'Bleedin' orphans don't gerraway wi' givin' me the cold shoulder. I'll teach him to respect his elders, see if I don't. Aha!'

'What have you seen?' Tom asked breathlessly, panting along beside his friend. Sid was at least eight inches taller than he and could, he knew, see a good deal further ahead. 'What are they doin'?'

'They've been and gone and disappeared,' Sid said. He did not sound disappointed, however, but rather pleased. 'Now we've got 'em! They've nipped down under Houghton Bridge, so I reckon they're headin' for the Scaldy. Tom, can you remember if that kid . . . Geoff, isn't it? . . . can swim?'

'I never met a fellow yet what couldn't,' Tom said. He glanced up at his companion. 'If you're thinkin' of chucking half bricks . . .'

Sid snorted. 'Just you shut your gob and do as I tell you,' he advised the younger boy. 'I'm goin' to show 'im it ain't wise to cross a pal, that's all.'

As soon as the two boys reached the bridge, they were able to confirm that the children they were following had indeed gone in for a dip. It was soon obvious, furthermore, that Sid's guess had been right – Geoff could not swim but was being given a lesson. The two boys watched for some time as the youngsters splashed around in the water, apparently not in the least worried by the drizzling rain, but it was not until some other children had joined them, that Sid finally revealed his strategy to his companion. 'See where them canal boats is moored up?' he said. 'I'm goin' to slip in the water under cover of the boats and give that kid the duckin' he deserves. And you're goin' to help me.'

Tom, used to obeying his elder, looked doubtful but obediently followed him down the bank and on to the towpath, taking off his clothes as soon as they neared the water. 'Just remember the feller can't swim,' he advised, 'and the girl's only a kid, after all. We don't want to end up having to rescue him from drownin' and gettin' into big trouble, do we?'

Sid grinned but vouchsafed no reply and presently the two of them slid into the water and began to head towards the part of the canal already occupied by half a dozen other swimmers as well as by their quarry.

Lizzie was pleased with her pupil. It had not occurred to her, until they were actually in the water, that Geoff might be afraid to take his feet off the bottom and begin to use his arms and legs to keep himself afloat, but at first this was just what happened. Geoff insisted on keeping at least one foot on terra firma although he obediently splashed with his arms. After a very short time, however, with Lizzie's hand firmly cupping his chin, he seemed to gain confidence and

76

was actually frogging away quite competently in the shallower water near the bank when something very odd happened. His chin detached itself from Lizzie's hand, he took a deep gulp of air and emitted a strangled squawk before disappearing completely.

Lizzie, laughing, waited for him to re-emerge and when he had not done so after a few seconds, plunged under water herself to see what had happened to him. Immediately, someone seized her wrists and began to tow her out into deep water. Glancing wildly around her, Lizzie saw two figures nearby, one a great deal larger than the other, both struggling desperately. At the same moment, she twisted sharply in her assailant's grip and brought her feet up, kicking him in the chest with enough force to make him release her wrists. At once she bobbed cork-like back to the surface of the Scaldy and looked wildly around her; Geoff was still nowhere to be seen, but ten feet away she caught a glimpse of a horribly familiar face as its owner came up for air.

It was Sid.

For a moment, Lizzie could not imagine what he was doing in the water and then, as Geoff's head appeared briefly beside him only to be viciously thrust under once more, she realised. He was trying to drown her pal – probably did not even realise her friend could not swim – and had undoubtedly told his horrible little side-kick to do the same with her. She dived across the intervening water and felt around desperately, trying to find Geoff so that she could help him to the surface once more, but then Sid turned on her, grabbing a handful of her hair and doing his best, it seemed, to scalp her while still holding the unfortunate Geoff underwater.

Lizzie squirmed in his grasp and kicked as hard as

she could against his bony legs, making him release Geoff momentarily so that she had the satisfaction of seeing her friend's head emerge just long enough for him to take a breath before Sid pushed it under once more. Tom, meanwhile, had surfaced alongside Lizzie and was doing his best to pinion her arms to her sides while the murderous Sid tried again to reach Geoff and had indeed got him by the hair when mercifully there was an interruption. Someone gave a shout and dived into the mêlée of thrashing bodies. The unknown punched Sid squarely on the nose, freed Lizzie's arms by the simple expedient of dragging Tom away from her by his hair, and then brought Geoff to the bank, where he laid his limp form on the towpath and began to squeeze the water out of him as one would squeeze a sponge, first turning his head sideways on the grass.

Lizzie, bruised and shaken and very worried for her pal, scrambled out of the water and stood over Geoff, shivering with cold and fright. Out of the corner of her eye she saw Sid and Tom fleeing in the direction of the bridge, clearly intent upon escaping from the consequences of their actions.

Lizzie looked down at Geoff's recumbent form. Her friend looked awful and did not appear to be breathing, but presently he gave a great gasping choke, spouted water like a whale and began breathing normally though hoarsely. The boy who had been applying artificial respiration so ruthlessly said: 'Let him lie quiet for a moment to recover himself.' He sat back on his heels and glanced up at Lizzie. 'What was that all about?' he enquired, looking back towards the water. 'If that was a game, gal, it were a mighty dangerous one, but I guess it was no game. That feller, the tall one, meant business.

D'you know him? If so you ought to tell the coppers, 'cos he's a madman.'

'His name's Sid, and he's got it in for Geoff because they used to be pals and they aren't any more,' Lizzie said, rubbing her arms vigorously with her hands. 'We saw them earlier, Sid and Tom, I mean, but we didn't know they'd seen us else we might not have come down to the Scaldy. Not that I thought even horrible Sid would try to kill someone,' she added reflectively. 'I s'pose he just meant to scare us only things got out of hand.' She glanced curiously at the stranger. 'Where did you come from anyway? I'm terrible glad you saw us, I reckon you saved Geoff's life, but how did you know we were in trouble?'

'I was on that canal boat over there, *The Liverpool Rose*,' the boy said. 'I'd been down the Scottie to buy some sweets and I'd just climbed back aboard when I spotted the fight. If you could call it that,' he added thoughtfully, 'because from where I was standing, it were pretty one-sided. That feller – Sid you said? – must be my age or more, a lot older than you or your pal.'

'I reckon he's about sixteen,' Lizzie was beginning when Geoff, who had been lying with his eyes closed, opened them and hitched himself up into a sitting position.

'What's going on?' he enquired thickly. 'Who was that feller who was trying to drag me under? I were nearly dead, everything had gone black, when someone heaved me up and began pummelling me.' He gave a gigantic shiver, looking pathetically from Lizzie's face to that of his rescuer. 'What's going on?' he repeated.

The boy from the canal boat looked around him, then spoke decisively. 'Where's your clothes? Have you got a towel?' He turned directly to Lizzie. 'You'd best fetch all your stuff so the pair of you can get dried and dressed. Then we'll go to *The Liverpool Rose* because your pal could do with a warm up and a hot drink. He's cold as death and suffering from shock, that's clear, and the sooner we can get him warm and dry, the better for both of you. There's always a fire in the galley of the old *Rose*, and Priddy won't mind if we take advantage of it, seein' as how your pal's a bit under the weather, like.'

Lizzie, glad to be told what to do, headed along the bank to where they had left their food and clothing. She scooped everything up into her arms, carefully combing the ground to make sure she had left nothing behind, then turned and went over to the two boys. Once dried and dressed, if not warm, the three of them set out in the direction of Houghton Bridge so that they could gain the further bank of the canal.

Lizzie had never been near enough to the canal boats to take a really good look at them, but now she stared with all her might. *The Liverpool Rose* was brightly painted in scarlet and green with yellow trimmings and the name on her bows was picked out in gold leaf, with wreaths of stylised roses of every imaginable colour coiling about the letters. On the decking were buckets of earth in which various vegetables grew in profusion. Lizzie, always deeply interested in growing things, wondered whether she might be able to grow tomatoes and lettuces as this boat owner grew them – in buckets or flowerpots rather than in the garden, which neither the Greys nor the boat owner possessed. It had always been a sore point with her that, because the house in the Court was a back-to-back, there was not even the tiniest square of earth in which to set plants. Now she realised a little imagination – and some buckets of soil – meant you could grow things almost anywhere.

Having taken in the look of the boat from the outside, from the plants to the clean and shining walkway, the coils of plaited rope matting which prevented it from scarring itself on the canal bank as it was brought alongside, and the crisp white cotton curtains at the small windows, Lizzie followed the boys eagerly as they went into the cabin. She looked around her curiously as she entered.

It was tiny, but so beautifully arranged that one could only admire the thought and planning which had gone into it. Every surface hid drawers or cupboards; tables folded down flat against dresser tops or settles and, looking about her, Lizzie could not see so much as an inch of space which had not been utilised. What was even more remarkable to eyes used to the drabness of her aunt's home, with boxes pressed into use as cupboards and chairs fashioned out of any old bits of wood, everything here, even smaller objects such as buckets, plates and mugs, were all brightly painted. There was a stove, its doors now open so that warmth flooded the small space, and Geoff was in the act of being sat down on a cushioned settle as near to the fire as he could get while the owner – and the boy who acted as though he owned the boat – pulled the kettle over the flame and announced that he would make them all a hot cup of tea.

Lizzie, suddenly remembering that she and Geoff had not yet eaten their carry-out, rootled in her bag for the cheese sandwiches and plonked the greaseproof-wrapped package on to the table. 'Here's some grub to go wi' the tea,' she announced, glad to be able to make some contribution after this kindness. 'There's plenty for three.'

'They look very tasty,' their rescuer observed as Lizzie began to unwrap the sandwiches. 'It's always nice to have a bite of something to eat after a swim.'

'Who did the painting?' Lizzie asked, indicating the roses, castles and little scenes surrounding her. 'They're awful good, whoever did them. Don't I wish I could paint like that!'

'It were Priddy – she's very artistic as well as being a sort of doctor to the people and the horses on the canal and a good few of the dogs as well. Jake – that's her husband – told me she delivers babies and splints broken legs when there isn't a doctor handy. She's a grand lady is Priddy, but it's a good thing she and Jake aren't at home, seeing as the three of us is spreading out a bit,' he said chattily as he got a tea caddy from the cupboard beside the stove. The boy took mugs from the hooks on the wall, arranging them on top of the folding table. 'Priddy's gone to see an old friend so Jake stayed wi' *The Rose* while I did my bit of shopping, then he lit out to make final arrangements for a return load from Tate's, or at least I reckon that's where he's gone. They wouldn't mind you bein' here,' he added hastily. 'They're right hospitable are Priddy and Jake, but they're neither of 'em small and they would have made the cabin awful crowded.'

'Is Priddy and Jake your mam and dad?' Lizzie asked baldly. 'And who's you, anyway?'

The boy looked up, surprised, and grinned at her. Taking a good look at him for the first time since he had rescued them, Lizzie saw a sturdy boy of perhaps sixteen or seventeen, with dark curly hair falling over a broad forehead. His eyes were very dark as well and his mouth had a humorous tilt to it, but there was something . . . something . . . Subconsciously, Lizzie had been aware that he was not quite like the other boys she had seen on canal barges, nor quite like the youngsters who had been swimming in the Scaldy. What was different? Gazing curiously at him, she realised that he was very much paler than the boys on the canal boats, who tended to look very brown, summer and winter, because of the outdoor life they led. This boy had a flushed, almost tender look across his cheekbones and forearms, which seemed to indicate that he had only recently begun to spend time in the sun. But the boy had looked down again and was pouring the tea as he spoke.

'No, Priddy and Jake ain't my ma and pa, they took me to work for 'em when their nephew decided he could make more money in one o' the factories up north. My name's Clem Gilligan. I work the butty boat – that's the one we tow behind – and see to the horse, and help with loading and unloading, that sort o' thing.'

'I *thought* you didn't look like the other people on the canal boats,' Lizzie said triumphantly. 'You aren't all brown and leathery, like they are. It's only gypsies and canal folk what live outside all the year round who get so tanned. You don't have that look, not yet. What did you do before you joined *The Liverpool Rose*? And what did your mam and dad say to you going a-sailing on the canal, and by the way, where's your horse?'

Clem bent and took a tin of condensed milk from a tiny cupboard under the settle on which Geoff sat. He began to pour a small amount into each of the mugs. 'The horse is stabled 'cos there's no grass around here for him to graze. His name's Hal and he's a grand feller, so he is.' He turned to face Lizzie, his eyes serious. 'My parents are both dead. After my father died, Mam and I struggled on somehow. I worked in the pit, mostly with the ponies because you can't hew coal until you reach your full strength. After my mam went there didn't seem any point in staying in the village. I hated working underground and I've always loved the countryside, so I lit out from the village, meaning to go on the tramp while the good weather lasted. Then I reckoned I'd pick up work in one of the mills or factories round Bradford or Leeds, only I were lucky. I was sitting by the canal, eating bread and cheese, when the *The Liverpool Rose* came alongside and young Bert, the nephew, started to rant and rave that they weren't going to keep him aboard when he could earn more in a factory . . .'

Lizzie and Geoff listened, fascinated, as Clem told them with great relish of Jake's offer of the job and his acceptance, and then went on to tell them of the life he had lived over the past weeks. He made it sound exciting and adventurous and when at last he'd finished, Lizzie and Geoff stared at him with envious eyes. 'I wish I were in your shoes,' Geoff said. He took a long draught of tea then stood down his empty mug. 'That were great, Clem, you make a fine cup o' tea.' Suddenly, something seemed to strike him; he looked round at the other two, a slow smile spreading across his face. 'I've just realised something – you talk about coincidence!' He addressed Lizzie. 'D'you realise, queen, that we're all three of us orphans? Oh, we have very different lives but we've got that in common. When you think it's just like a story book how we come to meet, with Clem saving my life an' all. I reckon we ought to keep in touch, the three of us.' He turned to Clem. 'Are you in Liverpool regular, Clem? I mean, every two or three weeks or so? 'Cos if so, we could arrange to come down to the canal whenever we know you're docking here.'

'That'd be grand,' Clem said eagerly. 'It ain't easy to make pals on the canal 'cos most of the fellers were born and bred to it and they've known each other all their lives, just about. On the short runs, some of 'em get dropped off at a local school, so's at least they learn to read and write. Then they make friends with the local kids, so all along the canal they've got pals. It's different for me, being a stranger, like, so I'd be glad to meet up wi' the pair of you whenever we're docked in Liverpool.'

'The only snag is, Geoff ain't his own master. He lives at the Father Brannigan Orphan Asylum,' Lizzie said blithely, then clapped a hand to her mouth. 'Oh! Sorry, Geoff, I forgot you might not like . . .'

'S'all right,' Geoff told her, 'I don't mind me pals knowing – it's just strangers, like. When *The Liverpool Rose* docks, you can find a way to let me know without landing the brothers on me neck, I daresay. Mind,' he added, 'we're going to be down at the Scaldy most Saturday afternoons for a few weeks yet.'

'You won't want to risk going there again,' Lizzie said, scandalised. 'You were very nearly drowned, chuck! That horrible Sid will be watching the Scaldy now, and Clem here isn't always going to be around to gerrus out of trouble. I think we ought to steer clear of it for a bit.'

Geoff, however, shook his head obstinately. 'No, you couldn't be more wrong,' he declared. 'What happened today means I gorra learn to swim, and the sooner the better. As for perishin' Sid, he won't expect me to come back here. He thinks because I have me hair cut regular and wear the Branny uniform that I'm scared of me own shadow – but I'm not, you know. I'm going to come back here every Saturday I can get away, until I can swim really well, and next time it'll be me what does the ducking!'

'You're really brave, Geoff. And sensible as well, 'cos you're dead right about Sid,' Lizzie said. 'I don't say he thinks you're yaller, but I'm sure you're right and he won't expect to find you at the Scaldy again. If you ask me, he ain't the sort to go swimming without a very good reason, so we aren't likely to run into him again, particularly with autumn coming on. The Scaldy's always lovely and warm, but I suppose it's colder coming out, which puts the other kids off swimming once September starts.'

'Aye, you're both right,' Clem said, getting to his feet. 'As for meeting up again, you'll have to keep a look out for me, 'cos my time's not my own when we're loading and unloading.'

'Righty-ho,' Lizzie said. 'Me home's near enough to the canal so I can keep an eye out for you most weekends. I live wi' me Aunt Annie and Uncle Perce and me cousins; their name is Grey but mine's Devlin, 'cos my mam and Aunt Annie were sisters, so if you want to find me, just ask for Lizzie Devlin, anywhere on Burlington Street.'

'Her Aunt Annie's real nice,' Geoff volunteered. 'She lets me have me tea wi' the family sometimes, and I'm always welcome to stay in the house if young Lizzie here's busy doing chores. But her cousins aren't too friendly, and her Uncle Perce is a bit gruff, like.'

'Me Uncle Perce's a beast and a bully,' Lizzie said frankly. 'He don't touch the boys, 'cos they're all near as big as he is, but he gives Aunt Annie a clout whenever he's had a drop too much and he'd hit me an' all if he could. Only I take care to keep out of his way,' she finished.

'Right, mates,' Clem said cheerfully, 'I'll walk as far as the Houghton Bridge with you but I can't come no further 'cos it just isn't safe to leave the canal boat unattended. No offence but there's kids in the 'Pool what'd steal the socks off your feet while you were still wearing 'em – and not only kids, neither,' he ended darkly.

Lizzie and Geoff both laughed. 'I daresay every city is as bad,' Geoff said. 'I've never been outside Liverpool myself, but I've heard Leeds and Bradford can be pretty rough, and as for Wigan . . .'

'Aye, Wigan's got a bad reputation amongst the boat people,' Clem agreed, 'and truth to tell, when we're in the country we don't leave the boat unattended if we can possibly help it. Even high up in the Pennines, the three of us seldom go off together. We take it in turns, like.'

The three of them reached Houghton Bridge and Lizzie and Geoff climbed up to the road and leaned over the parapet to watch Clem retrace his steps and enter the barge, with a final wave in their direction. As they watched, they saw an elderly man with a sack over one shoulder coming slowly along the towpath. 'I wonder if that's Jake?' Lizzie said idly. 'Will you make me a bet, Geoff? I get a penny if I'm right and that old feller goes into *The Liverpool Rose*, and you get a penny if I'm wrong and he goes straight past.'

'No, I will not make a bet with you,' Geoff said roundly, just as the elderly man climbed aboard *The Liverpool Rose* and disappeared into the cabin. 'I guessed it were Jake, same as you did. Who else could it be, after all?' He shivered suddenly. 'I dunno whether it was my ducking or because it's getting late, but I'm beginning to feel chilly. Race you back to Cranberry Court!'

Later that night, in her own small bed in the partitioned-off piece of attic room, with the boys snoring beyond, Lizzie thought about her day. She had been delighted with *The Liverpool Rose* and thought Clem one of the nicest boys she had met. He was older than both she and Geoff, and had been working at a proper job for more than two years, but he had made no attempt to boss them around, nor had he seemed to feel himself superior.

Apart from the swimming incident, which had so nearly ended in tragedy, the day had been a great success. Lizzie was still downright proud of Geoff who had had a truly horrible experience yet had bounced back. She knew that he still intended to learn to swim, despite what had happened, and admired his courage. Bullies are always frightening and Sid, with his reckless disregard for everyone except himself, frightened her even though his venom had been mainly targeted on Geoff. She supposed, vaguely, that living in the Branny had made Geoff far more independent than living with Aunt Annie had made her.

It had been fascinating to hear about life on the canal boat, and Lizzie hoped that she and Geoff would see a great deal more of Clem. She could not help wishing that one day he might invite them to go along for a short cruise. That would be far more exciting than a ride on the ferry which crossed the Mersey and could take you over to New Brighton. This was a treat to which she had long looked forward, though without much hope of its ever happening.

Presently, still thinking about the canal boat, Lizzie drifted off to sleep, to dream of painted roses, flourishing tomato plants and a tiny self-contained world all packed into the canal boat's cabin.

As soon as Jake and Priddy returned to *The Liverpool Rose*, Clem told them all about his adventure and the two pals he had made. He had carefully cleared up all signs of their impromptu visit before Jake had come into the cabin, but did not intend to keep it secret. He had been sure that the old people would not mind his offering hospitality to two kids in distress, and so it proved. Priddy was horrified by the near drowning – despite having been born aboard a canal boat, she had never learned to swim – and told Clem approvingly that he had done right.

'There's a little flask of brandy in the cupboard above Jake's bunk,' she told him. 'You could ha' used that if the need had been there, but I daresay brandy ain't a good thing for a young feller. Probably hot tea were best. What were he like, this Geoff?'

'Oh, about fourteen, I suppose, short and stocky, wi' dark hair. He were from one of the local orphan asylums, so he spoke nice and was neatly dressed.'

'And the girl?' Jake asked, from his seat by the fire. 'Same age roundabout?'

Clem considered. He realised he had not looked particularly closely at Lizzie and now merely had an impression of a small pale face, dominated by huge, dark blue eyes and a mass of straggly, hay-coloured hair. 'Lizzie? Well, she must be about eleven or twelve, I suppose. She lives with an aunt and her dress was more like a rag than anything else. She was barefoot, and scraggy, but a nice kid, nevertheless. You'd ha' liked her, I'm sure.'

'Are you going to meet up again?' Priddy asked casually. She had been stirring a large blackened stewpot on top of the stove. Now she reached three plates down from the rack above her head. 'I know it's been difficult for you, Clem, to make pals amongst the boat people, 'cos on the canal everyone knows everyone else. Working aboard a barge is usually something you're born to, so it'll be nice for you to have a couple o' pals, even if you're older than they.'

'I daresay we'll bump into each other around the 'Pool when we're in this area,' Clem said, rather guardedly. He did not want Priddy and Jake to think that he was lonely or that he was suffering from any lack of friends. Indeed, he was so happy aboard *The Liverpool Rose* and so content with the companionship of Jake and Priddy that he could not imagine missing other friends. Even so, it would be nice to meet Lizzie and Geoff from time to time. We could go to the pictures, he told himself, or go shopping – even if it was only the window sort – in the big stores, whenever he was in the area.

And presently, when he went to the butty boat and took his place in the tiny cubbyhole, snuggling under his blankets, he went happily off to sleep and dreamed of roses and castles and scrawny little yellow-haired girls.

Chapter Three

AUGUST 1924

'Lizzie! Are you nearly ready, queen? It's a nice warm morning and I want to get to the shops early, to pick up any bargains a-goin'.'

Lizzie was in her room, vigorously plaiting her hair into a long braid, when Aunt Annie's voice came floating up the stairs. She went to the door and called out that she was coming, wouldn't be half a mo', then returned to her room, smiling to herself. She had taken to braiding her hair regularly since her thirteenth birthday, which was now some time past. It looked very much neater and more business-like and was a good deal less costly than the bob or shingle which was fashionable and for which she had yearned. Aunt Annie, however, had pointed out that haircuts were expensive. 'That hair of yourn is your crowning glory, queen,' she had said reprovingly when Lizzie had suggested bobbing it. 'Short hair may be fashionable but it ain't what the fellers like, nor what your mam would have liked if she'd been here to see you.'

So Lizzie had taken her aunt's advice and now was quite proud of the long, silky plait of blonde hair which hung down her back, almost to her waist. What was more, plaiting had made her hair beautifully wavy, so that when it was loose, it looked even nicer than before. Aunt Annie, Lizzie concluded now, slipping a rubber band round the end of the plait, was a knowing old bird.

Making her way down the stairs and entering the kitchen, Lizzie found that she was looking forward to the day ahead. She and her aunt were mounting an expedition to the shops for two reasons. The first was to replace the skimpy cotton dress which she had worn every summer for the past three years. It now strained so tightly across her chest and was so brief in the skirt as to be almost indecent, so Aunt Annie meant to go along to Paddy's Market and buy a replacement. While at the shops she also hoped to beg, or even buy, oranges and lemons so that she might make her famous fruit drink.

A year had passed since Lizzie and Geoff had nearly got themselves drowned in the Scaldy. Geoff now swam as well as anyone Lizzie knew, and she herself had begun to appreciate Aunt Annie more than ever. This was, she thought, entirely due to Geoff, who had made her realise that though Aunt Annie could never take the place of her own mother, she was doing her very best to see that Lizzie was as happy as she could be.

For instance, Aunt Annie had come to school on a couple of occasions to see the teacher about her niece's future; a good few real parents did not trouble to do as much for their offspring, but Aunt Annie told Uncle Perce, when he sneered at her for taking the trouble, that she was only doing what her sister would have done, had she been able.

At thirteen, starting work was something all the girls in Lizzie's class discussed. There were a great many jobs to be had in Liverpool if you were content with taking on shop or factory work. Such jobs did not call for any particular degree of intelligence, far less specialised training, but Lizzie's mother had hoped for better for her little girl and Aunt Annie, knowing this, cross-questioned the teacher as to possible careers for her niece. Lizzie, who was bright and had always done well at school, could have set her sights on office work, but an office junior was lamentably badly paid and she wanted to make some contribution to the household and to have some money to herself when she did start work. Furthermore, she was not at all sure that she wanted to end up working in a stuffy office. There must be other jobs which would allow her to spend at least some of her time out of doors, though she could not for the life of her, think of one at the moment.

However, right now it was a hot and sunny day in August and she was still only thirteen and not expected, as yet, to earn her own living. She was looking forward to acquiring a new dress, though it would be unlikely to fit without some alteration. Aunt Annie was dreadfully bad with her needle and could not sew a straight seam to save her life, but Lizzie had long ago realised that in the courts off Burlington Street, skills could be exchanged. Aunt Annie was an excellent cook and would make a big stew or a family-sized apple pie and the recipient would respond by altering a dress, or mending shirts and darning socks. So one way or another, Lizzie would get her dress and Aunt Annie would see that it was altered to fit without a penny changing hands.

When Lizzie had entered the kitchen, Aunt Annie had been sitting at the table, apparently writing a list, but now she stopped, thrust the paper into the pocket of her stained and unlovely black dress, and surged to her feet. 'Good gal,' she said briskly, waddling towards the door. 'Get the big canvas bag, would you? It's all I can do to carry me own weight, so you can tek the bag and bring home the spoils of war.' She chuckled richly. 'I mean to do well wi' the fades today 'cos Mrs Buckingham's kids have all got the measles so they'll need a deal of me fruit drink to cheer 'em up. And you know what your Uncle Perce's like if he thinks I'm wasting housekeepin' money on any belly but his'n.'

Together, aunt and niece left the house, crossed the court and emerged on to Burlington Street and turned right. Despite the early hour, the pavements were crowded and Lizzie shouted a greeting to her pal Sally Bradshaw, who was sauntering along the opposite pavement, a small child clinging to either hand.

'I thought you said the Buckingham kids had measles,' Lizzie remarked as she and her aunt set off towards the Scottie. 'It looks as though two of 'em escaped anyhow.'

Aunt Annie stared across the road. 'Them's not Buckinghams, them's Harrisons,' she said reproachfully. 'Surely you can tell 'em apart, queen?'

Admitting that she could not, Lizzie apologised and bit back the retort that, to her, one snotty-nosed kid looked remarkably like another. Besides, the Harrisons lived on one side of the Bradshaws and the Buckinghams the other, and since all the kids of the court played up and down the stained and filthy paving it was unlikely that anyone, apart from Aunt Annie, bothered to differentiate between the various children whose shouts and laughter resounded around the court daily.

Presently Sally, towing the little boys, came across the road. She greeted Aunt Annie politely and asked where they were heading. 'Because we're going along to the sweet shop on the corner. Mr Harrison's brother, their Uncle Mark, docked yesterday and he's give me tuppence to keep an eye on the kids for the morning. He's give the boys a ha'penny each an' all.' She smiled beguilingly at Aunt Annie. 'Do you really *need* our Lizzie? Only I'll share my tuppence – a penny each – if she comes along o' me.'

Lizzie was secretly relieved when Aunt Annie smiled back but shook her head. 'No, chuck, you ain't gettin' round me that easy,' she said. 'We's got a deal of serious shoppin' to do and I need Lizzie's strong arms to carry it all back home. Besides, baby-sittin' ain't much in our Lizzie's line, eh, Liz?'

'Oh, well, it were worth a try,' Sally said resignedly. 'We'll walk along o' you until we reach M'Larky's Confectionery, and then I'll be on my own.'

The three of them chatted inconsequentially until they reached the sweet shop and saw Sally and the boys disappear inside. Then Aunt Annie gave Lizzie a conspiratorial grin. 'Mr Harrison's brother! Who do that woman think she's kiddin'? Everyone knows the "uncles" who turn up to call on Suzie Harrison ain't nothin' o' the sort. I admit they's sailors, but relatives they ain't. That Suzie will find herself catchin' more'n a cold one of these days, you mark my words.'

Lizzie nodded sagely; she did not know precisely what her aunt meant by her last remark, but she did know it was common knowledge that, during her husband's long absences with the merchant fleet, Suzie Harrison entertained a great many young men, all of whom were known as 'uncles'. That this was something to be frowned upon had been made clear by the attitude of other women in the court. They would willingly baby-sit for friends and neighbours without expecting more than thanks and reciprocal help when they needed it. Since they disapproved of

Suzie's morals, however, it was usually left to her visitors to bribe some child to take the Harrison kids out of the way for a few hours.

Because of her size and the heat of the day, Aunt Annie was a slow walker. Presently, they reached the Scotland Road and turned towards Paddy's Market, and began to make their way between the stalls. Aunt Annie knew everyone and was soon exchanging shouted greetings and comments as she pawed through the second-hand clothing on her favourite stall. After much cogitation, she picked out a blue gingham dress with smocking across the chest, a bright red cotton frock with a white 'Peter Pan' collar, and a fine wool frock, navy-blue with white trimming. 'They's all good material,' Aunt Annie hissed beneath her breath, waiting until the stallholder was serving another customer before making her comment. 'Choose which you like best, queen, then I'll start in a-bargainin'.'

Lizzie looked longingly at the three dresses. Aunt Annie had chosen well. She loved the blue gingham, adored the red cotton and knew she would look delightful in the navy-blue wool. Of course, the garment was supposed to be for summer, so she should discount the navy-blue, but it was such a delightful dress! It had a white lawn collar, the popular dropped waist and three square pleats, front and back. Lizzie just knew that it would wear well and would be beautifully cosy in winter, compared to the shrunken wool skirt which had been her best garment for some while.

'Best tek the gingham,' Aunt Annie hissed. 'That smocking will be all right for now, but mebbe we could unpick it as you gets fatter. Why, in another year, queen, you'll be earnin' your own livin' and buyin' your own dresses, so this one will only have to do a twelve-month, less in fact . . .'

'Yes, all right. I've always liked blue,' Lizzie admitted.

Aunt Annie nodded, glanced towards the stall-holder, then back at the navy dress. Then she leaned over the counter and spoke to the stallholder in what she no doubt imagined to be a confidential murmur, though Lizzie heard every word plainly. 'Look, Missus, what sort of deal will you gi' me if I buys two of 'em? Only in a couple o' months, she'll need the wool dress – the gingham's fine for now, I grant you, but summer's more'n half over . . . and the smocking's already been unpicked down either side of the chest and I can't do nothin' about that, 'cos I ain't too clever wi' me needle and the gel's worse. So what do you say?'

The stallholder named a price which seemed reasonable to Lizzie but Aunt Annie hissed her breath in through her teeth, closed her eyes, clapped a hand to one enormous breast, and staggered back as though she had been physically assaulted. 'Two and tenpence?' she wheezed. 'I take it that's for the pair of 'em?'

The stallholder shook her head. 'Two and tenpence for the wool and one and six for the gingham, and at that price it's little enough profit for me. Why, I must ha' paid the gal what brought 'em in near on as much as that, an' I've bin . . .'

'Feedin' 'em ever since, I suppose,' Aunt Annie said with rare sarcasm. 'It don't cost you nothin' to keep a pile o' dresses on your stall, you can't fool me.' She stood before the other woman, breathing deeply and calculating on her fingers, at last announcing triumphantly: 'Four and bleedin' fourpence! Why,

97

that's a week's rent in some parts o' the city! However, I'll stretch a point and make you an offer. Would three shillin' do you?'

'Three and six,' the stallholder said promptly, and then regretted it – Lizzie could tell by the sudden widening of her eyes that she had not intended to give in so easily. 'And that means me ole man won't be gettin' mutton stew for his dinner for many a long day.'

Aunt Annie grinned and fished around in her pocket, producing a handful of small change. Carefully counting it out into the stallholder's palm she remarked: 'Mutton stew, eh? Well, now that I've parted with three and six – I think you'll find that is three and six – it'll be blind scouse for the next year most probably.'

'When I say mutton stew, a' course I only buys best end o' neck,' the stallholder said defensively, carefully checking the handful of pennies, ha'pennies and farthings with which her customer had presented her. 'Ho, yes, me ole feller likes a nice bit o' neck, stewed till the meat falls off of the bones.' She jammed the two dresses into a brown paper bag, sighed deeply and handed it to Lizzie. 'I can't say it's a pleasure doin' business wi' you, 'cos you strikes a hard bargain, Missus. Next time you comes a-buyin', I'll keep me trap shut until you reaches a proper figure.'

Aunt and niece left the market together, Lizzie clutching her bag delightedly. The gingham dress hardly needed any alteration and was made of good, strong cotton, while the wool dress was, if anything, a bit too large. When she had a few coppers, she would buy a sash, she decided, preferably a sash of white lawn to match the collar. She would look so smart that none of her friends would recognise her. She could imagine how Geoff's eyes would widen when he saw her decked out in navy-blue wool.

Walking along the pavement and heading for the nearest tram stop, for Aunt Annie could not possibly walk all the way to St John's Market, Lizzie suddenly started giggling. Her aunt shot her a suspicious look. 'What's mekin' you grin like a perishin' clown?' she demanded.

Lizzie giggled again. 'That poor woman's face!' she said weakly, still fighting laughter. 'D'you realise, Aunt Annie, that you got the gingham dress for eight-pence? And – and when she said she only bought best end o' neck for her old feller, I thought you were going to say, why didn't she try for worst end of neck if she were so hard up.'

Aunt Annie laughed. 'I'll 'member that next time,' she said. 'That old woman weren't a bad sort though, queen. There's many a stallholder would ha' fought me up, penny by penny, until we'd got nearer what she wanted for the perishin' dresses. Tell you what, next time I does a bake, I'll take her in a couple o' buns, just to show her I 'preciate her kindness.'

'You could make her a mutton pastie,' Lizzie suggested but though Aunt Annie grinned she vouchsafed no reply and presently, they climbed aboard a number twenty-three tram and soon found themselves heading for St John's Market. When they descended from the tram in Lime Street, the day was still both warm and sunny and Aunt Annie hummed a tune beneath her breath as she waddled along the pavement. Lizzie knew that her aunt adored bargaining and would be looking forward to squeezing as many oranges and lemons out of the stallholders on St John's Market for as little money as she could possibly pay. It was not that Aunt Annie was mean –

quite the opposite, since most of the fruit would be given away once it had been transformed into liquid form. But she knew, as did Lizzie, that fruiterers were always anxious to get rid of the bruised and split fruit since otherwise these would be thrown away as a dead loss at the end of each day. In these circumstances, any money that Aunt Annie paid would be unexpected profit, so clearly it behoved her to swell the pockets of the rich – and to Aunt Annie, all stallholders were rich – as little as possible.

When Lizzie had first moved in with Aunt Annie, she had been mortified by the older woman's hard bargaining, for her own mother had not been made of such stern stuff. She had paid the asking price for almost everything, and had, Lizzie supposed, thought it beneath her to argue over cost. But very soon, Lizzie had realised that her mother's circumstances and those of her aunt were totally different. With Uncle Perce spending all his money on drink and the boys grudgingly contributing as little as possible of their wages to the household, Aunt Annie could not afford to pay the asking price for food if she could get it cheaper. For the first time in her life, Lizzie had visited markets when they were about to close, shops at the very end of their trading day, and had even haunted such places as slaughter houses, where, if one were lucky, the men coming off duty might have odds and ends of offal which they would sell cheaply to passers-by. Since her mother had been dead now for eight years, Lizzie was well and truly used to making a little go a long way and regarded Aunt Annie's bargaining with profound approval. She only wished she could do as well, but knew that kids had their own methods of getting bargains.

Half an hour later, Aunt Annie and Lizzie emerged from St John's Market, the canvas bag which Lizzie carried weighted down with damaged oranges and lemons as well as with some bruised and battered apples which Aunt Annie said would still make an excellent apple tart. They caught the next tram home and, within a very few moments of reaching Cranberry Court, Aunt Annie was peeling the fruit, chopping it into segments and throwing it into one of her large saucepans. There was so much that she had divided up the oranges and lemons and meant to make lemon barley as well.

'So if you'll just nip along to Addison's on the corner and buy me a pound of pearl barley, and I suppose you'd best get another pound of sugar as well, then you can go off with Sally and amuse yourself for the rest o' the day,' she said. 'I daresay she'll be rid o' the Harrison boys be now.'

'I'm just going to try my dresses on,' Lizzie said, picking up the brown paper bag and holding it defensively close to her chest. 'I daresay I might wear the blue gingham, if the fit's good enough. I'd like Sally to see it,' she finished.

Aunt Annie was agreeable so Lizzie whipped up the stairs and presently descended them again and went into the kitchen, feeling as smart as any fashionable young lady in her blue gingham. She paraded round the room under her aunt's approving eye, holding out the skirt to show how full it was and admiring her reflection in the lid of the old biscuit tin which Aunt Annie kept propped on the sideboard for just such moments.

'That dress looks a treat on you,' her aunt admitted, having scrutinised her niece from every angle. 'Next time you've a ha'penny to spare, queen, go along to

Paddy's Market and buy a length of blue-checked ribbon. It'll just add that finishin' touch.'

'Yes, I thought that myself,' Lizzie said, taking her aunt's purse from the table and holding it out to her. 'How much is pearl barley, Aunt Annie? And sugar?'

'Oh, tek the purse, there's only a few pennies left in it,' Aunt Annie said. 'I know I said a pound weight of both, but you may find the brass won't run to it, so get as much as you can for the money.'

'Right,' Lizzie said, pushing the purse into the pocket of the gingham dress. 'D'you want me to come straight back, Aunt? Only sometimes there's sugar to be had off the canal barges, if a sack leaks.'

'I think you'd best come straight back,' her aunt said after only a moment's thought. 'I want this fruit drink bottled and out o' the way before your uncle gets in from work. You know how crabby he can be if he thinks I'm wastin' money which he'd rather spend on drink – and I don't mean fruit drink, either,' she added with mordant humour.

So Lizzie hurried out of the court and down the road to the little corner shop where she purchased pearl barley and sugar and then turned for home, hoping that everyone had noticed her smart new dress. When she entered the kitchen again it smelt wonderfully of the cooking fruit, and Lizzie hoped that her aunt would let them all have a drink with their supper that evening. Then there was a perfunctory knock on the door and Sally came bouncing into the kitchen, sniffing appreciatively and exclaiming that she wished her mam was as good a cook as Aunt Annie. Lizzie felt really proud of her relative, and when Aunt Annie pointed wordlessly to the blue gingham and Sally exclaimed that her friend looked wonderful, Lizzie could only thank her aunt with a speaking look.

She and Sally then left the house and wandered along Burlington Street with linked arms, chatting of this and that. Sally knew all about Lizzie's friendship with Geoff, having met him on several occasions, and was deeply interested in his plans to rise with meteor-like brilliance in the world as soon as he got clear of the orphan asylum. However, at the moment, both girls were more interested in Lizzie's new dress and in the fact that Sally, the possessor of largesse both from Suzie's sailor and from her own mother, intended to mug the pair of them to see the show at the Rotunda.

'We'll buy half a pound of broken biscuits to eat while we watch the screen, and then you can come back and have your tea wi' us,' Sally planned busily. 'It's a pity your Geoff can't get out much, 'cept at weekends. Wharrabout that feller what's on a canal barge? Clem, was it? You ha'n't seen him for quite a while, have you?'

'Now you come to mention it, I haven't,' Lizzie agreed, having given the matter some thought. 'Cripes, it must have been June when we last met up. The thing is, *The Liverpool Rose* don't always dock at weekends, when me and Geoff is free to come down to the Scaldy. I reckon we've only met up wi' Clem four or five times since that first time. In June he were downright goshswoggled at how well Geoff swims now. No need for him to be afraid of a ducking any longer. He could beat most o' the kids who swim in the Scaldy – not that he would, Geoff ain't like that.'

'He's growed a lot, your Geoff,' Sally said. 'They feed 'em awful well in orphan asylums, even if the food is dull, like what he says. There ain't many kids in Cranberry Court what are as broad and strong as your Geoff.'

'I know what you mean, but he ain't my Geoff exactly,' Lizzie objected. 'Oh, he's my pal all right, but that's because he likes visiting an ordinary home and being with ordinary people. I think I'm more like a sister to him really, and Aunt Annie's more like an aunt.'

'Well, that's what I meant,' Sally exclaimed. 'Don't I call Herbie and Denis and Henry your Herbie and Denis and Henry when I'm talkin' about 'em?'

She sounded innocent, even aggrieved, but Lizzie shot her a suspicious look before neatly changing the subject. 'I wonder what's showing at the Rotunda?' she asked. 'And I wonder how many of our pals will be going there today? I'm that pleased with my new dress that I want everyone to see it. Oh, and did I tell you, Aunt Annie bought me another one for winter? It's really lovely, even better'n this one. It's navy-blue, wi' a lawn collar . . .'

Chattering happily, the two girls continued along the road.

It was evening before the two girls returned from their cinema trip. They had seen Louise Dresser and Rudolp Valentino in *The Eagle*, and both fallen irrevocably in love with the latter. Crossing the court, still starry-eyed from their recent experience, it occurred to neither of them to so much as glance at number nine. They went straight into Sally's home where Mrs Bradshaw had a grand tea ready. Mr Bradshaw came in from the back yard, already washed, and sat down expectantly at the table. 'What have you got for us tonight, Mother?' he asked jovially. 'I see we've gorra visitor – and how's young Miss Devlin on this bright summer's day? I like your dress so I do.'

'I'm fine, thanks, Mr Bradshaw,' Lizzie said. 'And Mrs Bradshaw's got fried fish and chipped potatoes in, for a special treat. Oh, I do love fish and chips.'

'I love 'em meself,' Mr Bradshaw assured the girls. They all sat round the table, enjoying the meal, Lizzie thinking smugly that though Aunt Annie was a wonderful cook, no one could make fish and chips like they made them in the shop. Besides, she knew very well Aunt Annie had planned a gravy and potato pie; missing it would not be as hard as if she had managed to buy some meat.

After supper, Lizzie and Sally played a noisy game of cards, so that it was growing dusk when Lizzie finally dragged herself away from the Bradshaws' cosy kitchen and began to cross the court towards her own home. She was within six feet of the door when it was opened violently from within and a missile flew out, travelling with the speed and velocity of a cannon ball. It whizzed over Lizzie's head, still travelling upwards, and hit the brick wall of the house behind her, to be closely followed by another and another. These projectiles were accompanied by feminine shrieks and masculine curses so that Lizzie was not surprised to discover, when one of the missiles fell short and landed at her feet, that it was a lemon. Uncle Perce must have come home and discovered Aunt Annie still slaving over the production of her fruit drink. Why he should subsequently have begun to hurl lemons, however, was still a mystery unless he had taken it into his head, in the odd befuddled way that drunkards did, to assume that his wife was making lemonade instead of cooking his supper.

Lizzie edged closer to the open door and peered inside. She could see Uncle Perce, poised in the kitchen doorway, one hand holding a lemon above his head while with the other he attempted to thump Aunt Annie, who was circling him very much as an angry wasp might circle a piece of rotten fruit. Even as she watched, wondering whether to interfere, her uncle flung the lemon, turned round and began hitting Aunt Annie across the head and shoulders with all his strength, hands bunched into vicious fists.

'You're a wicked old bitch, spendin' me hard earned cash on filthy fruit for a lorra bleedin' kids,' Uncle Perce roared. 'Actin' the Lady Bountiful wi' money that you've never earned, whiles I have to leave the pub early 'cos I ain't got a penny-piece to bless meself with. And where's me supper? A man needs a good hot meal when he's been slavin' at the docks all day, but what do I get? Bleedin' lemonade, that's what's on offer, and it ain't good enough, Annie Grey.'

As he spoke, he continued to thump any bit of Aunt Annie that he could reach and Lizzie, having begun to approach the doorway, hastily backed down the steps again and into the court. Her uncle's face was bloated and scarlet with rage and she guessed that if she got near enough, he would simply start on her. She had best get some help or very likely her uncle would kill Aunt Annie stone dead, and then where would they be?

'I told you and told you, only you're too bleedin' drunk to listen,' Aunt Annie shrieked, as soon as her husband had stopped speaking. 'There's scouse and dumplings on the back of the stove and an apple pie in the oven and I swear, if you hit me once more, I'll send our Lizzie for the scuffers and you'll find yourself behind bars, which is where you bleedin' belong.'

Uncle Perce gave a derisory bellow of laughter. 'That little runt? You won't find her hangin' round our place when she can be with her smart friends. She'll be wi' them snooty Bradshaws, mekin' up to that ginger-headed brat what she plays out with. And if she were here, I'd ring a chime round her ears an' all.'

Incensed by this, Lizzie marched boldly up the three steps and stared directly into her uncle's rolling, bloodshot eyes. 'I *am* here, Uncle Perce,' she said, keeping her voice as steady as possible. 'And I'll go for the scuffers like a shot if you raise a hand to my Aunt Annie once more.'

Uncle Perce roared with rage and took two enormous strides towards his niece who, despite her brave words, backed hastily away. In fact, it was a good job she did so since Uncle Perce's second step took him out through the doorway. Apparently expecting to find solid ground beneath his feet, he stepped into thin air and fell heavily forward, crashing full length on to the flagstones, narrowly missing Lizzie, who leapt back still further, her heart bumping with fright. She wondered for a moment – almost hopefully – if her uncle were dead, but a deep groan and a good many mumbled curses told her that the devil looks after his own. She had heard that drunkards could have quite nasty falls without doing themselves any particular damage and this, it seemed, was such an example.

However, Lizzie supposed that she had best try to get her uncle back indoors and, glancing round her, saw that the commotion had not gone unnoticed; just about every door in the court was open and ringed with faces. Lizzie bent over her uncle and began to heave, rather ineffectually, at his beefy shoulders.

'Give us a hand someone, would you?' she asked plaintively. 'He's a big bloke and I'm not really up to his weight.'

A couple of neighbours, Jack and Dan from number three, came across and pushed Lizzie aside. Jack took Uncle Perce's shoulders and Dan took his feet, and Lizzie saw, with some amusement, that her uncle was stiff as a board. The two young men carried him into the house and Lizzie followed, thanking them profusely for their help as she did so. Aunt Annie gestured them to carry Perce into the front room where he was dumped unceremoniously on the prickly horse-hair sofa.

'He'll do there until the boys come home,' Aunt Annie told them. 'Of course it's only Herbie and Denis who live at home now, but they'll gerrim upstairs if he's wantin' a bed.' She glanced across at Lizzie as the two young men left the house and blew out her cheeks in a long whistle. 'Phew! When he's had one too many, your uncle's a rare handful – I've gorra pain like a knife in me head and me arms feel as though someone's tried to pull 'em out of their sockets. I'm for me bed, queen, and I'll lock the bleedin' door and put a chair under the handle. If the boys want to bring him upstairs, he can sleep in their room 'cos he ain't likely to try to damage a couple o' husky lads like Denis and Herbie. What's more, on second thoughts, I reckon you'd best sleep wi' me tonight, chuck. The door of your room's awful frail, and I wouldn't put it past him . . .' Aunt Annie gave Lizzie a shifty look, then concluded: 'Yes, you'd best share my bed tonight.'

Lizzie looked searchingly at her aunt. The older woman's thinning grey hair had been yanked from its bun and hung in witch-locks around her pale, bruised face. Her aunt's lower lip was split open and a thin trickle of blood had dried across her chin. She had a black eye and there were what looked like blue finger marks around her fat, white throat. If any man treated me like that, I wouldn't just threaten to get the scuffers in, I'd do it, Lizzie told herself as the two of them re-entered the kitchen. Aloud, she said: 'I'll make you a hot cup of tea, Aunt Annie, and it wouldn't hurt you to have a bit of that apple pie. I don't reckon you've touched that scouse yourself.'

The kettle was already simmering on the side of the fire and Aunt Annie agreed that she would be all the better for a drink of tea, but shook her head at the suggestion that she might try to eat. 'Me gob's too bleedin' sore for anything solid,' she said frankly. 'Wharr I really need is a good long sleep. Then tomorrow I'll be able to take on the world.'

'You're really brave, Aunt Annie,' Lizzie said admiringly, handing her aunt an enamel mug of tea with a generous amount of conny-onny to sweeten it. 'If someone treated me the way Uncle Perce treats you, I'd have him up before a magistrate if it were the last thing I did. You're ever such a good wife to him. You're the best cook in Cranberry Court, you make and mend, and lerrim gerraway wi' using you like a punch ball. It won't do, Aunt Annie. If you let this go on, one of these days you're going to wake up dead.'

Lizzie half expected her aunt to deny this, but instead Aunt Annie nodded gloomily. 'I know you're right, queen,' she admitted, 'but the plain fact is, I'm mortal fond o' your uncle – when he ain't drunk, that is. When we was first wed, I were the envy of all me pals, honest to God I was. Percy were the best-looking lad in the whole of Liverpool; he were polite and thoughtful, he spent a mort o' money on me, when the kids came along he were that proud . . . then the drink took hold of him and he began to change. Only – only I can't ever quite forget the feller I married, see? That's why I haven't ever said a word to the scuffers, 'cos I think of the old Perce what's underneath this braggin', bullyin' feller, and – and I can't bring meself to hand him over.'

Lizzie nodded sadly and presently accompanied her aunt up the stairs and into her room, where the two of them removed their outer garments, bolted and wedged the door and climbed into bed. Lying there in the half dark, Lizzie looked sadly at her beautiful new dress, neatly folded over the back of Aunt Annie's wooden kitchen chair. She could not really understand her aunt's attitude to Uncle Perce, yet she had sense enough to see that the older woman's feelings were genuine. Nevertheless, if Uncle Perce continued to beat up his wife whenever the boys were out of the house, she could foresee both trouble and tragedy ahead.

Sighing, she pulled the blankets up round her ears and was soon asleep.

Clem had visited Liverpool many times over the past year, but it had been only rarely that they'd docked on a Saturday, so he had not seen very much of either Lizzie or Geoff. Recently, indeed, he had been far too busy when they tied up alongside Tate's to do more than have a hasty look round and then go up to the shops for any messages which Jake or Priddy might find for him.

Right now, *The Liverpool Rose* was making her way back to Leeds and Clem was looking forward to the moment when they would be in the country once more, far from the hot and dusty streets and the many troubles which were apt to beset the boats and their crews, as they passed the long series of locks in the industrialised area of Wigan. They had already gone by Wigan Pier, which had once been the butt of many northern comics but which was now in a sorry state of dilapidation, and also the large coal wharves alongside the canal and were fast approaching the long series of locks and bridges which started at Britannia Bridge and ended, nearly three miles later, at Withington Lane. Now, as the golden afternoon slid into evening, they entered the first lock on the stretch of the canal which Clem particularly disliked because of the young toughs who patrolled the towpaths, trying either to thieve from the boats or simply to make trouble as they ascended the locks. He had fallen foul of these gangs on several occasions and knew that they kept a look-out for him, hoping to be able to pay him back in his own coin for the times he had foiled their attempts at theft and disruption.

Once, because Jake had kept *The Liverpool Rose* well clear of the sides of the lock, thus making it difficult for anyone to climb aboard unseen, one of the ragged, wild-eyed lads had dived into the water with a length of slimy rope which he had wound round the boat's rudder, beneath the water. Had Clem not spotted him, they might easily have had an accident as the boat tried to change direction to follow the course of the canal.

Jake usually tried to time his trips so that they traversed this particular part of the canal at nighttime. Then, although navigating was more difficult in the dark, at least they should not be troubled by active interference. But unfortunately it was not always possible, and on this occasion Clem realised they would be passing through the dreaded area in daylight, which almost certainly would mean that the Wigan Wolves, as he had christened them, would be on patrol. During the school holidays, these gangs of ragamuffins liked nothing better than to distract the boat crews while snatching anything loose aboard the barges. At this point, the canal was bisected by bridges and locks at frequent intervals, and from these ambushes, the boys could either drop on to the boats and snatch anything loose, or throw down heavy objects to damage and distract. Buckets, coils of rope, mops, dishcloths, even a line of washing, strung up carefully from one end of the barge to the other, could fall prey to the the Wigan Wolves, and though he, Priddy and Jake did their very best to keep the boat clear of anything portable, they usually had something stolen on a daylight voyage through this area.

The nuisance of it was, Clem reflected as he hurried about the boat, stowing away everything portable, that it was a beautiful evening, the sort he would otherwise have thoroughly enjoyed. Hal, well fed and groomed that morning, had been led out of his stable, seeming downright eager to get back to work once more, and Priddy had been shopping at St John's Market and had promised them a pork stew with apple dumplings once they had cleared the industrial areas – it was not a good idea to tie up for a meal while negotiating the Wigan locks. When they had a hot meal, Priddy would be in the cabin for a good deal of the time, which meant, in its turn, that Jake and Clem would have to manage both *The Liverpool Rose* and the butty boat, as well as leading Hal along towpaths.

Still, you never knew; this afternoon might be the exception which proved the rule, as the teacher used to say in school. Maybe they would have a clear run through the locks, Priddy's tomato plants would not be ravaged, nor her young vegetables torn from their bucket homes. The towpath might be clear so that Hal could negotiate it without help and the Wigan Wolves might have decided to spend an afternoon pestering someone else.

They were in luck – the bottom lock gates were open and they could go straight in. Accordingly Clem disconnected the tow rope from *The Liverpool Rose* to the butty boat which he tied up at the side of the canal. Then he urged Hal on to greater effort and soon the boat was safely inside the lock with the walls seemingly towering above her. Jake and Clem pushed hard on the lower lock gates, using their backs to get a greater effort until the gates were firmly shut. Then they each took a windlass handle, and going to the top gates began to wind up the paddles in the gates to let the water into the pound. *The Rose* began to rise steadily in the lock. When the water in the lock was level with that in the canal above they swung open the top gates and Hal pulled *The Rose* clear. Now we've got to repeat the whole procedure again with the butty boat, Clem thought grimly

As they left lock number seventy-eight there was a clear stretch of water with the Peel Hall Bridge ahead of them. Clem could see that the towpath was crowded with youths while on the bridge itself several young lads leaned over, looking down into the water as though in innocent admiration of the glittering ripples. Even from here, he could see what looked like a pile of broken bricks spread across the path and, with a sigh, he led Hal across to the edge of the lock and shouted a warning to Priddy that there were difficulties ahead.

When both boats were through the lock and had

been tethered once more to Hal, Clem took hold of his bridle and began to lead him along the towpath. The big horse knew almost as well as Clem did that the boys hanging about meant trouble and, though he was a gentle and amenable beast, began to roll his eyes and fret with his bit.

'It's all right, old lad,' Clem said gently into the pricked ear, well above his head. 'I'll not leave you. Jake and Priddy will fend off on both boats and you and me will just keep walkin' steady, like, until we reach those confounded bricks. Then we'll go round them, or over 'em, or you can take a bit of a paddle if there's no other way. Whatever happens, you'll be safe wi' me.'

Accordingly, he began to lead Hal towards the next bridge, occasionally glancing behind him at the canal boats. As he had promised the horse, Priddy was aboard *The Liverpool Rose*, Jake the butty boat, and they were using their long, hooked poles to keep their craft in mid-stream. Satisfied on that score, Clem looked ahead once more and realised, as the pile of bricks drew closer, that the Wigan Wolves were actually using them as missiles, were hurling them with all their force at something in the water ahead. It might have been a large can or kettle or something of that nature, he thought, and continued to take more interest in the path until he heard a shriek of triumph from one of the boys, followed by a yell, apparently directed at the lads on the bridge. 'Go rahnd and gerrim you idle little buggers, else he'll climb out and run orf,' the boy yelled. 'Move your perishin' legs or I'll come up there and knock your bleedin' heads together. I won't see 'im escape, not twice I won't.'

This made Clem look with more attention at the object in the water and he realised, suddenly, that it was alive. A duck, perhaps? It was too small to be anything else . . . and then Clem remembered that even a man or animal, swimming in the canal with only its head showing, would look a good deal smaller than it really was.

The boys on the bank ahead of them were still hurling their missiles and now Clem saw that those on the bridge were descending to the further bank and running along it. At the same moment, he came almost level with the object in the water and realised, with a pang of pity, that it was a large and shaggy dog which, by the look of it, was already in a bad way.

Clem gave an indignant shout. 'Jake, Priddy, they're stoning a dog to death!' he shrieked. 'I've got to – got to –' He let go of Hal's bridle even as the dog was struck by a particularly well-aimed brick, and sank. Clem had been barefoot and clad only in a light shirt and faded cotton trousers, so it was no particular hardship to dive straight into the water. The dog, now an inert bundle of fur with its nose scarcely breaking the surface, was drifting down towards him and he grabbed it by the scruff of the neck and swam as quickly as he could, towards the canal boats. Reaching them, he swam behind them to get out on to the bank, since that would mean both he and the dog would be out of sight of their enemies for a short while. Fortunately Jake, who had taken Clem's place beside the horse, pulled the big animal to a halt and came back to give Clem a hand, for the dog proved to be a gaunt, but enormous, Alsatian, and left to himself, Clem doubted he would have been able to get the sodden creature to safety without inadvertently letting go of it as he scrambled on to the bank. As it was, he and Jake between them heaved the animal on to the grass where it lay supine, its eyes half-closed and its tongue lolling. To Clem's relief, however, it was still breathing, though shallowly, and did not seem to have inhaled any water.

Oddly enough, the Wigan Wolves did not seem to realise what had happened to the dog. They must have seen Clem dive into the water, but possibly the brick throwers had been too intent on persuading the younger boys on the bridge to go round and prevent the dog from scrambling ashore, actually to realise what Clem was doing. The dog being so low in the water, they had probably not even seen that he was towing it to safety, and had gone on assuming it was still trying to get ashore along the further bank. At this particular point, there were reeds growing along the right-hand bank of the canal which meant that, had the dog gained their shelter, it would have been much more difficult to pick out.

Jake must have realised at the same moment as Clem that they were being granted a breathing space; the Wigan Wolves continued to shout to one another and the younger boys began to search the bank, diligently poking around with sticks and shouting insults to the bigger boys, who were half-heartedly lobbing bricks.

'Gerrim aboard the butty boat,' Jake hissed, taking in the scene with a swift glance. 'No need to court trouble. If they don't know we've got him, likely there'll be no fuss.'

Clem's indignation was such that, for once, he would have been quite glad to square up to a Wigan Wolf, or even to a crowd of them, but he realised that Jake was right; it did not do to court trouble. Even if he won a fight with the Wolves, they would hold it against him and lie in wait for *The Liverpool Rose*, very likely with a paving slab balanced on the parapet of the nearest bridge, ready to tip it down on to the deck, quite prepared to sink a canal boat, even if it meant drowning the crew.

Despite the drama of the situation, it had only taken a couple of minutes from the time Clem had first recognised the dog for what it was. Having bundled the creature into the butty boat, he took up his post by Hal's head, Jake jumped nimbly aboard, and they set off once more towards the groups of youths lining the bank. There were the usual shouts and jeers as they approached but, since all the younger boys were still on the further bank and their elders were busy shouting advice and criticism and desultorily lobbing bricks, the little caravan of boats and horse passed them without further incident. One boy, indeed, asked them if they'd seen 'a ugly great brute of a dog with a rare, mean look to its gob', but Clem merely gave him a disdainful look, as though he thought the boy had gone mad, and continued to trudge stolidly along the towpath. The boy spat, narrowly missing Clem's bare wet feet, but said nothing more. The pile of bricks was considerably diminished by this time, and it was not necessary for Clem to lead the horse around them; they picked their way past and then they were under the bridge, and for a miracle no one threw anything at them or hurled insults. Indeed, Clem thought with a wry smile, they had escaped remarkably lightly, especially when you considered that they carried, in the butty boat, the very fugitive for whom the Wigan Wolves had been seeking.

The lock-keepers did their best to keep control in the area of their locks but could not manage the stretches of bank as well and many a running battle ensued when an inspector was not present to augment the lock-keeper's efforts.

It was a good distance from the Peel Hall Bridge to Withington Lane; they passed through another thirteen locks, ascending all the time, and when they came out of the Top Lock, Jake judged it safe to moor up for five minutes so that they could examine the dog more closely. He was fully conscious now and keeping well to the back of Clem's tiny cabin in the butty boat. Every time anyone looked in at him, he showed his teeth and the whites of his eyes, but made no move either to escape or attack.

'You'd best go into him first, young Clem,' Jake said thoughtfully. 'It were you what rescued him, when all's said and done, and he'll mebbe know it. Dogs is a lot wiser than we give 'em credit for. As soon as he's quiet, I reckon Priddy will want to take a look at him. She's as good at doctoring dogs as she is with horses, so provided he don't need stitchin' up or physicking, he can go his ways while we're still in an area he knows.'

'Go his ways?' Clem said, amazed. 'But the moment we let him loose, the Wigan Wolves will be after him, sure as eggs is eggs. Why, Jake, you can see he's a stray without a real home of his own – I could feel his ribs even through that thick fur when we dragged him out of the water. That feller hasn't had a square meal since – since he were a pup. He's nobbut skin and bone, for all he's so big.'

Priddy, approaching along the towpath, grinned at Clem over her husband's shoulder. 'Having rescued him, I daresay you'll be wantin' to keep him, young feller,' she observed shrewdly. 'I think you're right not to want to leave him here. He'll go back to the only place he knows, like you said. Dogs do, 'specially if they've been fendin' for themselves and rootin' round dustbins and rubbish tips for any food.

they can get. The thing is though, Clem, he's awful big and mebbe he'll turn out vicious an' all. You can see we couldn't have a dog like that aboard, can't you?'

'I know he's big, but your old Zip was big and we need a big feller who'll put thieves off robbin' stuff from the boats,' Clem pointed out. 'And he curls up pretty small – look at him now, all scrunched up in the back of the cabin. So I wouldn't mind sharin' with him. As for vicious . . . well, we'd best not judge till I've got him out o' that.' With these words, Clem jumped aboard the butty boat and went boldly into his tiny cabin. The sight of the dog curled up so protectively, its huge ears pricked and its eyes fixed upon him, was a little daunting, but Clem had always been fond of dogs and telling himself that this creature was unlikely to attack him, he crouched down on the floor by its side and, picking up a blanket off his bed, began to rub the thick coat, murmuring explanations as he did so.

'Well, and ain't you a fine feller, then? When you're dry and a bit more respectable, like, we'll go outside and you can meet Priddy and Jake. You'll like 'em, they're grand folk and Priddy can take a look at you and see if you need doctorin', 'cos she's grand with animals, so she is, and if you've got any nasty deep cuts, she's the person to make sure they don't go bad on you. Then, of course, you'll need something hot inside you to make up for bein' half drowned and you're welcome to my share of the pork stew 'cos Priddy sees I get a good meal twice a day and I daresay you'll let me have the apple dumplings.'

The dog, though it could not have understood a word, seemed very conscious that here was a friend. He stood up under the brisk rubbing of the rough cotton blanket and after a moment cautiously extended a long, pink tongue and licked Clem's nose. Clem laughed, put an arm round the shaggy ruff and gave the dog's neck a slight squeeze. 'You're a fine feller, so you are,' he said again. 'Even though you're nobbut skin and bone, it's easy to see you'll make up into a real powerful animal, once you've got good grub inside you and someone to protect you from those bullying Wolves. As for turnin' you out to fend for yourself, that I'd never do – and nor would Priddy and Jake, not when they see you'll be gentle as a lamb when you're wi' friends.'

Once the dog was thoroughly dry Clem accompanied him off the butty boat and on to *The Liverpool Rose*. With his thinness hidden by his newly fluffed out coat, the dog did, indeed, look magnificent, though there was a deep cut over his right eye which still oozed blood and Clem suspected that there would be other wounds where missiles had hit him during the recent skirmish. To Clem's relief, as soon as the dog saw Priddy and Jake, his long shaggy tail began to wag gently from side to side and he came aboard and down into the small cabin, flattening his ears as he did so in an ingratiating manner, as though he was well aware that he was among friends.

Priddy had prepared a meal in a bucket, consisting of a great many potatoes, some rich pork gravy and a little of the stewed meat. Putting it down before the dog, she said: 'It don't do to overfill a starving stomach, nor to allow anyone what's been hungry for a long time, to eat rich victuals. But this should do him a treat . . . Oh!'

Clem looked down enquiringly at the dog, wondering whether he had not dared to eat the food. Instead, he saw an empty bucket while the dog looked up at him with a rim of potato across its nose and its eyes shining adoringly.

Jake, eating his own stew at a great speed as though he feared Priddy might seize it from him and feed it to their new-found friend, grinned. 'Sit ye down, lad, and get outside o' this,' he said, pointing to Clem's well-filled tin plate. 'He don't look vicious to me, the poor devil's just starved and neglected. Priddy will take a look at him once we've ate, but I don't reckon we'll be turnin' him off w'out a shillin', as the saying goes. I think this chap will be a grand friend to us and *The Liverpool Rose* 'cos just the sight of him, standin' on the cabin roof and showin' his teeth when anyone gets too near, would be enough to put off most thieves.'

Clem felt an enormous wave of relief wash over him. He leaned across and ruffled the dog's fur affectionately. 'You're a member of the crew, old feller,' he said exultantly. 'You ain't the captain, 'cos that's Jake, and you ain't first mate, 'cos that's Priddy. I'm the bo'sun, so you'll have to be a deckhand. Deckie learners, they call newcomers aboard the trawlers, but I don't reckon much to that for a name.' He turned to Priddy. 'What'll we call him, Priddy? He's a big feller, so he'll need a big name with a bit of dignity to it.'

'Them 'orrible Wigan Wolves called him an ugly brute, so how about Brutus?' Priddy suggested. 'He were one of them Roman generals, I seem to remember, one o' them fellers what wore a laurel wreath and had a damn great conk. And this feller, you must admit, is similarly blessed.'

Looking at the dog's profile, Clem had to laugh. The Alsatian did, indeed, have an enormous nose, with a patrician hook to it. 'Brutus,' Clem mused, continuing to stare at the dog. 'Yes, I like it. I think he's going to be a grand addition to our crew, and Brutus suits him just fine. Deckhand Brutus of *The Liverpool Rose*, just the feller to keep the Wigan Wolves at bay. And I reckon he'll do that, all right.'

Clem was speedily proved right. Brutus proved to be both intelligent and sensitive. He seemed to know by instinct when a person footing it along the towpath was a casual farm worker, probably setting snares for rabbits and therefore harmless, or a young fellow bent on stealing anything he could lay hands on aboard a canal boat. With the former he was gravely polite, wagging his tail if greeted and even condescending to allow himself to be patted, but with the latter he was a different animal. His hackles would rise, his lips would curl back to show his excellent set of teeth, and he would growl in the back of his throat in a manner which left little doubt that had the intruder taken a step towards either *The Liverpool Rose* or her butty boat, he would speedily find himself badly mauled.

At night-time, he curled up beside Clem in his tiny cabin, but even though he appeared to be sleeping, he was clearly alert for the smallest noise or unusual happening. He would sit up, growling softly beneath his breath, and the moment he became convinced that someone was around, his deep, rumbling bark would be enough to scare off the most intrepid burglar.

With the introduction of Brutus into their lives, things became very much more comfortable aboard *The Liverpool Rose*. Within a matter of days, Priddy and Jake felt that they could snug down the boat and go off for a beer at a canalside tavern without worrying over what they might find on their return. For his part, Clem had found the perfect companion. He had always loved the countryside and enjoyed walking and exploring, and when the canal began to wind its way across the Pennines he had often longed for someone with whom to explore. Now he had Brutus. Jake was a real dog lover and insisted that sauntering along the towpath, hard on the heels of man and horse, was not sufficient exercise for a big dog like that. 'He's your responsibility, young Clem,' he said severely. 'You took him on and you must see he gets proper exercise and the right sort o' grub. He's only young – Priddy thinks no more 'an twelve months – so he needs good food, a few nice bones if you can pick 'em up from a butcher in one o' the villages, and walks to strengthen his muscles and keep him fit.'

This was the very advice that Clem wanted, and once the dog was well enough the pair of them enjoyed many rambles up into the high hills and the quiet places, where they could be by themselves, sometimes looking down on the shiny ribbon of the canal, far below them.

By the time they reached Leeds, Priddy's wonderful ointments and tender care had completely transformed Brutus from the shabby fugitive they had carried aboard the boat to a gleaming, bright-eyed dog, sure of himself and apparently without fear. Indeed, when they returned through the Wigan locks, with Brutus standing on the prow of the boat as it moved along the length of the canal, there was not one comment from the Wigan Wolves to indicate they recognised him. They certainly respected him, however. Whether aboard the boat or walking sedately at Hal's heels, he was a force to be reckoned with, and one which the young ruffians from the slums did not intend to take on. They kept their distance – and their thieving hands to themselves – and the crew of *The*

Liverpool Rose knew that the worst of their troubles were over while Brutus was aboard.

'Class dismissed!'

Brother Laurence, who taught the boys of St Mark's school mathematics – 'For my sins,' he was apt to say gloomily – had been trying this particular October afternoon to get into the heads of the older boys some basic facts about bookkeeping. Geoff pitied the teacher in some ways but knew him to be an excellent mathematician from whom he, himself, could learn a great deal. Accordingly, he did his utmost to see that the other boys in the class behaved themselves. He realised that this was selfish rather than public-spirited, but felt it was the only way that he would ever master the subject, for he saw clearly enough that his chances of succeeding in the world would be far greater if he had a good grasp of bookkeeping. Every post in an office seemed to require a knowledge of the subject and, should he be fortunate enough to get a job in a bank, he knew that he would be expected to take – and pass – bookkeeping examinations, so it behoved him to learn as much as he could from Brother Laurence. What was more, he genuinely liked the teacher and knew that Brother Laurence liked him, too. At any rate, although the rest of the boys had rushed to the door as soon as Brother Laurence had dismissed them, the teacher was still seated behind his desk and Geoff had remained in the classroom. He was hopeful that Brother Laurence might take a look at the work he had been doing in his own time.

Some weeks earlier, Brother Laurence had kept Geoff back after a particularly rowdy classroom session and had told him, approvingly, that he had a better grasp of the work the class had been doing than most of his fellow pupils. 'If you would like to advance a little further, I'd be happy to work with you for half an hour after class on Mondays, Wednesdays and Fridays. You're a bright lad and I think, with coaching, you might do well for yourself and get a good job. I know mathematics seems a dry and dusty subject to most lads, but it strikes me that you've a good grasp of the work and would not be afraid to venture further.'

Geoff had accepted the suggestion eagerly and now he had begun to enjoy the sessions a good deal more than the actual classes, which were so often disturbed by the less able boys.

'Well, Gardiner? Did you manage to do the work I set you?' Brother Laurence said, pushing his glasses down his nose so that he could look at Geoff over the top of them.

Geoff grinned and delved into the front of his shabby school bag, producing a sheaf of papers and laying them on the teacher's desk. 'No problems, sir,' he said, trying not to sound smug. 'I gorrin a bit of a muddle over question ten, but I had a good think and realised I were looking at it from the wrong angle. Once I knew that, I was able to work it out for myself.'

Brother Laurence took the papers, pushed his glasses up on to the bridge of his nose once more and began to mark the sheet with his red pen, nodding approvingly as he did so. 'You're forging ahead at a grand pace, young Gardiner,' he said. 'If you keep this up, by the time you're ready to leave school next summer, I'll be able to recommend you as the ablest boy to pass through my hands for some time. You may not think that this will help you to get a well-paid job, but you'd be wrong. I've placed many of my best pupils in positions of responsibility and now they, as employers, are willing to take my word when they need a new member of staff themselves.'

'I know it, sir,' Geoff said, taking back the pages which Brother Laurence was holding out. 'The other fellers wouldn't believe it but I enjoy working out answers to puzzles, especially puzzles with numbers. Maths is so – so logical, sir. I don't understand why the others think it's so hard.'

Brother Laurence nodded, pulled a clean sheet of paper towards him and began to write. He and Geoff went and sat at one of the big double desks at the back of the class and the coaching session began.

When Geoff left the classroom half an hour later, he was carrying a further set of problems which he would work out before he had his next maths lesson. He was looking forward to this much as another boy might look forward to a game of football, but that did not mean he was not interested in football; simply that he could enjoy both. He went to the cloakroom, took his brown Father Brannigan coat off its peg and struggled into it, slung his satchel across his back and set off for the orphan asylum. No one would query his lateness – they never did – since most of the boys dawdled home, taking as long as possible between Carver Street and the far end of Shaw Street where Father Brannigan's was situated.

Truth to tell, when he was not having extra maths classes, Geoff dawdled too. There was such a lot to see and do that everyone stretched the walk home as much as possible. Usually, Geoff crossed Islington Square and made a beeline for Whitley Gardens, where a chap could kick a ball about or play tag or relievio with anyone who happened to be around. Then after Whitley Gardens there were the big houses. Geoff always walked fast past Mr Carstairs', the dental establishment, remembering the horrors of visiting the school dentist, who seemed indifferent to the miseries he caused his patients and had once pulled out a perfectly sound tooth which Geoff had been jiggling in his jaw with much enjoyment for several weeks and had planned to sell to a boy in school who was going to make a necklace for his mam for Christmas. The dentist, however, had put a stop to such money-making schemes by throwing the tooth disdainfully into his rubbish bin and ushering Geoff out while his mouth was still too full of blood to protest.

This evening, as Geoff made his way along Shaw Street, however, he was not thinking of dentists or the Brannigan Asylum, or even of mathematical problems. He was thinking of Lizzie Devlin and of their last encounter.

He did not see as much of Lizzie as he would have liked now that they were both growing up. In summer they went bathing in the Scaldy a couple of times a month, but Lizzie was growing self-conscious because she was nearly always the only girl in the water. What was more, her attitude towards Aunt Annie had changed considerably since Geoff had first met her. Something must have happened, he realised, to make his little friend protective towards her aunt instead of merely fond of the older woman. It was something, he thought, which had happened last August, because ever since then Lizzie had seemed worried about leaving her aunt for more than the odd hour or so. Geoff knew that only two of her sons were now living at home and guessed that this put Aunt Annie more at risk from Uncle Perce's occasional bouts of violence. So the expeditions which Lizzie and he had planned to make, meaning to go by tram to

Seaforth or even by ferry to New Brighton, had had to be shelved. Lizzie still talked of going, but he could tell by her lack of enthusiasm, that she would not enjoy such outings unless she could guarantee her aunt's safety.

He had suggested that Aunt Annie might come along with them, but though Mrs Grey had pinched his cheek and said, 'You're a kind lad,' she had explained that such a trip would likely kill her in the heat of summer. Geoff had noticed that she had grown stouter over the past few months and that even a short shopping trip up the Scotland Road would cause her to breathe fast and short, while perspiration trickled down her face to be impatiently mopped away with the back of a sleeve or a piece of rag.

He had met Lizzie the previous weekend, however, and they had had a pleasant afternoon. They had caught a tram up to Princes Park, fed the ducks, chucked a ball about and talked. The talk was the best thing. Lizzie was growing to be both pretty and sensible – he admired the long rope of fair hair which she always kept beautifully clean and neat – and because she was growing so fast, Aunt Annie had actually bought her a couple of neat dresses which had greatly improved her appearance. He gathered from Lizzie that her best dress spent a good deal of its time in J. O'Hare's establishment on Scotland Road, being 'rescued' on a Saturday night and returned to the pawn shop on Monday morning. Not only was the money useful, but, as Aunt Annie put it, it stopped Uncle Perce's mouth. He had been furious at what he called the 'waste of money' over the purchase of the dress, but became reconciled to it when Aunt Annie explained that she could borrow money on it. The sort of clothing Aunt Annie herself habitually wore would not have brought in so much as tuppence, even from the most generous-minded 'uncle'.

However, it was not of clothing that Geoff and Lizzie had talked as they wandered across the sun-bleached grass of Princes Park. Despite the fact that there was two years between them, they would both leave school the following summer, so what they mostly talked about were their future plans. Lizzie had thought about going into an office, but was now resigned to factory work. It paid a great deal better and Geoff gathered, reading between the lines, that it was becoming increasingly important for her to earn a decent wage. He had no idea how much Denis and Herbie contributed to the household but guessed that now he had two sons earning and at home, Uncle Perce was simply drinking all his own money and contributing nothing, save kicks and blows when he was unable to find more money to pour down his neck.

Geoff knew that he was lucky, in a way, to be in the orphan asylum. He was well fed, well clothed and well housed. Lizzie, who had the advantage of a real home life, was seldom any of these things. Yet she was bright and lively and was just as ambitious as he. The factory would do, she told him, until she had made enough money and had had enough experience to try for something better. In the meantime, she would look after her mother's sister, who had been good to her, and would endeavour to see that Uncle Perce never laid a finger on any of her wages.

Geoff doubted whether Lizzie would be able to stop Uncle Perce from stealing any money he found in the house, but guessed that she had plans to keep her savings – when she had any – well away from all her relatives. Denis was a silent and taciturn young man, already running to fat and reluctant to shift himself, even in his mother's defence, but Herbie was sly as a fox. He disliked Lizzie, being jealous of his mother's affection for her niece, and would no doubt be keen to treat his cousin badly if he got the chance.

Not that he ever would. Lizzie was being raised in a rough school and was probably more capable than he, Geoff, of watching her own back. She was well aware that Herbie disliked her and would do her a mischief if he could, so wherever she chose to hide her wages, it would be somewhere that was safe from Herbie as well as her Uncle Perce.

When he reached the YMCA building, Geoff glanced towards the lower windows, as he always did. A face loomed briefly behind the glass and a hand was raised in greeting. Grinning to himself, Geoff returned the salute. He knew a good few of the youths living at the YMCA because when a lad left the protection of the Father Brannigan Orphan Asylum, he was quite often offered a place in that establishment. It meant that an ex-Branny boy could still visit his old pals up the road, often have the odd meal with the other lads in the orphanage's big old-fashioned dining room, play a game of footie in the battered backyard and generally feel less isolated than those boys who chose to move into lodgings in some other part of the city.

Reggie Phelps, the lad who had waved to Geoff through the window, was a case in point. Brighter than most of his fellows, he had got a good job as a clerk with the L & NWR at Waterloo Goods Station and spent each day sitting in a large, untidy office, working on the ledgers and chaffing with the rest of the staff. Reggie was a tall, thin boy with hair so frizzy that, from the back, he looked like a gorse bush. He was extremely short-sighted and peered myopically at the world through a pair of steel-rimmed spectacles. He was also an asthmatic and his struggles to get his breath had caused his shoulders to rise up so that he looked as if he were perpetually shrugging. He had never been any good at games, yet despite these drawbacks, he had always been popular with his fellows and Geoff was able to view a future spent in the YMCA with equanimity, since he would be sharing a roof with Reggie once more.

When Geoff thought about the future, mind you, it was apt to take on a rosier hue than the reality which he knew lay before him. He planned to stay at the YMCA until he could afford a place of his own and despite being, on the whole, a practical person, a vision of a cottage with roses round the door, a long garden full of flowers, fruit and vegetables and a river running nearby, persisted in putting in an appearance in his imagination. If he allowed his mind the luxury of a real daydream, there would be a woman in the cottage, or rather a girl. She had a long plait of corn-coloured hair and bore a remarkable resemblance to Lizzie Devlin, and when he *really* got going, his imagination also supplied his dream girl with a beautiful rose-coloured dress, covered by a snowy white apron, to whose hem clung two idyllically pretty children.

However, at this point Geoff usually pulled himself up short, scolded his imagination for running riot and turned it back severely to more practical matters; what he would do to earn himself a place in the sun, for instance. Banking was a grand starting point, but due to his upbringing Geoff had few illusions and knew that there were a great many bank clerks and tellers and very few bank managers. So he intended to save his money until he could buy himself a small business of some description – at this stage he had no idea what – which he could nurse and nurture until it began to earn him the sort of money he needed. Only then would his dream of a country cottage – and Lizzie – begin to look possible.

Sometimes, in one of his more down-to-earth moments, he would remind himself that if Lizzie had to wait for him to earn the money for his cottage, she would be old and grey and well past child-bearing before she ever got to sniff the roses, but since daydreams were what kept a fellow going, he pushed more practical considerations to the back of his mind and enjoyed the fantasies.

Chapter Four

LATE JUNE, 1925

It had rained all day, but when Lizzie and Sally emerged from school and began on the walk home, the rain had stopped and warm, late-afternoon sunshine was falling on the wet cobbles which steamed gently under its rays.

Lizzie and Sally, arm in arm, came gaily into the court, talking busily about the work which they would both start very soon. They had been lucky; they had both got jobs in the bottling department at Cantrell & Cochrane's in Atlas Street, and were looking forward eagerly to the new life which would open up for them shortly, and to their first wage packet. This was to be their last week in school and since they had already been given their examination results and knew that they had done well, it should be an enjoyable week, too.

'Are you coming round to mine for a cuppa?' Sally asked, as they drew level with her front door. 'Or does your Aunt Annie want messages? Oh, Lizzie, if it doesn't rain tomorrow, what do you say we go over to New Brighton for the day? My mam's ever so pleased wi' my exam results and my dad's fairly fizzin' over with pride because we're going to be working at C and C's, so they'll give us our ferry fares and a bit more, likely. What d'you say?'

'I'd love it,' Lizzie said honestly. 'I don't think Aunt Annie would mind if I took a day off for once. We do seem to have spent the whole summer so far working

– I'm right for a bit of a spree, to tell the truth. And though I usually work at Mayall's on a Saturday, I'm sure she'd be happy to let me have the day off because she's got a niece who stands in for me if I can't work weekends.'

Lizzie had got herself a job in Mayall's shop, on the corner of Lime Kiln Lane and Gildarts Gardens, which had been a great help moneywise but which had considerably shortened her free time. She went straight to Mrs Mayall's shop after school and worked there until seven o'clock, and sometimes later, and all day on a Saturday. She made up orders, carefully weighing out the small amounts of butter, sugar, flour and other dried goods which the customer had ordered. Then she priced the items and made out a neat bill and after that she delivered them, usually walking but occasionally riding on a borrowed bike, for Mrs Mayall had a son of twenty-two who seldom rode his machine now that he worked in Birkenhead.

She did not mean to put a damper on her friend's enthusiasm but it had been on the tip of her tongue to remind Sally what a dreadfully wet summer it had been and how unlikely it was that the weather would improve on a Saturday. Everyone knew it always rained weekends, so why should this one be different? Still, you never knew, and a day out with her best pal would be prime.

'I'll just pop in and see if Aunt Annie wants any help,' Lizzie said as they reached her home. 'Are you coming in for a mo', queen?'

'Might as well,' Sally said gaily, and the two girls ran up the steps and through the front doorway. They burst into the kitchen, expecting to see Aunt Annie in her usual chair by the fire, but the room was empty. 'She must be queuing for the lavvy,' Lizzie remarked, turning back towards the front door. 'Unless she's gone next door, of course. She might have gone to get her own messages, only she usually waits for me to do that. I wonder whether . . .'

The two girls had reached the front door. As they emerged on to the steps, Mrs Clarke from next door was coming towards them. Her face bore the expression of one about to impart momentous tidings and Lizzie, who liked Mrs Clarke but knew her to be a born gossip, smiled and went to pass her. Mrs Clarke, however, shot out a pudgy hand and seized Lizzie's elbow.

'Lizzie, love, your aunt's been took to the 'orspital,' she said importantly. 'None o' them boys was in, nor her old feller, so the doctor telled me to tell you you'd best get round there as fast as you can. She were mortal bad, fair doubled up and groanin' like a foghorn.'

'Oh, my God!' Lizzie said, one hand flying to her heart. 'What was it, Mrs Clarke? Was it her appendix? Or did she have a fall? She's awful big, so if she fell she could do herself a deal o' mischief.'

Mrs Clarke looked at her pityingly. 'You mean to tell me you didn't *know*?' she said, incredulously. 'You mean to say your Aunt Annie never telled you? Why, queen, she were in the family way. I reckon somethin' went wrong . . . she's a bit long in the tooth for babbies, is your Aunt Annie.'

Lizzie stared, eyes rounding in total astonishment. For a moment, she had not been able to think what Mrs Clarke meant by being 'in the family way', and even now she understood, she could scarcely credit the truth of the statement. Her knowledge of babies and the making of them was hazy, but surely Aunt Annie and Uncle Perce were both far too old for the sort of carryings-on which having a baby implied? And then there was Aunt Annie's weight; if Mrs Clarke was implying that the additional weight was due to a baby, Lizzie couldn't see it. Aunt Annie's figure was always so generously swathed in petti-coats, skirts, blouses and shawls and scarves, that it would have been impossible to notice a little bump like a baby. However, Mrs Clarke said she was to go to the hospital, and go she most certainly would.

She was about to fly down the steps and out of the court, shaking off Mrs Clarke's grip, when it occurred to her that she did not know to which hospital her aunt had been taken, nor whether Aunt Annie needed anything brought in. She turned to Mrs Clarke, the questions almost on her lips, but that competent lady forestalled her. 'They've taken her to the Maternity Hospital on Oxford Street and she'll need a night-gown and a bit o' towel and some soap,' she said instructively. 'I doubt your aunt will have the sort o' thing that the hospital expects, if you know what I mean. I'd lend her one o' mine, but she's twice my size . . .' She paused delicately, eyebrows jerking upwards. 'I could say a word to Mrs Bedford, if you think your aunt wouldn't object?'

Lizzie doubted whether Mrs Bedford's nightgown could possibly stretch to cover Aunt Annie's enor-mous frame, but telling herself philosophically that this would be a problem for the hospital to solve, she agreed with Mrs Clarke's suggestion and presently, with soap, towel and a borrowed nightgown in a paper carrier bag, she and Sally set off at their fastest pace in the direction of Oxford Street.

Lizzie stood in the kitchen, washing the pots and thinking, crossly, that it was about time one of the

136

boys gave a hand with the drying-up. Come to that, it would have been fairer if they had helped with the preparation of the meal, since she had her work cut out to cook anything, what with school, her job, and visiting her aunt.

For despite the fact that three days had elapsed since her aunt had been taken into hospital, no member of the Grey family had yet made any attempt at any sort of household task. It was true that both Herbie and Denis had visited their mother, Herbie with a paper bag of striped Everton mints and Denis with a large bunch of roses, but this was not exactly helpful to poor Lizzie, coping alone at home.

Sadly, Aunt Annie had lost the baby quite soon after reaching hospital. By the time her niece was ushered into the long ward, she was lying back on the hard, high bed, looking exhausted and trying to come to terms with what had happened to her. As soon as her eyes had fallen upon her niece, however, her expression had lightened and a wide smile had spread across her face. 'Eh, our Lizzie, I knew you wouldn't let me down,' she had said, a world of relief in her tone. 'You'll look after me lads and your old uncle whiles I'm kept in here, won't you, queen? Only they's so bleedin' useless about the house that they'd likely starve to death before I were let out.'

Her expression was so pleading and her face so pale that Lizzie would not have had the heart to refuse her, even had she wanted to do so. As a result, Lizzie now found herself, not only buying and preparing all the food for their meals, but making the boys and Uncle Perce's snap each morning before she went off to school then hurrying home from Mrs Mayall's emporium with her arms stretched almost down to her ankles with the weight of the bags of potatoes, bread and other groceries which she carried. Since neither boy had seen fit to give her any money and Uncle Perce would not have dreamed of doing such a thing, she had been forced to buy on tick. Fortunately, Mrs Mayall was an understanding woman and knew Aunt Annie of old. 'She'll pay me back as soon as she's better,' she said comfortably, adding up the items on the special pink lined paper which she used for credit customers. 'And just you take a nice bar of Fry's chocolate in to your aunt when you go to see her tonight. Tell it's a present from her old pal Edie Mayall, and I hope she gets better right quick.'

Thinking about this as she grimly washed pots, Lizzie felt that she echoed Mrs Mayall's sentiments; the sooner Aunt Annie got well, the better pleased Lizzie would be. Finishing the washing-up, she decided to let the pots drain and crossed the kitchen to make her preparations for the night and the next day. Despite the month being June, she damped down the fire and closed down the damper; she would need the fire tomorrow morning if she were to get breakfast and reach school on time. It was already ten o'clock and she was bone weary and tempted to shriek up the stairs and force Herbie or Denis to come down and give her a hand. They could at least have filled the buckets with water before they sneaked off upstairs, she thought resentfully, taking a pail in either hand and heading for the tap at the end of the court. If Aunt Annie had been at home, she would certainly have insisted that they do the heavy work.

Since she had not thought to collar either lad before they went up to bed, however, she would simply have to make the best of it. Accordingly, she filled both buckets at the tap and staggered back along the court in the frail light from the solitary gas lamp, slopping water as she went. Climbing the steps to the front door so heavily burdened was not easy, but Lizzie managed it with the loss of only perhaps an inch of water. Nevertheless, she was glad to park the buckets under the washing-up bowl on its rickety table and straighten her aching back. She checked with her eye that everything was now ready for the morning: fire damped down, water brought in, coal in the hod so that the fire might be freshened without having to leave the house, and her cousins' sandwich wrappings laid out ready on the central table. Yes, it looked as though it was safe to go to bed at last, and pray heaven Aunt Annie would soon be discharged from hospital so that she might take up her usual place once more. She doused the lamp, lit her candle and left the room, closing the door behind her.

Making her weary way up the stairs, Lizzie reflected that she had never realised just how hard Aunt Annie worked. When you considered that, in addition to everything Lizzie had been doing, Aunt Annie also both cooked and washed bedding for anyone who could pay her a small sum to do so, it was a miracle that her aunt ever got into bed before midnight. Lizzie knew that, of late years, her aunt made it a rule to be upstairs and in bed before ten, if possible. The pubs closed at half-past ten and if she were out of the way when Uncle Perce returned, he would either fall into a drunken sleep on the sofa in the front room or, if he was in a nasty mood, take his anger out on the furnishings, such as they were. Uncle Perce was responsible for the battered panels on the front door and for the marks on the walls where objects, flung in a drunken rage, had gouged holes in the plaster. Lizzie followed Aunt Annie's example and always tried to get to bed before Uncle Perce returned. Now she hurried up the two flights of stairs to her attic room, went inside and sank thankfully on to the bed. Usually, she brought up water so that she could have a good wash as soon as she awoke, but since Aunt Annie had been in hospital and she had had to be downstairs so early, she had given up the habit and washed in the kitchen.

Presently, having rested for a moment, she got reluctantly to her feet and began to take off the large calico apron which, earlier in the evening she had donned to protect her blue gingham dress, and hang it on the hook behind the door. Then she began to unbutton the blue gingham, reflecting as she did so that it was getting extremely tight across the chest. Idly, she looked down at her front; there were darts in the dress which could be unpicked if she were clever enough. She could not bear the thought of having to give the dress away when she had had it for such a short time and had just decided she would take it round to one of the women who was renowned for her sewing skills when she heard a very odd noise, coming from the direction of her narrow truckle bed. Frowning, she lifted her eyes from the dress and examined the bed, then bent down to look beneath it. The sound had been just like an animal breathing, or perhaps it was a bird which had flown through the open window and, having exhausted itself in trying to find a way out again, collapsed beneath the bed. A large crow had done this the previous summer and Lizzie had had great difficulty in catching the bird and ejecting it. So she hoped very much that the sound had been caused by almost anything other than that.

To Lizzie's relief there was nothing under the bed.

Putting the matter out of her mind, she began to unplait her hair, removing two hairpins and placing them carefully on her washstand where they would be easy to find in the morning. Picking up her brush, she began the evening task of untangling her locks, idly examining herself in the mirror as she did so. Absently, as she worked, her eyes fixed themselves on the reflection of a small dark patch on the partition behind her. It was odd, she thought, that she had never noticed the mark before. Goodness knows, she must have eyed the thin partition wall between her room and the boys many times over the past few years. She was still staring at the mark when it seemed to change. There was a flickering white flash, just for a moment, and in that instant Lizzie realised, with fury, that it was not a mark, it was a hole in the partition which had certainly not been there that morning, and unless she was very much mistaken, glued to the hole there was a round and protuberant eye. The hated Herbie was spying on her! Though why he should bother to do so, she thought resentfully, she could not imagine.

Seconds later, she chided herself for an idiot. Herbie might see her at all times of day in the kitchen, but then she was fully dressed. The horrible, sly, disgusting boy, who was incapable of getting himself a girlfriend, was trying to find out what went on below calico aprons and print dresses!

Lizzie usually slept in the raw in summer and realised with horror that had she not noticed the hole, she would by now have stripped off. As it was, she was still respectable, though the top two buttons of her dress were undone. She turned her back on the hole, trying to decide what best to do, for if she did not discourage Herbie firmly, he might well start selling peeps at a penny a go. Glancing around her for a weapon, she spied the hairpins, sitting on the washstand, but a moment's reflection caused her to dismiss them as a weapon. Herbie was a beast all right, but she did not fancy being responsible for a one-eyed cousin. If she made her little finger rigid . . .

Walking back towards her bed, more alert now that she knew about the spyhole, she heard sounds which she was easily able to identify: Herbie was trying to see where she had gone and what she was up to. Smiling grimly, Lizzie sidled up to the wall. Then she took careful aim and pushed her little finger through the hole with as much force as she could muster. Almost immediately, she felt a horrid squelchy sensation and drew back her hand hastily, half expecting to find Herbie's eyeball impaled on her nail. Indeed, judging from the gasp and gurgle which he gave, her fear was not altogether unfounded, but her finger proved to be only sticky . . . Yuck, yuck!

There was a terrible scream from the other side of the wall, followed by a stream of obscenities and a thump and a squeak of springs as someone – Herbie, obviously – collapsed on to his own bed. Lizzie heard Denis saying sleepily: 'Whazzup, wozzer marrar?'

'That bleedin' little bitch has bloody blinded me,' Herbie moaned. The bed creaked again, as he rocked to and fro, probably clutching his eye, Lizzie thought with grim satisfaction. 'Oh, oh, me mam'll kill her when I tell 'er Lizzie's put me eye out. Oh, gawd, the pain! If I could lay me hands on her now . . .'

There was a thump of heavy feet crossing the boys' room and Lizzie hastily went to push the washstand across her door, but it turned out that there was no need. Denis, seeming to come wide awake, said thoughtfully: 'What on *earth* are you talkin' about,

142

young Herbie? If you're grumblin' about Lizzie, she ain't in here, that much I do know, and if you're moanin' about supper then you'd best give her a hand another night. I thought it were okay meself. She's learned a thing or two from our mam, has Lizzie – that meat an' potato pie were prime.'

There was a longish pause, then Herbie said: 'I banged me head on the partition. I must have been having a bad dream – I thought I heard Lizzie scream out.'

'That were you screamin' out,' Denis said dryly. 'I never heared anyone make such a fuss over bumping their head. Now just you get back into bed, our Herbie, 'cos I needs me beauty sleep if I'm to get to work on time tomorrow.'

Lizzie listened joyfully as Herbie grumbled his way back into bed. It was clear that he had decided not to own up about the hole, nor to tale-clat on her about being poked in the eye, and it was probably for the best, she decided. She had nipped his little plan in the bud; tomorrow she would get some putty and close up the hole and she supposed she would then do best to forget the whole incident. But aren't boys queer? she thought to herself as she settled down to sleep. He must have seen girls swimming in the Scaldy from time to time. She had seen boys, and certainly wouldn't bother to make a hole in a wall in order to see them again. Bodies were only bodies after all, she was thinking as she fell asleep.

By the time Aunt Annie returned from hospital, Herbie's eye had begun to improve and though his mother commented that he seemed to have got himself a real shiner, she made no other remark. Clearly, Herbie had decided to keep his little adventure to himself, though every time he saw Lizzie looking at his scarlet and painful eye, he gave her a malevolent glare out of the other one.

Since her aunt had only spent a week in the Maternity Hospital, Lizzie was able to take up her new job on the day appointed. She and Sally set off together, both neatly dressed in summer frocks and sandals, with their carry-out in identical scarlet tins which Sally's mother had bought for them from Paddy's Market.

The work in the despatch department was not onerous, though one had to be both quick and accurate. As the belt moved the goods around, the girls checked that all was well with each item before sending it on its way. They found the other workers and the supervisors both friendly and helpful. The money was a good deal better than anything the girls could have earned in an office, and though Lizzie had always seen herself doing the sort of work which the teacher had talked of, she soon settled down at her bench and became a reliable – and happy – worker.

She and Sally often took their carry-out to the banks of the canal and sat there for the thirty minutes they were allowed. They were doing this one day when the familiar shape of The Liverpool Rose came into view, with Hal pulling it, Clem leading him, and the large and shaggy dog, which Lizzie had never met, close at Clem's heels.

'Look, Sal, it's The Liverpool Rose and that young feller I told you about,' Lizzie said excitedly. 'I wonder if they're going to dock quite near us. They look as though they're coming in for a cargo, wouldn't you say?'

Sally screwed up her eyes against the sunlight and peered. 'I don't know how you can tell one boat from another, let alone one horse or one young feller,' she grumbled. 'All I can see is *a* boat and *a* feller. Still, I reckon you're right so now you can introduce me. Do you think they'll let us go aboard? I've never seen inside one of them little cabins; it's a miracle to me how they get one person in there, lerralone three.'

'I don't think they invite ordinary people aboard much,' Lizzie said. 'Me and Geoff only got took aboard because he'd been half drownded. Still an' all, I'd like a chat with Clem. They go all the way across the Pennine hills to Leeds – imagine the adventures they must have, Sally! If ever Aunt Annie turned me out, or I lost my job, then I reckon I'd give a lot to work aboard a canal boat. Instead of just a street outside your front door, with the same cobbles and the same house opposite, you would see different fields and woods and waterways every day of your working life. I reckon that would be grand.'

Sally's round and placid face took on a horrified expression at her friend's words. She pushed her fingers through her chestnut curls, lifting them off her neck and exhaling in a deep sigh. 'Lizzie Devlin, you're mad!' she said decidedly. 'Cramped up in a tiny cabin, wi' no room to swing a cat, no nice shops, no neighbours – and all that mud what they call earth surrounding you. If that's what you'd rather have than a decent kitchen, with a proper fire which don't tip about every time you take two steps, then you really are mad.'

'You've got no spirit of adventure, that's your trouble,' Lizzie said. 'I thought you said you'd like to see aboard *The Liverpool Rose*? If you despise it so much, what's the point of a visit?'

'I'd like to see inside a gypsy caravan, or a charcoal burner's hut, but that doesn't mean I'd fancy living in

145

either,' Sally pointed out. 'I want to know how the other half lives. Ain't that natural, our Lizzie?'

'You mean, you're curious as a cat and want to be able to criticise,' Lizzie said crossly. 'Well you can't . . . hey up, here they come.'

The two girls got to their feet and walked down to where Jake was winding the mooring rope around the nearest bollard. Clem was unfastening Hal but turned to greet Lizzie and look enquiringly at Sally. 'Well, if it ain't Lizzie,' he said, grinning at her. 'Who's your pal?'

'Oh! This is Sally. Sally, this is Clem what rescued Geoff from a watery grave. Sally and I work together now at the bottling plant at Cantrell's, just a tiddy way further back from the Britannia Warehouses on Love Lane,' Lizzie explained. 'She lives near me, so we walk to and from work together every day, and usually bring our carry-out down here if it's fine.' She glanced at the enormous dog by Clem's side and stepped back nervously, one hand flying to her throat. She had never seen such a big dog, nor one who looked more like a wolf. 'Is – is he yours, Clem? I wouldn't like to meet him on a dark night! Hasn't he got a lot of teeth, though? Where did *he* come from? Is it a he?'

'Hello, Sally,' Clem said. 'First things first, young Lizzie. As to how I got Brutus here – and he's as meek as a lamb with folks he likes – it's a long story. When do you have to be back in work?'

She gave a squeak of dismay, grabbed Sally's arm and the two of them snatched up their belongings and prepared to leave. 'Oh, Lord, I forgot all about the time – we're going to be late,' she gasped over her shoulder, as the two of them began to run. 'Will you be here this evening, Clem? We finish work at six – we could come back.'

Over her shoulder, Lizzie was dismayed to see the dog begin to leap after her, lips curling back from his excellent white teeth. Hastily, she slowed her pace, guessing the dog was worried by her sudden flight, but Clem uttered a sharp word of command and the dog returned to his side at once.

'We'll be here till tomorrow, likely,' Clem said cheerfully. 'See you later then. I'm just going to stable Hal, then I'll do some messages for Priddy, and after that I guess we'll start loading. 'Bye for now.'

His words barely reached Lizzie's ears but she guessed their purport and shrieked that they would return soon after six, and by a dint of hard running, she and Sally got back to the factory just in time to clock on for the afternoon's work.

She fully intended to go back and see Clem again, she just wished that he had not acquired that huge dog. Once, long ago, when she had been no more than three or so, her father had been taking her down to the sands when they had passed a pair of huge, cast-iron gates. Through them, the small Lizzie had glimpsed what, at that age, she had simply thought of as 'a doggie', and she had pulled away from her father to throw herself at the gates, calling out to the dog as she did so. The next moment the gates had shaken like leaves in a gale as one of the huge animals hurled itself at what then seemed a frail barrier, tongue lolling, teeth bared, as it snarled a warning right into her small, frightened face. Lizzie's father had pulled her back in time, so that those sharp white teeth had snapped on empty air, but it had coloured Lizzie's whole attitude towards all dogs, particularly Alsatians. And now, if she was to remain friendly with Clem, she would have to try to overcome her fear.

She did not tell Sally she was dreading another face-to-face encounter with the big dog, but in the event it was only Lizzie who returned to the canal that evening, Sally wanting to get home to help her mam with supper so that they might go along to see the film at the Burlington Cinema on Vauxhall Road. Sally's mother had told her daughter that she would mug her to a cinema seat and then to a meal at their restaurant because they were showing Frederick Norton and Betty Blythe in *Chu-Chin-Chow*. 'Me mam's got a weakness for Frederick Norton,' Sally explained. 'And I like Betty Blythe – she's a cracker, ain't she? – so it should be a good evening. I'll nip in and tell your Aunt Annie that you're going to be late.'

Lizzie thanked her. She was quite anxious to have a word with Clem on several subjects and told herself severely that she could not even consider upsetting him by confessing her fear of the dog; he was obviously both proud and fond of the animal. She had confided in Sally about Herbie's strange behaviour some time before and Sally had said she ought to tell Aunt Annie. 'Fellers who start behavin' like that go on to do other things,' she had said darkly. 'You don't want no trouble from Herbie, so best tell Aunt Annie.'

But Lizzie was reluctant to worry her aunt with anything so trivial because ever since coming home from hospital Aunt Annie was not her usual cheerful self. Lizzie often came home from work to find the evening meal still not started and Aunt Annie sitting in her old basket chair, staring blankly ahead of her. A couple of times she had walked into the kitchen and found her aunt crying, which was totally unlike the cheerful, placid person she had always known her to be. She had mentioned the matter to Sally, who had merely shrugged and said that if she had given birth to

Herbie and Denis, she would probably cry a lot as well, but Lizzie thought it was more important than that.

Finally, really worried when Aunt Annie had taken herself off to bed one fine evening, leaving a blind scouse half made on the kitchen table, she had gone round to Mrs Buckingham's house and tried to explain how worried she was. Mrs Buckingham listened to her halting explanation and then nodded wisely. 'You're too young to understand, and Sally's mam hasn't ever lost a child,' she told Lizzie. 'But your aunt has, chuck. Losing one can have a terrible effect on a woman, especially a woman of your aunt's age. She must know, you see, that there won't be no other chance. And in her heart, like, she'll blame herself and believe it were something she done that made the baby die. Perhaps she never truly wanted the kid – one more mouth to feed – but even so, losin' it would be a terrible blow.'

'Then what'll I do, Mrs Buckingham?' Lizzie had asked, greatly disturbed to realise that her aunt was actually mourning for the little dead baby she had not even seen. 'The hospital took the baby away so she never set eyes on it – are you sure she could miss something she never knowed?'

Mrs Buckingham's rather small grey eyes suddenly looked larger, softer, and Lizzie realised that the older woman was restraining tears. 'I am sure, queen,' she had said gently. 'I've lost a little 'un, and I know the – the hurt of it. But time's a great healer, they say, and you've gorra be patient. Then, as time passes, the hurt grows easier to bear, easier to push to the back of your mind. Right now, it's all your aunt can think of, but as the weeks go by you'll find she'll come back to you, the same Aunt Annie that you knew before . . . before her bit o' trouble.'

'And is there nowt I can do to help?' Lizzie had asked, greatly distressed to think of poor Aunt Annie bearing such a burden alone. 'If I tell her I understand how she feels, wouldn't that help?'

'Norrif she's tryin' to deny she's sad,' Mrs Buckingham assured her. 'But do your best to tek her mind off of it, give her other things to think about. Not more worrits,' she added quickly, 'but good things . . . a day out, perhaps, or say you'll cook a meal or two, to give her a break. And then someone'll get took poorly and they'll go to her for help and she'll be right in there, graftin' away, and you'll see quick enough that her cure's begun.'

So as soon as *The Liverpool Rose* had come into view, it had occurred to Lizzie that Clem had told her that Mrs Pridmore was a sort of doctor, and there might be something she could do to help bring Aunt Annie round. She realised she could not possibly involve Clem himself in her aunt's troubles, but another woman . . . well, that would be different.

So, when she had finished work Lizzie had set off for the canal, and very soon she and Clem, with the big dog sitting beside him and looking as though butter would not melt in his mouth, were perched on a low wall and chatting comfortably, as though they had known each other well for years. Lizzie saw that Clem, who had once been as pale as she, was now as tanned as a gypsy and looked very much stronger and even taller than he had done when last they met. She also realised that he was wearing what she thought of as boatmen's clothes: the dark blue corduroy trousers, the white, collarless shirt and a dark blue garnsey. She remarked on the garnseys and Clem told her, with evident pride, that Priddy had knitted him two such garments on the long winter evenings when they sat below in the small cabin, yarning and playing cards by the light of the little oil lamp.

'I'm right proud to be seen as a boatmen, too,' he assured Lizzie. 'Priddy and Jake have been real good to me, Lizzie, but I'm useful now they've taught me a thing or two. Why, I were raw as – as an onion when they first took me aboard, but I'm a good listener and a quick learner and now I guess I'm near as good as they are at working the old *Liverpool Rose*. I can tack up the horse, steer, handle the locks, crack the whip – though I'm nowhere near so good with that as Jake is – and do most other things aboard. What's more, I love it. I wouldn't want any other sort of life. When I think back to that bleedin' pit, and the poor little ponies . . . well, I don't know how I stuck it, I tell you straight.'

Lizzie looked into his peaceful dark eyes and saw that he was speaking no more than the truth and presently Clem produced a rustling paper bag and offered her a Cornish pastie. 'Priddy makes 'em,' he explained through a mouthful, 'and when I told her you were coming straight from work, she said as how you were bound to be hungry and would likely welcome a mouthful. They're mutton pasties, and Brutus here loves 'em, so if you just save him a corner with a bit of gravy still in, he'll be your pal for life.'

'Suppose someone doesn't have anything to give him?' Lizzie said, swallowing nervously. 'He's a huge dog, Clem – I don't know as I've ever seen a bigger – so I wouldn't like to get on the wrong side of him. What is he, anyroad? I – I were attacked by a dog just like him once, when I were only three. It – it's made me a bit nervous, like, of big dogs.'

'I guess he's a cross-bred – Alsatian crossed wi' a

151

werewolf, Jake says. Now Priddy, she's more practical, she says his mam were an elephant. As for being friendly, a boat dog what would let anyone aboard wouldn't be no manner of use to us. He's trained to keep people away, you see, so he has to be pretty fierce wi' strangers. Once he knows you're a pal, though, he'll let you do anything with him. Soft as a kitten, aren't you, old feller?'

Brutus, knowing himself addressed, turned to stare adoringly up into Clem's face and when he bent towards the dog, licked him on the chin with a long, pink tongue. The affection between them was plain, Lizzie thought, but was unable to feel at ease with the great dog so close. She had always longed for a pet of some sort herself, but would never have considered Brutus as such. She thought more of kittens or small puppies, or perhaps a cage bird, but she guessed that being without close neighbours or friends of his own age must mean that Clem valued Brutus immensely. 'Tell me how you found the – the old feller,' she said, and then plucked up her courage and held out the last corner of her pastie, rather gingerly, towards Brutus. She hoped he would not accept her fingers as well as the titbit but he proved to be both gentle and mannerly, taking the proffered food with such careful delicacy, that he never even touched her hand. 'I can't imagine anyone handing over a – well, shall we say a guard-dog? – like this one without expecting something in exchange.'

Nothing loath, Clem told her the story of Brutus's ordeal and subsequent rescue and Lizzie's admiration for Clem grew in the telling. Clem had not said that he feared the Wigan Wolves, but it must have taken considerable courage to rescue the dog from under their noses, knowing that he would be plying back and forth in *The Liverpool Rose* for years to come. And when she thought of him grabbing the enormous dog by the scruff her blood ran cold. He could easily have savaged Clem in his fright, she thought wonderingly, and wished with all her might that she was not so scared of dogs. But there you were, she had had a bad experience and not all the wishing in the world could change her feelings.

'I reckon Brutus owes you his life, so no wonder he loves you,' Lizzie observed when Clem's tale was told. 'Does he take a lot of feeding?'

Clem grinned, one hand ruffling the smooth hair between the dog's enormous ears. 'When we're in open country, he not only fends for himself, he brings rabbits home,' he said proudly. 'I s'pose it's because he spent his first eighteen months or so of life fending for himself, though how many rabbits you get up by the Wigan locks, I'm sure I couldn't say. Priddy buys extra bread and cooks up more potatoes so's I can mix them in with any meat he brings back, and she gives him the cod liver oil that she gives Hal – she says it keeps his coat shiny – and other boat people save him bones and such. He's a big lad, but he earns his keep, I can promise you that.'

'You know you said Priddy gives Brutus and Hal cod liver oil?' Lizzie said tentatively, after a moment, seeing an opening for the question she most wanted to ask. 'I were going to ask you if I might have a word with her. The thing is, me Aunt Annie's been under the weather and even though she's better now, she – she's that depressed and miserable, she'll make herself ill again if we're not careful. I remember you saying once that Priddy doctored animals right well, and people too sometimes. Do you think she'd mind if I had a word?'

'We'll go over right now,' Clem said with commendable promptitude. 'You can talk to her while I get Brutus's grub ready and make sure that Hal's got everything he needs for a night in the stables. Last time we were here, there were black beetles in his manger, jigging about all over the hay, and the poor old feller wouldn't touch a mouthful.'

He got up as he spoke and the two of them walked along to where *The Liverpool Rose* was moored. As they drew closer, a delicious smell came wafting up from the tiny cabin and, despite the Cornish pastie, Lizzie felt her mouth water. 'That smells wonderful,' she whispered under her breath. 'Me Aunt Annie is a great cook, but your Priddy is even better 'cos she don't have the space of a big kitchen to do her cooking in. What *is* the smell, Clem?'

'Roast rabbit wi' onions and potatoes, all cooked in the same tin in the oven until they's sort of blended together,' he said with relish, after an approving sniff. 'I'll just give Priddy a shout . . .'

Upon hearing her name, Mrs Pridmore appeared, a wooden spoon in one hand, and Clem explained briefly that this was his friend Lizzie whose aunt was ill. Then, accompanied by Brutus, he set off briskly along the towpath, leaving Lizzie to explain her errand to Mrs Pridmore.

'Come below. And you must call me Priddy as Clem does,' the older woman said. 'So you're our Clem's little pal, eh? I'm right glad to meet you, having heard the lad mention you from time to time. Now what can I do for you?' She sat Lizzie down by the fire and began to stir the big black pot which was bubbling on the stove.

Lizzie glanced around her at the comfortable, crowded cabin; at Priddy's neatly parted grey hair, skewered into a tiny, hard bun at the back of her neck; at the brightly painted furniture and the dried herbs hooked to the ceiling. Priddy's leathery brown face looked as old as the hills, as though the wisdom of Egypt could be hidden behind her seamed forehead, but there was kindness and humour in the glance which she bestowed on her guest. 'Clem's made hisself scarce so I guess it's women's problems and there's no need for shyness twixt you and me 'cos we's both women, though I've been around a tad longer 'n you.'

Lizzie began, haltingly, to tell Priddy about Aunt Annie's loss and subsequent illness, if you could call it that. Very soon the fact that Priddy listened without comment but with deep, unspoken understanding made it easier to continue. In ten minutes, Priddy knew as much about Aunt Annie's strange behaviour as Lizzie did herself. The old woman had nodded approvingly when Lizzie had related Mrs Buckingham's words and now she turned away from the pot on the stove and sat down opposite Lizzie. 'Your pal's right, she do need something to take her mind off what's happened,' she said broodingly. 'Now we can't give her a babby, nor she wouldn't want one what ain't her own.' She grinned across at Lizzie, her face suddenly mischievous. 'You've seen our Clem wi' that great soft dog? It's better'n a brother to him, so for all it's so huge we welcomed it, Jake and meself. Clem's lost his mam and his da, you see, and though he didn't know it, we wasn't enough for him. He needed . . . I reckon he needed Brutus.'

'I'm sure Aunt Annie would love a dog,' Lizzie said, crossing her fingers behind her back and trying not to sound as horrified as she felt at the thought. A little puppy, she now realised, could turn into a

155

monster in no time at all if it chose to do so. 'The trouble is, we live in a back-to-back so there's no yard, nowhere a dog could go to do his business, and what's more, Aunt Annie don't gerrout much. I'm working all day now, so the poor animal would either roam the streets by hisself or be shut in all day wi' me aunt, and that don't seem right somehow.'

'Wharrabout a cat?' Priddy suggested, but Lizzie, though her eyes shone at the thought of a dear little kitten, shook her head.

'Me Uncle Perce hates cats worse than poison,' she said. 'He's scared of them, in a way – I think he'd kill one if it walked near him – *that* sort of scared. Then there are me cousins, Herbie and Denis. They hate cats an' all. There's ever such a pretty grey and white one what lives two doors from us and Aunt Annie lives in fear that one of them will wring its neck one dark night, if it rubs up agin them as they're coming back from the pub.'

Priddy sighed. 'A goldfish ain't the same,' she muttered. 'It's gorra be something young and sort o' fluffy. Wharrabout a cage bird, queen?'

'I dunno,' Lizzie said. 'We might run to a canary or a budgie, I suppose. It'd be nice if we got one what could talk to her. It'd be company, like.'

Priddy nodded approvingly and got to her feet. She reached up to a tiny cupboard, brightly ornamented with painted roses, and drew forth a medium-sized brown bottle, firmly corked. She handed this to Lizzie. 'It's me cowslip wine, fortified,' she explained mysteriously. 'Just you tell her to take a nip or two of this whenever she's feelin' real down. It'll help. And don't worry, queen, a lot o' women in your aunt's position have to struggle for themselves before they get well again. At least your aunt's got you on her side.'

156

Thanking her hostess profusely, Lizzie left the canal boat and was walking along the towpath in the direction in which Clem had disappeared when she saw him coming out of a range of sturdy wooden buildings ahead, accompanied by Brutus dancing joyfully along, clearly anticipating the meal ahead. 'Going to come back wi' me while I feed the old feller?' Clem said hopefully. 'Then, if you're still at a loose end, we might take a walk round the shops.'

Lizzie longed to agree, but she had no desire to spend any more time in the company of Brutus, and besides, she knew that at home Aunt Annie would be waiting for her. On the other hand, if she were to walk just a little way with Clem, they might discuss the problem of a pet for her aunt. Clem struck her as an inventive sort of person – perhaps he could think of a pet which would not cost too much money. Lizzie herself handed over the lion's share of her wages each week to Aunt Annie and had already spent the little that was left on a piece of blue ribbon for her hair and some sweets. She did not think that cage birds would be cheap, and she would have to purchase a cage, too, since the Grays did not own such a thing. There were wild birds, of course, and rabbits in the fields, but she did not imagine that even the ingenious Clem would be able to produce one of those at a moment's notice, but perhaps, if they walked around the shops . . .

A couple of hours later, Lizzie returned to the court with the cowslip wine under her left arm and a rustling paper bag in her hand. The bag was rustling because it contained a present for Aunt Annie – the only one Lizzie had been able to afford. She had bought, for the sum of one ha'penny, two day-old chicks and a measure of the meal which the pet shop man had assured her was the best possible food for such tiny mites.

Much to her relief, Clem had agreed at once that a trip to choose a pet from one of the many pet-shops in the area meant that Brutus would be happier at home. 'Or the fluffy kittens and little canaries would be happier, at any rate,' he assured her. 'He's a grand feller, none better, but he'd put the fear o' God into pet-shop owners, never mind the pets.'

So the two of them had gone off on their search without Brutus, who had taken up his favourite position in the cabin between Priddy and Jake and had only looked a little mournful when Clem had told him to 'Stay' and had departed with Lizzie.

She and the chicks had parted from Clem on Houghton Bridge and had watched wistfully as, with a wave of the hand, he had disappeared into *The Liverpool Rose*'s cabin. Lizzie imagined the welcome that her pal would receive from his dog, and guessed that even now Clem would be eating delicious roast rabbit and no doubt telling Priddy and Jake all about Lizzie's purchase. He had told her that when he had lived with his parents in the little mining village they had kept poultry and had enjoyed a better standard of living as a result. 'The feller in the pet-shop assured me we got a cock and a hen,' he said instructively, 'because, unless you have one of each, you won't get no more chicks.'

'Why not?' Lizzie had asked, wide-eyed. 'I thought hens just laid eggs without needing anything except a good diet?'

'So they do,' Clem admitted. 'But the eggs don't turn into chicks unless there's a cockerel around, and a hen has to be a year old anyway before she lays any eggs. It's – it's kind o' like what happens wi' people, I suppose. Girls and fellers have to . . . to grow up before they get wed and that.'

Lizzie began to say that surely hens were nothing like people, but she was watching Clem's face as she spoke and saw a tide of pink spread across it, though he simply said, shortly, that she would soon realise he was right and that one day her aunt could easily find herself in possession of several good laying hens. 'Then she'll be able to sell 'em on, which can't be bad,' he concluded.

So now Lizzie crossed the court with a buoyant step and burst into the kitchen of number nine. Aunt Annie was sitting in her favourite chair, staring at the fire as though she could see pictures in the glowing coals. From the look on her face, they were not pleasant pictures. Lizzie banged the cowslip wine down on the table and placed the paper bag with great care next to it. Then she looked disapprovingly around the kitchen.

It was filthy. Dirty pots were piled up all around the washing-up bowl, the buckets which should have been brimming with water were empty, and the big kettle had been taken off the fire, which was burning low, and stood on the floor beside it. It was the first time that Lizzie had seen the fire without the kettle steaming gently over the flames and somehow this distressed her even more than the piled up dishes and the floor which, now that she looked at it, had not been brushed for a week. Fragments of vegetable matter, crumbs of stale bread and dirty linen lay on it in a way which the old Aunt Annie would never have allowed. However, this was clearly not the moment to berate her aunt for slovenliness.

'Sorry I'm late, Aunt Annie,' she said cheerfully. 'I guess Sally told you I was seeing my pal, Clem, the

159

one who lives on a canal boat? Mrs Pridmore, who owns the boat, has sent you a little present. She says to have a nip whenever you're feeling down, and it looks to me as if you could do wi' one right now.' She reached a chipped cup down from the sideboard, uncorked the bottle, and poured a little of the amber liquid into it. The smell wafted up to her nostrils, reminding her of grass bleached by the sun and of the flowers which spangled the meadows in June. Aunt Annie, who had glanced incuriously across at her as she entered, seemed to smell the drink as well for her eyes brightened and she lurched to her feet and sank down into a wooden chair by the table, holding out a plump hand and taking the cup from her niece's grasp.

'That's mortal good of Mrs Pridmore,' she said appreciatively, curling both hands around the cup as though to warm them. 'Wharris it, chuck? Don't it just smell good! I don't mind takin' a sip if it tastes like it smells.'

'I'm sure it does,' Lizzie said eagerly. 'Have a swig, Aunt Annie, it'll do you good. Mrs Pridmore is a wonderful cook and she makes wonderful medicines, too. Everyone on the canal knows it.'

Aunt Annie raised the cup to her nose and inhaled deeply; then she took a tentative sip. Lizzie watched as she rolled the liquid around her palate, finally swallowing it all in one gulp. 'My, I'd best keep this out of sight, where neither Perce nor the boys can find it,' Aunt Annie remarked, taking another sip. 'It goes down mild and gentle but when it hits your belly, there's a lovely hot, burning feeling . . . I guess a mouthful of this would bring a corpus back to life!'

A couple more sips and the cup was empty. Aunt Annie stood it back on the table and gave a squeak.

The paper bag had begun to move across the table towards her. 'Wharris it?' she whispered, never removing her eyes from the paper bag. 'Oh, our Lizzie, wharrever were in that drink? You've poisoned me, so you have – I'll be seein' pink elephants next! The bloody bag's dancin' a jig!'

Lizzie bit back a laugh and tipped the paper bag – or rather its contents – out on to the table. Two round balls of yellow fluff tumbled out and stared at Aunt Annie as curiously as she was staring at them with their round, boot-button eyes.

'Chicks! Day-old chicks!' Aunt Annie exclaimed, and Lizzie saw interest in her eyes for the first time since returning from hospital. 'Oh, Lizzie, ain't they just the sweetest little buggers? Are they your friend's?' Her hand reached out as though of its own accord and she gently picked up one of the chicks and held it against her face. 'So soft,' she said. 'I've always wanted to keep chickens, you know, queen. But we ain't gorra back yard nor nothin', and I daresay your uncle would take agin 'em.'

'He'd better not,' Lizzie said with real belligerence. 'Just think, Aunt Annie, one day those little scraps will be able to lay eggs and have chicks of their own. That's why me pal, the young feller off the canal boat, got one baby cockerel and one baby hen. And of course there'll be the eggs.'

Aunt Annie looked at Lizzie as though she had suddenly discovered that her niece was a genius. 'You've gorra point, chuck,' she said slowly. 'And what's more, it's a good point. Your uncle's always short of a bob or two, always complainin' that I'm idlin' here at home just because I'm not strong enough to take in washing, not yet I'm not. But if he knows these little fellers are goin' to grow up useful, proper little money-spinners, then I don't see him treadin' 'em underfoot nor slingin' 'em out to seek their fortunes, do you?'

'No, I don't,' Lizzie said. The thought of the tiny chicks, with a stick over each shoulder upon which dangled a bundle tied up with a red and white spotted handkerchief, *à la* Dick Whittington, was a delightful one, but she suppressed her smiles and stared solemnly back at her aunt. 'In fact, once Uncle Perce realises that they'll help out the housekeeping, I daresay he'll grow as fond of 'em as you or me.'

'But what'll we keep 'em in?' Aunt Annie asked plaintively. 'We ain't got no crate, nor even an old parrot cage. Besides they'd slip out through the bars of a parrot cage while they're so tiny.'

'The feller in the shop said to get 'em an old shoe box, lined with cotton wool for sleeping in night-times. In the day, I reckon they can scrat around the kitchen, provided you keep the door closed and watch where you're treading,' Lizzie said. 'The only alternative is the front room, and you want them with you really, don't you? They can pick at crumbs and that which fall on the floor – they'll be as good as a couple of housemaids, Aunt Annie!'

'Well, we'll give it a try and see how it goes,' her aunt decided. She looked around her. 'We don't have no shoe boxes, but I guess one of me saucepans will do the trick if I line it with a good, thick piece of blanket. Well, fancy you buyin' me these two little fellers – I can see I'll have me work cut out just watchin' that they don't come to harm.'

A month later, Sally and Lizzie were working side by side at their bench, snatching up the items as the belt moved past them, sealing them and replacing them, to be whisked along to the next stage in the process.

'How's the chickens?' Sally enquired, shooting a glance at her friend. 'I know your aunt were tickled pink with 'em at first, 'cos you told me so, but I suppose as they grow up, they'll start trying to gerrout and explore the court. What'll she do then, eh?'

'They are getting bigger,' Lizzie acknowledged. 'They're getting feathers instead of fluff and their legs seem to have got awfully long. They're tame, though, not like the chickens you see in folk's backyards. They've been brought up in our kitchen and I suppose they think they're people, only littler of course. When Aunt Annie's cooking, they jump up and down by her feet, cheeping for scraps, and of an evening when she's sitting in her basket chair cobbling socks – you can't call it darning, not the way she does it – they sit on her lap, the way a cat would. She talks to 'em as if they understood every word and saves them special treats – they love boiled potato mashed up with cabbage – and the other day, she went out to the pet-shop and bought a bag of corn. They won't eat it yet, I think they're too little, but it goes to show she thinks a deal of them.'

'Wharrabout your Uncle Perce? And horrible Herbie? Wharrabout Denis an' all?' Sally asked. 'Don't say they like 'em too?'

'Well, they do then,' Lizzie assured her friend. 'To tell the truth, Sal, it's so grand to have Aunt Annie cheerful again, the same as she was before she went into hospital, that they would be prepared to put up with something a lot harder to take than a couple of chickens.'

'Have those birds ever seen the outside world?'

Sally asked ten minutes later as the two of them were hurrying out of the factory after the whistle had gone. 'Hens are supposed be outside, you know, not in a kitchen.'

Lizzie giggled. 'The way Aunt Annie treats them, she'll be taking them out on a lead for an airing any day now,' she observed. 'Did I tell you she calls one Sausage and the other Mash? She says it's because she don't know which is the cockerel and which the hen, but I ask you – naming chickens! She'll be having collars made for them next.'

The two girls emerged from the bottling plant gates on to Atlas Road, turned along Love Land and then left into Burlington Street. 'It were your pal Clem who got the chicks for you, weren't it?' Sally asked, as they made their way along the crowded pavement. 'Has he been to see them, now they're growing up? He can't keep hens aboard a canal boat, that's for sure.'

'That's all you know, clever clogs,' Lizzie responded smartly. 'Priddy was so taken with the idea of keeping a few hens that she's fenced off a section of the butty boat with wire netting and she's got half an orange crate full of hay in there and four grand pullets – that's what they call hens when they ain't chicks, nor yet fully grown – and whenever Clem takes Brutus across the fields, he brings back a few ears of corn or some nice young shoots for Priddy's birds, and they're doing fine.'

'Well, I never!' Sally said. 'I didn't know you'd seen Clem recently. Has he been round to the court a-visiting? Since the chicks were his idea, I suppose he's interested in 'em.'

'He's not been round. But last Saturday, when I was doing messages for Aunt Annie, I crossed the

Houghton Bridge and saw the old *Rose* drawing up alongside Tate's wharves, so naturally I climbed down for a word wi' him. I walked up to the stable with him and we talked about our chicks and his pullets. He says they've had several tiny eggs from their fowls already, so it won't be long before Sausage – or Mash – will be looking for a nice nest to lay in.'

Sally laughed. 'Sausage and Mash!' she said derisively. 'I know you said the boys and your uncle gerralong okay with the chickens, but how do they feel about having to keep the kitchen door closed all the time, even in this hot weather? Doesn't it fret them? And wharrabout watching where they tread?'

'It were a bit awkward at first,' Lizzie acknowledged. 'But now the birds keep out of the way of your feet of their own accord. I always thought hens were uncommonly foolish creatures, but they aren't, you know. They don't want to be trod on any more than you or I would.'

'And how's your other flame?' Sally enquired roguishly as they entered Cranberry Court. 'The one from the Branny, I mean. He used to come around regular at one time, but we've not seen so much of him this summer.'

'If you mean Geoff, he's a friend not a flame,' Lizzie said defensively. 'The trouble is, he doesn't work in a factory, he's in a bank, and they open Saturday mornings, you know. But he and I are going off on a spree together in a week or so. He's going to take me across the water, and we'll have a grand day out in New Brighton. That's why I'm saving all my pennies because the fun fair is one of the best ever, Geoff says.'

'If he's mugging you for a trip to New Brighton and goes on the fun fair, then he's a flame not a friend,' Sally said firmly. 'No feller spends money like that on a girl if he ain't seriously interested, queen. Besides, you like him, don't you?'

'Oh, like!' Lizzie said scornfully. 'I like ever so many people, but that doesn't mean to say I'm serious about any of them. How are you getting on with young Dougie Fairweather?'

'Oh, him!' Sally tossed her mass of red-brown curls, kept back from her face with a piece of bright green satin ribbon. She was getting prettier and prettier as she got older, Lizzie thought enviously. She always felt pale and rather plain beside her friend, longing for striking dark eyes instead of her own blue ones, and for curls and vivid colour instead of the soft waves of light hair which had to be plaited and bound round her head in a coronet at work. But despite envying Sally her vivid looks, they were still best friends and seldom parted for long. 'Dougie's all right – in fact he's a nice feller – but he isn't ever going to set the Mersey on fire. Clerks in the booking office don't, you know. Still, he earns a fair wage and he's not mean, I'll give him that. I haven't had to pay to go to the cinema once in the last four months.'

'You mercenary woman,' Lizzie said, climbing the steps to her own front door and pushing it open. 'See you tomorrow then, queen.'

Lizzie and Geoff enjoyed themselves so much on their day out that they planned to make it a once-monthly affair. She came home, alight with the pleasure of her day, and spent a pleasant hour in the kitchen, giving Aunt Annie a blow-by-blow account of the treat.

'I've been on the ferry before, of course, when I were a kid and Mam and Dad took me to New Brighton for a day on the sands. But this were different. Geoff and I went below and had a pot of tea and some biscuits in the bar. It seemed ever so strange, eating and drinking aboard a great big ship – I felt like a princess, to tell the truth, Aunt Annie – and then we went up on deck and he told me all about the other shipping which we passed. He knows ever such a lot, but he never lectures you. He tells you in an interesting way which makes you want to know more.

'Then when we got to New Brighton, we walked round the funfair, choosing what to spend our money on and being really careful to make sure the rides we chose were the best. Geoff is like that – he doesn't do things on the spur of the moment, he thinks them out. Before we had our dinner, we had a go on the Big Wheel. It was wonderful, Aunt Annie! We could see for miles and miles, right across to the blue mountains in the distance – and then we had a go on the bumper cars, which was ever so exciting . . . didn't I just scream every time there was a collision!'

'Your Uncle Perce took me to the New Brighton funfair when we first started to go steady,' Aunt Annie said, a reminiscent gleam in her eyes. 'We went on the pier an' all. Is it still there?'

Lizzie tried, unsuccessfully, to imagine her aunt and Uncle Perce squeezing into the tiny cab of a bumper car; she even found it difficult to imagine them walking along the pier, but she supposed that was how you felt about old people – that they did not begin to live until you yourself were born. 'Yes, the pier's still there,' she confirmed. 'It's a grand place, full of amusements and with a concert stand at the end. We sat there after we'd had our dinner and listened to the band playing excerpts from Gilbert and Sullivan.

'We had fish and chips at the Avondale Café on the

prom and then we walked to where the Wall's ice-cream man stands and Geoff bought us a special each. You should have seen it, Aunt Annie, it had lovely strawberry syrup all over it and a blob of cream on top.'

'And what did you do in the afternoon?' Aunt Annie asked. She was sitting with both Sausage and Mash on her lap and paused to give them an affectionate stroke. 'I'm sure these here hens would have enjoyed the day out as much as you did.'

'After we'd watched the concert, we went back to the funfair and had several goes on different amusements,' Lizzie told her. 'And then we went to the Tower Ballroom, which is ever so posh, and had a marvellous high tea with cold chi— I mean, cold meat sandwiches and scones and all different cakes and a huge pot of tea, of course. And after that, Aunt Annie, we went to the Tivoli Theatre on the prom and saw a wonderful variety show. There was a comedian and acrobats and some black and white minstrels . . . oh, all sorts. And when we came out we walked along the pier again, in the dark, and watched all the little lights flickering and fizzing, and ate candy floss until it were time to catch the last ferry home.'

'It sounds ever so nice,' Aunt Annie said, so wistfully that Lizzie was impelled to say: 'Well, what's stopping us, you and me, Aunt, going over there one Saturday? We can save up our pennies and have ourselves a nice day out. Only,' she added with a twinkle, 'I don't think we can possibly take Sausage and Mash.'

Aunt Annie laughed too, but she said that having a day out now and again was a good idea, so she would certainly save up some money for the treat. 'And I'll mebbe start doin' a bit o' cookin' for them as can afford it, though I don't think I'm up to launderin' sheets yet awhile,' she said. It was yet another encouraging little sign, Lizzie thought, that her aunt was fast regaining her former spirits.

Lizzie told Geoff all this the next time they met, and he offered to lend her some money so that she could take her aunt to New Brighton before the bad weather came. 'You and me can go somewhere cheaper next time,' he said vaguely. 'We said we'd go each month, on my Saturday off. Well, what say we go into the country on this side o' the Mersey next time? You said Clem and Priddy were telling you that hens need green stuff in their diet, and that Clem takes a bag with him when he walks that great dog and collects dandelion leaves and that. Why don't we go on a foraging expedition for grub for Sausage and Mash?'

Lizzie thought that this was a very good idea and agreed, after only the slightest hesitation, to accept the loan from him.

She and Aunt Annie had had a grand day out, though Lizzie was guiltily aware that it was not quite such fun to share a day out with her slow-moving and overweight relative as it had been to be with Geoff. He had taken good care of her, fed her, amused her. Now it was her turn to do these things for Aunt Annie and though she did enjoy herself, she came home after it very tired. And feeling, somehow, a little flat.

She suspected that she was, quite without meaning to, comparing this trip home on the ferry with her previous one because, when she and Geoff had travelled home together, he had put his arm round her shoulders in a manner both casual yet intimate, and had murmured: 'Dear little Lizzie, you get prettier and nicer every time I see you.' And then he had kissed her.

It had not been much of a kiss, just a light little touch, soft as a moth's wing, on her still parted lips as she had turned towards him, about to tease him for such a patently untrue if flattering remark. Nevertheless, it had been a kiss, and her very first what was more. So that sitting beside Aunt Annie in the big lounge bar below decks, drinking a last cup of tea before docking, she had felt that this day lacked . . . oh, something.

When she and Geoff set off together for their next outing, towards the end of September, the best of the summer weather definitely over, she wondered whether the day in New Brighton had been such a success because she was with Geoff, who thought her pretty, or because it was such a novelty to have a day out anywhere, or simply because they had done such lovely things and never had to worry once about what they were spending. Or whether, when it came down to brass tacks, it had been such a magic and memorable day because of that kiss.

On this September day he called for her early, as arranged. Aunt Annie had baked her a couple of very large and delicious-smelling mutton pasties and she had cut a pile of cheese and pickle sandwiches for their carry-out.

They caught an early bus as they had planned and went to a suitably rural spot near Crosby. They jumped down from the bus and Lizzie, following Geoff over a stile, glanced admiringly around. He had certainly chosen a beautiful spot, for although it was still very windy, in the shelter of the wood, with the sunshine dappling through the leaves overhead, they could have been a thousand miles from civilisation. She had brought two large string bags for the greenery they meant to take home with them and a stout canvas one containing their carry-out.

'I know clover because the leaves are so pretty, like the clubs on a pack of cards,' Lizzie said as they began to pick some leaves around the edges of a sloping pasture. 'But unless it's gorra yellow flower, I wouldn't know a dandelion leaf if it bit me on the knee. How do you tell 'em from all the other leaves, our Geoff?'

Geoff showed Lizzie the selection of leaves he was picking which included a good few he couldn't name, though he thought they were probably all edible so far as birds and rabbits were concerned. 'When we came to visit the grand house round here, one of the farmhands used to take us foraging for his rabbits,' he explained. 'You mustn't give them fresh green stuff – I don't know why because they must eat fresh stuff in the wild – but he used to let us pick a big bag of leaves and then, when they had wilted next day, he'd let us feed the rabbits ourselves, by hand. I've never forgotten it, but I didn't expect it would come in useful. It just goes to show, Lizzie, that nothing you learn is ever wasted.'

Companionably, the two of them moved along the autumn-bright hedge, filling their string bags. They reached a mossy gate leading to a field which contained a pond. Standing next to it, they saw a water-vole scudding quietly along, only its nose showing above the water. Bulrushes grew in thick clumps along the further bank and as they approached a kingfisher took off in a blur of turquoise and blue. Lizzie gasped and sat down on the bank. 'It is so beautiful,' she said, her voice almost reverent. 'I wish Aunt Annie could see it. Oh, Geoff, what's that?'

As Lizzie had sat down, she had kicked out a wedge of the dark, water-softened earth which surrounded the pond and revealed a number of tiny, blood-red worms, wriggling in the rich soil. 'They're worms, the sort that fishermen use as bait,' Geoff said. 'Gosh, there must be hundreds. Tell you what, Lizzie, didn't you once tell me that Clem dug worms for Mrs Pridmore's hens? What say we collect some of these for Sausage and Mash? Why, what with all this lovely green stuff and lots of wriggling worms, they'll think it's their birthday!'

Lizzie agreed. 'Because neither Sausage nor Mash will eat corn yet, and I'm sure I've read somewhere that chickens love worms,' she said. 'What a treat it will be for them – sort of meat and two veg, wouldn't you say?'

Geoff laughed and began the task of extricating the worms from the rich and peaty soil, dropping them into a sort of nest of greaseproof paper which Lizzie made in the bottom of the canvas bag. Then, as the sun sank behind the distant hills, they turned their faces towards the road and their bus home.

That evening, Sausage and Mash were given their first taste of real greenery, chopped up small and mixed in with the breadcrumbs and fine meal which they usually ate. They seemed to enjoy the change and gobbled it up with great enthusiasm, so Lizzie tipped about half the wriggling mass of worms into their bowl and stood back to watch.

The leggy young chicks, looking odd now that their fluff was being replaced by tiny, brown feathers, stared anxiously at this strange phenomenon, jumping back every time the worms seemed about to attack them. Aunt Annie made chirruping noises and picked a worm out between thumb and forefinger, dangling it in front of the chicks' eyes. Neither Sausage nor Mash made any move to grab the tantalising titbit; in fact they both drew back, looking as outraged as though Aunt Annie was offering them cyanide. 'Come on, fellers,' she said coaxingly. 'This 'ere's the most delicious thing you've ever tasted, and there's a whole heap more of 'em, what's more. If one of you don't make a move soon, your Aunt Annie will have to eat 'em all herself.'

Lizzie gave a protesting squeak and smothered a gasp as Aunt Annie pretended to eat a worm, smacking her lips and telling the chicks how delicious it was, before dangling it front of their eyes once more. And presently, to Lizzie's relief, for she guessed that Aunt Annie would insist on keeping the worms until Sausage and Mash decided to try them, Sausage leaned forward and grabbed one end of the worm. In the blink of an eye it was gone and soon both chicks were tucking into their lively supper, crooning and cheeping and clearly enjoying the unusual meal.

'I reckon wherever there's soil, there'll be worms,' Aunt Annie said later, as the two of them made their way up the stairs to bed. 'I know we ain't got a backyard, but there's earth all over the place. Wharrabout the canal bank? Could you dig there if you had a little spade, or a spoon, or something?'

'I suppose you could,' Lizzie said doubtfully. 'Only I don't think it would be a good idea. Tell you what, Aunt Annie, there's allotments out at Seaforth and some of the fellers who own them are really old and might be glad of a hand in exchange for a few worms. Next time I've got a day free, I'll take a tram out there and see if I can do a swap. Come to that, when it's low tide, you see chaps down on the sand, digging for bait. Bait's only worms, isn't it? The shore doesn't belong to anyone, so I guess Geoff and I could dig there and bring the worms back for Sausage and Mash.'

'I'm going to ask round St John's Market whether they can spare me old cabbage leaves and that,' Aunt Annie said dreamily. 'They're only little now, but one day they'll be needin' a good deal of food, 'specially when they start layin'. Folks are pretty good on the whole when you explain you've gorra couple of young hens. I'll see what I can do.'

And Lizzie, continuing up the attic stairs, thought that Aunt Annie would probably do very well. Everyone liked her and would be keen to do anything they could to help her, especially if the food they gave for the hens would otherwise have been thrown away.

Going into her own attic room, Lizzie thought what a lovely day she had had and was grateful to Geoff, both for his companionship and his kindness in giving her another day out. Most young men of his age – for at sixteen he really was a young man and not a boy – would not have wanted to spend a whole day with a kid of fourteen. Still, Geoff had been her pal for a long while now, and never mentioned their age difference, so perhaps it did not matter after all.

Entering her attic, she checked with a quick glance that Herbie's peephole was still firmly puttied over and that there was nothing untoward in the room. Then she undressed quickly and slid between the blankets. She intended to relive her lovely trip to the country in that delicious time when she was not quite asleep nor fully awake, but it had been a long and exciting day in the fresh air. Very soon Lizzie slept, revisiting the country only in her dreams.

Chapter Five

It was a sunny day and Chinky was sitting on the grass feeling placid and even a little sleepy. It was too much to say that she was happy because she had come to Toxteth Park Cemetery to visit the grave of one of the few people who had been kind to her. Old Mrs Muggeridge, who had lived three doors further along from Chinky's foster mother and had always been good to the small unwanted child, had for the past year or so been asking her in and often the two of them would share a simple meal. It had seemed like heaven to Chinky to have a friend who not only fed her but seemed to like her as well. Mrs Muggeridge had even given her clothing from time to time – a faded blue skirt, several sizes too large, a much-patched white blouse, even clogs on one occasion. The clothes had once belonged to Mrs Muggeridge's daughter, Evie, but she had died in the influenza epidemic of 1919 so Mrs Muggeridge had been happy for Chinky to have them.

She had been glad to have Chinky's companionship as well. It was lonely for an old lady whose daughter had died and whose only other child, a son named Cuthbert, had married a Scottish fishergirl and now lived in Aberdeen. He wrote quite often, describing the beauties of the granite city, Mrs Muggeridge was apt to tell Chinky wistfully, but letters weren't the same as a nice chat. She seemed fond of her daughter-in-law, Kirsty, and of her two grandchildren, but assured Chinky that she would never consider leaving Liverpool to go and live in Aberdeen. 'It doesn't do to change your whole way of life when you're nudgin' seventy,' she told her young friend. 'What's more, it's hard on the young folk to have an old 'un thrust upon them, especially since I wouldn't know a soul up there apart from me own family. No, no, I'm better livin' in the house my dear husband brought me to when we was wed, surrounded by neighbours who've known me fifty years, and with me little friend Chinky to keep me company now and then.'

But a week ago, when Chinky had gone round to the house with a present for Mrs Muggeridge – three pretty good cooking apples which she had acquired from a stall in Great Homer Street – a strange person had answered the door. She was a tall, raw-boned woman in her fifties, her reddish hair streaked with grey, wearing a black dress and shawl. She stared down at Chinky without saying a word and the girl stared back, completely bemused. Who could this be? The woman was not young enough to be Kirsty, and besides Mrs Muggeridge would surely have told Chinky had she been expecting a visit from her daughter-in-law.

'Who's you after?' the woman said suddenly, peering through sandy lashes at Chinky. 'If it's Mrs Muggeridge, she's no' here. She's in the hospital.'

Her accent was so strongly Scottish that Chinky had to listen hard to understand a word but as soon as she did so, her heart jumped into her mouth. Her friend was in trouble – this must be a nurse, or perhaps a relative of the landlord, come to take possession of the house. Chinky's hands flew to her mouth and the bag of apples dropped to the paving.

'H-h-hospital?' she quavered. 'Is she ill? What's happened? Has someone sent for her son? And who – who are you?'

Seeing Chinky's obvious distress, the woman unbent a little and actually smiled. 'You'll be the wee girl that m'son-in-law says his mammy talked about in her letters,' she said, enlightenment dawning. 'I'm Kirsty's mother, Mrs McTavish. You'd best come away in, lass, and meet Cuthbert. My daughter's back home wi' the wee ones, so I came doon wi' the laddie to do what I could.' As she ushered Chinky into the well-remembered little parlour, she added: 'Your pal's had a stroke. She's very ill and does nae even know her ain wee son. They doot she'll last the day oot.'

Chinky couldn't help herself and began to cry, big shuddering sobs that shook her small frame. Mrs Muggeridge had been more than just a friend to her, she had been a refuge, a port in a storm, the only person upon whom Chinky could rely. If she died . . . but the thought was too terrible to contemplate. She turned tear-drowned eyes to Mrs McTavish. 'I dunno what I'll do if anything happens to her,' she gulped. 'She's me only real friend in the whole world. She often gives me food and bits o' clothing, but it ain't just that. She – she *likes* me, Mrs McTavish, which is more'n me foster mother does. I'm just a nuisance to *her*, she'd lambast the hide off of me if I didn't keep out of her way. Surely Mrs Muggeridge might get better?'

Before Mrs McTavish could answer, another voice spoke. 'You'll be young Chinky,' it said, in a familiar Liverpool accent. 'Me mam's often writ about you in her letters, so I feels I know you. I'm Cuthbert Muggeridge, but I daresay you've guessed that much.'

Chinky turned. In the doorway stood a tall young man, smiling down at her with a good deal of sympathy in his dark eyes. He was wearing seamen's clothing – a dark-blue jersey and trousers, with a blue and white spotted handkerchief knotted round his neck. But instead of sea boots he wore a pair of cracked black shoes. He had a square chin and a dimple in one cheek, yet he was so like Mrs Muggeridge that Chinky thought she would have guessed who he was even if she had met him in the street and not in this house. 'Hello, Mr Muggeridge,' she said shyly. She scrubbed the tears away from her eyes with the back of both hands, then wiped her nose on the sleeve of her ragged jersey. 'Are you going to the hospital? Can I come? I's real fond of your mam. Mebbe if she saw me . . .'

'Of course you can come, we'll all go together,' he said heartily. 'What's in the bag?'

Tears welled up in Chinky's eyes afresh. 'I – I brung your mam a few cooking apples,' she said brokenly. 'She's a grand cook, your mam. She used to say if I'd bring her fruit, she'd make a pie and then we could share it. She were awful good to me, were your mam.'

'Tell you what, lassie,' Mrs McTavish said, her tone gentle, 'yon puir widow woman will nae know me from Adam, so why don't I stay here and bake a pie ready for when the two of you come back from the hospital?'

Cuthbert agreed that this seemed like a good idea and he and Chinky set off for their visit.

They were too late. When they reached the ward, Sister came bustling towards them, a brown paper parcel in one hand. She told them that Mrs Muggeridge had died only a few minutes before, without regaining consciousness, and handed over the bag containing the dead woman's possessions, saying briskly that the body would be released for burial the following day.

Cuthbert and Chinky trailed home, both so miserable that they scarcely exchanged a word until they reached the court once more. Then Cuthbert told Chinky that she must come to the funeral, and to the wake afterwards, because he knew she had been one of his mother's dearest friends. 'I'll kit you out respectable,' he assured her. 'Kirsty's mam is a grand needlewoman and, God knows, there's enough black gear in me mam's wardrobe to clothe half Liverpool. After our Evie died, mam didn't wear colours for a long while. She used to say black were easier, didn't need washin' so often, but in her heart, she were always in mournin' for my little sister. From what she said to me, you kind o' took the place of our Evie for me mam, and I'm grateful to you for that, so when the wake's over, you must take a memento for yourself – something to remember her by, like.'

He had been as good as his word and Chinky had attended the funeral decently dressed in black, from the bow which held her hair away from her face to the scuffed boots on her feet. And afterwards she had not only helped to serve the funeral tea – ham, egg and cheese sandwiches, sausage rolls and a quantity of iced cakes – she had also eaten a good deal of it. Her memento was an ornament she had always greatly admired: a ship in a bottle which Mrs Muggeridge's sea-faring husband had made when he retired from the sea. In addition, Cuthbert had given her a great many odds and ends which she had put into a coarsely woven hemp sack, so that she might carry them away easily. She left the sack in the cupboard under the stairs at the Muggeridge house until Cuthbert and his mother-in-law, having sold or otherwise disposed of all his mother's goods and effects, set out for Aberdeen once more. Only then had Chinky dragged the sack back to her foster mother's, choosing to do so late at night in the hope that she might hide it somewhere safe until she had decided what to do with the contents. She meant to keep the ship in the bottle, but knew she would have to sell or pawn the rest of the stuff, or lose it to her foster mother's greedy and unprincipled children.

That first night she had covered the sack with her thin blanket, but because she had come in so late she had overslept, a most unusual occurrence, and when she awoke, the sack was gone. She had searched the whole house desperately, without success, and when she told her foster mother, the woman merely said that it would be one of the older boys and advised her not to make a fuss. 'I never axed your mam to leave you with me,' she reminded Chinky for the hundredth time. 'So you've lost a few bits and pieces? Well, you'll lose more than that before you're growed. Now get along wi' you, I've work to do even if no one else has.'

Burning with indignation, for the contents of the sack, when pawned, could have kept her in food for a month, Chinky had made her way to the cemetery. She urgently desired revenge on whichever of her foster brothers had prigged her sack and intended to beg Mrs Muggeridge to haunt the thievin' bugger and make him regret his dishonesty. But somehow, when she reached the cemetery, revenge seemed a petty and unworthy thing. Instead, she reached the grave and settled herself on the grass next to it and began to chat to Mrs Muggeridge as though the older woman were still alive and listening. She told her how kind Cuthbert and Mrs McTavish had been, and how someone had stolen her sack, and she drew from the bosom of her blouse the ship in a bottle, the only thing she had managed to save from the thief. And because it was quiet and peaceful in the cemetery, with the sun shining and a little breeze caressing her cheek, the burning anger which had brought her here faded away and she was only aware that folk other than Mrs Muggeridge had been kind to her, that neighbours at the wake had told her she might pop in and share a meal with them, now that her old friend was dead, and that, though she would miss Mrs Muggeridge horribly, life was not as bad as it might have been. She was growing up, and once she was fully grown and no longer in fear of the schools' inspectors, she could get a proper job and earn proper money and perhaps even have a room of her own, far away from her thieving foster family.

She was musing thus when a hand fell on her shoulder and a voice said in her ear: 'And why aren't you in school, chuck?'

Chinky twisted round, ready for flight, and saw above her the rubicund face and dark helmet of a policeman. The scuffer was not looking at her unkindly but the grip on her shoulder was so firm that his fingers dug into her flesh and she knew, instinctively, that he did not intend to let her go. She would have to talk her way out of this one, and talk pretty cleverly too. His grey eyes were sharply intelligent and she had a horrid feeling that he would not be easily fooled.

'Well? Why aren't you in school, young lady?'

A number of good excuses flashed through Chinky's mind. A recent bereavement – her presence at the newly dug grave lent authority to such a statement – a bad stomach upset, a sick mother? She took a deep breath and began to talk.

A week later, a very different Chinky sat on a small iron bedstead in the orphan asylum of Our Lady of the Immaculate Heart, gloomily contemplating the neat brown lace-up shoes upon her feet, the brown cotton stockings which were attached to her brand new liberty bodice, and the hem of her mauve gingham dress. The scuffer had been every bit as difficult to fool as she had feared. He had listened politely to her story of a recent bereavement, had nodded comprehension when she indicated the newly dug grave and the black riband around her arm which she now wore instead of her borrowed funeral attire, and had then asked her which school she attended – so that he might check up on her story, of course.

Chinky, long prepared for some such question, had answered glibly that she attended St Anthony's on Newsham Street. Indeed, so far as it went, it was truer than most of the things she had told him, since she had attended that school for almost a month when her foster mother had got her some boots and had sent her off in the care of an older child each day. But then hard times had come again, the boots had been pawned, and Chinky's school days had ceased as abruptly as they had started. She also gave him her real address, secure in the knowldege that this, at least, was provable. If he hauled her off to St Anthony's, as seemed likely, she would have to rely on her native wit and considerable turn of speed to get away from him before their destination was reached.

The scuffer, however, must have divined her

intention, for he took her wrist in a kindly, but firm grip, and did not give her the slightest opportunity to escape. The teachers at St Anthony's declared she had not attended school there for at least three years, but the final and worst blow came when Constable Perkins took her home to the court. Her foster mother, forced to accompany the policeman up the stairs and to show him where Chinky and the other children slept, leapt to the conclusion that the girl had grassed regarding the theft of her sack. Seeing that this could mean real trouble, she told the policeman shrilly that the child was no relative of hers, had been dumped on her when her prostitute mother had got sick of her, and demanded that the policeman take her away. 'I oughta have purrer in one of them orphan places years ago 'cos I got kids of me own what I'm hard pressed to feed, wi'out adding a half-Chinese brat to me string,' she said, with a vicious glance at Chinky. 'And don't you go believing a word she said, hofficer, because she's one as lies as easily as she breathes. If she says we ain't done right by her then she's lyin' again, same as always.'

Chinky had been outraged and hurt by these dreadful remarks, calculated to get her into trouble even deeper than she was already, but Constable Perkins was a sensible man and as he escorted Chinky from the house, told her that he was too old a hand to believe half of what her foster mother had said. 'Why, apart from them clothes you're wearin', which you say were given you by a neighbour after her own daughter died, there weren't a stitch of clothing, nor so much as a clog, in that house which would have fitted you,' he said, looking kindly down at her. 'I doubt that woman ever gave you a square meal in the whole of your life, so I'm not likely to believe anything *she* says either. But you can't go on like this, queen. Your foster mam don't want you. If you try to go back there, she'll send you off with a flea in your ear and you'll be walkin' the streets or beggin' on the docks and end up with your throat cut, like as not. But there's folk in Liverpool with hearts as big as your foster mother's is small. The sisters at the convent of Our Lady of the Immaculate Heart have a home for girls like you. You may know it as the Mackie Orphan Asylum because that's what most folk call it, it being less of a mouthful than the full title. The sisters aren't rich, but they're real good to the children in their care. You'll be happy there, I promise you.'

Chinky agreed to go to the orphanage, fully intending to stay a day or so and then to flit, but it seemed the nuns knew very well that new girls would try and do just that and Chinky was never alone for a moment. An older girl, Rosemary O'Reilly, took care of her and when Rosemary was unable to be with her, Sister Theresa, who was the house sister and in charge of the girls when they were not in school, made sure Chinky was kept under her eye.

Not that she was known as Chinky here – that was one advantage of the Mackie. When Mother Superior had asked her her name on that first terrifying day, Chinky had looked down at the faded blue skirt and the much-patched white blouse which had belonged to Evie Muggeridge and had said instinctively: 'Evie. Evie Evans.'

Mother Superior had not questioned the name – why should she, indeed? She had simply entered 'Evie Evans' on her roll, and now it was the name which was written, in indelible ink, on all her new clothes. The staff called them her 'nice new clothes' but to Chinky – only she was really Evie now, even thought of herself as that – they were no better than prison gear. They marked you out as an orphan as clearly as though the word had been written across your forehead, and since nobody at the Mackie possessed any ordinary clothing at all, escape became impossible.

Gazing gloomily down at her shoes now, however, Evie knew that no matter how much she disliked the thought of being held here, she was unlikely even to try to get away. Humiliating though it might be to admit it, three good meals a day and a proper bed of one's own, with clean sheets and blankets, had already softened her attitude to the Mackie. She might tell herself that life on the streets was freedom, but what sort of freedom was it really? The freedom to feel freezing cold in winter or to have one's stomach constantly growling a reproach because it was seldom comfortably full, was scarcely worthy of the name. What was more, although she had only been at the Mackie for a week, Evie was learning. The nuns were not rich, as the scuffer had implied, so the girls had to do their share of domestic tasks. Evie dusted and polished, cleared tables after their meals, washed dishes and made beds. She also attended classes and was learning both to read and write, and finding, to her pleased surprise, that the lessons she had been taught at St Anthony's so long ago were still in her head. The teacher had taught her her letters and it was remarkable how quickly she learned to string these together and to read the resultant words. 'You are going to be reading and writing by the end of a month,' Sister Catherine had told her, only the previous day. 'How come you're so quick, my child, when you've been – well – somewhat neglected?'

'I were friendly wi' a neighbour, a Mrs

Muggeridge. She used to read to me from the papers and she read slow, usin' her finger to point out each word. I reckon I took in more than I knowed,' Evie said, having given the matter some thought. 'And I want to learn to read awful bad – does that help, Sister?'

The nun agreed that she was sure it did, so that now, sitting fully dressed on her bed while around her the five other girls who shared the room got themselves ready for the walk to the park, Evie told herself that she would stay for a bit. She would learn to read and write, to keep house and do sums. She had little understanding of money but each orphan was given tuppence on a Saturday morning and allowed to spend it as they wished. What was more, arithmetic lessons were practical affairs since the main aim of the Mackie was to send their girls out into the wide world, when they were sixteen, able to fend for themselves. Arithmetic lessons therefore dealt with practical matters such as marketing, the costing of various household jobs, budgeting on a small income and the like.

'How come you're ready so long before us, Evie Evans?' The remark came from Sarah, a bouncy, freckled red head whose bed was next to Evie's. 'We walk to the park in what they call a crocodile, you know, that means walking in pairs. We have to choose partners, so will you walk wi' me? They don't mind if we talk, so long as we do it quietly, only we mustn't run or shout – not until we get to the park, that is. D'you know Princes Park? It's a fair old walk, but it's a grand place, so it is. If we are really good, Sister lets us go round the aviary and if you've any pocket money left, there's ices for sale at the kiosk. You can get a cone for a ha'penny.'

'Yes, I'll walk with you,' Evie said, trying for a nonchalance she was far from feeling. The other girls had been pleasant enough, but this was the first real overture of friendship which had been made. Evie had watched the other girl covertly and realised Sarah was popular with both children and staff; it was nice to think the other girl had chosen her of her own accord.

Somewhere below them a bell tinkled. Sarah jumped off her bed and grabbed Evie's hand. 'Come on, gerra move on,' she said, hauling her out of the dormitory. 'We'll make straight for the cloakroom 'cos though it's a nice day we'll have to wear our hats and coats. Wonder which Sister's in charge today? I hope it's Sister Edna. She's me favourite 'cos she's young and jolly.'

Chattering and laughing, Sarah and Evie descended the stairs and headed for the cloakroom.

By the time Evie had been at the Mackie for two years, she had begun to realise what a very good turn Constable Perkins had done her. Looking at herself in the small mirror which hung at the end of the wash-room, Evie saw that she was scarcely recognisable as the tattered little waif who had been admitted here. An ordered life, with good but plain food, regular bedtimes and, best of all, no worries concerning her personal safety, meant that Evie had blossomed. Her hair, which was black as night, was also glossy with daily brushings and weekly washing, and though the Mackie's rules meant that she had to wear it braided, when it was loose it reached almost to her waist. Her skin was clear and creamy with a flush on her cheeks, and the long, liquid black eyes sparkled with health. Her figure, which had been of scarecrow-like thinness when she had lived in the court, was burgeoning now, her small waist emphasising the curve of hips and tiny breasts.

I'm getting to be a woman, Evie told herself, flicking her braids back over her shoulders and setting off for the dining hall downstairs. If only we knew how old I really was, the nuns might let me start looking for a job. But then suppose I'm younger than I think, that'd hold me up for longer, so best stick to what they decided when I was brought in. Only sometimes it irks me being told what to do every moment of every day and never being able to please meself any more.

It was odd, she thought later that morning, that she should have been thinking about her old life on the very day that it caught up with her. For when she went to the music room – she was learning to play the piano, and had proved herself an apt pupil – she found that Miss Mather, the music teacher, had not arrived. Evie enjoyed her piano lessons so sat down at the instrument and began to tinkle out a little tune, only to stop in dismay after the first few notes for there was clearly something wrong with the instrument. When struck the keys seemed reluctant to rise again and the notes she knew she was playing sounded weird and off-key. She was staring down at her fingers, perplexed and startled, when the door of the music room opened and Sister Maria came in. 'Ah, Evie! I searched for you upstairs but you must have come down before me,' the nun said. 'One of the girls was polishing the piano this morning and overturned a vase of flowers. The water got into the works and I understand the instrument can no longer be used, but Miss Mather has a pianoforte in her front room and says if you go along to her home, you may have your lesson there.'

Evie had thought the restriction of never being allowed outside the orphanage unless accompanied by a nun or some other member of staff irksome, but now she looked at Sister Maria with something akin to panic. 'Go – go to her home?' she quavered. 'But I don't know where she lives, Sister. Is it far? Is anyone else having a music lesson today as well, or are you coming with me yourself?'

Sister Maria laughed. 'Evie Evans, you're a big girl now, you must be almost fourteen! Why, I remember when you first came to us you were furious because you could no longer roam the streets at will. Surely you'll be glad of an opportunity to go out alone? Anyway, I'm far too busy at the moment to accompany you and there is no other member of staff available to do so either. If you really feel you cannot find Prospect Street, then I suppose you will have to miss your lesson.'

'Prospect Street?' Evie said thoughtfully. 'Isn't that near Erskine Street, Sister? I know that area all right, but it's a fair old walk from here.'

'I'm to give you your tram fare,' Sister Maria said briskly, producing a small purse from the folds of her habit and handing Evie two shiny pennies. 'If you walk down to Lime Street, you can catch a tram which will take you up the Scotland Road as far as Tenterden Street – Miss Mather lives at number sixteen – and when you come home, you just do the same journey in reverse. I'm sure I don't need to tell you not to talk to anyone in the street and to behave with decorum. You know, Evie, Mother Superior is placing great trust in you, letting you go out alone in this way. Mackie girls are never usually allowed to roam the city, but Miss Mather says you are the most promising piano pupil that she has taught in all of her forty years. She thinks it possible that if you persevere with your studies, you might end up teaching music as she does. So naturally, Mother Superior is keen that you should continue with your lessons.'

'But what about practising, Sister?' Evie asked anxiously. The nuns, she knew, only possessed one piano, in the orphanage at any rate, though there was a harmonium in the chapel and might, for all she knew, be other instruments in the convent itself. 'Will it take long to mend this one?'

The nun sighed and pulled a face. 'Mr Benedict came in earlier and says he thinks the piano too old and too badly damaged to repair,' she said mournfully. 'As you know, child, we are a poor Order and have very little money coming in, so the price of a new piano will be beyond us for some time to come. But Miss Mather has very kindly said that, until we replace the instrument, you may go to her house for half an hour's practice three or four times a week.'

'It's awfully good of her,' Evie said rather doubtfully. She guessed that the practice would be taken out of the only time the children had to themselves, which was evenings, when they played games in the garden in summer or gathered in the playroom in the winter, to do jig-saws or crossword puzzles until bedtime. However, this was something which need not trouble her now, so she thanked Sister Maria, pocketed the tuppence and went to the cloakroom for her mauve jacket and the straw boater, with its silver and mauve ribbon, which the girls always affected to hate but which most of them secretly thought becoming.

So it was that Evie found herself walking down Brownlow Hill, heading for the bustle of Lime Street. It was a fine, sunny day and as she walked, a delicious sense of freedom invaded her. She could not believe she had actually felt nervous of a solitary expedition – she who had spent the first ten years of her life roaming the Liverpool streets alone! She knew that she would relish every moment of this unexpected treat. She reached the tram stop and joined the short queue of people waiting. She saw that people recognised her uniform and several smiled at her in a friendly fashion; clearly they did not realise how unusual it was to see a Mackie girl out alone. And then a number twenty-three came roaring and rattling along the road, screeching to a halt alongside the queue, and everyone scrambled aboard.

Evie settled herself on the slatted wooden seat and looked curiously around at her fellow passengers. It would have been nice, she reflected, to see someone she knew, a neighbour perhaps or one of the stallholders on Byrom Street who had been kind to her, but there was not a single face she recognised among the tram passengers, so she settled down to look out of the window as the well-remembered streets passed by outside.

When they neared Tenterden Street and the conductor rang his bell, she got up with several other passengers and climbed down on to the busy pavement. As she walked towards her destination, she reflected how strange it was that nothing had altered; the very shops into whose windows she had peered as a hungry street urchin were still there, although they looked smaller and less splendid than they had once done. Their windows still looked appealing, however, with the apples and oranges in their boxes on the pavement gleaming in the morning sun. But I am very different, Evie told herself, studying her reflection in the polished panes of glass. I look very grown up and well dressed; in fact, I look better than almost anyone in the street. Goodness, I'd quite forgotten what a poor area this is. You hardly ever see an old shawly in Brownlow Street because it's a residential area, I suppose, but they're still here, haggling with the shopkeepers and trying to sell passers-by bunches of flowers or a few fades from the fruit stalls in St John's Market.

Despite her determination to go straight to Miss Mather's house, she found herself lingering, gazing at children playing on the pavement in the hope that she would recognise one of them, so when someone coming towards her seemed vaguely familiar, she smiled delightedly, before realising with a sinking heart that he had looked through her as though she were a total stranger. 'Sid?' she said tentatively. 'You *are* Sid Ryder, aren't you?'

The young man stopped short and stared incredulously, taking her in from the top of her head to the tip of her brown lace-up shoes. 'I'm sorry, Miss,' he began, 'but I think you must be mistaken. I'm Sid Ryder, all right, but who the hell are you?'

She opened her mouth to tell him that she was Evie Evans and realised, just in time, that the name would mean nothing to him. Feeling the heat rush to her face and knowing that she was as red as any rose, she said rather crossly: 'Oh, Sid, I can't have changed that much! Around here they used to call me Chinky Evans because my dad was Chinese. But my real name's Evie. *Now* do you remember me?'

Sid stared for a moment, then a broad grin spread across his face and he seized Evie's hands in a firm, delighted grip. 'Well, I'll be damned!' he said. 'I thought you was dead, queen, 'cos you disappeared one day and weren't ever seen in this area again. I felt real guilty 'cos I'd not done more for you and now here you are, walking up to me, bold as brass and lookin' . . . like a Queen.' He beamed down at her. 'Come along o' me and I'll mug you to a cup of tea and a bun whiles you tell me what's been happening to you this past couple o' years.'

Evie laughed but gently detached his fingers from her wrist. 'I'm sorry, Sid, but I'm on my way to see a teacher who lives in Prospect Street,' she said. 'If I'm late, there'll be an awful row because I'm on my honour to go straight there and back and not to talk to anyone on the way. I'm at the orphan asylum attached to the Convent of the Immaculate Heart – the Mackie they call it – and we're never allowed out alone as a rule, so I don't want to be in trouble on my very first trip. Sorry, but . . .'

'Prospect Street? Then I'll walk along o' you and you can tell me what happened as we walk,' Sid said cheerfully. He took her hand and tucked it into the crook of his arm, smiling benignly down at her. 'I'm a feller as don't desert his pals, and you were always me pal, though you were one of the filthiest kids I'd ever clapped eyes on. Now come on, give us the low down.'

Among the many things the convent had taught her was the ability to collect her thoughts and tell a simple, straightforward story. Remembering Sister Bernadette's oft repeated injunction in English lessons to begin at the beginning of every tale, she started her story with Mrs Muggeridge's death and her subsequent capture in the cemetery. It was soon told and by the time they reached Prospect Street, Sid was in possession of Evie's life story over the past two years.

He pulled her to a halt on the pavement and once

more his eyes raked her from top to toe, the expression in them now undoubtedly admiring. 'Well, you've turned into a right little cracker and I'm proud to know you,' he told her. 'I'm not going to lose touch with you a second time either. As for me, I'm in a good way of business in me own right, making money hand over fist and savin' for the future. You're a real good-lookin' gal now, and I reckon we could help each other. How long do they mean to keep you in that orphan asylum?' His eyes raked her again. 'Why, you must be all of fifteen or sixteen, old enough to gerra job, and a good one too.'

Evie laughed. She was excited both by his obvious admiration and by his worldly and knowing attitude. She knew that she must be more like fourteen, but guessed that good living and the self-confidence that the convent had given her made her look older than her years. 'I'm probably around fifteen,' she said, crossing her fingers behind her back. 'The nuns want me to teach music, which I quite like, but that won't be for a good few years yet.'

'What, stay in that place for years, shut in like another nun? You can't *want* that,' Sid said incredulously. 'Why, you've gorra smashin' figure, kiddo, as well as the prettiest face I've seen in ages. Don't you want to earn some money?'

Evie looked at him doubtfully. She did not think that the sort of money a girl of her age could earn would be enough to keep her in lollipops; certainly it would not be enough for her to live on. She said as much, but Sid wagged his head reprovingly at her. 'Ah, you'll be thinkin' of work as a shopgirl or in a factory somewhere,' he said knowingly. 'Still, perhaps you're right, perhaps you'll be better with a year or two more under your belt. Then, what say you and

I go into partnership, like? I'd see you right, Evie, you can trust me for that.'

Evie thought of the ha'pennies which he had handed to her when she had been desperate, the ends of loaf and the bits of cheese he had occasionally saved her from his carry-out, and wavered. But she also remembered he had been quite an accomplished thief and though the young Chinky had admired this very much, the older and wiser Evie knew that such behaviour did not pay in the end. If Sid was still on the shady side of the law, then the less she had to do with him, the better.

'Thanks, Sid, I'll think about it,' she said. 'But I've got to go now or Miss Mather will be reporting back to the convent that I must have been chattering to folk because I was late for my lesson. 'Bye!'

'Oh, but . . . when will I see you again?' Sid called after her disappearing back. 'You can't just walk out on me when we were such pals once. I want to see you again.'

Evie turned. 'Well, you can scarcely call at the convent,' she remarked cheerfully. 'We'll meet up sometime, Sid. And now I really must go.' And with that she hurried along the street, found Miss Mather's front door, and was soon being ushered into her teacher's small front parlour

Evie expected that this would end the matter but an hour later, when she emerged on to Scotland Road, Sid was waiting for her. He had bought her a bar of Nestle's chocolate and said, as he boarded the tram beside her, that he had meant to buy her flowers but realised that she could scarcely take them back to the orphan asylum without a good many questions being asked. He then demanded to be told when she was having her next music lesson and, despite the uneasy conviction that she should not tell him, Evie found herself admitting that, for the rest of the month, she would be spending an hour in Prospect Street at around this time every weekday. She also told him that this was only possible while the piano at the convent remained unplayable, but Sid said now that she had a leg loose, surely she would not want to be incarcerated once more, and Evie knew he was right.

'We'll invent an old aunt what you met while walking up the Scottie,' he said breezily. 'I know orphans are allowed out once a week or so to see relatives, if they've gorrany, so I daresay the sisters will be glad enough to release you every now and then. I've gorra real respectable aunt – Auntie Madge, that is – who'll write a note for me, tellin' the nuns she's your mam's sister and asking permission for you to visit in Cazneau Street, a couple of times a month. How does that suit you?'

Evie thought that, had Aunt Madge really been respectable, she would not have gone along with her nephew's lies, but was not bold enough to say so. She merely nodded and murmured agreement and reminded him that for a while at least, she would be coming and going to Prospect Street on a lawful errand and would not need anyone to lie for her. At this Sid took her hand and squeezed it, eyeing her reproachfully. 'It's all right, I'm not aiming to get you into trouble,' he said reassuringly. 'But that bleedin' piano might get mended tomorrer, and then where would we be? Best plan ahead, that's my motto, but we'll leave Auntie Madge for a while, if you like.'

At this point, they reached Lime Street and Evie got down. Though Sid accompanied her on to the pavement, she refused to allow him to go a step further with her. 'If I'm seen with a feller, I'd be in the most awful trouble,' she said earnestly. 'They'd shut me in a prison cell for a hundred years, I should think. So just you buzz off back on the next tram, Sid. 'Bye for now.'

She turned resolutely away, and was relieved when he made no attempt to follow her.

Chapter Six

February 1927

Lizzie and Sally emerged from the factory to find themselves in a different world. Even within doors they had known that it was snowing, glancing up from their workbenches from time to time to see the flakes descending outside, grey against the white sky. But now, looking around them, they realised that this was a blizzard, no less.

'Glory!' Lizzie said. 'I hope Aunt Annie's done her messages before this lot came down – she's never been completely well since she lost the baby, and being so big, a bad fall could do her a lot of harm. Still, she's got me to pick up anything she's forgot at the shops.'

Sally bent down and picked up a handful of snow, beginning to form it into a ball. 'You're too old to . . .' Lizzie began, but it was too late; Sally took aim and the snowball cut the sentence in half. Spluttering, Lizzie wiped snow off her face and, with a vengeful gleam in her eye, began to make a snowball of her own. She hurled it at Sally, but half-heartedly, and saw without much interest that her friend had dodged so the snowball whizzed over her shoulder and broke in the roadway.

'Acting like kids is all right when you *are* a kid, or when you've got really thick gloves on, but all it's done for me is make my chilblains ache,' Lizzie said, balling her hands into fists and shoving them into the pockets of her thin coat. 'My gloves are more hole than finger, if you see what I mean, so I left them in the kitchen 'cos Aunt Annie said she'd get Mrs Threadgold to do a good darning job on them.'

'Pity you to chose to leave them behind on a day like this when you could do with them,' Sally said. She pulled off one of her own thick scarlet gloves and offered it to Lizzie, then shoved her bare hand into her pocket. 'There! Now you'll be a bit warmer.'

'Thanks, Sally, you're a pal,' Lizzie said gratefully. 'Although the first thing I'll do when I get indoors is to put my own gloves on – if Mrs Threadgold has finished with 'em. I don't reckon our house is a lot warmer than out in the court, unless you park yourself right in front of the fire, that is. The draughts are chronic and no matter how carefully we shut up before we go to bed, there are times when Uncle Perce comes in late after the pubs have closed and leaves every door in the perishin' house wide open. Aunt Annie's told him and told him, but it doesn't make any difference.'

Sally stared at her friend through the whirling flakes, hunching up her shoulders so that the scarf round her neck obliterated everything except her round, brown eyes.

'Mam and I saw him coming out of the pub the other night,' she said, shooting a sideways glance at her friend. 'We'd been to see Clara Bow and Gilbert Rowland in *The Plastic Age* – oh, Lizzie, it were wonderful, and ever so romantic. We'd not seen your uncle for ages and were real surprised because he looked quite smart. I don't believe he was drunk. He didn't fall down or shout abuse or anything like that, at any rate,' she added.

Lizzie chuckled. 'Now you mention it, he keeps himself a deal tidier than he used to,' she remarked.

'As you know, Uncle Perce's gorra fearful temper and he used to hit out at Aunt Annie or me on any excuse, but now he's usually not home until after we're in bed, and he leaves for work later than I do so I scarcely ever see him. But he doesn't seem to be so – so angry all the time, and it's ages since he and Aunt Annie had a real barney, with flying fists and screechings, that sort of thing. Oh, he still gets pretty drunk from time to time, but he's doing well on the docks and though the family don't see much of the money, at least he doesn't keep stealing from the rest of us. In fact, apart from mealtimes when he comes in and eats everything in sight, we hardly know he's sharing the same house, particularly as he always sleeps in the front room so Aunt Annie can have the big bed all to herself.'

'My mam told me, as we were walking home, that your Uncle Perce used to be a right handsome feller. She said all the girls were after him and really envied your Aunt Annie when the pair of 'em got wed. Your aunt were ever so pretty, Mam says, with lovely red-gold hair and a peaches and cream complexion. It's a real shame what too many kids and too much hard work can do to a woman, and then there's the drink. Once a feller starts on that . . .'

Lizzie nodded agreement, trying to stop her teeth from chattering as the wind hurled fresh handfuls of snow into her face. 'When you see Aunt Annie's thin grey hair and that little bun on the back of her head, it's hard to realise it was once so long she could sit on it,' she observed. 'I don't suppose I'll ever marry, but if I do it won't be for looks or charm or anything of that nature. I'm going for money and power meself.'

Sally laughed. 'Ain't we all?' she said derisively. 'Has it ever crossed your mind, queen, to wonder why your uncle's smartenin' hisself up and goin' easy on the drink?'

'Oh, aye, I reckon it's because old Mr Latimer, what was one of his drinking companions, died of the booze last August,' Lizzie said wisely. 'It's enough to put anyone off, 'cos Mr Latimer had been in school with Uncle Perce, so they were about the same age. Aunt Annie reckoned it scared the old feller because he began to take more care and to drink less from then on.'

'Maybe, but I did wonder . . .'

At this moment, they turned into the court and as they did so there was a wild shriek and snowballs came flying through the air, hitting the two girls with enough force to make them stagger back, laughing and trying to catch the little imps who had laid in wait for them. By the time they had dealt out punishment and sent the children scampering off to ambush the next court dweller to come within reach, Lizzie was so cold that her only thought was to get within doors before she froze solid. Handing back Sally's glove, and promising to meet her so that they might walk to work together next day, she ran up the three steps, pushed open the front door, closed it carefully behind her, and made for what slight warmth the kitchen offered.

Aunt Annie was standing at the table, making dumplings. She had bought a large lump of suet from the butcher and was crumbling a handful of dried herbs into her mixing bowl. She looked up and grinned as Lizzie entered the room. 'Well, who is under all that snow?' she asked jovially. 'Just you go back outside, my fine lady, and shake it off your coat and scarf. My goodness, if this is going to keep up, you'll want a pair of Wellington boots – I reckon those thin little shoes, for all they've got extra cardboard soles in 'em, won't last long in weather like this.'

Lizzie, aware of wet and ice-cold feet, nodded agreement and said through chattering teeth: 'I'll put fresh cardboard inside 'em as soon as they've dried out. Did you get my gloves mended?' She went to the front door as she spoke, rid herself of the quantity of snow on her coat and scarf and returned, shivering, to the kitchen, which seemed quite warm after the chill outside. 'Are there any messages, Aunt Annie? Have you brought water in? Only there's no point in my taking off me coat and scarf if I've got to go out again later.'

Aunt Annie turned and peered at the buckets beneath the sink and Lizzie saw that despite the warmth from the fire, there was cat-ice forming on the surface of the biggest bucket. She knew that in her own little room there would be icicles hanging from the curtain rail, and that the water she would take upstairs when she went to bed would probably be solid ice by morning. 'I brung a bucket of slack in to heap the fire up once the food's cooked,' Aunt Annie said. 'Young Ivan Carruthers – he's a good lad, he is – filled me water buckets earlier, and your cousin Herbie brung in a sack of coal yesterday. I dunno where he got it and I ain't goin' to ask,' she added hastily, seeing the question in her niece's eyes. 'And, yes, Mrs Threadgold brought your gloves back an hour since – she's made a real good job of them, too.'

'That's grand. My hands are covered with chilblains. The damned things burn when I'm cold and itch like crazy when I begin to get warm,' Lizzie said. She lowered the wooden rack and spread her coat and scarf across it, then hauled it back to ceiling height once more. By tomorrow morning, her thin coat and threadbare scarf would be dry enough to wear. Having done this, she rooted about in the cupboard to the left of the fireplace and found a sheet of stout cardboard and the rusty old scissors which her aunt used to cut out inner soles for thinning boots and shoes. Using the old, wet inner soles as a pattern, Lizzie soon had two fine new ones, which she laid carefully on the cupboard shelf, intending to insert them into her shoes when they were dry. In the meantime, she padded barefoot around the kitchen, laying the table for the evening meal.

Sausage and Mash, who usually made a dash for the kitchen door as soon as it opened, were ensconced in Aunt Annie's basket chair looking, Lizzie thought, extremely smug and self-satisfied. Clem's confident assertion that one was a cock and one was a hen had proved false for they were both hens and now laid eggs on a fairly regular basis. The previous spring, Aunt Annie had somehow managed to smuggle a neighbour's cockerel into the house for an amatory half hour, and as a result Sausage had become broody and had produced, and reared, ten fine little chicks. Aunt Annie had wanted to keep them, but there had been a terrible scene with Uncle Perce who flatly forbade her to turn his kitchen into a poultry yard and threatened the chicks with a grisly fate if they remained on his premises. However, Aunt Annie had sweet-talked a neighbour further down Burlington Street into letting her rear the chicks in his backyard and had sold them as six-month pullets for a respectable sum the previous September.

'I see you know when you're well off, you great fat idle blighters,' Lizzie said, breaking off a leaf from the cabbage she had just taken from the cupboard and handing it to the two birds. 'It's wickedly cold out there. You ought to be very grateful you aren't ordinary hens, forced to live outdoors and find a living pecking around someone's backyard. You're a couple of prima donnas, you are!'

By the time the lads got home, both freezing cold and loudly cursing the snow, Lizzie and Aunt Annie had the food prepared and the table laid for five people. Herbie worked for a local coal merchant, hefting sacks up on his shoulders and emptying them out into the yard of whoever had bought the coal. It was hard, sweaty work. In the summer he came home black, hot and exhausted, but in winter, because of the heavy weights he carried, he could not wrap up against the cold so usually came home grumbling that he was freezing but with runnels of sweat making white pathways through the coal dust. Aunt Annie always made him wash thoroughly before allowing him to sit down for the evening meal and today he was glad to do so, for the kettle of hot water which his mother had prepared warmed him up in a way nothing else could.

'Had a good day, you fellers?' Aunt Annie said, as the four of them took their places around the table. 'We won't wait for your dad 'cos his'll keep hot in the back oven bein' as it's a nice mutton stew, and I never know from one day to the next what time he'll be in.' She shivered as she spoke then began to heap potatoes on to the four tin plates. 'Ain't it cold, though? I hates the winter worse than I hate anything, I think. I piles on the shawls indoors and I puts two coats on and me thickest scarf and gloves when I goes out to do me messages, but me breath wets the scarf and freezes solid, and when I've got a basket in either hand and me nose runs, that freezes solid an' all. Even bed ain't the comfort you'd think, 'cos the draughts whistle in round the window frames and the door and somehow they find their way into bed with me, no matter how many old coats and shawls I piles on top of me blanket.'

'You want to do a job like mine, sloggin' uphill and down dale with a bleedin' great sack of coal over one shoulder and your feet slippin' and slidin' at every step,' Herbie said morosely. 'The only warm thing is the bleedin' horse and he ain't much comfort in Havelock Street. I delivered there this afternoon, to the mad old biddy what lives almost at the top. I parked the cart in Netherfield Road, 'cos I'd had a customer or two along there, but what with the snow and the ice, I judged it best to carry the coal up sack by sack. Honest to God, Mam, I were clingin' to them metal handholds set into the houses and heavin' meself along, but by the last sackful, I were crawlin' on all fours, more like a bleedin' dog than a feller.'

'Poor old Herbie, it's a hard life you've chose,' Denis said, looking smug. Lizzie guessed that the ticket office at Exchange Station, where he was working at present, would seem a haven of warmth and comfort compared to Havelock Street on an icy day. 'But you're always tellin' us the money's good, and the perks can't be bad. I see Mam's burnin' best coal again an' I don't suppose they asked you to pay full price, eh?'

'You mind your own bleedin' business,' his brother said immediately. He dug his fork into a large potato and conveyed it whole to his mouth. Speaking in muffled tones, he added: 'Old Jones won't miss a few lumps of coal. After all, there's spillage to take into account – I reckon I lose half a sack every time I parks and goes out of sight to the bleedin' kids. They're always on the look-out for somethin' to nick.'

Lizzie, who had never taken so much as an empty lemonade bottle without first asking permission to do so, knew that she was in a minority here. Most of the girls working at the factory considered that they were underpaid and thought it perfectly fair to go home with the odd bottle of lemonade or gingerbeer tucked away in a pocket or handbag. And now that she thought about it, she decided that Herbie was probably right. To be sure, he was better paid than his brother, and she knew he could buy slack or the very lowest grade of coal for considerably less than Mr Jones charged the public, but it seemed a small enough thing to prig a sack of best from time to time so that his family might have a decent fire when the weather was so cold.

If Aunt Annie needed something desperately which I could get from the factory, I reckon my principles might slip, Lizzie told herself, cutting her potato into bite-sized pieces. Come to that, when Aunt sent me on messages years ago, many's the time I was so hungry for fruit that I prigged the odd apple off a stall and never even thought I was thievin', though I was, of course. She remembered a teacher at school, telling them the old saying, 'Necessity is the mother of invention', and remembered also, with a secret smile, how she had held Aunt Annie's shopping bag below the level of the stall, and reaching up for the goods she had just bought, had carefully knocked into the open bag some other item of fruit which was within her reach.

Herbie was beginning to tell Denis what he thought of clerking as a career when the kitchen door opened and Uncle Perce appeared. He stood in the doorway for a moment to shake the snow off himself, for he was so covered in the stuff that he could have been a snowman. Lizzie noticed that Aunt Annie did not order her husband to get rid of the snow outside but hurried at once to the stove to fill his plate with stew, then went over to help him off with his wet outer clothing. However, Uncle Perce pushed her rudely aside and dropped his wet things on to the floor. 'Gerrout of me way, you stupid fat cow,' he growled, and took his place at the table, looking round at his sons and niece from under bushy, lowered brows, though he did not greet any of them. Aunt Annie picked up his wet clothing and hung it before the fire.

'I hope it's something decent for once,' he growled as she carried his well-filled plate across to the table. 'None of that blind scouse muck you're so fond of givin' me.' He snorted as his wife put the food in front of him, then picked up his spoon and fork and began to eat. Speaking through a full mouth – his sons had obviously learned their table manners from him, Lizzie thought – he went on grumbling about the meals his wife provided until Lizzie said sharply: 'We've not had blind scouse more than a couple of times since I've been working, Uncle Perce. Now that Aunt gets money from the three of us, she's able to buy meat of some sort four or five times a week, which is a lot more than most families get. And there's the money she gets for cooking for other folk in the court, and for laundering all that table linen for the dining rooms on the Scottie . . . I tell you, we do better'n most.'

This was bold of Lizzie, who rarely said anything to Uncle Perce let alone anything critical, but although he gave her a long and thoughtful stare, he neither challenged the remark nor asked her why she had not mentioned his own contribution to the household. Which was as well, Lizzie thought savagely, eating her mutton stew as slowly as possible to make it last, because, so far as she could make out, he contributed almost nothing. If he was unloading a shipment of sugar from the Indies or bananas from the Canaries, he might occasionally bring such items home, but this happened very rarely. Once, a year or so ago, he had brought home a length of black cloth and another of tartan wool for his wife to get made up into a dress or shawl, but that had only happened once. Uncle Perce, Lizzie concluded, took a good deal more than he gave and she wondered, not for the first time, why Aunt Annie continued not only to put up with him, but to feed him well, wash, iron and darn his clothing, and see that he got the lion's share of any food going.

A moment later she thought she knew the answer to her unasked question. Aunt Annie took her place opposite her husband and said affectionately: 'Did you have a good day on the docks, love? Was you workin' in the hold or out on the quay? I hopes as it was the hold 'cos that's warmer, ain't it? And this 'ere's brass monkey weather, no question.' Lizzie, glancing at her aunt as she spoke, saw the expression in her bright little eyes and recognised it as love. It was an odd thing, she told herself, that her aunt could continue, obstinately and against all the odds, to love this unlovable pig of a man, but there could be no doubt that she genuinely did so.

Mentally shrugging, Lizzie continued to eat her stew. It was no use being sorry for Aunt Annie because from the way she acted Lizzie assumed she wasn't sorry for herself. Lizzie remembered the affection between her own parents, the way her mother had felt after her father had died, and knew that whether Uncle Perce returned her feelings or not, Aunt Annie could not stop loving him just because he clearly had no feelings left for her. It was dreadful but her aunt who was very dear to her was as trapped by her affection as though Uncle Perce had physically locked her into number nine.

Uncle Perce's spoon clattered round his empty plate. Before he could say anything, Aunt Annie whisked it away and replaced it with an enamelled dish filled to the brim with suet pudding. Uncle Perce glanced around, but once more Aunt Annie was before him, holding out an almost full tin of conny-onny. 'Tek as much as you like,' she said eagerly. 'I didn't make custard 'cos I know you like this best.'

Uncle Perce grunted and poured the sticky condensed milk over his pudding with a prodigal hand. Lizzie, who also liked conny-onny, saw the tin passed next to her cousins and guessed that if she got any, it would be a thin scraping indeed. However, the suet pudding with apples in its centre, all soft and sweet, was delicious even without the addition of condensed milk and Lizzie ate eagerly, finishing as soon as the others despite having been served last.

Uncle Perce's chair grated on the tiles as he pushed it away from the table, but before he could speak Aunt Annie jumped in once more. 'I've gorra kettle over the fire and the teapot nicely warmed. You can have a nice cup of tea before the cat can clean her ear,' she said anxiously, watching her husband with such a dog-like and devoted glance that Lizzie might have laughed had the circumstances been different. Uncle Perce, however, did not consider it amusing.

'I'm goin' to the pub,' he said roughly. 'I'm not curdlin' me stomach wi' bleedin' tea when I could be enjoyin' a pint of strong ale.'

'But, Perce, your outdoor things is still wringin' wet and the snow's still fallin' fast. If you go out again, you'll likely catch your death,' Aunt Annie pleaded. 'Just for tonight, just for once, love, why not sit in your cosy chair by the fire 'til it's time for bed? We could have a game of cards or I could run and borrow a copy of the *Echo* from Mrs Leggatt at number thirteen. Her daughter usually brings one home after the shop closes.'

Uncle Perce did not reply but went over to where his son's coat hung from the pulley and jerked it down. He tried to struggle into it while Denis, who was considerably narrower across the shoulders than his father, stood by, a half grin twisting the corners of his mouth. 'Don't you go splittin' the seams of me only coat, our Da,' he said warningly. 'Because I ain't goin' to go to work in rags. I'm always up before you in the mornings so I suppose I'd have to use yours, which is a deal thicker'n mine anyhow.'

Uncle Perce gave a snort but tossed his son's coat down across the table and headed for the back door. 'It's nobbut a step to the pub from here, I won't bother wi' a coat,' he growled, snatching a big muffler and a ragged old cap from the hooks on the kitchen door. 'As for stayin' in, this place ain't no home to me. Why, I'm not even welcome in me wife's bed no more. I'm chucked into me front room to sleep on the sofy like an old dog, and it's mortal cold in there come the early hours.'

Aunt Annie's large face flushed with distress. 'Oh, Perce, me love, you're as welcome as flowers in spring to sleep along o' me in the big bed,' she said eagerly. 'Why, it's only because you can't always manage the stairs when you're a bit befuddled like that we've took to leavin' beddin' on the sofy in the front room. Many's the time I've come down and tried to heave you up the stairs, only you'd get so fightin' mad when your elbows caught in the banisters, I was scared you'd break your bones afore ever we reached the top landin'. Why, if you've a mind to sleep in your own bed tonight, there's no one would be happier than meself.'

She gave him a flirtatious glance and put a tentative hand on his arm, but Uncle Perce shook it off and headed for the kitchen door. 'I know when I'm not wanted,' he growled. 'Why, you think more of them bleedin' hens than you do of me,' and before Aunt Annie could say another word, he had wrenched open the kitchen door and was crossing the hallway.

Lizzie, unable to control her wrath, shouted after him: 'At least the hens lay bleedin' eggs, and don't just guzzle down their dinners and walk out on us,' but she was speaking to thin air. Uncle Perce had gone, coatless, into the storm, slamming the front door viciously behind him and leaving Lizzie to mutter beneath her breath that she hoped the cold would kill him and then they'd all be better off.

Aunt Annie had turned away, her lip quivering, and the boys seemed so embarrassed by their father's behaviour that they could only sit in their places, staring at the empty pudding bowls before them. Lizzie jumped to her feet and went and shut the kitchen door, through which a mean and biting draught was coming. Then she went over to her aunt and, putting both arms around the older woman, gave her a comforting squeeze. Aunt Annie hugged her back, then broke away to go over to the fire where she began to make the tea, saying in a small voice: 'He don't mean half he says, it's just . . . well, I ain't the girl he married and that's the truth. I wish I weren't so fat, but somehow, when you're alone in the house and your husband's down the pub each night, eatin's about the only comfort you have left. I gets so low in me mind, queen, that I wonder how I'm goin' to go on. If the baby had lived . . . or if I could have another . . . well, things would have been different. There would have been . . . oh, I dunno. Something to – to look forward to, I s'pose.'

'You've gorrus, Mam,' Denis said bracingly. Crossing the room, he gave his mother a quick hug and Lizzie reflected that though they said little, the boys must realise their mother had a pretty hard life. 'Our Dad don't mean half what he says, you know. He's fond of you. It's – it's the drink. It puts words into his mouth what he don't mean and makes him hit out without thinkin'.'

Aunt Annie gave a huge sniff, then fished in the bosom of her dress and withdrew a large square of cotton waste upon which she blew her nose resoundingly before grinning, a trifle wanly, at her son. 'He ain't drunk now, chuck, norreven on tea,' she said with a wry smile. 'Still, I knows what you mean. I reckon he's more or less pickled in the stuff. Mebbe you're right and he don't mean half of what he says. At least he didn't have a go at Sausage and Mash, because I hates it when he shouts at me hens.'

Lizzie, who had been quietly clearing the table and piling the dishes into the washing-up bowl, began to pour boiling water over them, not wanting to seem to be watching Aunt Annie's distress nor the boys' efforts to comfort her. But presently, as she had guessed they would, Denis and Herbie got their outdoor things and made for the kitchen door. 'We'll just stroll down to the Black Dog on the corner of

Vauxhall Road and get ourselves a bevvy afore bedtime,' Denis said, half apologetically. 'You go off to bed, Mam. By morning, none of this will matter.'

'Aye, you know what they say,' Herbie chimed in. 'It'll all be the same in a hundred years, our Mam. D'you want us to pop back wi' a jug o' porter so's you can drown your sorrows afore bed?'

But Aunt Annie, though she laughed, shook her head. She seemed to have recovered her equilibrium without having to resort to strong drink, Lizzie saw thankfully. And indeed, once her sons had gone, Aunt Annie sat in her favourite chair before the fire with her beloved hens nestling in her lap, and she and Lizzie talked of other things until it was time for bed.

The blizzard of February had ended in torrential rain and Geoff had got soaked to the skin coming home from work but he did not repine. The YMCA had a drying room in which the lads could hang out their clothing, secure in the knowledge that the next time they needed to go out, they would once more be warmly and dryly clad.

It had been Geoff's turn to clear away after supper and since he and Reggie intended to go to the cinema once this was done, his friend had helped him. Now, Geoff peered out through the rain-smeared window, trying to judge whether it was still pelting or had begun to ease off a little. Truth to tell, he was not particularly keen to get another soaking just in order to see *Win that Girl*, which sounded suspiciously like a romance to him. He and Reggie preferred westerns or gangster films – Reggie would go miles to see any film with Victor Varconi starring in it. The only reason, in fact, that either of them had considered seeing *Win that Girl* was because it was showing at the

Popular Picture House on Netherfield Road which would mean a short walk in the rain rather than a long one. The other acknowledged reason was that girls usually preferred a romantic film, and Reggie was searching for a girlfriend.

Geoff, although he secretly admitted to himself that he was very fond of Lizzie, also knew that she was too young, as yet, to take anyone seriously. He and Reggie had had long discussions about girls, work and life in general, and had both come to the conclusion that before settling down with anyone, no matter how delightful, they should get some experience under their belts.

'Not tarts,' Reggie had said hastily, seeing Geoff's rather shocked expression. 'I didn't mean tarts, you fool. I mean decent girls what'll take us serious – but not too serious – and let us kind of – of – practise on them. There must be girls like that about, else no feller would ever get his leg over.'

'I don't know as I'd want to go all the way,' Geoff said cautiously. 'I can't see a nice girl lettin' us for starters, and the other sort might give us something nasty.'

Reggie laughed. 'Look, we go to dances and to the flicks to meet gels, right? I reckon we ought to agree that if one of us gets lucky, he'll tell the other all about it. What d'you say?'

Geoff, having thought the matter over, decided that Reggie's suggestion was sensible, and agreed. But so far, though they had assiduously attended dance halls and picture houses, they had never met what Geoff called 'a nice girl' willing to do more than allow them to walk her home and give her a peck on the cheek.

'Well? You've been staring out of that window as

though a procession were going past. I daresay you've got mesmerised by the rain, eh? Still pelting, is it?'

Geoff dragged himself away both from the window and his thoughts, and turned to grin at his friend. 'If you look in the puddles, you can see it's still raining cats and dogs,' he said. 'What a winter it's been, Reggie. First there was the blizzard and now it looks as though the Lord wants us to build an ark. I'm damned if I want to go and shiver in the cinema in a wet coat only to come out and get wet all over again. What's more, I could do wi' an hour or two of extra study. I know the exams aren't until June, but I've heard tell that when Mr Babacombe leaves, they aren't going to bring anyone in from outside, they're going to shuffle all the senior staff up one grade. Now that's all right for the seniors, it's all cut and dried, but there'll be plenty of us clerks ... tellers ... call us what you will, who'll be fighting for a better job, and in my view it'll be the chap who comes top in the exams what gets it.'

'And that chap's going to be you,' Reggie said, nodding. 'Well, old feller, you work so bleedin' hard that you deserve promotion, and I know you're probably right to stay in tonight and do some extra study. But what if I nips down to the Jug and Bottle for some porter? Then when you've swotted for long enough, we can have a jar or two and a hand o' cards perhaps.'

Geoff, getting out his books and spreading them across his rickety table, brightened. 'I'll come with you, get a breath of fresh air before I settle down,' he said, and though Reggie laughed at this blatant attempt to put off the evil hour, the two of them donned mackintoshes, Reggie carrying the white enamel jug which they had bought for just such a purpose, and set off into the downpour, heading for the nearest pub.

There was quite a crowd in the Jug and Bottle and the two elderly ladies taking orders and pulling steadily on the pump handles to fill the various receptacles offered were flushed and sweating, though still good-humoured. Idly watching the people ahead and wondering how long it would be before they reached the counter, Geoff heard someone else enter the small room behind them. 'Cor, if I were a duck, I reckon I'd be flapping me bleedin' wings and crowing like a cockerel,' a voice which sounded vaguely familiar remarked, almost in Geoff's ear. 'I wish you'd thought to bring a brolly, young Evie. As it is, I bet you're wet right through to your knickers, same as what I am.'

'I am pretty wet,' a girl's voice replied; she sounded rather sulky. 'And if this is your idea of a nice evening out, it isn't mine! What's more, for all your big talk, it's me who'll be in trouble if I'm not in my bed when I'm expected. You've simply got to get me back by the time the concert is supposed to end. Oh, sometimes I wish I'd never met up with you again, Sid.'

'Don't be like that, queen. I said I'd get you back home before you're missed and so I shall. Have you ever known me break me word, eh?'

Geoff, with a sinking sensation in the pit of his stomach, turned his head just enough to catch a glimpse, out of the corner of his eye, of the speaker. Groaning inwardly, he turned his eyes front once more. He had been right. Standing behind him, with a flat cap cocked to one side and raindrops gleaming on his sharp and narrow face, was Sid Ryder.

The queue of people shuffled forward and Sid

continued to talk to his companion without, apparently, recognising Geoff. Very soon, a lively quarrel began to develop between Sid and the girl and, despite himself, Geoff listened with interest. It seemed as though Sid was trying to persuade her to do something which he thought was in her best interest, though she was plainly not so sure. What was more, Sid's oft-repeated remark that she was too beautiful to hide away from the world like a bleedin' nun seemed to infuriate her. Several times Geoff thought she would have walked out on Sid, had he not kept a firm hold of her arm.

The quarrel was at its height and Geoff was telling himself, thankfully, that Sid was far too involved with this girl Evie to notice him, when the two people at the counter turned to leave the pub and the queue shuffled forward again. This brought Geoff level with the counter, his profile now clearly in view both of Sid and his companion. He was not unduly surprised when he heard Sid mutter to the girl: 'Let's not quarrel, Evie. Everything I've done for you, I've done for the best. You know I wanted to introduce you to me pals, and if I'm not mistaken there's a familiar face. Now who on earth . . .?'

Geoff heard Sid give a sharp, rather stagey exclamation. 'Well, if it ain't an old school mate of mine.' A hand seized Geoff's shoulder and swung him round.

Geoff stared hard at the other lad, remembering their last encounter, but it appeared that Sid had forgotten it, or at least intended to pretend that he had done so, for the older lad suddenly remarked to the girl, 'It's Geoff Gardiner what was at school with me.' He stuck out one large hand and seized Geoff's in a firm clasp. 'How you doin', old mate? I reckon you're

217

workin' by now, eh? Well, if this ain't a turn up for the books, I don't know what is. Fancy me meetin' an old pal in the Jug and Bottle when all we come in for were some porter.'

In the face of such obvious and disarming friendliness it was difficult to remain cool, but Geoff did his best. 'Hello, Sid,' he said. 'Who's your friend?'

Sid ignored this remark, instead turning to Evie and telling her how he and Geoff had, as he put it, 'frisked around the streets, gettin' up to all sorts of mischief, the bane of all the shopkeepers along the Scottie in the old days'. Then he turned back to Geoff. 'What are you doin' now, young Geoff?' His eyes flickered knowingly across the shiny waterproof, trilby and neat black lace-ups. 'Wharris it, then? Solicitors? Insurance office? Or a bleedin' bank clerk?'

Geoff, ruffling up indignantly, was about to tell his erstwhile enemy to mind his own bleedin' business when Sid clapped him affectionately on the shoulder and said with a laugh, 'Don't mind me, old feller, I'm only kiddin'. And if I remember rightly, you've gorra grudge to pay off agin me for foolin' about in the Scaldy that time and near finishin' you off. By God, I were a mad young fool in them days, never gave a thought to the consequences of wharr I did. Well, I'm right sorry, old pal. Can we be friends again?'

In the face of this outright admission of what he had done, Geoff felt it would be downright uncivil to snub Sid, so he grinned, returned the handclasp and said: 'I'm a bleedin' bank clerk, actually, you cheeky dog, and me pal Reggie Phelps here is an insurance clerk so you've managed to insult the pair of us. What do you do? Nothing much, I daresay!'

Sid grinned good-naturedly, pushing his loud tweed cap to the back of his head as he did so. 'I'm a runner for Drelincourt the bookmaker at Aintree, but that's only race days of course. They sends me all over the country and one of these days I'll have me own nice little business and make a fortune out of . . .' he grinned wickedly '. . . out of bleedin' bank clerks and the like, what puts their gelt on a gee with a pretty name and don't study form 'cos they don't know how.' He turned to Geoff's companion, who had been staring round-eyed at the girl, Evie, and stuck out his hand. 'How d'you do, Reggie? Nice to meet you. I'm Sid Ryder and this is me – me cousin, Evie Evans.'

'How do you do, Mr Gardiner, Mr Phelps?,' she murmured. 'It's fortunate we met you because it's time I was making my way home and you'll be able to keep Sid company in my place.'

'No, no, Evie, we've made our arrangements and we'll stick to 'em,' Sid said firmly. 'Mind you, it's a rotten wet evening. If Geoff and his pal are agreeable, why don't we all go back to my place? I've gorra flat of me own only a couple o' streets away. What say we goes round there, the four of us, and has a chat about old times and mebbe a bite to eat? There's a chippie just up the road – or we could get something from one of the canny houses, if you've no taste for fish and chips.'

Geoff looked thoughtfully at Sid, then let his eyes stray to Evie. She was, he thought, the most beautiful girl he had ever seen. Her night-black hair was tied back from her face with a wide black satin ribbon; her eyes, dark and almond-shaped, still sparkled from the argument with Sid, and her smooth, creamy skin bore traces of an angry flush. But when she smiled, a dimple appeared beside her mouth and the small teeth the smile revealed were white and even. A fashionable hat with a tiny half veil was perched at a dashing angle on her gleaming head. She wore a full dark raincoat with the collar turned up, showing a glimpse of scarlet silk scarf at the neck, and her feet were clad in well-polished half-boots. Realising he was staring, Geoff turned his eyes back to Sid. The older lad had not changed very much, though he was a good deal taller and broader than Geoff remembered, but he still had the cocky, self-confident air of one who goes his own way, regardless of others, which meant he was still dangerous company.

Half regretfully, Geoff began to shake his head, to explain that he and Reggie were studying for exams and must get back to the YMCA, for despite Sid's friendliness he knew the older boy to be what Father Brannigan would call 'bad company', when Evie leaned forward and put a small hand on his arm. 'Don't say no, Mr Gardiner,' she said in a soft voice. 'I don't really have to be home this early and I'm sure I don't want to lose Sid a friend.' Here she gave Sid a look so charged with annoyance that Geoff blinked and even the hardened Sid looked a little embarrassed. 'He hasn't got that many friends, I shouldn't imagine. I've not visited his flat, but I'm sure he has a pack of cards and we could have a game of gin rummy or something. I don't drink porter myself, but you fellows can have a glass or two and I'll make myself a nice cup of tea.' She shot another venomous glance at Sid. 'I suppose you do possess a teapot,' she finished coldly.

Geoff hardly knew which way to look; if Evie had spoken thus to him, he would have curled up and died, but Sid merely grinned and reached out a hand to chuck the girl under the chin. ''Course I got a teapot,' he said breezily. 'No use gettin' your rag out at me, young Evie, just because it's a rainy night and

I didn't fancy trudgin' all the way to the Gaiety to see some silly romantic fillum.' He turned back to Geoff. 'Come on, you can study any time,' he said, his tone half wheedling, half commanding. 'Remember what I said? We'll stop off at the fried fish shop on our way and buy ourselves a nice fish supper. Then we'll have a real cosy evening, gettin' to know one another again.'

'Well, I don't know . . .' Geoff began.

'Please,' Evie said, her voice low and husky, and now that he looked at her again, Geoff thought that she seemed vaguely familiar, as though he had known her, too, sometime in the past. He looked hard at her, staring at the big, dark eyes, but she glanced down shyly, as though such an inspection embarrassed her and he looked away at once. She was astonishingly pretty and he realised that, despite Sid, he would like to spend more time in her company. He glanced interrogatively at Reggie, who nodded enthusiastically. It was clear that he would far rather spend an evening with Sid and Evie than back at the YMCA.

'Well, if we come back wi' you, Sid, then Reggie and me will buy the grub,' Geoff said. 'I'd planned to study this evening, but I daresay I can put it off for the sake of such an old friend.' He had meant to sound sarcastic but Sid took the words at face value, beaming and seizing his arm. In fact, in his enthusiasm, he would have forgotten all about the porter he had come to purchase, had not Mrs Nettlebed shouted: 'Come along, young gentlemen, hand over those perishin' jugs. You're holding up me commerce, and that I *don't* allow.'

So it was with two jugs of porter and a large paper of fish and chips that the four young people presently let themselves into Sid's 'little place', which turned out to be a very cosy flat over a fishmonger's shop in Cazneau Street. Sid relieved the men of their wet coats and hats in the tiny hallway, and took them into a large and pleasant living room where he put a match to the gas fire and bustled about, fetching plates and cutlery for the fish and chips and tall glasses for the porter while telling Evie to spread her wet coat across a chair in the kitchenette. Very soon the room began to warm up and Evie returned to the living room, clad now in a dark-collared wool jacket and matching skirt. Geoff thought she looked very nice, though rather severe, but before he could comment, they were passing round the plates of food, the salt and vinegar and porter, and beginning their meal.

Very soon the four of them were eating and drinking and talking as if they had known one another all their lives. Geoff remembered that Sid had always been good company, and tried to forget that he had also been thoroughly dishonest. He told himself, however, that most street urchins, particularly those from poor families, were scarcely able to be upright citizens – not if they wanted to eat regularly, that was. He and Reggie, with the security of the Father Brannigan Orphan Asylum behind them, had been more privileged than most. In fact, considering the circumstances, his own behaviour had been a good deal less honourable than Sid's. Sid stole because he had no other means of making sure he ate regularly; Geoff had stolen – or if not stolen, connived at stealing – because he wanted to be like other boys, and be accepted by them.

Sid kept them amused with tales of his racecourse experiences while they ate, and interested Geoff greatly by recounting the many wins he'd had at various racecourses throughout the country. He had been working with Drelincourt's for two years and had got to know both jockeys and stable lads, as well as some of the trainers and almost all the bookies. He explained, disarmingly, that such people were willing to give him tips – advice as to which horse would most probably win – and whenever he felt sufficiently confident that they were right, he put as much money as he could afford, acquire or borrow upon the horse in question. In the nature of things he sometimes lost, but more often he won, and used the money either to put on the next likely nag or to add to his savings account towards the day when he should have a business of his own.

In his turn, Geoff told them stories of his life in the bank, some of which were amusing and made both Sid and his cousin laugh. Geoff liked it when Evie laughed; her mouth turned up at the corners and her small white teeth showed and her cheeks bunched her eyes into gleaming slits. The trouble was, whenever she opened her mouth to speak, Sid rarely let her get out more than half a sentence before he interrupted. It was he who told them that Evie worked in Lewis's, showing off dresses, coats and skirts in their big restaurants, to encourage the customers to buy. 'She's what they call a mannequin,' he said proudly. 'She makes good money at it, and when she isn't parading up and down, wrapped in furs and silks, she works in gowns. Ain't that so, queen?'

'Oh, Sid, I don't . . .' Evie began, but was once more interrupted.

'Naturally, she's only part-time as a mannequin because it ain't no use paradin' around in fancy gear when there's nobody in to watch,' he said. 'But the day will come when she's doin' it full-time and earnin' enough to have a decent flat of her own, like mine,' he finished. 'Now wharrabout a game o' gin rummy, fellers, seein' as there's four of us?'

'I'm not playing for money because I haven't got any,' Evie said baldly. 'I know you, Sid Ryder! You and your betting – you'd see us all without a coat to our backs and think yourself a really sharp operator.'

Sid pretended to be much hurt by this remark, though Geoff could tell he was secretly rather pleased and considered it a type of compliment. However, Sid denied that he would dream of betting for money in his own house and produced a large box of spent matches which he doled out to each of them before seating himself at the table and beginning to shuffle the pack with an expertise which would, under different circumstances, have made Geoff extremely nervous.

The four of them continued to talk and play cards until Geoff suddenly realised that it was almost half-past ten. Fortunately, they had just finished a hand and Sid, who seemed as lucky at cards as he was with horses, was counting his matchsticks with as much satisfaction as if they were tipped with solid gold when Geoff jumped to his feet. 'We've gorra go, me old pal,' he said, indicating the clock on the mantel-piece. 'We're supposed to be in before eleven and I dunno about you and Evie here, but Reggie an' me's in work for eight-thirty tomorrer, same as usual. But thanks for a grand evening, I dunno when I've enjoyed meself more.'

Evie had jumped up as Geoff did, one hand flying to her mouth. She had almost run into the kitchen and was struggling into her damp coat before Geoff and Reggie had so much as taken their own off the fender.

'I've got to go as well, Sid,' she said breathlessly. 'Oh, why didn't I notice the time? I shall get into the most awful trouble and not be allowed out of an evening again.'

Sid shot her a reproachful look. 'They'll think you missed the last tram and had to walk,' he said. 'But you won't be late, 'cos I'll take you home in a taxi. Now stop worryin', chuck, and get yourself ready while I see me pals off.'

The three young men descended the stairs, all in very good charity with one another. 'We must do it again,' Sid said, leading the way up the hall. 'You might come out to the race track wi' me sometime – I'll bet you've never visited Aintree, have you? – and I'll tell you which gees to back to make yourself a nice little bit o' money. I put all me pals in the way of makin' some gelt on the side from time to time.'

Geoff said that it sounded like a nice day out and asked Sid whether it might not be easier if he and Reggie went out and hailed a taxi which could then return Evie to her home before taking them on to Shaw Street. He grinned at them. 'Don't you worry about Evie, I'll see her right,' he said genially. 'It ain't that I don't trust you two fellers – why, Geoff's been me pal since we was kids in school together – but she's my responsibility.' They had reached the front door by now and he opened it with a flourish. 'I'll be in touch, don't you worry about that,' he said. 'Night, both.'

Evie stood in the middle of Sid's cosy sitting room, simmering with annoyance, both with herself and with him. She should have known better than to come back to his flat, even in the company of the other young men. When Sid had met her, as arranged, outside St George's Hall and had said that his aunt had been unable to get tickets for the concert, she had been immediately suspicious. But she had been disarmed by his profuse apologies and by his immediate suggestion that they should go out for a meal, or perhaps see a film at the nearest picture house, so that her evening should not be altogether ruined.

She had known, of course, that the nuns would not approve; they had given her permission to attend a piano recital by Arthur Rubenstein, in the company of a woman they believed to be both respectable and her aunt. In fact, Aunt Madge, who was a relative of Sid's, had come in very useful. She had come to the orphanage two years ago, when Sid had first taken up with Evie, and told such a plausible story that the nuns had had no hesitation in releasing Evie to her care, two or three times a month.

Mostly, these outings had been with Sid. They had gone to cinemas and theatres, had picnicked in the parks, had gone rattling into the countryside by bus or train, so that Evie might see more of the world than the convent allowed. She had been grateful to him but always, in the back of her mind, there had been a tiny, niggling doubt. *Why* was Sid being so kind to her? He must have spent a considerable sum of money upon her, and now she realised that she had been right to worry.

This evening he had come clean, or as clean as he was likely to, at any rate. He had told her that they were going back to his flat. He had a proposition to put to her and thought the flat was more private like to do so. Evie, sensing danger, had refused his suggestion point blank. There was a look in Sid's eye which told her it would be extremely unwise to be alone with him and presently she had soon realised that she was right. He had taken her to Fuller's Cafe where he proposed that she should leave the orphan asylum and take a job in Lewis's. This would enable her to help him with 'clients' who wanted some sort of social life when racing finished.

'They's respectable people,' he assured her. 'But when the racing's over for the day, they don't want to go meekly back to their hotel rooms. They want to see a bit o' life in the company of a pretty girl. Mostly they're respectable, so there won't be no funny business, but they are prepared to pay, and pay well, for feminine company, if you see what I mean. Evie, you could do it on your head.'

Despite her doubts, she had never expected anything as bad as this; indeed, she could hardly believe her ears. 'Why, Sid Ryder, I'm not going to prostitute myself for anyone! You can talk about your business acquaintances wanting company, but what you mean is you want me to sell myself! I truly think you must be mad. And as for married men being more respectable than bachelors, no decent married man would even consider paying for a girl's company. Oh, you make me sick!'

She had tried to leave then, but Sid had pushed her back into her chair and promised humbly never to mention the matter again. 'I thought I were doin' you a favour, puttin' you in the way of earning a decent living,' he had said. 'I wouldn't hurt you for the world, Evie, you know that! Don't let's fall out over me plan, because I meant it for the best, honest to God I did. And we mustn't waste this evening. Tell you what, we'll nip into the Jug and Bottle so's I can get meself some porter. I'm real proud of me little flat and I'd love you to see it. Why, if you took the job in Lewis's, you could have one just like it.' But I can tell by your expression you'd never come to me flat so how about if we go back to Aunt Madge's? Then she and I can share the porter since I know you won't drink it. Me aunt's done a lot for you, queen, lettin' you change your clothes in her house, keepin' your school stuff safe, tellin' the nuns a pack o' nonsense so's you can get out from time to time. She'd enjoy an evening wi' us and it wouldn't be no skin off your nose to give her a little treat.'

Evie was forced to admit that she did owe Sid's aunt a good deal. Surely there could be no harm in going back to his Aunt Madge's until the piano recital ended? Across the small, white-clothed table she had stared searchingly at Sid and had seen in his anxious face only a desire to please. Half grudgingly, therefore, she had agreed to go to Aunt Madge's, though she had warned him that one step out of line or one attempt to persuade her to leave the orphan asylum would result in their friendship ending abruptly. But once the boys had joined them in the Jug and Bottle – she had recognised Geoff at once – there had seemed no harm in going to Sid's flat which she was curious to see.

Now, standing in the centre of the room waiting for him, Evie heard the front door slam shut and knew the other two young men had gone. Telling herself that the evening had been quite a success, she adjusted her little hat on her head and pulled on her black woollen gloves. She was crossing the room when the door opened and Sid came in. He took a deep breath then expelled it in a long whistle. 'Phew! Thank God that's over,' he said genially. 'Take off your coat, queen, because you ain't goin' nowhere. I've tried to treat you right, to offer you a good job and the chance to get rich, and you throwed it back in me face. You've left me no option but to use a stronger argument. What'll you tell the nuns when you turn up tomorrer mornin', eh?'

Evie stared at him, round-eyed. 'You wouldn't *dare* keep me here,' she gasped. 'Why, I'd go straight to the scuffers as soon as you let me out. And don't pretend you can keep me here forever, because you can't.' She made for the door, only to find her way barred by Sid's strong arm. He was grinning most unpleasantly and, catching hold of her shoulders, pushed her into a chair, snatched the hat off her head, and began unbuttoning her coat so roughly that she grew afraid and clutched the garment round her. 'Get off!' she squeaked. 'Leave me alone, Sid, or it'll be the worse for you.'

Sid chuckled breathlessly, wrenched her coat off and threw it across the room after her hat. 'I should have done this long ago, when you were just a nasty little slum kid,' he said. 'But how was I to know you'd turn into such a little cracker? Now shut your face or I swear I'll beat the livin' daylights out of you.'

Geoff and Reggie made their way along the puddled pavement in thoughtful silence. The rain had stopped, but Cazneau Street was deserted and both young men were immersed in their own thoughts. When they turned left into Richmond Row, however, Geoff put a hand on Reggie's arm to slow his pace. 'What's Sid's game, eh?' he asked. 'If that gal's his cousin, I'm a bleedin' millionaire. Well, she may be his cousin,' he amended, 'but there's more to it than that. I don't reckon they're livin' tally, but do you think that Sid's planning on marrying her, having a permanent relationship, like? They were certainly quarrelling like a married couple when they came into the Jug and Bottle. And if so, why couldn't he tell us? I don't mind admitting I'd be downright proud to have a girl like Evie. Why, any feller would! Though if he meant to marry her, he'd have telled us straight off, don't you think?'

'Yes, of course. He'd tell you as soon as you clapped eyes on her, so's you wouldn't go gettin' ideas,' Reggie said thoughtfully. 'It's real strange, because she's a respectable girl in a good job, and Sid's clearly makin' a bob or two, yet . . . Hey, where's you goin'?'

Geoff had turned back the way they had come and was heading for Cazneau Street, pulling the protesting Reggie behind him. 'I'm going to see whether she leaves with Sid or whether she stays the night there,' he said grimly. 'Sid's about as reliable as a perishin' weathercock. He'll swing from one thing to another until you're fair dizzy with it, and that Evie's a decent kid; she doesn't want to get mixed up with the likes of him.'

They turned into Cazneau Street once more but here Reggie pulled his friend to a halt. 'Look, old feller, they must have left. Evie already had her coat on and unless Sid manages to persuade her to stay, they'll be long gone. Besides, it's none of our business. I don't know about you, but I'm ready for me bed. What's more, you met the girl for the first time this evening and you're always tellin' me you're stuck on some other Judy – Lizzie, ain't it? So what call have you got to go chasin' after a girl you don't really know? You don't want to go makin' a fool of yourself over a pretty face.'

Geoff took a deep breath and let it out in a long, whistling sigh. Then he linked arms with Reggie and turned back towards Richmond Row. 'You're right and I know it,' he admitted. 'The trouble is, Reggie, that girl wasn't happy with Sid. Oh, I know you could say it were just a lover's tiff, but I know Sid and he isn't a feller it's wise to cross. If Evie thinks she can lead him round by the nose, then she's in for a great disappointment – might be in danger even. It's an odd thing, but several times this evening I got the feeling I knew Evie, had known her for years. It can't be so, of course, because no one could forget a face like that – she isn't just pretty, she's beautiful – but you *are* right. It's none of my business what Sid or Evie does, and as you say, I've been stuck on Lizzie for years. Only – only, there's something very appealing about Evie. I know you'll say she can look after herself, but can she? She didn't mention her family at all, did she? I got the feeling she were probably alone in the world, like you and me, Reggie. And she's a deal younger than both of us, if you ask me.'

They had reached Richmond Row by now and were trudging along the pavement, sloshing through the puddles, eager to get back to the YMCA and their beds. Reggie shook his head reprovingly. 'Gals mature much earlier than fellers do,' he said wisely. 'Besides, if she'd needed any sort of help from us, she could have said. She could even have left the house when we did, telling Sid it would save him a journey in the wet. If you're still worried about her, go along to Lewis's in your dinner break tomorrow and have a word with the gal when Sid ain't around to make things difficult, like. If she's really just a pal o' his, she'll tell you then and you can be easier about her. If there's more to it than that, I guess you'll get the nod quick enough.'

Geoff agreed that this was sensible and by the time they'd reached Everton Brow, was resigned to spending some time in Lewis's, trying to get in touch with the delectable Evie. It began to rain once again, just as they were passing the YWCA on Shaw Street, and both boys glanced wistfully at the building as they always did. It housed a great many pretty working girls and the inhabitants of the YMCA sometimes met them at dances or the cinema and walked them home, so that Geoff and Reggie were getting to know several members of the opposite sex.

'For all we know, Evie might live there,' Reggie remarked as they hurried past. 'Although I daresay we should have noticed her. Come to that, there's other YWs all over the city – she might be in any of them.'

'Or she might not,' Geoff almost snapped. The long evening, the lateness of the hour and the soaking rain were beginning to get to him. What was more, they were supposed to be in before eleven, which meant they would have to enter the house via the pantry window. If they were caught they would be in hot water, so it was stupid, he decided, to worry about a girl as lovely and as self-confident as Evie Evans, especially considering how he felt about his own dear Lizzie. What he ought to be worrying about was his reputation, if anyone found out that he had come home after lock-up, without first getting permission, he would be in trouble.

And on this thought, he and Reggie headed down the side of the YMCA, squeezed through the carefully unlatched pantry window and made their weary way to bed. They met no one on the way and as Geoff snuggled beneath the sheets he vowed never to be such a fool again. If they had only come straight back and not returned to Cazneau Street they could have been in bed at least twenty minutes earlier.

But despite the lateness of the hour and his tiredness, Geoff found it difficult to go to sleep. His mind kept returning to the elusive likeness to . . . someone . . . which had made him think he recognised Evie. And the more he thought about it, the less sure he became that Sid had told him the truth about the girl. If, as Sid had said, she was a shopgirl and a mannequin at Lewis's, then why had Sid taken up with her merely as a friend? Unless Sid had changed almost beyond recognition, he was unlikely to do anything which did not benefit him in some way, yet for the life of him Geoff could not see how friendship with Evie could be of the slightest use to the other fellow. These thoughts kept tumbling around in his brain until at last he slept, but it was an unsatisfactory and restless sleep, haunted by dreams in which Lizzie and Evie flitted to and fro, both reproaching him, the first for his faithlessness and the second for not helping her out of some dreamlike, but terrible, fix.

When his alarm went off at six-thirty, Geoff was downright glad to get himself out of bed and to start the new day. He decided that he would make a real effort to find out just what Sid was up to over the course of the next week. If, at the end of that time, he was still no wiser, then he would walk away from the problem and try not to see Sid again.

Much relieved to have made a firm decision he went down to the dining hall, settled himself beside Reg, and ate a good breakfast. Then he made his way to the bank, determined to stick to his resolve to contact Evie and find out what was happening, or else to forget the whole business.

Clem had not much enjoyed the snow, although it had not been severe enough to ice up the canal. The icing up of the water was dreaded by all the boatmen since it meant that it took twice as long to get the cargoes to their destination. Sometimes they had to wait for an ice breaker to clear the canal, sometimes they were actually iced in themselves and had to work hard to free their own particular craft. The favoured method was for two members of the crew to take up position on the gunwales at each side of the boat, where they would shift their weight from side to side until the ice creaking, began to loosen its grip. Because this was hard on the wooden hull, most of the men deemed it politic to make sure that the ice never became too thick, which meant rocking the boat at regular intervals whenever she was moored up. In addition to the hazards of the ice, furthermore, tackling the locks with the snow thick on the ground was a nightmare for both horses and crew. Bad visibility, the weight of snow on decks, locks and tow-paths, as well as the difficulties of both horse and crew pushing their way through perhaps several feet of snow, made such conditions all but intolerable.

However, this year the snow had cleared quite quickly under the torrential downpours which had followed it. Though rain, Clem thought now, peering ahead through the fast-falling drops, was almost as bad as snow. It made the decks slippery, even though the clogs which most of the boatmen favoured gave them a good grip, and it made steering a nightmare. With the best will in the world, a steersman could not see further than a few yards in weather like this which meant that when approaching locks or bridges, one was almost on top of them before the boatman could crack the great leather whip to announce his arrival.

Jake and Priddy were both experts with the whip. There was a knack to using it which Clem had not yet mastered, but he had decided that when the weather was finer, he would sneak off and practise in a nearby meadow when they were moored up for the night. Whip cracking was important because not only did it announce your arrival at locks or bridges, it also gave you the right to enter the lock or go under the bridge first. Where the bridge was narrow and low only one boat could pass through at a time so it was important to men carrying perishable merchandise to have their right of way clear. *The Liverpool Rose* always carried clean merchandise because Priddy and Jake, living on board as they did, had no desire to fill their beautiful boat with coal, lime or manure, and since they worked for themselves, they always chose their cargoes carefully. Wool, groceries, fruit and vegetables, sugar, whatever it might be, they took good care of it and made sure that it arrived at its destination in perfect condition. They preferred long hauls to short, too, so they usually arranged to take a cargo from the Liverpool docks all the way to Leeds, and then the return load from Leeds back into the city of Liverpool, and because they were known and trusted, they rarely had to wait long for a cargo.

Now, however, Clem was thinking less about their cargo than about the hot meal which Priddy was preparing in the forward cabin and the fact that very soon they would pull in and moor up for the night. Tomorrow they would tackle the Bank Newton and Cargrave locks and would refill their water barrel, for the water piped from the Winterburn reservoir above was famous for its purity and taste and was much valued by the boatmen. Jake always made sure that they rewatered at that point on their journey if they possibly could, and because it was in the heart of the Pennines Clem usually took Brutus for a long walk up on to the hills while the boat was taking on water. The countryside was beautiful, although he acknowledged now, peering ahead through the driving rain, no one could think the countryside was at its best when February was living up to its name of 'fill-dyke' and seemed intent on turning the entire landscape into one enormous lake.

'Wasn't that the best, the very best, fillum you ever did see? Oh, I'd see it all over again just to get another look at Ramon Navarro, wouldn't you? Me mam said as it were the best picture show she'd ever seen – all them bare chests probably went to her head – but I think she was right. Oh, Lizzie, weren't it just grand?'

Lizzie and Sally had just emerged, blinking, from the Derby cinema on Scotland Road. Lizzie, linking her arm with her friend's, shook it chidingly. 'If that isn't just like you, Sally Bradshaw,' she declared. 'Every blessed picture becomes the greatest film of all time, and your mam's every bit as bad. You shouldn't work in a mineral water bottling plant, you should go to the *Echo* offices and get them to make you their cinema reviewer. The only trouble would be you'd never admit to seeing a bad picture, norrif you live to be a hundred.'

Sally giggled and shook her head. 'If I never see a fillum I don't like, it's because I'm choosy about what I go and see,' she insisted, trying to ignore her friend's stifled giggle. 'Well, what'll we do next, eh? The night's young, as they say, and we were paid yesterday. We could go into the Acacia Ballroom because it's after interval time so it's cheap, or we could have us a paper of chips. Ain't it a nice fine evening, though?' She looked along the crowded pavement ahead, glistening in the gaslight. 'I daresay they had an April shower earlier, but you'd never know it now, it's so mild.'

'After all the excitement of *Ben Hur*, I don't think I've got the energy to go prancing around the floor, especially with some foreign seaman, who only knows three words of English and pretends he doesn't understand "no", no matter how forcefully you say it,' Lizzie said. 'Tell you what, let's get some chips and go and sit down by the canal to eat them. We might run to a bottle of ginger beer as well, between the two of us, and if we go down by the Scaldy, there's a bit of grass and a wall we can sit on. I bet the canal's real romantic by moonlight.'

'Oh, you'd think the canal was romantic in a bleedin' blizzard,' Sally said, getting her own back, Lizzie thought, for the remarks she had made earlier on her friend's uncritical attitude to the cinema. 'Still an' all, it'll be a change from sitting in me mam's kitchen – or your Aunt Annie's – trying to talk while they're listening to the wireless.'

'Which chippie shall we honour with our custom, then?' Lizzie said presently, as they came level with Burlington Street. 'We get to Mr Jones first, but if we go a bit further, we can go to Joe's place. Aunt Annie reckons he has the freshest fish in Liverpool.'

'We might as well join the queue here before the pubs come out,' Sally observed. 'I thought it was quieter than usual along here; it's still ten minutes before chuckin' out time, that's why.'

As she spoke, both girls saw a gap in the traffic and plunged across the road, managing to join the tail end of the queue just ahead of a gang of young seamen who wolf-whistled and jeered but took their places behind the girls with a fairly good grace.

Talking animatedly about the film they had just

seen as the queue edged slowly forward, Lizzie's eyes roamed the passers-by. Having spent most of her life in this area, she knew a good few of them and exchanged waves and smiles with several girls who had once been at school with her and Sally. Right opposite the chippie was the Eagle pub, on the corner of Collingwood Street, and even as she watched, the doors opened and men and the occasional woman began to stream on to the pavement. Several of them made straight for the end of the queue, including a tall and heavy man who, at first glance, Lizzie had taken for Uncle Perce. She realised her mistake, however, when she saw that the man was accompanied by a young woman with peroxide blonde hair, a very short skirt and shoes with heels so high that she seemed in perpetual danger of falling on her nose.

Lizzie's attention was about to return to the queue, which was shuffling forward once more, when she did a double-take. It *was* Uncle Perce, looking almost smart in navy trousers and jacket with a red spotted handkerchief tied round his throat and tucked into his shirt. Telling herself that the girl hanging on to his arm must be the daughter of a friend, who was clearly in need of support, having equally clearly drunk too much – for the girl was weaving and cackling as they approached – Lizzie was about to turn away, when the couple drew level with her. Looking more closely at the woman, Lizzie realised that she was not as young as the bleached hair and short skirt had led her to suppose. She would be in her forties, Lizzie decided and wondered, with considerable distaste, if Uncle Perce had picked up a tart and having mugged her to a night on the ale, was seeing her home.

By her side, Sally was staring fixedly ahead and there was something in her friend's attitude which led

Lizzie to guess that Sally, too, had spotted Uncle Perce and his friend. She nudged Sally, drawing her attention to Uncle Perce and the woman, who was staring at the queue probably considering joining it, but before Sally could say a word, Uncle Perce remarked loudly: 'I ain't waitin' here all night, queen. We'll go along to Joe's place, see if the queue's shorter there.' And with that, the two of them lurched away down the road and were soon lost to view in the hurrying crowd.

Lizzie turned, round-eyed, to Sally. 'Did you see that?' she hissed. 'It were my Uncle Perce with some horrible little dock-side tart clinging on his arm! Well, I just hope he doesn't catch something nasty, that's all. I guess he picked her up in the pub and bought her a few drinks and now he's hoping to do . . . Well, whatever men do with tarts, before going home to Aunt Annie. I hope he doesn't go taking a liking for low company, because my Aunt wouldn't stand for that as she's still mortal fond of him. Only I'm sure it's just because he's had a few. Aunt Annie was saying only the other day, that since he got a permanent job on the docks, he's been keeping himself real smart and scarcely ever coming in drunk. He goes out a lot, mind, but she says that's for companionship more than for the drink.'

Sally cast her a long and thoughtful look. 'It's that yaller head and short skirt which makes you think she's a prossie, ain't it,' she said in a low voice. 'But – well, I've seen your uncle with her several times before. Of course, it may mean nothing,' she added hastily. 'Men go for cheerful, common women like her when they're out for an evening. She's good company, they say . . .'

'Are you trying to tell me that Uncle Perce's seeing

a lot of that woman?' Lizzie said, scandalised. 'But he's a married man, Sal! Married men aren't supposed to have friends of the opposite sex, are they? Who *is* she, anyhow, and how come you know her?'

'Oh damn, I didn't ought to have said a word,' Sally moaned, looking guilty. A pink flush was creeping up her face from her neck. 'The fact is, queen, that it ain't me that knows her, it's me mam. She and Flossie were at school together, out Everton way and although she's bleached her hair and wears no end of make-up, me mam recognised her as soon as she clapped eyes on her. Flossie's married to Willie Sharpe, an old geezer what keeps an ironmonger's shop on Heyworth Street, but he must be nearing seventy now and I suppose he doesn't take her out much because my mam says he's as tight as a fish's arse at forty fathoms, and never spends a penny if he can get away with a farthing. Flossie has a miserable sort of life, Mam reckons, so – so, perhaps you can't blame her for wanting a bit of company, like.'

'But I still don't understand,' Lizzie said slowly. 'How come you and your mam have been discussing this Flossie? Do you mean your mam's seen her with Uncle Perce as well?'

Sally nodded unhappily. 'Aye, chuck, it's us going to the cinema so often, you see. We usually come out before the pubs – well, just like we did tonight – and several times we've been passing by a doorway when your uncle's come out wi' – wi' – Flossie on his arm. Of course, we both know it's not right, but what can you do? If they's only friends . . .' The queue began to move forward again but Lizzie broke away from it and Sally followed her, clutching at her arm. 'What are you doing?' Sally said urgently. 'We can't follow them!'

'We can. In fact, we're going to do just that,' Lizzie said grimly, towing her friend along the pavement at a smart pace. 'Why, Sal, if he's seeing this – this woman often, who knows what might happen? He might . . . oh, I don't know, but I've gorra follow them, even if you won't.'

'Well, don't let 'em see us,' Sally said urgently, tugging on Lizzie's arm to slow her down. 'Honest to God, queen, they mustn't see us. That Perce's an ugly customer, I've always thought so, he could turn real nasty if he knows you've rumbled his little game. Not that I'm at all sure he's playing a game,' she added quickly. 'Just let's keep our eyes open and stay well back!'

'All right, if that's what you want,' Lizzie agreed. In truth, she was not reluctant to follow her friend's advice. Now that she came to think about it, she herself had seen Uncle Perce in an ugly and violent mood too often to want that violence turned on herself. And of course he had a perfect right to be pals with a woman, she supposed, though it had not previously occurred to her that Uncle Perce was the sort of man to crave female company. In fact, she'd thought his only interests were to have money in his pocket, a full belly and as much ale as he could hold. As for his wife being all the female company he should want, she had to acknowledge that Aunt Annie would never even think of accompanying her husband to the pub. Her aunt very rarely left the house, being self-conscious about her size and saying that neither the cinema nor the theatre had seats into which she could comfortably fit, and to Lizzie's knowledge Uncle Perce had never even suggested an outing of any sort. It was not that the two of them were enemies, precisely; rather, they were no longer either lovers or friends.

241

Lizzie had just reached this conclusion when the couple ahead of them paused outside the fried fish shop. Since the queue there was even longer than that in which Lizzie and Sally had waited, however, they walked on.

'They've gone past Cranberry,' Sally said huskily after a few minutes. Lizzie privately thanked her stars. She could not imagine that her uncle would take his fancy woman – if she *were* his fancy woman – back to number nine to meet his wife and sons, but with someone as wild and strange as Uncle Perce, you could never be sure. And presently, she began to have the uncomfortable feeling that she could guess where he and Flossie were bound.

'Oh, Gawd, Sal, they're heading for the bleedin' canal,' she said, her voice full of foreboding. 'Aren't I glad we didn't get into the queue earlier? If we'd been sitting calmly on the wall with our papers of chips he might have walked straight into us . . . and then what would I have said?'

'You'd have said, "Evenin', Uncle Perce. Whatever are *you* doing here?" Sally said, in a fair imitation of her friend's voice. 'What else should you say, chuck? That's what you'll say tonight, I hope, if we happens to meet 'em. But it's not too late, we can turn back right now and no one the wiser.'

For a moment, Lizzie was actually aware of a craven desire to do just that; to turn back, pretend she had seen nothing, and return to the Court and Aunt Annie's undemanding presence. But she knew that if she did so she would never forgive herself. Whatever Uncle Perce was up to, she had been given the opportunity to find out and find out she must and would. So she frowned and shook her head at Sally, and continued to walk quietly in the wake of the two older people.

As they neared the Houghton Bridge, there were fewer and fewer people to be seen. Sally hissed that they should fall back a little further, but Lizzie disagreed. 'They won't expect to see us so they won't assume that it *is* us,' she stated. 'If they look back – and I don't see why they should – they'll just assume we're a couple of girls walking back home. They may even think we're a courting couple because your hair's almost as short as a boy's and we're both wearing long coats.'

Sally, who was proud of her newly bobbed hair, said smugly: 'You're just jealous, you, because you're stuck wi' that bleedin' great plait when all us fashionable folk are gettin' bobbed or shingled.' But for once Lizzie did not rise to the bait.

'I don't happen to want to cut off me hair and look like a perishin' feller,' she said, imitating the voice of one of their bosses at work. 'Look out, they've disappeared!'

'Don't try to foller,' Sally advised. 'They've gone down on to the towpath on the nearside of the bridge. We'll creep up to the bridge and peep over.'

They did so only to be disappointed for there was no one in sight, though the dark waters of the canal reflected the great silvery moon overhead in a fashion just as romantic as Lizzie had imagined. 'Where did they go?' she whispered, putting her mouth close to Sally's ear. 'Keep your voice down, sound doesn't half travel well over water.'

'They'll be under the bridge,' Sally mumbled, having looked long and hard at the canal and its environs. 'It's the only place they could be, when you think about it. Well, now you know the worst, so let's go home and forget we ever saw 'em.'

'The worst? I don't see . . .'

'They'll be kissin' goodnight, probably,' Sally said, trying to pull Lizzie away. 'Do come home now, queen! I wouldn't like to be caught spyin' on your aunt's old feller and that's gospel. Come home!'

'Tell you what, you put your arm round my waist and I'll kind o' lean my head on your shoulder and we'll walk a little way along the towpath so they'll think we're just another courtin' couple, like you said,' Lizzie whispered. 'I know you said they'd be kissing goodnight, but they might just be – be talking, like. And I've got to know what's going on, Sal, for Aunt Annie's sake.'

'We-ell, remember, she's a married woman, so wharrever they're gettin' up to, it won't be too bad 'cos she won't want her old feller findin' out,' Sally whispered back. 'All right, all right, don't pull me coat off me back, I'm comin' as fast as I can.'

The two girls descended cautiously on to the towpath, arms round each other's waist, Lizzie's head leaning, very uncomfortably, for the two girls were much of a height, on Sally's shoulder. They ignored the bridge completely, walked along the path for perhaps five minutes, and then turned back. They covered the return journey much more quickly, and presently bolted up the side of the bank and back on to Burlington Street, both rather breathless from climbing its steep side at speed.

'Well, I never!' Sally said as they regained the road. 'Well, the shameless baggage! I call that disgraceful, Liz, considerin' the pair of 'em's married – to other people, I mean. What'll she say if she falls for a baby, that's wharr I want to know? The rotten tart – I knew me mam didn't approve of her, but I didn't know she were *that* bad!'

Lizzie, agreeing, thought this was proof positive

that Sally was a good deal more experienced and worldly wise than she. To be sure she had seen the two dark figures under the even darker arch of the bridge, but left to herself she would probably have assumed that they were merely standing very close and probably talking intimately. Indeed, had she not been able to see the bright yellow of Flossie's hair, she might even have assumed that the tall, heavy figure of Uncle Perce was simply leaning against the stonework of the bridge and looking down at his own feet. Sally, however, made no such innocent assumptions.

'What'll you do, queen?' she said presently as they walked back along Burlington Street. 'Surely you aren't going to say anything to your Aunt Annie? I know what your uncle's doing is wrong, but when it comes down to it, I reckon telling your aunt would only make things worse. My old gran often says, "What the eye don't see, the heart don't grieve over", and I reckon your poor aunt has had enough grief without us adding to it.'

'I wouldn't *dream* of telling Aunt Annie. It would hurt her most dreadfully because I know she's still fond of the beast,' Lizzie assured her friend. 'But think on, Sally. If Uncle Perce's seeing a lot of this Flossie then sooner or later everyone will know. Why, you and your mam guessed what was going on ages ago, didn't you? And you know what the courts are like for gossip. It only takes one person to see them making for the canal, and the next thing you know, tongues are wagging the whole length of the Burlie, and folks will be giving Aunt Annie funny looks, and when she turns away she'll hear the whispering start.'

'Folk are real fond of your aunt,' Sally said rather reproachfully. 'They wouldn't want to hurt her, not deliberate. She's respected as well as liked.'

'Oh, aye, I know that. But folk can't help talking and sooner or later Aunt Annie will find out. What I've gorra do, Sally, is find a way of stopping it before it goes any further.'

'The gossip, you mean?'

Lizzie snorted. 'No, idiot, the carryings-on. I don't know quite how I'll do it yet, but there has to be a way. If I tell Uncle Perce I know and will tell the boys if he doesn't stop, that might work, mightn't it?'

By now they had reached the court and paused outside Sally's door, lowering their voices instinctively as they did so. 'It might,' Sally said cautiously. 'The trouble is, queen, once you've told him you know, you've shown your hand, like. Wharrabout tackling Flossie first? She's the one wi' more to lose, when you think about it. Her old feller's rich as the Lord Mayor of Liverpool so she won't want to be chucked out of that there lovely house they've got.'

This advice struck Lizzie as being profoundly sensible and she said as much before the two girls went their separate ways. Number nine was in darkness, for their nocturnal adventuring had taken longer than Lizzie had realised, so apart from a sleepy cluck from either Sausage or Mash when Lizzie hung up her coat on the back of the kitchen door, no one greeted her arrival at the house. The kitchen was still warm from the day's activities, the fire in the range damped down so that it would smoulder quietly until morning. Lizzie made herself a hot drink, for the kettle on the hob still steamed gently, and then cut herself a hefty slice of bread off the long loaf. She spread it with jam and began to eat, reflecting that however you looked at it, Sally's advice to go for Flossie rather than Uncle Perce was sound. For a start, she had never met Lizzie, would not know her from

Adam, which meant she was unlikely to tell Uncle Perce that his wretched niece was on their track. Indeed, if Flossie had any sense, she would say nothing at all to him but would solve the dilemma by ending their relationship.

Lizzie finished the bread and jam and drained her cup, then set off up the stairs to her room. She had no desire still to be in the kitchen when Uncle Perce came back from his clandestine meeting, though she knew he usually went straight into the front room and made himself comfortable upon the sofa there. Once in bed, she lay listening for his footsteps outside in the yard, but she was so tired that sleep overtook her before her uncle returned to the court.

Chapter Seven

Despite Lizzie's hopes, it did not turn out to be as simple to approach Flossie Sharpe as she had expected. For one thing, she had not realised that Flossie worked in the ironmonger's shop, nor that her husband worked with her. Her first couple of attempts at speaking to the woman were foiled when Mr Sharpe came forward, smiling ingratiatingly, and sold her a small milk saucepan and a dozen six-inch nails, neither of which she wanted. In the end, she decided to consult Geoff so popped into the bank where he worked. They arranged to meet on a Saturday morning when both of them were free since he said that he too had a problem which he would be glad to share.

Accordingly, Lizzie helped Aunt Annie with some of the chores and then said that she and Geoff were off for a day out together. Aunt Annie, who was hard at work baking gingerbread for a neighbour who then sold the cake, cut into squares, to the stallholders in St John's Market, passed a hand over her flushed forehead and gave Lizzie a gap-toothed grin. 'That's all right, chuck, 'cos I thought I might take a bit of an outing meself, seein' as it's such a nice sunny day,' she said. 'Myrtle's asked me if I'll go with her and the kids to Bootle, to visit her sister Amy what I were in school with. But there'll be a beef stew and dumplings ready for supper at the usual time so if you want to bring Geoff back, he'll be welcome. I like young Geoff. He's what you might call a solid citizen.'

Lizzie laughed and slung the light jacket which she had recently bought from a stall on Paddy's Market over one shoulder and set off across the kitchen. 'Thanks, Aunt Annie, Geoff loves to have a meal with us so you can expect us back at the usual time. Have a nice day.'

She left the house at a run for she and Geoff had agreed to meet at the clock tower on Great Homer Street and she would be hard pressed to arrive on time, having slept late that morning. Despite this, however, she reached the clock tower moments before Geoff arrived and naturally pretended she had been waiting for hours.

Geoff grinned. 'I saw you coming round the corner of Cazneau Street,' he said triumphantly, 'so don't you tell me no stories, young Lizzie.' He took her arm. 'Where do you want to go for this here talk? We could have a cup of tea and a bun on Homer, unless you want to go somewhere a bit more exciting? It's the first really sunny day we've had, we might as well take advantage.'

After a short discussion, Lizzie decided that she wanted to have her cake and eat it, so they went to the nearest tea-room and settled themselves into a window table, ordered a pot of tea and two iced buns and waited in silence until their order had been delivered. Geoff's story must be as sensitive as her own, Lizzie decided, pouring tea for them both into dainty china cups.

The tea-room was crowded but since there was only room in the bay window for one table, the one at which they sat, Lizzie concluded that this was about as private as they could get and, resting her elbows on the table, leaned towards Geoff. 'Well? Who's going to start? I never imagine you as having problems,

Geoff, unless you count all those dreadful exams you have to take, that is.'

'It isn't exactly my own problem,' he confessed. 'It's – it's to do with Sid. Do you remember him, Lizzie? He's the feller who tried to drown me in the canal that time.'

'Oh, Geoff, you haven't got mixed up with that awful Sid again, have you?' Lizzie said, much shocked. 'He's a *horrible* feller. I wonder you even speak to him in the street as you pass. I wouldn't, I'm sure.'

Geoff laughed. 'Sid's a reformed character,' he assured her. 'Why, he's gorra decent job and a right cosy little flat above a fishmonger's shop on Cazneau Street . . .' And he proceeded to tell Lizzie the story of how he and Reg had met Sid and Evie and about their evening together. 'But it sounded fishy, the story of her being his cousin,' he concluded, 'so I did as Reggie suggested and kept my eyes open every time I was anywhere near Lewis's. And the fact is, Lizzie, that wherever she may work, it isn't there. I've tried the other big stores, even some of the smart dress shops in that area, but there's not a sign of her. What's more, I've not seen hide nor hair of Sid and I just can't make out what he's playing at. What do *you* think?'

'I dunno,' Lizzie said doubtfully. She picked up her plait and began to nibble thoughtfully at the ends of her hair. 'Didn't she give you any sort of sign that Sid was lying, Geoff? Didn't she look uncomfortable when he said she was a mannequin and worked in Lewis's? Surely, if she's an honest girl, which you seem to think, she wouldn't have wanted to go along with his lies. I know I wouldn't, in her shoes.'

'The thing is, Lizzie, there was no point in Sid lying, so far as I can see,' Geoff said, after a moment's thought. 'If he and the girl were living tally, where's the shame in that?' He caught Lizzie's scandalised glance and grinned sheepishly. 'Well, it isn't what you and I consider respectable but I'm sure Sid would think it perfectly all right, so why the lies?'

'Why are you so interested?' Lizzie countered. 'You said she was very pretty, but that doesn't mean she's a respectable person, our Geoff. For all you know, she might walk Lime Street every Saturday night or go down to the docks and pick up foreign seamen. She could be a real bad character, just like Sid.'

She half expected Geoff to rip up at her, tell her she had a nasty suspicious mind, but instead he just grinned ruefully and shrugged his shoulders. 'You may be right,' he admitted. 'She is pretty – beautiful, in fact – but I had the feeling she was a decent girl, a girl just like you, Liz, and what's more, when we first met I thought I recognised her. When Sid said she worked in Lewis's, I thought perhaps I'd seen her when I'd been into the store, but now I don't think it was that. Oh, I dunno, I s'pose I'm making a fuss about nothing really. Only it's a mystery, Lizzie, and I do hate unsolved mysteries.'

'I know what you mean,' she admitted. 'But I don't see how I can help you. I can ask around, of course, but not knowing what the girl even looks like, I could walk past her in the street and never know it, whereas you at least have the advantage of having seen her. What do you want me to do?'

'Asking around's a good idea,' he said, 'but I dunno as I had anything definite in mind, I just wanted to see what you thought. Reggie's fair sick of the subject, though he was keen enough at first. There aren't many girls who look like Evie Evans, I can tell you.'

'Describe her,' Lizzie said, but though Geoff did his best, she still had to shake her head. The girl certainly sounded stunning but there was nothing in Geoff's description, not even the almond-shaped eyes, which was sufficiently unusual to jog her memory. 'No scars or tattoos, not even a third eye in the middle of her forehead,' she said regretfully, when Geoff had finished. 'Never mind I'll put the word around amongst me mates and let you know if I get a nibble. Want another cup of tea?'

Geoff promptly accepted her offer and ordered two more cakes, then asked Lizzie to tell her own story. Lowering her voice, she did as he asked. When she'd finished, Geoff gave a low whistle. 'That's a facer and no mistake! What'll you do, Lizzie? No point in telling him you know. From what you've said he isn't the sort of feller to be shamed into good behaviour. Any hope of the woman being more – well, more easily threatened?'

Lizzie regarded her old friend with admiration. 'Fancy you thinking of that first go off, our Geoff! But yes, that's what Sally and I decided it would be best to do. The snag is that I'm in work daytimes. Saturdays I'm free so twice I went up Heyworth Street and into Sharpe's Ironmongery, hoping to be able to get a word alone with her. Only she and Mr Sharpe both work in the shop and he's pretty quick to come forward . . . anyway, both times I tried to get served by her and ended up being served by him!'

'Hmm. The answer is to find out where she goes socially . . . oh, I suppose when she does go out it's with your uncle, and you don't want him to know you've been interfering, that's for sure. An ugly customer, your uncle.'

'You're right, but that's the beauty of tackling her

rather than him,' Lizzie said eagerly. 'She's never seen me, won't know me from Adam, so she won't go telling Uncle Perce that his niece has been trying to warn her off.'

Geoff stared at her. 'My dear girl, she's only gorra set eyes on that yellow plait of yours . . . you're not exactly a mousy little nobody, you know!'

Lizzie stared at him; she could feel a rich tide of heat rising up her face, and it was dismay as much as anything else which caused it. Why had she and Sally never thought of that? The minute Flossie told Uncle Perce that they would have to stop meeting because a girl had threatened to tell Mr Sharpe what was going on he would surely ask for a description, and there were not many girls of her age with fair, waist-length hair. Even if she did it in a bun, or coiled it up under a hat . . .

'Tell you what, why don't I tackle Flossie for you?' Geoff asked. 'And then if I do get a lead on young Evie, perhaps you could tackle her for me? Well, not tackle precisely, but just have a word wi' her, find out what's up. Only if I do it meself it'll get back to Sid . . . and he's a bad enemy, I'd say. How about doing a swap, like?'

Lizzie was so relieved she jumped up from her seat and gave him a hug. 'You're a real pal, so you are,' she said breathlessly. 'And now let's go down to the Pier Head and catch a ferry to Woodside and walk there while we discuss how you're going to get to talk to Flossie without her husband hearing, and how I'm to get friendly with this Evie Evans of yours.'

Oddly enough, within three days of talking the matter over with Lizzie and agreeing that she should try to find Evie while he concentrated on Flossie, Geoff walked slap-bang into Sid Ryder. Geoff was just coming out of Lime Street Station, where he had gone to buy a newspaper, when someone cannoned into him. Geoff started to apologise at the same time as the other fellow did and was astonished to find himself addressing Sid – and a very smart Sid, too, wearing a short, dark brown Burberry, with a trilby instead of a flat cap slanted over one eye, expensive-looking tweedy trousers and brown brogues on his feet. Furthermore, he was carrying a hide suitcase in one hand and a Gladstone bag in the other.

'Sid! Where are you off to?' Geoff said, very startled. 'That's a big suitcase to be taking to the races! Come to that, you don't want Lime Street Station for Aintree!'

'I'm not going to Aintree,' Sid replied after only the slightest hesitation. 'I'm headin' for pastures new, feller! London first, and if that pays off the way I think it will, then it's the United States of America for this Scouser! There's no future for fellers like me in this country – I'm headin' west, as they say in the movies.'

'That wasn't what you said a few weeks back when Reg and I came round to your place,' Geoff said mildly, but his mind was racing. 'Are you going alone, Sid? Not taking that pretty little gal . . . what was her name? . . . Eva, was it? Something like that, anyroad.'

'Her? Aw, she's past history,' Sid had said airily, but his eyes suddenly stopped meeting Geoff's and began darting about in a very uncomfortable manner. 'Well, I can't stand here chattin' to you, I've gorra train to catch.'

'Hang on a minute . . . if you aren't interested in that girl, I am,' Geoff said, suddenly desperate to get any information he could before Sid was swallowed up by first London and then America. 'Where does she live? Where does she work, for that matter? She seemed like a nice kid . . . looked sort of familiar, too, I wondered . . .'

But Sid had pushed past him and was heading for the platforms so Geoff turned round and followed him doggedly, determined not to miss this opportunity. Sid pushed through the crowd and to Geoff's annoyance actually showed his ticket at the barrier then headed for the train which was getting up steam, though there were still people hurrying aboard. 'Look, Sid, if you aren't interested . . .' he began again, but the porter on the barrier put out a stout arm to detain him. Geoff slid him half-a-crown, begged him to buy a platform ticket and then hurried after Sid while the porter stood staring, as if mesmerised, at the money in his grubby palm. Geoff saw Sid get into a carriage and slam the door shut but arrived in time to wrench it open again just as Sid was taking a corner seat, having clearly assumed that his 'old friend' would not be able to get past the porter. The other occupants of the carriage, three businessmen and a portly matron in a navy suit, nursing a large handbag and using the seat beside her for the rest of her luggage, looked curiously at the two young men, clearly wondering why, if they were friends, Sid had closed the door almost in Geoff's face.

Grimly, he climbed into the carriage and sat down opposite Sid. 'If you want company all the way to London and a fair old fuss when the ticket collector comes along and discovers I've not even got a platform ticket, then you just keep your gob shut and I'll stay right here until you open it,' he said, ignoring the dangerous look in Sid's eye. After all, what could Sid do to him with so many onlookers? 'Now what's up wi' you and young whatsername? And how can I gerrin touch wi' her?'

He spoke as Sid did, in the same accent, and was pleased to see that it had had its effect. Sid looked thoughtful, almost wary, but no longer dangerous. Geoff also noticed that his former friend had the fading marks of a black eye and a half-healed split lip and guessed it probably had something to do with a racecourse fracas. He would have liked to question Sid, but the other was already speaking. 'Well, if you really want . . . and you didn't reckernise her? Why, you must ha' knowed her once, same as I did.'

'I thought she looked familiar,' Geoff said. 'But I couldn't remember how or why.'

'No? Do you 'member that little kid who used to foller us around when we was youngsters? Filthy, she were, and always dressed in rags. Lived wi' some old woman in the same court as wharr I did – Cumberland Court. The other kids called her Chinky because her mam was a prossy and her da were a Chinese coolie, worked in an engine room on one of the Transatlantic liners they say. Only her mam abandoned her when she were no more'n a year or so old. And a real little trollop she's turned into, just like her mam. I wouldn't have anything to do wi' her if I were you. Anyroad, I dunno where she lives nor where she works . . .'

'You said she was a mannequin in some shop,' Geoff said. He could have strangled Sid with his bare hands, but still retained enough commonsense to know that if he tried to do so he might be the one spending the night explaining to the scuffers that he had gone temporarily off his head. Also Sid probably carried a knife, would certainly fight dirty, and Geoff was out of practice after several years working in the

256

bank. 'I remember you tellin' Reggie and me that she had a real good job . . .'

'Oh, aye, in Blackler's, that's right. Only she quit,' Sid said airily. 'I'm tellin' you, Geoff, for your own good more'n anything else, that the gal's gone missin', I don't know or care where, and if you've gorra grain o' sense you'll leave well alone. Now you'd better be gerrin' off or you really will come to London wi' me! Hear that whistle?'

The whistle had been genuine and a porter was coming along the platform, slamming doors, and the train was actually rocking a little . . .

Geoff cursed beneath his breath and left his seat in a hurry, jumping down on to the platform and standing back as the train began to move off. No use trying to force Sid's hand, he would give nothing away now. Indeed, he had the cheek to come to the carriage window and wave to Geoff through it as though they were indeed old pals, before pulling the leather strap to bring the window closed and taking his seat once more. His smile was mocking; was he hiding Evie away somewhere or had they really quarrelled? As he walked back along the platform, Geoff decided that for once Sid had probably tried to persuade Evie to do something which was anathema to her and the girl had got away from him and would not renew their acquaintanceship. Glumly, he retraced his steps, the paper still tucked under his arm. When he reached the barrier the porter had disappeared, which meant that the half-crown had disappeared too. Not that it would have mattered had Geoff been lucky enough to get a lead on Evie from the slimy and disgusting Sid.

Still, he had known, really, that Sid was not likely to put him in touch with the girl. It was now clear that he had lied to Geoff when he had told him Evie worked in Lewis's. Geoff doubted that she worked in Blackler's either, but he would take a look in there in his lunch-hour and keep an eye out for a while.

And I've got Lizzie on my side, helping me, he reminded himself. He mulled over what Sid had told him; that Evie had once been known as Chinky, but he could not remember. . . and then, as he settled back into his desk at the bank and reached for his big black accounts book, it all came back to him. A chilly winter day, fading towards dusk, he, Sid and Tom wandering back through the streets, Sid with a pocketful of cash for they had acquired a pretty gold chain from a jeweller's shop and had sold it, probably for a tiny portion of its real worth, to a fence he knew. A little girl had approached them, one hand cupped hopefully, and Sid had tipped a few small coins into it, had grinned at her breathless thanks and strolled on as she disappeared, barefoot but at great speed, towards the shops. She had been a tiny, skinny, filthy creature who could have been almost any age, dressed in rags with thin, dust-laden black hair and long, almond-shaped black eyes. He had seen her before, usually watching them hopefully, her hunger plain and worse than most in a city where hungry children were no rarity. Her skin, he recalled now, had seemed yellowish beneath the dirt, but it was difficult to tell . . . Chinky! But surely that little scrap could not have turned, as if by a miracle, into the doe-eyed beauty Sid had introduced as his cousin?

Yet why should Sid lie? And now that Geoff had remembered the child, he could see some resemblance, if only in the long, almond-shaped eyes and a certain look in them when they had rested on him. Not amusement exactly . . . yet definitely recognition.

Well, perhaps it would help that he now knew not only her real name but the nickname which had been common currency when they had all been kids. Satisfied, he pulled the ledger towards him, dipped his pen into the ink and began to write. The more he knew about the girl, the greater the chance he had of tracing her. Determining to tell Lizzie all about his encounter with Sid as soon as possible, he continued with his work.

It was a hot August day and Geoff was pretending to look in the window of the shop next door to Sharpe's Ironmongery. He was heartily sick of pursuing Flossie and was beginning to think he would never catch her alone. He and Lizzie had met several times to discuss their progress but neither of them had anything to report. However, he had managed to ascertain that when the shop was quiet, Flossie occasionally left her husband in charge while she visited a friend on Mere Lane and, because of the heat and the bright sunshine, there were fewer shoppers than usual crowding the pavements, so Geoff thought today might be his lucky day.

By half-past three he was beginning to contemplate giving up and going to the nearest tea-room for a drink, when the shop door swung open and Flossie emerged. She had shed the dark brown overall which she wore in the shop and was clad in a light floral print and open-toed sandals, with a wide-brimmed straw hat perched on her Marcel-waved hair. She looked cool and comfortable and set off at a good pace in the direction of Mere Lane, making Geoff think, wistfully, that there were advantages to being a woman; his grey flannel trousers and jacket seemed horribly hot, but he dared not shed the jacket since he wanted Flossie to think him a person to be reckoned with.

Geoff knew that her friend lived a good way down the lane but he had missed catching Flossie alone too many times to risk it happening again, so he speeded up, got in front of her and then turned, as though he thought he had just recognised someone he knew. 'Afternoon, Mrs Sharpe,' he said breezily, though with banging heart. 'Can I have a word?'

Flossie Sharpe did not looked pleased, neither did she stop walking, though she did slow her pace. 'Are you a customer?' she said baldly. 'Because if so, me husband's mindin' the shop. If you want somethin' he'll be there till six, later if business is brisk – which it ain't, or I wouldn't be off to see me pal.'

Geoff looked round desperately but there was no tea-room, or garden where he and Flossie might talk; it would have to be here and now, on the pavement, with people passing by. Fishing a handkerchief out of his pocket, he mopped his damp forehead and spoke the words he had been secretly rehearsing for weeks: 'Mrs Sharpe, I know you've been seeing Mr Percy Grey of an evening, and I know Mr Sharpe wouldn't like it if he knew. I daresay you'll say you and Percy are only friends, but I've followed you more than once and I know different. I want . . .'

He had been about to say that he wanted the relationship to stop before Percy Grey's wife heard of it, but he was not given the opportunity. Flossie Sharpe stopped dead in her tracks and swung back her right arm as far as it would go. Before Geoff had realised her intention, she had brought her arm round and clouted his head with her open palm and with sufficient force to knock him off balance, so that for a moment he saw stars and was fully occupied in keeping his feet. 'You dirty, blackmailing little tyke,' Flossie Sharpe hissed as Geoff, with tears in his eyes, righted himself and stared indignantly at her. 'If you think you'll gerra penny out of me, you're very much mistaken. As for seein' some feller in the pub of an evenin', what makes you think Mr Sharpe don't know – and approve – of wharr I do?'

For a moment Geoff was so astonished that he could only gape, then he realised that Flossie assumed he wanted money in return for his silence on the subject, and took fresh heart. 'No, no, you've gorrit wrong, I just don't want you to go on seein' him,' he said breathlessly, for his face and head still stung from the violence of her blow. 'I'm a friend and neighbour of Annie Grey, Perce's wife, and – and she's – she's mortal fond of him. It would break her heart to know he's carryin' on wi' you, an' I – I guess Mr Sharpe would feel the same, so I thought if I saw you, asked you to stop seein' Mr Grey . . .'

'Don't waste your time, sonny, because I ain't admittin' nothin', nor I shan't stop seein' me pals at your say so,' Flossie said decisively. She stared hard at Geoff, her bright little eyes taking in his every feature. 'And I knows you now, young feller. If I ever sets eyes on you when I'm wi' Perce, I'll see he gives you the hidin' of your life. Now gerrout of me way. And don't you think I've not noticed you hangin' round the shop, either! I've already telled Mr Sharpe I reckoned you was waitin' the chance to thieve from us, and if you keep it up I'll tell the scuffers that an' all. Now clear orf!'

That evening Geoff and Lizzie met to exchange news. She was distressed to learn that Flossie had been, to say the least, indifferent to Geoff's threats of revealing all, but accepted that he had done all he possibly could.

Because of the heat, the pair of them were sitting on the edge of the canal, dangling their bare feet in the cool water. Now Lizzie kicked an arc of dazzling spray into the air, aiming at a couple of ducks who were passing by. 'Damn and damn and damn!' she said explosively. 'This summer weather makes Aunt Annie more likely to come out of the house of an evening, 'cos it's wickedly hot in the courts. Suppose she walks down to the Travellers' Rest on the corner of Burlington Street and the Scottie and sees them coming out – or going in for that matter? She'd be bound to guess there was something up, and it would break her heart.'

Geoff, however, was more sanguine. 'I know I didn't do a very good job of scaring Flossie off, but she's no fool. I think she'll tell Perce she wants to go to some other pub and they'll probably keep clear of Houghton Bridge as well,' he assured Lizzie. 'After all, no one wants to court trouble and since she seemed to think I intended to blackmail her, she won't deliberately stick her head into a trap. No, I reckon your Uncle Perce will keep his fancy woman well clear of our area, for a while at any rate.'

'And what else can I do about finding Evie?' Lizzie said rather desperately. She had picked up no clues at all since the other girl seemed to have disappeared off the face of the earth. 'I'm beginning to think Sid Ryder isn't the only one who's left Liverpool. In fact the only thing which has kept me searching is the fear that something bad might have happened to her, and if it has, I don't know that there's much we could do about it. I think it's time we both put Evie out of our minds. If she turns up, we'll certainly find out about it but there's no point in continuing to search when we've already covered just about every avenue.'

'I know you're right,' Geoff sighed. In his turn, he began to kick spray at the ducks. 'Have you seen Clem lately? I bet it's lovely and cool on the canal, walking along the towpath, leading Hal in the daytime and sleeping aboard the butty boat of a night. Better than boiling in that beastly bank.'

'Better than the bottling plant, I can tell you,' Lizzie said. 'When it's hot like this it really gets you down. I haven't seen Clem for months and months in fact not since Sausage and Mash were quite young, but I often think of him. I'd love a week or two travelling up the canal and seeing all the beautiful countryside spread out around me. I wonder what he's doing at this very moment? Something nice, I bet.'

'Do you wish you were with him?' Geoff asked idly. He rolled up a trouser leg which had begun to descend dangerously near the water, and kicked more spray.

Lizzie thought this over, then shook her head. 'No, because he'd have that bleedin' great dog in tow and I'm scared stiff of it.' Across the water came a faint tinkling and she raised her head. 'That sounds like the "stop me and buy one" crossing the Houghton Bridge. Do you fancy an ice cream?'

'Phew! I reckon we need a break,' Jake remarked as *The Liverpool Rose* emerged at the top of Bingley Five Rise Locks. 'That's eight locks we've come through in the last couple o' miles and locks is hard work when you've two boats to take through.' He grinned at Clem, who was at Hal's head, encouraging the big horse to lean his full weight into the collar, for although the horse got a rest when the boat was coming slowly up the five rise, it was a hard job to get it moving again from the 'at rest' position.

Clem enjoyed going through the locks, though it meant a good deal of hard work for him. He had to take the horse ahead, tether him to a convenient post and then run back to help with the gates and paddles of the locks, for with two boats it needed the full crew – Jake, Priddy and himself – to get through them as quickly as possible and without fouling *The Liverpool Rose* on either the sides or gates of the locks.

Not that he minded any of this running about. Indeed, in cooler weather it was good simply to be on the towpath without having Hal breathing down his neck, and this had not been a particularly fine summer. Rain had fallen most days and it was only as August edged into September that the sun had begun to shine, allowing Clem to appreciate the breathless beauty of the Pennines as the canal wound its way amongst the hills.

But right now they had made their way carefully through the locks, both the Bingley five rise and the earlier three, and Jake was steering *The Liverpool Rose* into one of the wider sections where she could be safely moored without obstructing other craft. The boat bumped gently against the bank, its rope fenders already out and protecting its sides from the contact. And Priddy's face, rosy from the heat, emerged from the cabin. 'What's up?' she said in a slightly aggrieved tone. 'It ain't dinnertime yet, is it? I've got a mutton stew simmerin' over the fire which makes it mortal hot down here, so if we want to keep movin' I'm in favour.'

'Well, I thought we'd have a sandwich for us midday meal and save the stew for this evenin', when it's cool,' Jake said, half apologetically. 'Hal gets his nosebag on for a feed and has a snooze while the water's goin' up or down in the locks but it's perishin' hard work for the rest of us.'

'I think we could all do with a break. This hot weather's hard on both horse and man alike and I reckon old Brutus wouldn't say no to a run in the hills, eh? With a bit of luck, he might find his way crossed by a rabbit – or even a nice plump hare.' Jake smacked his lips reminiscently for the dog had brought a hare in only a month previously and there was nothing Jake enjoyed more than jugged hare. 'So what do you say to a bit o' bread and cheese, Priddy, and a mouthful of ale, if there's any aboard?'

'I'm agreeable,' she said at once, emerging thankfully from the cabin and fanning her hot face with a large red handkerchief. She looked round approvingly at the spot Jake had chosen, at the trees and dappled shade beneath which the boat rested. 'This is a grand place. I'll get the grub out as soon as I've cooled down a bit and we'll eat it on the bank – have a picnic, like.'

Clem began to take off the tack from Hal's enormous body. He removed the swingle tree and laid it down on the bank, then took off the heavy collar and hung it over one of the tethering posts. He left the bridle in place since they would not be stopping here for much over an hour and began to rub Hal down with a handful of long hay which he had taken from the kennel where the horse's food was stored. Then, hooking his fingers into the ring beside the bit, he led Hal to where the grass was at its most lush and left him there to graze. Some horses, he knew, would have needed a tether to stop them straying too far from the boat, but Hal was a placid and obedient animal and would stay within sight of *The Liverpool Rose* while they had their meal.

Presently, the three of them were sitting on the bank with their feet dangling in the water and their clogs on the decking of the boat. Brutus sat beside Clem, his dark and melting eyes fixed hopefully on his young master, for the big dog knew very well that Clem always handed over the last mouthful of whatever he was eating.

Having finished his bread and cheese and a couple of swallows of ale, Clem fed the Alsatian the last bite and got to his feet. 'I'll just take Brutus for a run, get the fidgets out of his legs,' he said. 'I won't be gone no more than ten minutes. I know you said we were early and didn't need to hurry because we had help with loading, but I'd like some time in Liverpool, if that's possible. I want a word with that girl Lizzie.'

Priddy, who had been lying on her back gazing up at the blue sky, sat up and turned to stare at him. 'Lizzie? Ain't she the one you brought on board? Why, it must be a year or two ago. Haven't you seen her since?'

'Not to speak to, not for more than a few moments,' Clem said rather guardedly. 'The trouble is, she's scared stiff of Brutus, though heaven knows why. You know how gentle he is, Priddy, but she's got it into her head that, given half a chance, he'd tear her limb from limb. I've tried to talk sense into her but I never see her for long enough to convince her that he's harmless. Come to that, I'm pretty harmless meself,' he added with a grin, 'so I'd like to persuade her she won't come to any harm seeing me now and then, either.'

Jake, who had not appeared to be listening to this exchange, turned as well then and beckoned Clem to his side. 'I've been meaning to have a word wi' you for some time, lad,' he said, removing his short clay pipe from his mouth and examining the bowl critically. 'It's time you was paid a wage and not simply your keep because the truth is Priddy and me couldn't possibly manage wi'out you.'

'I manage all right,' Clem said awkwardly. 'I often get the odd penny for helping other boats through the locks, you know I do, and Priddy gives me a bit for runnin' messages and doing odd jobs for her from time to time.' He had never questioned the economics of running *The Liverpool Rose*, but imagined that, by the time all their expenses had been paid, there was not a lot of money left over. Priddy made sure they were well fed, that the horse was in excellent condition and that their clothing was adequate for any weather. Jake saw to the boat, caulking the planks in dry weather so that when rain followed there were no leaks below decks, and he made new rope fenders when the existing ones were worn. He kept the tarpaulins which protected the cargo in good condition and saw that the cargo itself was protected from wind and weather. Clem knew that there were a great many boats working the canals which were in a lamentable state compared with *The Liverpool Rose*. Some men neglected their horses and used their children as slave labour while others ignored the condition of their boat until it grew so bad that no one would employ them to carry goods. Because of this *The Liverpool Rose* was highly regarded and never short of a cargo. Due to her skill in doctoring, Priddy sold her medicines to most of the careful horse owners, though she seldom charged half as much as the farriers and horse doctors with premises alongside the canal, and she always paid Clem when he gathered herbs for her.

'I knows all that,' Jake said patiently. 'Me and

Priddy make sure you've a few coppers in your pocket when we are near towns wi' shops, but it ain't good enough, Clem. You do a man's work, and – and pretty soon, you'll be havin' a man's needs. When did you last go to a picture house, eh, or visit a dog track? Or go out to Aintree to watch the racing? I'm not sayin' you want to do such things, but I am saying that if you do want to see a fillum or take a pretty girl dancin', then you should be able to do so. Priddy and me talked it over and we decided you should have a third share in the profits. It ain't a lot, because we pays all expenses first, but it'll be money of your own and you'll get it at the end of each trip. All right?'

'You don't need to do that,' Clem mumbled. 'You've been so good to me, you couldn't have been better if I'd been your own son. Besides, what would I spend money on? Priddy makes my clothes and my food and you feed Brutus here . . . I don't deny I'd like to see more of Lizzie when we're in Liverpool, maybe treat her to a show or a meal, but other than that . . .'

'You can save your money for your future, if you've no better use for it,' Priddy put in. 'One of these days, you're goin' to want to get married, a good-looking lad like you, and then you'll be surprised how the money goes. And I only provide you wi' workin' clothes, you know. If you were to go dancin', you'd want a suit, wouldn't you?'

'I don't know,' Clem said helplessly. In the old days when he had lived with his parents in the little mining village he had had a grey flannel suit for wear at weddings, funerals and Sunday services. The canal people always tried to get to church or chapel on a Sunday but attended such services in their working clothes, though the women would shed their practical aprons and don straw hats in summer and clean, dark head scarves when the weather was bad. 'Still an' all, Jake, if you truly think I'm worth it and it won't make things difficult, it 'ud be grand to be earnin' a wage. Now I'd best be off or poor old Brutus won't get his run.'

As he made his way past a rippling stream, he stopped for a moment to let the dog slake his thirst in the clear, dappled water. He could see tiny fish beneath the surface, darting in and out of the tumble of rocks which formed the floor of the stream, and wondered idly as he climbed higher, making his way amongst the slender saplings of silver birch and willow, whether there were trout lying in the deep pools further down stream. If there were, it would be fun to bring his rod up here and see if he could get a fish or two for supper. It would be even better, he thought dreamily, skirting the moss-covered piles of rock which abounded in this area, if he could catch some fish and take them to Liverpool for Lizzie. He knew this was not a practical dream, however. Fish caught up here on the moors would be well and truly past its best by the time *The Liverpool Rose* arrived in Liverpool docks.

Having emerged from the trees, Clem felt the breeze on his face as he climbed higher and was glad to be in open country once more. He let his thoughts dwell lovingly on what Jake had said to him: that he was doing a man's work and would, in future, be paid a man's wage. He had always liked Lizzie, thought her the prettiest girl of his acquaintance, and even now, when he was on friendly terms with a good many of the young women who worked other boats on the canal, he liked her best. But because of Brutus and the difficulties of working the canal, he rarely had an opportunity to seek her out. Either they met by chance, or they did not meet at all, and he had a shrewd suspicion that since his acquisition of Brutus, Lizzie no longer came down to the canal when she thought *The Liverpool Rose* was berthed there.

But now that he would be earning a wage, all this would surely change. He could leave Brutus with Priddy or Jake and ask Lizzie to go dancing or to a picture house or simply to accompany him when he went shopping for the various commodities which Priddy needed. Because of his own hard work and that of the others, they really did have more time at either end of their journey now. Jake paid any strong young lads loafing about the dockside, to help them load and unload and this gave them free time which had not been possible when there were only two of them to do the heavy work.

A muffled yap from Brutus made him look round. The dog was staring at a fox which trotted across a clearing before disappearing behind a tumble of boulders. 'You're a good lad not to chase him . . .' Clem was beginning when he suddenly remembered his own duties, gave a guilty start and turned back towards the canal once more. He had best get back. He must tack up the horse and re-attach the tow rope before they could move on, and now that he knew a wage awaited him in Liverpool, he was even keener to arrive there.

Whistling the dog to heel, he set off down the hill once more.

Lizzie stood just inside the front door of number nine, looking out disgustedly at the rain which was being blown almost horizontal by the wind which came howling in at the narrow entrance to the court. She had meant to go down to the canal to see whether *The*

Liverpool Rose was yet berthed, for she thought the boat might be coming in some time during the next two or three days, but now the weather was making her wonder whether it was really worth the wet and windy walk – and presumably a wetter and windier wait, for there was never any guarantee that the boat would be in at the time Clem had suggested. What was more, since she would not go aboard either *The Liverpool Rose* nor the butty boat in case she met Brutus face to face, she would not get the pleasant gossip with Priddy and Jake nor a comfortable half-hour in the cabin which was one of the attractions of going down to the canal. Lizzie considered, standing in the doorway and watching the rain while behind her Aunt Annie sat, hens on her lap, and darned socks for her sons.

'Well? Are you goin', chuck, or ain't you? Only there's a right mean draught comin' through that door and me hens aren't keen on draughts.'

Sighing to herself, Lizzie closed the door and turned back into the kitchen. She said: 'It's awful wet and windy. I was supposed to be going to meet Clem down at the canal, but it'll mean hanging about . . . I thought I might get a tram up to Shaw Street and see whether Geoff's at a loose end. But that seems as though I'm letting Clem down, 'cos I know he sets a deal of store by a bit of an outing when he's docked in the 'Pool. What d'you think?'

'Oh, I'd go and see Geoff,' Aunt Annie said comfortably. She was rather fond of Geoff, telling Lizzie frankly that he was a steady chap who would make some lucky woman a good husband one day, and suggesting that it might just as well be Lizzie as another. And the only time she had met Clem she had made it clear that she thought all canal folk were wanderers, gypsies almost, and therefore not as reliable as bank clerks.

'I'll think about it,' Lizzie said guardedly now. She went and fetched her waterproof off the back of the kitchen door and shoved her feet into her cracked Wellington boots, then wrapped a scarf round her head. 'I'll nip round to Sally's, see whether she's doing anything this afternoon. A walk to the canal wouldn't be so bad if she came along.'

She set off, head down, still undecided what to do, and Sally was no help. She was in the act of leaving the house as Lizzie crossed the court and told her that she and her mother were bound for the home of an aunt, bidden to tea to celebrate her cousin Nellie's fifteenth birthday.

'Oh, well. I'll mebbe get a lecky up to Shaw Street then,' Lizzie told her friend. 'See you later, Sal. Geoff's probably studying, but I might be able to persuade him to come out for half an hour.'

As she made her way to the tram stop, Lizzie thought of Geoff with a good deal of affection. For several weeks after her pal had tackled Flossie, Lizzie truly thought the confrontation must have done the trick. She kept her eyes open but saw neither her uncle, nor Flossie, either going into or coming out of any local hostelries. When she told Geoff this, he looked rather smug, but then reminded her that had the relationship ceased, Uncle Perce would have returned to his old haunts, albeit grudgingly, without the lady. Because both parties had disappeared he was inclined to think they had merely gone to ground, but since this suited Lizzie's book almost as well as the ending of the relationship would have done, she did not repine and was grateful to Geoff for his intervention.

The Indian summer which had followed the long wet months of June and July had ceased in mid-September with squalls of violent rain. Earlier, Clem had come visiting, telling Lizzie of his new status on board *The Liverpool Rose* and suggesting that the two of them might have some fun together when he was in the 'Pool. Lizzie was reluctant to admit that she was still terrified of Brutus, but realised Clem was unlikely to bring the dog along if they went to the picture house or a dance hall so had agreed to his suggestion.

Unfortunately, however, it was not always possible for their free time to coincide. Aunt Annie had never fully recovered from the illness she had suffered after losing her baby, and Lizzie found herself with more and more of the housework, shopping and cleaning to do when she arrived home from work. Sally was a great help, keeping her company when she was slaving over a hot stove and going shopping with her to search for bargains along Great Homer Street and the Scottie, and Aunt Annie did her best to see that her niece had some time to herself, but Lizzie knew she was still longing for her husband to take a bit more notice of her, so did her best to ease the burden her aunt carried by continuing to work as hard as she could in the house. Her cousins, when they had lived at home, had been simply useless save for such tasks as the bringing in of water and coal. However, since they had moved out of number nine a month or so before, they could not even be counted on to perform these tasks, and though Lizzie was glad not to have to feed them or clear up after them any more, financially Aunt Annie was considerably worse off, for Uncle Perce had got into the habit of not contributing anything to the household and, despite his wife's pleas, continued to keep his wages to himself.

Both Herbie and Denis were courting young women who lived on the opposite side of the city, and had decided to leave home after a tremendous row with their father over his refusal to help with the household expenses. There had actually been a fight, Aunt Annie had told Lizzie when she had returned from a day out with Geoff. Uncle Perce had laid about him with a cudgel and the boys had sworn never to cross his threshold again until he apologised. 'Which means never,' Aunt Annie had said tearfully to her niece. 'I know Percy, he'd die sooner than say he was sorry, though I'm sure he misses our lads as much as I do.'

Lizzie suspected that Herbie and Denis were aware of their father's affair with Flossie, but took it more or less for granted that a man with their father's appetites would seek female companionship elsewhere since his wife would not go out with him nor share his interest in drink. Lizzie knew that a great many men were unfaithful to their wives and that the women, though they were aware of it, did nothing to prevent such affairs. Indeed, she had heard more than one neighbour commenting that she was grate-ful her husband occasionally went with other women since it saved her from his unwanted attentions.

Despite the amount of work that Lizzie did in the house, however, she and Sally managed to find time to enjoy themselves one way or another. When they were free to do so, the two of them went about together, dancing at the Grafton Rooms in West Derby Road when they could afford the sixpence which was charged to go in after ten o'clock and frequenting the many picture houses in the city centre when they had the money for admittance. When Clem was in Liverpool, therefore, Lizzie felt she could not simply drop her old pal in order to go about with him, for Sally still had no regular boyfriend. Once or twice Lizzie had thought of inviting Geoff to make up a foursome, but the trouble was, because of Clem's inability to give her any advance warning that he would be in the city, arranging a date was difficult, if not impossible. So though Lizzie and Clem did manage the odd meeting, it was still rather hit and miss.

What was more, even when Brutus was not present, Lizzie always felt a little in awe of Clem. He was a lot older, and a great deal more experienced, and she could not for the life of her imagine why he still wanted to go around with her. The last time she had been down to the canal to meet him, he had been talking to a breathtakingly pretty girl with a cloud of dark hair and melting brown eyes. Clem had introduced her as: 'Suzie Raxton, who works *The Cumberland Lass* with her mam and dad,' and Lizzie had envied her her neat print dress and navy blue jacket, and her air of knowing her own worth. Despite the fact that Lizzie had been earning money now for a while, she seldom had anything left over to spend on clothes, certainly not on new or fashionable ones. She sometimes thought she paid more than her fair share towards household expenses, but realised that Aunt Annie was powerless to get money from her husband.

In fact her aunt frequently suggested that Lizzie might pay her less, but if she had done so they would have gone hungry towards the end of each week and this was something Lizzie felt she could not allow, so she continued to hand over the lion's share of her wages to her aunt every week, and to buy clothing from Paddy's Market whenever she needed something desperately and had a shilling or two to spare.

But right now she was heading for the tram stop, having made up her mind that she *would* go and see whether Geoff could play – no, not play, come with her down to the canal to see if *The Liverpool Rose* had docked. Now that she thought about it, she remembered that Geoff and Clem had met several times before. So there would be nothing strange in suggesting that the three of them might spend a few hours together.

With this thought in mind, Lizzie climbed aboard the first tram which came along, and when it had deposited her in Islington walked through to Shaw Street and along to the YMCA where she found Geoff not studying, but playing a rather half-hearted game of chess against a bespectacled young man who seemed to be winning at an amazing rate. When Lizzie suggested that Geoff might consider coming out with her to see Clem, he jumped up with alacrity.

'Solly here's a wizard at chess and I'm just a beginner,' he explained as the older boy, with a shrug of his shoulders, began to pack the men and board away. 'Sorry, but we'll play another time – if you can't find someone a bit better'n me, that is. Come on, Lizzie, or we'll not reach the canal before dark.'

Lizzie was delighted with this response, though when they got as far as the front door and Geoff saw the rain, he looked a little less pleased to be rescued from what was obviously a humiliating game of chess. 'It's pouring perishin' cats and dogs,' he said, sounding aggrieved. 'Are you sure you want to go visiting this feller, queen? Wouldn't you rather see a flick? There's a western on at the Paramount Theatre in London Road. We could grab a lecky and be inside in the dry before the cat can lick her ear.'

Lizzie, who quite liked westerns, had to struggle with herself before replying: 'Oh, but I did arrange to meet Clem, Geoff, and it isn't often the boat is due to arrive when I'm not in work or doing something for my Aunt Annie. Besides, he may not be there. If he isn't, you can come back to number nine and we'll have cocoa and a bit of Aunt's seed cake by the fire . . . or we could go to the flicks then if you're really keen.'

'Oh, all right, then. I'll fetch me waterproof because a raincoat's norra lorra good in rain like that,' he said, heading for the cloakroom. 'How come you aren't soaked, young Lizzie? Don't say you're thin enough to run between the raindrops!'

Lizzie laughed. 'No, but as I got off the lecky it stopped raining for just long enough for me to reach you,' she assured him. 'If you take a look at me legs, you'll see I splashed a good deal of mud up them as I ran, though.'

Geoff laughed too. 'Oh, all right, if you don't mind the weather I suppose I shouldn't,' he remarked. 'And I'd like to see that feller again. I wonder if he'll remember that afternoon when he just about saved me life, all them years ago? As I recall, he landed Sid a tidy one, too. I'll never forget it, even if Clem has.'

Outside the rain had eased off a little. Lizzie looked enquiringly up at her companion. 'Do you want to walk, Geoff? I don't mind if you do, 'cos we can both get under that umbrella of yours, but of course the tram would be a lot quicker.'

Geoff, who had been holding his big black umbrella over the pair of them, grinned back. 'It had better be the lecky since there's a number thirteen bearing down on us right this minute. It'll take us as far as Islington, then we can nip through and catch another the rest of the way.' He lowered his umbrella, shook it briskly and raised it again to hail the tram, jumping aside with a muttered curse as it drew to an abrupt stop, sending a bow-wave of water from the gutter on to the pavement. 'Come on, Lizzie, look lively! If we're lucky with our connections, we'll be at Houghton Bridge before you know it.'

Clem sat on the side of the butty boat, peering out from under the brim of his sou'wester, in the direction of Burlington Street. It was just his luck, he thought morosely, that the weather should have turned sour on him on the very day they reached the 'Pool, so that now Lizzie might change her mind about meeting him. He knew her address, of course, and could have strolled up to the court despite the driving rain, but hesitated to do so since her aunt had made him feel uncomfortable on the only previous occasion that he had called for Lizzie. He had thought at the time she had no call to look down on him because he was so tanned, since she herself was a great untidy whale of a woman who looked as though she never brushed her hair or changed her clothing. But she had managed to make it plain she did not think him a suitable friend for her niece and Clem had been both upset and irritated by her attitude. Because of this, he preferred to meet Lizzie down by the canal, but if there was no alternative, and if she had not arrived in the next twenty minutes, he would have to grit his teeth and go up to the court where he meant to counter Mrs Grey's rudeness with such civility and charm that she must surely unbend towards him.

The twenty minutes were almost up and he was just turning to tell Brutus to stay and guard the boat when he saw a figure in a waterproof, huddled beneath a huge umbrella, coming along the towpath. Immediately, he felt a smile spread across his face. 'Stay there, Brutus, and guard!' he said, trying to ignore the disappointment writ clear in the dog's dark brown eyes. 'I'll buy some chips, old feller, when I come back, so just you be good. I'm off to see my pal and if we go to the picture house, or even dancing, they wouldn't want a chap like you along.' He had never told Brutus how Lizzie felt about him, but knew the dog's sharp intelligence to be considerable and was sorry that Lizzie could not get over her fear. However, the big dog settled down on his blanket, curling round till his nose was covered by his bushy tail, and Clem slid off the gunwhale and began to walk along the towpath.

He had only gone a few yards, however, when he realised that there were two people beneath the umbrella and not one, as he had supposed. He was about to turn back to the boat when a voice hailed him. 'Clem! It *is* me under this brolly – and Geoff's come along as well. Do you remember him?'

By this time the couple had reached him and Clem was able to recognise Lizzie, even when swathed in a waterproof with a dark scarf hiding her golden hair. He looked at the two beneath the umbrella, and felt the short hairs on the back of his neck bristle. He had half expected that she might be accompanied by her friend Sally, but he had definitely not thought to meet her with a young man. What was more, this young man had his arm about Lizzie's waist in a manner which made Clem want to punch him on the nose. How dared this stranger be so familiar with Lizzie? Were not Clem and she about to go out together?

'Clem?' Lizzie's voice was hesitant. 'What's the

matter? Don't you remember Geoff? He's the feller you fished out of the Scaldy when Sid Ryder was trying to drown him.'

Clem looked more closely at the other boy, but could see very little resemblance to the frightened, half-drowned kid he had hauled up the bank and pumped clear of water. It would not do to say so, however, so he put as much enthusiasm – which was not much – into his voice as he could and stuck out a hand. 'Sorry, Geoff, you've changed a good deal since that day. I was a bit surprised to see Lizzie with someone else, to tell you the truth, because I thought she and I were going to the flicks. Still, I suppose the three of us can go together.'

Lizzie looked uncertainly from one to the other as Geoff replied, in a stiff voice, that it had not been *his* idea to come along this evening, but Lizzie's. 'She knew there were a good chance you might not turn up at all,' he said. 'And since I don't suppose you'd want her to go to the flicks alone, she thought she'd bring a pal along. But if you'd rather I made meself scarce . . .'

'No, of course he wouldn't,' Lizzie said, sounding scandalised. 'It isn't as if me and Clem were courting, Geoff! I meant to ask Sally to come along so there'd be four of us, but she's gone to tea with her cousin 'cos it's her birthday – the cousin's I mean – and won't be home till nine or ten, I daresay.'

'You can come along and welcome,' Clem said, knowing his voice was as stiff as Geoff's had been. 'I'm sorry if I sounded a bit . . . well, taken aback, like. Only I don't see Lizzie here that often and I thought – well, I thought we might talk a few things over, like how things are going at home . . . how her life's going along, like.' Towards the end of the sentence he thought that his voice sounded more normal, less aggressive, but knew that he was still hoping Geoff would take the hint and make himself scarce. How could Lizzie put him in a position like this, he thought, really rather cross with her. When the two of them were alone they took the opportunity to discuss all sorts, which they could scarcely do with a third party along! He did not imagine that she confided in other people about her uncle's unfaithfulness and her aunt's unhappiness.

This, however, was disproved almost immediately. 'I don't have any secrets from Geoff,' Lizzie said, sounding almost accusing, Clem thought miserably. 'Him and me's old pals, Clem – I've known him even longer than I've known you, and because he's always around, not on the other side of the country half the time, I've had to rely on him a good deal. Why, the problem with my uncle's as good as solved, thanks to Geoff. And that means my aunt's a great deal happier, of course, and *that* means that I'm happier as well.'

'I didn't know. If I could have done anything to help, I would have,' Clem stammered, feeling guilty. Not that it was his fault he wasn't in Liverpool on any sort of permanent basis, he reminded himself. 'Only you know I've got my living to make, Lizzie, and that means travelling.'

'Oh, I'm not *blaming* you for not being around, I'm just pointing out that Geoff's always here when I need him and you aren't,' Lizzie said. She still sounded as though she were criticising him for his long absences, he thought resentfully. 'So anything you want to discuss, feel free to do so in front of Geoff. He's been a good friend to me, honest to God he has.'

'I'm sure he has,' Clem said glumly. 'I didn't mean to – to pretend . . . it was just that I thought . . . oh, dammit, what does it matter? What do you want to do, the two of you?'

Lizzie shrugged and glanced at Geoff. They were still huddled under the umbrella, making Clem feel very much an outsider as he stood out in the downpour with the rain hammering on his waterproof. Because of the weather, he knew that Priddy and Jake would stay on board *The Liverpool Rose* this evening which meant he could scarcely invite Lizzie and Geoff to join them in their living quarters. The butty boat had a nice little cabin though the tiny stove was rarely lit, but he had no intention of turning Brutus out into the cold in order to entertain a young man he hardly knew – and did not want to know, furthermore. The more Clem thought about the cinema or a dance hall, the less he fancied visiting either, particularly in a threesome. No matter how you looked at it, they would have to dispose of their wet clothing somewhere and he guessed that the cinema would be full of damp and steamy people and their raincoats and jackets and did not wish to add to their number. As for dance halls, he could just guess what would happen if the three of them went to one together, he thought resentfully. Lizzie would dance with her old friend Geoff while he either stood and glowered at them from the sidelines or danced with some strange girl in whom he had no interest in the hope of making Lizzie jealous.

'I don't care what we do,' Lizzie said. Clem thought she sounded bored and cross. 'We're in the city all the time, me and Geoff, so you can choose, Clem.'

He shrugged, making the rain channel off his waterproof in great streams. 'It's not the sort of evening for doing much,' he observed. 'I can't ask you aboard *The Liverpool Rose* because there wouldn't be room for all of us in the cabin. Jake and Priddy are staying at home because of the weather and, of course, Brutus is in the butty boat.'

'I suppose we could go back to number nine,' Lizzie said doubtfully. 'Only it'll be pretty dull, sitting round and chatting to Aunt Annie. On the other hand, it'll be awful steamy and hot in the flicks because everyone in there will be as wet as us.' She turned to her companion. 'If Clem doesn't want to choose, Geoff, why don't you say where we'll go?'

'I think I'd better go back to the YMCA,' he said gruffly. He was staring down at his boots, not meeting Lizzie's eye even though she was staring into his face. 'After all, I only came along with you in case the barge still hadn't arrived, and I don't know I much fancy going dancing anyway. As for spending the evening at your place, what about Aunt Annie? What'll she say to having her kitchen invaded by boots and waterproofs and brollies?'

'She won't mind . . .' Lizzie was beginning, when Clem was struck by a brain-wave. 'Tell you what, while we were coming through Wigan, I bought a bag of really big spuds off of an old market woman selling them at the canal side. She'd growed them in her garden and was selling them for a ha'penny a piece. What say I fetch four of them out? Your Aunt Annie always keeps a fire going in the kitchen, doesn't she? We can put them in the embers and have a game of cards or something while they're cooking. And if we pick up a couple of bottles of beer on our way back, then we'll be paying our way, so to speak.'

Lizzie agreed to this at once and Geoff also nodded, albeit grudgingly, so Clem got back aboard the butty boat, selected four enormous potatoes and a chunk of Cheshire cheese, dropped them into a brown paper bag and rejoined the other two on the towpath. 'There we are, a meal in a moment,' he said cheerily, indicating the paper bag. 'Aunt Annie, here we come!'

At ten o'clock that night, Lizzie waved the two lads off at the front door then returned to the kitchen where Aunt Annie was sitting at the table, thoughtfully eating one of the plums which had been her contribution to the feast. She looked up and gave her niece a gap-toothed grin as Lizzie approached the table. 'Well? And what were all that about?' she asked. 'I bet you felt like a worm being pulled in two different directions by a couple o' greedy hens, didn't you?'

Lizzie took a deep breath then blew out her cheeks in a long, whistling sigh. 'Phew! Oh, Aunt Annie, wasn't that the most uncomfortable evening you ever spent? I'm so sorry I brought it down on your head, but I had no idea how dreadful things would be. What on earth was the matter with them? They've not met for ages but I thought they'd be real pals – after all, Clem did save Geoff's life a few years ago. But instead of liking each other, it was just the opposite. I'm not saying they were enemies exactly, but . . . oh, I don't know, you would have thought they hated one another!' She pulled out a chair and joined her aunt at the table, reaching over and selecting one of the few remaining plums. 'I feel as tired as though I've run ten miles, just from trying to stop them actually coming to blows. Aunt Annie, do *you* know what was the matter?'

Aunt Annie chuckled. ''Course I does,' she said robustly. 'They was both jealous as a couple o' cats, that's what. What did you expect, our Lizzie? You know Geoff's got his eye on you and now you know

Clem has an' all. Each sees the other as competition, and they always will. Them two boys will never be friends – leastways not until you chooses between 'em. And there's no guarantee they won't carry on being jealous even then.'

'But Aunt Annie, I'm not courtin' with either of 'em,' Lizzie objected. 'In fact, after this evening . . .' She was interrupted by a loud knocking on the door and got to her feet with a sigh. 'I wonder if that's Sally? She ought to be back from her party by now. Perhaps she's come round to see how my evening went.'

She crossed the room, went into the little hallway and opened the front door. Clem stood on the step. The rain had stopped and he was carrying his hat in one hand, so that the pale moon, peeping between scudding clouds, cast its light on to his dark, rumpled curls. He grinned at her. 'Lizzie, can you come out for five minutes?' he asked urgently. 'I left in such a hurry, I forgot to tell you when we will be docking in Liverpool next.'

Lizzie looked doubtfully at the puddled court. 'It's awful wet out there, although the rain's stopped,' she said. 'Can't we talk here? Will you still be in the city tomorrow? Only I could come down to the canal . . .'

But Clem, clearly not wanting to waste time in argument, caught hold of her wrist and pulled her down the steps, then tucked her arm into the crook of his elbow and set off across the court. 'I can't talk properly when I know your aunt's listening,' he said frankly. 'She doesn't like me, Lizzie, and that makes me feel awkward. As for your pal Geoff . . . but never mind that. Come down to the canal, I've something to show you.'

'Hang on, Clem, I've not even got a coat and it

285

might come on to rain again any minute,' Lizzie objected. 'Why the rush?' But he would only pull her onwards.

It was midnight before Lizzie got into bed, and when she got there she was so tired and so distressed she did not think she would ever sleep. She and Clem had had the most almighty row, ending with her flinging away from him and almost running along the tow-path and up on to the Houghton Bridge. He had caught her up a short way along Burlington Street, grabbing her shoulder and spinning her round towards him. Lizzie, still hot with fury, had slapped his face so hard she had almost knocked him sideways. 'Why, you spiteful little . . .' Clem had said, fingering the red wheals which were already beginning to show on his moon-whitened face, but Lizzie had not waited either for retaliation or whatever it was he wanted to say, but had merely run towards her home as fast as she could go.

When she rounded the corner into the courts, she had glanced back, not sure whether she hoped or feared he might be in pursuit, but the street was empty. She had slowed to a stroll, determined not to let anyone see the state she was in, and had found that in her absence Aunt Annie had closed the front door, damped down the fire and gone off to bed. Lizzie had made herself a cup of cocoa and sat at the kitchen table drinking it, half hoping even now that Clem would come knocking on the door to apologise for the things he had said, about both Aunt Annie and Geoff. But he had not done so and as her temper cooled Lizzie realised she had no right to expect an apology from him. Thinking it over coolly, or as coolly as she could, she knew she had done little or nothing to make the evening a success and that Aunt Annie had purred over Geoff and been extremely off-hand to Clem. There had been good reason for his outburst, for his request that she should never bring Geoff to the boat again nor expect him to be treated like an outcast by her aunt.

At the time, however, she had simply resented his criticisms and thought him unfair to blame her for Geoff's antagonism and her aunt's prejudices. She had said she would ask Geoff to go with her whenever she wanted, since he was her good friend, and Clem would have to learn to put up with it or stop seeing her altogether. She had also said that Aunt Annie had not been nasty to him, even though she knew this was patently untrue. She had said her aunt was old and did not understand canal folk and merely wanted a secure future for her niece.

'You mean, she wants you to marry a bleedin' bank clerk so the pair of you can look after her in her old age,' Clem had replied contemptuously. 'I thought you had more to you than that, our Lizzie. I thought you were a girl who wanted to see a bit of life, who was prepared to work hard and play hard – not the sort to sit back on your bum and count the shekels some feller brings in after sitting on *his* bum all day in a nice clean office, writing in a ledger. Because that Geoff hasn't ever done a real hard day's work in his life, nor he isn't likely to, working in a bank.'

After that, things had simply gone from bad to worse; by the time Lizzie had turned and run for the Houghton Bridge, she had ripped Clem's character to shreds, said unkind things about Priddy and Jake, and told him that she never wanted to see him again. She marvelled now that he had bothered to run after her, had clearly meant to try to put things right. She had been unfair, unkind and untruthful, she could acknowledge that now she was calmer. Even so, Clem had said some pretty unforgivable things himself. Geoff might be a bank clerk but he worked extremely hard, if not physically. As for Aunt Annie, Lizzie supposed ruefully that she had a right to prefer Geoff to Clem, if she truly thought that Geoff was the better prospect. The fact that she had let it show was unfortunate, but surely Clem, who was the oldest of the three of them, should be more understanding of an old woman's prejudices. Aunt Annie had actually called the barge people 'water gypsies' – though not in front of Clem – and Lizzie knew that a lot of people thought the canal folk strange and unreliable, though even knowing this, she acknowledged Aunt Annie should never have let Clem see how she felt.

For some time Lizzie tossed and turned in her bed, finally falling asleep when dawn was already streaking the sky. She awoke late and bad-tempered, rushing downstairs and out of the front door without so much as a cup of tea. She had grabbed her hat and coat in passing, having the forethought to yell to Aunt Annie before she slammed the door behind her that she would be back late that night. Still sore from the thought of the previous evening's encounter, she meant to go round to the YMCA as soon as she finished work, to pour out her troubles to Geoff.

Fortunately, Sally had clocked in for her so she was not actually late for work, but she had a horrid day. She had told Sally what had happened the previous night and had received little sympathy. 'What did you expect?' Sally had said. 'Don't be so daft, Lizzie. Two fellers and one girl isn't likely to make for a pleasant evening.'

By four o'clock, Lizzie was so tired she could

scarcely keep her eyes open after her restless night and very nearly decided to give her visit to the YMCA a miss. However, having told Aunt Annie she would be late, she went round there and met Geoff just as he was leaving and very soon the two of them were seated opposite one another at a window table in Lyon's Corner House and Lizzie was leaning forward to tell her tale.

An hour later Lizzie, pink-faced and furious, was hurrying down the road a good deal faster than she had gone up it. I hope I never see Geoff Gardiner again as long as I live! she told herself, angry tears forming in her eyes and spilling down her cheeks. He's smug and self-satisfied and the last person on earth I'd want to marry. So far as I'm concerned, he and Clem can go to the devil together. And on this pious thought she returned to the court, where Aunt Annie, dishing up supper, asked no questions, merely said that she was tired out and needed an early night.

'Me too,' Lizzie said, going into the kitchen and hanging her coat and hat up on the hooks. 'See you in the morning then, Aunt Annie.'

'Well? Did you have a good time wi' the young lass?' Priddy asked next morning, when Clem came aboard *The Liverpool Rose* to get his breakfast. 'We'll be off in half an hour, so you won't be seein' her again this trip, but next time we'll hope for better weather, eh, lad?'

'We quarrelled,' Clem said briefly. 'She brought another feller along, a chap called Geoff. We – we didn't get along.' He was ashamed, now, that he had not managed to hide his annoyance and disappointment over Geoff's presence. After all, the younger boy was not to blame because Lizzie had dragged him along, and come to that Clem could scarcely blame her for wanting a pal with her on such a wet and lousy evening. Had the barge not berthed, the poor kid would have spent a pretty miserable time, keeping a look-out for him on the towpath. What was more, he knew the canal could be a dangerous place for a young girl out on her own. Most of the boatmen were grand fellows, the salt of the earth, but there were some – the Trelawney brothers for instance – who might try to take advantage of a girl alone, or even rob her if they were short of beer money.

'Quarrelled? What, with Geoff? But you went to meet Lizzie, she's your pal . . . you didn't quarrel with her surely? You were lookin' forward to . . . what about the present, then?'

Priddy's voice was surprised, even a little disappointed, which was no wonder when Clem thought how hard she had worked over Lizzie's present. He had spent his first wages on it, though he had not told Lizzie that. How could he, when she was being so aggressive and cross, and perhaps not even taking in that he was showing it to her because it was *for* her, had been 'specially chosen, 'specially made in fact?

'Oh, I quarrelled with Lizzie later, when I brought her back here. I meant to give her the present then. The trouble was, I forgot old Brutus was in the butty boat. I more or less dragged her on board . . . she began to struggle . . . I thought she was just messing around, you know . . . and then Brutus came out of the cabin like an arrow . . . he was only going to greet me but she shrieked . . . don't say you didn't hear . . . and then he jumped up at me, you know how he does, so glad to see me back . . .'

'We heard,' Priddy said. There was grim humour

in her voice. 'We'd ha' had to be deaf as postses not to hear – your young leddy's got a shriek on her wuss'n a steam train a-goin' into a tunnel. Only we didn't know what had caused it. Well, wi' some young fellers we might ha' made a guess, like, but we knows you better. Whatever your faults, Clem, you're a gentleman where gals is concerned. So it was Brutus, eh? But he didn't growl nor bark nor nothin', so we never guessed . . .'

'He never barked or growled because he wasn't attacking anyone,' Clem said patiently. 'Anyhow, I bundled him back into the cabin and fetched out the fancy Fair Isle jumper what you knitted so beautifully, Priddy. I showed it to Lizzie, meaning to tell her that it was your work and that I'd only paid for the wool, but she never even gave me a chance. She pushed it aside and started saying she'd had a horrid evening anyway and I'd just about crowned it by encouraging the dog to attack her. Attack her! I kept telling her that Brutus was meek as a lamb but she wouldn't listen, just kept saying he might have killed her, and in the end I got cross, too, and said that if he'd meant to hurt her, she wouldn't be standing there yelling at me, she'd be a hospital case.'

'Oh, Clem! I know you're a gentleman, like what I said, but I don't believe you've got an ounce of tact,' Priddy said reproachfully. 'She's such a lovely girl and I'm sure she's fond of you. Why not nip round to her house right now and take the jumper? There's time before we sail.'

But Clem, with the image of Lizzie's pink and furious face still dancing before his eyes, decided that discretion was the better part of valour. If he left it a few weeks and then went round to the court with his present, surely she would have cooled down and be in a more receptive mood? He still liked Lizzie better than any other girl he knew, even though he now acknowledged she had the devil's own temper when she was crossed. He would let her simmer down before approaching her again, and what was more, in a few weeks the autumn weather would have begun to edge towards the bitter chill of winter, which would make the Fair Isle jumper a far more appropriate gift.

He said as much to Priddy, who nodded a trifle doubtfully. 'But what about this other feller?' she demanded. 'Will he use these few weeks to fix her interest? You don't want to leave it too long, not if you're serious, that is.'

'I don't know whether I'm serious or not,' Clem said, having given the matter some thought. 'I think we're too young to be serious, Priddy. Well, no, that's not right. The trouble is, we don't see enough of each other. It's like the girls I meet on the canal – we can spend a couple of evenings in each other's company, then we may not meet again for three or four months. It makes courting kind of difficult.'

'Oh, canal people all have the same problem,' Priddy said comfortably. She was cooking breakfast in the tiny cabin and preparing to serve it to her menfolk before *The Liverpool Rose* cast off her moorings. The smell of bacon and fried tomatoes was very tempting and presently Clem sat down at the tiny table, with Jake opposite him, and began to eat, telling himself that it was useless to worry over Lizzie. The boat would be back at the 'Pool in two or three weeks; he could decide what best to do then.

After the quarrel with Lizzie, Geoff told himself that women were creatures he would never understand

and flung himself into his studies with more enthusiasm than ever. In fact, a little thought convinced him that both he and Clem were to be pitied. They were the victims of the contrariness and illogicality of the feminine mind. However, the fact that Lizzie and he had quarrelled so bitterly did not put him off women altogether. He had tried very hard to banish the recollection of Evie Evans, but she kept appearing in his mind's eye as though she were appealing for his help and he became even more determined to try and find her.

The quarrel with Lizzie had, in fact, come about because he had tried to explain to the girl that he could see Clem's point of view. If Clem was keen on Lizzie, and he obviously was, then his reaction to finding another feller included on their date was a natural one. Geoff had thought this a perfectly feasible argument, but it had caused Lizzie to go off like a rocket. She had yelled at him that Clem didn't own her any more than he, Geoff, did and said she would go around with any feller she fancied and they could both put that in their pipes and smoke it.

Geoff, very startled by her words, had said reasonably that he had not meant to offend her. 'I like you a lot, Liz,' he had said. 'I thought you liked me too, which were why I were a bit stiff when Clem's hackles started going up at the sight of me. But I've thought it over, and I reckon I never should have gone along wi' you on a date. No wonder Clem wasn't too thrilled . . .'

For Lizzie, that had seemed to be the final straw. 'No one bleedin' well owns me,' she had informed him, pink-faced and furious. 'All *I* wanted was an evenin' out wi' two of me pals. It were you and that stupid Clem who turned it into a sort of contest. Well, I've had enough of both of you. If you feel so sorry for him, then you and he can get together and cry on each other's shoulders, because I'm off.' And with that she had stormed out of Lyon's, leaving Geoff feeling hot and bewildered. If that was how women behaved when you had the least little misunderstanding then he wanted no part of them, he decided, returning thankfully to his books. Only he was certain Evie Evans was not like that. One day, he suddenly felt sure, he would find her again – and in the meantime he would let Lizzie see that he could manage very well without her.

Chapter Eight

DECEMBER 1927

'What do you want from the greengrocer's, Aunt Annie? I know you said I were to get some scrag end for a stew, but surely you'll want turnip, carrots and so on as well? And how about a couple of pound of spuds? I might as well get all your messages in one go, because Sally and I thought we'd go round the shops and look for Christmas presents this afternoon.'

Lizzie and her aunt were in the kitchen; Aunt Annie sitting in her usual chair, knitting industriously. She was making Uncle Perce a pair of the thick woollen socks which the dockers liked to wear in winter to keep off the chill as they worked. Since this meant using four needles, Aunt Annie needed all her concentration and did not even look up when her niece spoke but answered with her eyes fixed on her work. 'Oh, aye, there's not half a dozen spuds in the old sack so if you can get the veggies as well as the scrag end that'll be all I need. Just check in the cupboard for me, will you? I told your uncle I'd do a marmalade pudding for afters, so make sure I've gorra jar not opened. He's rare fond o' marmalade pudding is my Percy.'

There was a comfortable smugness in her voice which made Lizzie smile to herself, but there was no doubt that of late Uncle Perce had been very much pleasanter to his wife. Before, Lizzie sometimes thought, there had been faults on both sides. Because of her aunt's unhappiness, number nine had not been a good place to return to after a hard day's work, so Uncle Perce had stayed away as much as he could, but over the past few weeks, Aunt Annie had begun to make a real effort to turn their home into a pleasant place to be. Aunt Annie had recently inherited some money upon the death of an aunt and now she had what she described as 'a little nest-egg' tucked away in the bank though Lizzie thought that Aunt Annie had only confided in herself and possibly Uncle Perce since no one else ever mentioned her good fortune. She had bought new cushions for the sagging wicker chairs in the kitchen, had changed the draggled and dirty curtains for fresh clean ones, and had even attacked the parlour, putting down pretty floral rugs on the floor and re-upholstering the sofa on which her husband spent so many nights. Upstairs, she had bought thick woollen blankets for the bed and feather pillows with clean, crisp pillow cases. Ever since their arrival Uncle Perce had been sleeping upstairs.

Lizzie thought hopefully that this might well prove to be the salvation of Aunt Annie's marriage for now Uncle Perce actually complimented her aunt on the delicious meals she served and usually remained for at least half an hour in his wife's company afterwards before going off to the pub. In fact, so pleasant were things at home that Lizzie no longer regretted so deeply the rows she had had with Geoff and Clem. She still had Sally to go around with and it was fun to sit in the kitchen with a cheerful and optimistic Aunt Annie, knitting away, and discuss her work, her life, the young men she met at dances and the cinema shows she and Sally enjoyed. Even Herbie and Fred had noticed the change in the atmosphere when they came round to see their mother, and had taken lately to stopping for a meal and then remaining to chat with their father about affairs of the day.

Lizzie went across the room and checked the level of the marmalade; there was a full jar and another with just a scraping in it – plenty for a marmalade pudding, she decided. 'As I'm in the butcher's for the scrag end, shall I see if I can get a lump of suet?' she enquired, struggling into her coat and wrapping her warmest scarf around her neck. 'You could do a suet pudding with treacle for tomorrow – I know Uncle Perce loves a treacle pudding. Besides, it's so perishin' cold we all need to line our stomachs with something warming.'

'Good idea. A pound of suet would make a huge puddin', and if you could get some fades from the market while you're buying the carrots and that, then I could do an apple puddin' for Monday,' Aunt Annie said. She turned her knitting and Sausage, seated on her left knee, got knocked to the floor, flapping and squawking loudly. 'Shurrup, you silly old hen, I didn't knock you off a' purpose,' Aunt Annie said indulgently, patting one large knee encouragingly. 'Come on, me little feathered friend, me knee's quite cold without your nice fat feathers coverin' it up.'

'Okay, I'll see if I can get some fades,' Lizzie said, pulling on her thick woollen gloves and picking up her canvas bag. She had already taken Aunt Annie's purse from its place on the sideboard and now clicked it open and examined the contents, checking over pennies, ha'pennies and threepenny bits and noting the presence of a shiny florin amongst the other coins. Yes, there would be sufficient money for all her purchases, she decided, tucking the purse into her overcoat pocket. 'Cheerio for now, Aunt Annie. I'll be as quick as I can because the cold's wicked out there, but I doubt I'll be back in under an hour.'

Opening the front door, she actually hesitated for a second before plunging across the court. It was bitterly cold; above the blackened chimney pots she could see that the sky was blue and clear. Even so, she shrugged the scarf up to cover her mouth because the air was so icy it snatched her breath away, making her cough through the thick white mist forming around her mouth. She turned right on to Burlington Street and almost immediately saw Dolly Stewart ahead of her, also carrying a canvas bag; clearly, Dolly was also doing the messages for her mother. Lizzie quickened her pace and caught up with the other girl. 'Morning, Dolly!' she said cheerfully, through her muffling scarf. 'Going up to the Scottie, are you? If so, we might as well walk together. Are you going up as far as St John's Market? Me aunt wants veggies and some fades for a puddin' as well as some scrag end from Staunton's.'

'I'm to get the biggest bag of spuds I can carry and an ox tail as well as some veggies, so it looks as though we're bound in the same direction,' Dolly said cheerfully. 'Me mam told me to go up to Sharpe's the ironmonger's for a can of paraffin, but that'll have to come later. I ain't a perishin' donkey, I told her. Norreven your daughter can carry that much. How's the family, Lizzie? I've not seen you for a few weeks so I'm behind with all your news. Someone told me they saw Herbie and Denis round your place the other night, though. Don't say they've moved back home again?'

Lizzie's ears had pricked up at the mention of Sharpe's the ironmonger's. She had been neither near nor by the shop for months, and had almost forgotten about Flossie and her friendship with Uncle Perce. Now she said airily: 'No, the boys were only visiting. And things are grand at home right now, thanks. But why did your mam want paraffin from Sharpe's? There must be nearer places than that what sell the stuff.'

'Oh, didn't you know? Me mam is second cousin once removed to old man Sharpe's daughter Millie, so the old feller always gives us a discount, like. But, as it happens, he's in hospital. Me mam told me the doctor says he ain't expected to live for more than a few days, and that wife of his ain't likely to give me the time of day, lerralone a discount. Have you heard what the old devil's been and gone and done?'

'No?' Lizzie said on an interrogative note. She had had no idea that Dolly was in any way connected with the Sharpe family. 'Go on, tell us the worst.'

'He's been and gone and left the shop, the flat above it and all his perishin' money to his daughter, Millie,' Dolly said triumphantly. 'That painted Jezebel what he married is going to be mad as fire when she finds out. Norra penny, that what she's gettin' – and what she deserves,' she added with more than a trace of spite in her voice.

'Norra penny?' Lizzie echoed. 'But why ever not? I thought husbands always left their money and that to their wives. Isn't it the law or something?'

'Dunno. All I know is, he told his daughter, and she told my mam, that he'd found Flossie out after all these years. Says she's got a fancy man what she meets most nights and carries on with somethin' awful. Says he's set a detective on 'em, like in the fillums, and the chap caught them red-handed. Imagine! Cor, I wish I'd been a fly on the wall,' she added.

'What an awful thing,' Lizzie breathed. 'Did – did Millie say who the feller was? I wonder if it's anyone we know?'

'She never said, so I suppose the detective chap just saw her with a man and that were enough proof for old Sharpe to change his will,' Dolly said airily. 'My mam thinks the shock of findin' out that Flossie was unfaithful is what purrim in hospital. Why, when you think about it, it's almost as bad as murder, that.'

Lizzie was relieved to hear that her uncle's name was not being linked to Flossie Sharpe's and extremely glad that she herself had kept quiet on the subject. The only people to whom she had mentioned it had been Clem and Geoff, and even though they had quarrelled, she knew they would never let her down by breathing a word to a soul. Sally's mam, however, was a different kettle of fish, but since she and Sally had both assured Mrs Bradshaw the previous summer that happily the affair had ended, she doubted whether her pal's mam would start any unfortunate rumours.

All the way to the shops, Lizzie and Dolly chatted about other things, having exhausted the topic of the Sharpes. After all, Dolly had no idea that Lizzie's family were in any way connected with Flossie Sharpe so would naturally assume that Lizzie's interest in their affairs would be short-lived. But all through the shopping expedition and their discussion of films, film stars and boyfriends, there was a nasty little niggling doubt in the back of Lizzie's mind which would not go away. In some way she felt vaguely threatened by the thought of Flossie's fury when the details of her husband's will came to light. It was useless telling herself that old man Sharpe might live for years; after Dolly's calm reiteration of the doctor's remark, she could not believe it.

'Here's Staunton's. Oh, look, they're queuing right out on to the pavement,' Dolly said, giving a groan. 'I only hope no one else is after ox tail, 'cos there's only one to each carcass and I do love an ox tail stew.'

Joining the queue, Lizzie giggled. 'I may not be a country girl but I reckon you're right. One tail to a cow seems to be what most of 'em have,' she said. 'Oh, good, Joe Lidd's serving as well as Mrs Staunton. If we can get him, he'll always pop a few marrer bones into the parcel. He's nice, is Joe.'

'He lives in your court, doesn't he?' Dolly said. 'Ain't he courtin' Bessie Pye? She lives close by us so if anyone gets free marrer bones, it oughta be me.'

'Well, Joe's a nice feller, so if there's any to spare I daresay we'll both get one or two,' Lizzie said philosophically. 'By golly, this queue's moving slowly! Ah, now it'll speed up. Mr Staunton's coming through from the back and he's a dab hand with the cleaver. He'll joint the meat for the other two and we'll be served before you know it.'

Lizzie was right and a quarter of an hour later the two of them were making their way towards St John's vegetable market, talking about mutual acquaintances and discussing the various means by which young ladies like themselves could remain reasonably warm at dances while clad in their flimsiest dresses. Lizzie was in favour of piling on as much underwear as would fit under her dance dress whereas Dolly thought that a fluffy spangled shawl or a bolero jacket kept her warm enough, in the dance hall at any rate. The talk then moved on to the dresses which both girls owned. No one in their position could have more than one dance dress, of course, but with a little guile that dress could be made to appear different at each wearing, so that even though one's intimates recognised the garment unerringly, strangers – and young men – would think it a different outfit. Lizzie's dance dress was of black ninon, with a dropped waist, which she sometimes wore with a blue velvet sash adorned with a huge silver buckle. At other times, she pinned a pink artificial rose to one shoulder, or donned a light and gauzy gold scarf which she tied in a bow at the nape of her neck, allowing the ends to dangle below her waist. This poodle bow, as it was called, was the height of fashion and Lizzie had three: one in gold tulle, one in silver gauze, and one in cream-coloured crêpe-de-chine, patterned with rosebuds.

Dolly's dance dress was brighter and more striking than Lizzie's, being of pale blue artificial silk with a deep 'V' neck-line and a layered skirt. But it was far more difficult to disguise its appearance so, generally, she pinned an artificial rose to the waist or relied upon her jacket and scarves for variety.

Discussing clothes kept the two girls busy until they reached the market, whereupon the search for bargains took over once more and they prowled amongst the stalls, examining the goods for sale and finally choosing one of the country stalls where the stallholder sold her own vegetables and was consequently cheaper than some of the more professional market women.

'Well, I reckon we done all right,' Dolly said breathlessly, as the two of them lugged their heavy bags back along Scotland Road. 'Ain't it freezin' though, queen? It's cold enough for two pair o' bootlaces, as me dad would say. And you have to watch the gutters where the water's froze hard – me mam went a terrible purler only yesterday 'cos one of the boys had slopped water on to the steps when he brung it in and, o' course, it froze solid, didn't it?' She chuckled. 'Me mam reckoned she sailed through the air like a seagull. Lucky she weren't hurt when she landed, that's what I said to young Ivan, 'cos it were him that spilt the water.'

'I hate this weather because it gyps up my chilblains something cruel,' Lizzie said, as they made their way along the crowded pavement. 'It isn't too bad while you're out in the cold, because you're so numb you can't feel anything anyway, but when you get back in the warm and the blood starts flowing, ooh, isn't it agony?'

'Do you get 'em on your hands?' Dolly enquired. 'I get 'em on me wrists something awful. But it ain't long to Christmas and me mam's promised me a fur muff for me Christmas gift. I'll wear me old woollen gloves underneath it, of course, but we're hopin' to get rid of the worst chilblains wi' that. What are you gettin' for Christmas, queen, or is it to be a surprise?'

'I don't know,' Lizzie said rather guardedly. Usually, she and Aunt Annie discussed Christmas presents in great detail, but this year her aunt had not been so forthcoming. Knowing she had a little more money to spare, Lizzie was quite hopeful that her aunt might buy her something to wear. A new dance dress was too much to expect, she supposed, but perhaps a length of material might be forthcoming. She was quite looking forward to Christmas since she had decided that, at a time of goodwill to all men, she might expect a softening in their attitude from Geoff and Clem. Several times she had been sorely tempted to go round to the YMCA or to hang about under Houghton Bridge. She missed Geoff a lot but rather to her surprise it was Clem who was most constantly in her thoughts. She desperately wanted to heal the breach between them but was at a loss how to do it while he remained aboard *The Liverpool Rose* since it would be only luck which would take her to the canal when the boat was berthed there.

Christmas, however, was the ideal time for him to approach her to try to end their quarrel. Geoff, too, must surely consider the festive season a good enough reason for visiting number nine once more? So she was looking forward to Christmas on several different counts. Only the previous evening, Aunt Annie, who was a lot shrewder than most people gave her credit for, had suggested a Christmas party for those friends who did not have proper homes of their own – and anyone else who liked to come along. Lizzie had interpreted this, rightly she was sure, as a tactful suggestion that she should get in touch with Geoff and possibly with Clem also. The trouble was, she had gone down to the canal a couple of days previously only to find it completely iced over, save for a narrow channel kept clear by the constant passage of boats. She also noticed that there were fewer boats than usual moored alongside the bank, and those that were there were icing in even as she watched. She imagined that trade on the canals must slow down considerably in such weather and realised, with a stab of dismay, that finding Clem, let alone making it up with him, was not going to be easy.

'Lizzie! Don't go off in a dream, gal, I were askin' you whether you'd seen that feller you goes around with lately? He's at the YMCA, ain't he? Only my pal Andy works in the bank, same as your friend, and he says he's been awful down – your friend I mean.'

Lizzie jerked herself back to the present with difficulty. 'No, I've not seen Geoff for a couple of months,' she said briefly. 'We quarrelled. It was daft, a really stupid quarrel, but I've not seen him since.'

'But you still like him, don't you?' Dolly said shrewdly. 'Why not go round to his place, queen? Christmas is a time for makin' up differences.'

'Yes, you're right,' she said. 'I've quarrelled with me two best friends and the honest truth is, both quarrels were my fault, not theirs. So I'll be doing a deal of apologising in the next few days.' She smiled at Dolly, her heart lifting as she put the decision into words. What a fool she had been! But soon her lonely time would be over, and she would be back on good terms with Geoff and Clem once more. Taking both hands to the heavy canvas bag of groceries, she began to sing, carolling out the words at the top of her voice: '"Ain't she sweet, See her walkin' down the street, And I ask you very confidentially, Ain't she sweet".'

'Well, I never!' Aunt Annie, sitting before the fire in her favourite chair, with the *Echo* spread out on her lap, stabbed with one fat finger at the paragraph she was reading. 'You know old Arnold Sharpe, the ironmonger on Heyworth Street, the one who married a gal half his age? He's been and gone and turned his toes up! Now that sly little trollop is a rich widow woman, and much good may it do her.'

Lizzie, standing at the table rolling out pastry for a pie, stiffened, though her hands continued steadily with their work. So Dolly and the doctor had been right. Mr Sharpe was dead and Flossie was indeed a widow, though judging from what Dolly had told Lizzie, most certainly not a rich one. Well, it served her right for cheating on the old boy, Lizzie told herself, carefully lifting the round of pastry in both hands and tenderly placing it over the apples in the dish. She trimmed it to fit, thumbed it up round the edges, stabbed the middle a couple of times to let the steam escape and carried the apple pie over to the oven. With her back towards Aunt Annie, she said carefully: 'Poor old feller. Dolly Stewart told me he were poorly and not expected to live – he's a relative of hers, did you know? – but I didn't think it would be this soon.' She did not bother to correct Aunt Annie's assumption that Flossie was now a rich widow since that part of her friend's story might have been wishful thinking. After all, Dolly had not seen the will, had only heard tell of it through her second cousin, once removed, who stood to gain substantially if the story were true.

'Oh, well, I shouldn't grudge her. I had a deal of pleasure from me own little inheritance after me old aunt died. In fact, though I said it were a little inheritance because I didn't want no one gettin' ideas, it weren't that little, queen. It'll keep us comfortable for a year or two yet.' Aunt Annie grinned across at Lizzie as her niece straightened up and closed the oven door. 'Now suppose we have a little chat about Christmas presents, eh?'

A week later the news was out. Not that it appeared in the *Echo*, but the gossips were as good as a newspaper any time, Lizzie told herself, listening to the mutters and stifled giggles as she waited her turn to be served in the corner shop. Behind the counter, old Mrs Chadwick dispensed gossip – and received it – with almost as much speed as she sold sweets and newspapers. Now, she was leaning towards a skinny old woman with a seamed face and bedraggled grey hair and speaking in what was no doubt meant to be a confidential tone which, in fact, could clearly be heard by every customer in the shop. 'Mrs Grant in Heyworth Street were tellin' me all about the will reading. It seemed old Arnold Sharpe was as sharp as his name, 'cos he put one of these here new-fangled 'tectives on her trail and the feller caught her red-handed a-carryin' on wi' a seaman, most probably a black 'un, in the jigger right at the back of their house. Would you credit it? Talk about shameless, and her with her skirt over her head . . .'

'What did Flossie say when they told her?' the old crone said, gnashing her toothless gums with pleasurable excitement. 'Oh, I never did like that little tart – the times she's ordered me out of her shop, you wouldn't believe, sayin' I were dirty! There's nowt dirtier than an ironmongery, I used to tell her, but she'd bundle me out all the same. Whiles I were tellin' her my money was as good as anyone's.'

'So who's got the money then?' the woman behind the old crone put in eagerly. 'And wharrabout the law, eh? I thought a feller had to leave his money to his wife.'

'Ah, that's a common mistake folks make,' Mrs Chadwick said wisely. 'The money's gone to his daughter Millie, as it happens, and she told me that her father had pinned the detective's report to his will, just so there wouldn't be no argy-bargy like. Yes?'

Finding herself suddenly addressed, Lizzie fished a piece of paper out of her pocket and consulted it. 'Quarter of tea, quarter of sugar, and a half of rich tea biscuits, please, Mrs Chadwick,' she said glibly. 'So what'll happen now, Mrs C? Doesn't Mrs Sharpe get *anything*?'

307

'Norra penny,' the older woman said. She did not say it unpleasantly but as a simple statement of fact. 'I feel quite sorry for her in a way except you could say she got her comeuppance, like. Anything else, chuck?'

'No, that's the lot,' Lizzie said. Mrs Chadwick took her money and handed over her purchases. Lizzie made her way out of the shop and back towards the court. Her mind was seething with questions. Would this mean the end of the affair between her uncle and Flossie Sharpe? Surely it would! For a start, shame would make Flossie move as far away from Heyworth Street as she possibly could, and she would have to get work of some sort just to keep body and soul together. The knowledge that it was her own behaviour which had brought her low was no comfort, either. Come to that, the knowledge that it was also Percy Grey's fault would surely make her bitter towards him. Considerably heartened by this thought, Lizzie went under the arch and into the court, thinking thankfully that she would enjoy Christmas even more, knowing that her uncle was no longer sneaking out of the house to go to Flossie.

As she approached the door of number nine, however, a voice hailed her. It was Sally, wrapped up against the cold as thoroughly as Lizzie was herself. Clouds of steam surrounded her open mouth as she called her friend's name. 'Lizzie! Come here a mo, I want to talk to you.'

One glance at her friend's bright eyes and pink cheeks was enough to tell her that Sally, too, had heard the news. 'It's all right, Sal,' she said quickly, casting an anxious glance at number nine; the last thing she wanted was for Aunt Annie to share her own recent knowledge. 'I heard, at Chadwick's. Old man Sharpe's slipped off his perch and there's nowt but bad words for Flossie in the will. Isn't that what you were going to tell me? Only no one knows who the other man was – is – so least said, soonest mended.'

'No! Is that a fact?' Sally tucked her arm through Lizzie's and led her towards her own door. 'Well, my mam said Flossie were on the game before she caught old Sharpe, so perhaps she'll go back to that. There's plenty of customers down by the docks for a bottle-blonde with a sockin' great bust like Flossie's.' She giggled. 'No, I was going to show you the dress me mam bought me this morning. Ooh, Liz, it's ever so lovely! It's what they call a Princess dress – you know, with a layered skirt and lots of soft, unpressed pleats, and the back hem's longer than the front. It's georgette, with a square neck and no sleeves, but there's a lovely gauzy scarf to wrap around your shoulders if you feel cold. It's the new colour – dusky pink – with a bunch of deep purple violets pinned to one shoulder. Oh, Liz, wait till you see it!'

Lizzie followed her friend into her parlour and was soon admiring the new dress, though as she pointed out, it was so striking it would be hard to make it look different for future occasions.

'Oh, what does that matter? It's so pretty I wouldn't mind wearin' it a dozen times over the next few weeks,' Sally said exultantly, while her mother came bustling in with a tray of tea and a plate of smoking hot buttered crumpets. 'Are you comin' to the Grafton this evenin', Liz, or should we go to the Rialto? I know I shouldn't really wear it before Christmas, only Mam won't mind, will you, our mam? What'll you wear, Lizzie?'

The discussion over what she would wear and which ballroom they should frequent absorbed both girls to the extent that Lizzie almost forgot that Aunt

Annie would be waiting patiently for the packet of tea to arrive so that she might have a cup. She was reminded when her hostess offered her a refill and flew out of her chair, a hand going to her mouth. 'Lord above, me aunt's waiting for me to bring her back the messages so we can have a cuppa ourselves,' she gasped. 'Thanks for the tea, Mrs Bradshaw, but I'd best be getting back.'

As she hurried across the court once more, she reflected that though the interlude with her friends had not been planned, it was probably a blessing. She had managed to push Uncle Perce's behaviour to the back of her mind and now she would not be thinking about Flossie and her fate as she and her aunt enjoyed a cup of tea and some rich tea biscuits together. It was far better, she told herself, pushing open the door and calling out to her aunt she was back, that she simply stopped thinking about Flossie altogether. She would no longer be interested in a married man who could not possibly support her in the manner to which she had become accustomed during her marriage with old man Sharpe. In fact, Lizzie told herself as she entered the kitchen, this was an excellent excuse for going round to the YMCA and telling Geoff that her troubles in that direction were over . . . and asking him to forgive her for all the nasty things she'd said. Why, I'll go round there the first chance I get, she vowed, arranging the biscuits on a plate.

Warmed by her decision and by the fact that she need no longer worry in case her aunt discovered Uncle Perce's perfidy, she made the tea then cut two thick slices off the new loaf and sat down before the fire to toast them, telling her aunt gaily that they would soon be as fat as Sausage and Mash, what with hot buttered toast, tea and biscuits.

Aunt Annie, flushed from the warmth of the fire and by hot tea, said that she was a good deal fatter than either Sausage or Mash without the help of buttered toast, and the two women settled down in perfect amity to enjoy the unaccustomed treat.

'Geoff! There's a lady to see you.'

He looked up from his work. He and Reggie were in the shed, attached to the back of the YMCA. They were making skates from off-cuts of wood which Geoff had obtained from a friend at a local timber merchant's and hurrying to complete them before the frost relaxed its iron grip on the land. Geoff was in the act of attaching the blade to the base of the second skate, but when he saw who his visitor was, he stopped work, smiled rather stiffly and beckoned her in. 'Lizzie! Long time, no see, as they say. How have you been keeping?' He walked towards her, knowing that he sounded stiff and aware, as one always is, that his face would wear a guarded look. After all, the last time they'd met they had quarrelled and since then Lizzie had not made the slightest attempt to get in touch with him. 'What's up?'

He saw a tide of pink rise in her face and wished he had not asked the last question but told himself he had a right to wonder why she had come round after so long. He saw her take a deep breath and begin to speak and, impulsively, took her hand. 'Oh, Lizzie, it's good to see you! Do you want to talk here or would you rather come to the common room?'

Lizzie relaxed and the pink gradually receded from her cheeks. 'I wanted to say I was sorry for being so horrid to you the last time we met, and to tell you . . . well, that my worries over you-know-who are dead and buried, like her old man.' She glanced across at

311

the long wooden bench on which he and Reggie had been working. 'What's that you're making?' she asked curiously. 'It looks a bit like a skate.'

'First you apologise, then you insult me all over again,' Geoff said, grinning. 'It *is* a skate, you daft girl. Me and me pal Reggie's been toiling over them for a week now, scared stiff that the frost will go before we finish.' He turned to his friend. 'Reggie, this is Lizzie Devlin. I don't think you've met her but you've heard me talk of her often enough, I daresay. Lizzie, this is me old mate, Reggie Phelps.'

The two young people murmured hello and then Geoff took Lizzie's arm, addressing Reggie as he led her from the room. 'Shan't be more than ten minutes, old feller, so keep up the good work.'

Once he and Lizzie had reached the street, he grabbed her hands and gave them a squeeze. 'I've really missed you, young Lizzie,' he said. 'Let's not quarrel again, especially over something so silly. Now what's all this about your Uncle Perce – I take it that's what you meant?'

Lizzie told the story briefly but well. At the end of it, Geoff gave a low whistle and gazed into the distance, tapping his teeth with a forefinger.

'It *is* good, isn't it?' Lizzie said, a trifle apprehensively as the silence lengthened. 'It does mean that Flossie will have to find herself a new feller – one with money? And surely that means she'll leave Uncle Perce alone?'

Geoff frowned, looking down into her small, fair face and worried blue eyes. 'We -ell,' he said slowly, 'I daresay you're right and old Sharpe's death – and the will – should end the business. Only – only it gives me an uneasy sort of feeling. It's too neat somehow.'

He half hoped that Lizzie would disagree with him

but instead she gave a deep sigh and said: 'I know what you mean, actually. In fact, Uncle Perce's been quite different for weeks now, much nicer to Aunt Annie, and though he does go down to the pub of an evening, he isn't there long. They're sharing a bed-room as well, and he says nice things to me aunt when she makes a good dinner and doesn't harass the hens, either. And yet . . . and yet . . .'

Geoff gave a shiver and took hold of her shoulders, turning her back towards the house. 'It's too bleedin' cold to hang around out here, talking in circles,' he said. 'I'm sure you're right and everything's going to be grand from now on. If it isn't, it's something to face when it happens and not before. Now what are you doing Sunday morning? Only Reggie and me want to catch a bus which will take us up river a bit, so's we can find a frozen pond and try out the skates. Want to come along? There's only the two pairs of skates, but we can take turns.'

'I'd love to. Can I bring Sally?' Lizzie said eagerly. She smiled up at Geoff as they re-entered the work-room. 'We don't want to have another quarrel over a threesome, do we?'

He chuckled. 'You're right there, queen,' he agreed. 'Have you seen Clem since the quarrel?'

'No, we've not met,' Lizzie admitted. 'It's difficult, Geoff, because last time we were together, all I did was shriek at him. Now I've no idea when *The Liverpool Rose* is due back in again.'

'I reckon you've got a bit of apologising to do in that direction,' Geoff said, reaching out an affec-tionate hand and ruffling the rich gold of her hair. 'Poor old Lizzie, that'll teach you to lose your temper with us fellers.'

She laughed a trifle ruefully and then perched on a

tall wooden stool and watched as the boys carried on making their skates. Very soon the three of them were chattering away like old friends, full of the proposed expedition to try out the skates the following Sunday.

Aferwards Geoff walked with Lizzie to the tram stop and waved her off, then returned to the YMCA and went straight to his room. He was delighted that he and Lizzie were friends once more but the period that they had spent apart had taught him something. He liked Lizzie very much, she had been a good friend to him, but his affection for her was more like that of a brother for his sister. It had none of the restless yearning he had felt over the loss of Evie Evans. He still thought of her constantly, searched faces in the street for a glimpse of those lovely features, and believed that one day he would find her again. Until then, he was content to be friendly with Lizzie and to hope that she, too, would find someone she could truly love.

It was the creaking which woke Clem up. He had been cuddled down beneath his blanket in the butty boat with Brutus curled into the hollow of his body, their shared warmth making the cold bearable. At first, the creaking had merely entered his dreams and disturbed him not at all. Then it grew louder and somehow more threatening and he found himself sitting upright, his heart hammering, convinced that someone was attacking one of the boats.

The odd thing was that Brutus had not stirred until Clem sat up. Then he had stared, not out at the deck but at Clem himself, as though wondering why his master had awoken so abruptly. Knowing how the dog would rouse at a footstep on the towpath which no human being could possibly have heard, Clem relaxed a little. Whatever the creaking was, it could not be caused by an intruder. He was about to lie down again when realisation suddenly hit him. It was the ice! Before he went to bed, he had cleared a good two foot of ice from round the butty boat and *The Liverpool Rose*. Now, because of the extreme cold, it had formed again and was squeezing the hull, causing the creaking sounds.

In weather like this, no one undressed to go to bed though it was usual to remove one's garnsey and corduroy trousers. Clem was still clad in a thick woolly shirt, and underpants and his hand-knitted boat socks. Hastily, he heaved on corduroys, garnsey and clogs and reached for his jacket. He crawled out on to the deck and saw that he had been right. The ice round the boat was as thick as it had been when he had broken it up earlier; if he did not get a move on, they could easily find themselves trapped here until the boat was cracked open like a walnut shell, causing damage it would cost a small fortune to repair.

He seized the great iron bar which Jake kept for just this purpose and began hammering at the ice. As the first blow struck, he heard what sounded like an echo from the boat ahead and, glancing towards it, saw that Jake must have woken as he had and was freeing *The Liverpool Rose*. Brutus, making his way cautiously along the decking, was slowly wagging his plumed tail. Though Clem could see no one in the darkness, he realised the dog was greeting a friend and was not surprised when the boat heeled over as someone stepped on board.

'Clem? Want a hand wi' rocking her or is she too fast stuck already? Odd, ain't it, that we all woke at about the same time? If you get on to the stern, we can try what rockin' will do.'

'It's okay, Priddy, the ice isn't as thick as it looks, it's coming away in slabs now,' Clem shouted cheerfully. 'Any idea of the time?'

'Breakfast time,' she said. 'At least, it ain't breakfast time, it's more like five o'clock, but we might as well have our breakfast and then get moving since we're all awake. I've never wanted to own a fly boat – travellin' all night an' all day ain't my idea of a decent life – but in this sort o' weather, we'll be warmer moving than moored, I reckon. So when you've cleared the butty, p'raps you can get Hal out of the stable and tack him up. Leave his blanket on, 'cos it's mortal cold, and put an extra handful or two of oats into his nosebag, then he'll be ready to move when we are.'

'Right, I'll do that,' Clem said, and heard Priddy's footsteps retreating down the towpath. Presently he smelt the good smell of bacon frying. Away to the east he could see a lightening in the sky. He knew that dawn would soon be on its way and thought for the hundredth time how lucky he was. He had fled from a life in the coal mines, which he had hated, and fallen by the merest chance into a life he loved, for he knew he would not swap his place on *The Liverpool Rose*, not even for the job of King of England had it been offered.

Presently, with the ice cleared and a warm glow suffusing his whole body from the vigour with which he had attacked it, Clem took the lantern from where it hung above his make-shift bed, lit it, climbed on to the bank and went over to the dim bulk of the stables. Hal was in the end stall, sleeping on his feet as horses usually do, but he woke as Clem opened the half door and took down the harness from its hook on the wall. Clem led him down to the towpath with the tack over one arm since it would be far easier to tack the horse up out here, rather than within the confines of the stable. First he rubbed the horse down vigorously with a handful of hay and then buckled on the harness, slung the heavy collar round Hal's enormous shoulders then fastened on the swingle tree, from which the towrope would presently depend. Hal stood patiently while Clem worked, shifting his hooves occasionally on the iron-hard path, looking twice the size by lamplight that he did by day.

By the time Hal was tacked up, his nosebag satisfactorily full of good things and the towrope attached, Priddy was handing out thick cuts of bread, sandwiched together round equally thick cuts of bacon. Clem sat on the stern of *The Liverpool Rose*, with bacon grease running down his chin, while Jake told him that in future, because of the severity of the weather, they would have to have someone on watch whenever they were not moving, so that the boat could be rocked from side to side to discourage the ice from forming as it had done earlier.

'I dunno why I didn't think of it before,' he said, tipping his head back to look up at the fading stars. 'A clear night means a sharp frost and I knowed it would be a clear night, so what were I thinkin' of?' He sighed deeply and took a pull of tea from his tin mug. 'I'm gettin' old and careless, that's what,' he said sadly. 'You're such a good worker, young Clem, that I'm takin' it easy, leavin' you to do too much. But it won't happen again – can't be allowed to happen again – 'cos if we'd not woke when we did, we could have been drowned dead in our beds. That's what happens when a barge gets iced in an' cracked open. She just sinks when the water rushes in and because the water's so bitter cold, the crew don't get a chance to struggle out. They're dead before they know what's happenin',' he concluded.

Clem nodded soberly. He knew the old saying 'wooden boats, iron men', and had long ago realised that, though life on the canals was idyllic much of the year, it also involved very hard manual work and risks which landsmen never encountered. But even so, he reminded himself as the sky grew lighter, I wouldn't change it for a fortune, and nor would Jake and Priddy, whatever they may pretend.

Thinking about Jake and Priddy, who had spent all their lives on the canal, made him remember Lizzie and his half-formed hopes in that direction. Until he had acquired Brutus, Lizzie had seemed as fascinated by life on the canals as he was himself, and he had hoped that one day she might accompany them on a long-haul trip and see for herself the delights of the countryside he knew so well. He longed to show her Martin Mere, dreaming amongst the trees, home to a wide variety of water birds, whilst the small animals of the area had their homes within easy reach of it. Then there were the high moors and fells with a strange harsh beauty all of their own, brought about by the combination of the luxuriant, brilliantly coloured heather, gorse and broom which crowded every slope, and the great escarpments and obelisks of rock which pushed up through them.

But since the quarrel, Clem supposed that this trip was indeed nothing but a dream. Lizzie would never come with him now, even if he left Brutus with a friend aboard one of the other boats, and he could not see the dog agreeing to this. Like all Alsatians, the dog acknowledged only one master and, though he was strongly attached to Priddy and Jake, seldom left Clem's side unless ordered to remain behind. Then,

Clem knew, he would neither eat nor drink until his master's return, though he remained steadfastly at his post.

Trudging along at Hal's head with one hand looped through the cheek strap, Clem was aware of the dog at his side. He glanced down at Brutus and rumpled the fur behind his large pricked ears. 'You're a grand feller, so you are,' he said affectionately. 'If only Lizzie weren't so scared of dogs! But there's other girls . . . girls who've worked the canals all their lives and know how important it is to have a guard dog when you're passing through a bad area.'

Brutus looked up at him and grinned as though he understood every word, a cloud of steam escaping from his mouth as he did so. 'Who cares about girls?' Clem asked him teasingly, and tried to ignore the ache in his heart, surprised by how much he had missed seeing Lizzie when they had docked in Liverpool.

'It's still dreadfully cold,' Lizzie remarked as the two girls got off the tram on Scotland Road. They had just spent an enjoyable evening having a Christmas jolly with others from the bottling plant. The firm had booked the Rialto for the evening so that all the staff and their friends could have a Christmas party, providing refreshments when the dancing was over. It would have been even more fun had Geoff and Reggie been able to accompany them but with Christmas approaching fast Geoff had been working overtime at the bank, glad enough to augment his income at this time of year.

'Yes, I'm half-frozen, but it were a good evening even without the fellers. I do like them. Weren't the skating fun?' Sally said as they headed towards

Burlington Stret. 'If the frost holds we might do it again, I daresay.'

The skating party had been a great success. Lizzie and Sally had decided that their contribution to the day should be the nicest picnic they could afford. So Sally had made a mound of cheese, ham and egg sandwiches and Lizzie had contributed a large meat pie, a bag of rosy apples and a number of iced fairy cakes which she had made the previous day.

They had found a frozen pond easily enough and spent a glorious day taking turns on the skates which, despite being home-made, proved to be both sturdy and reliable. Neither Lizzie nor Sally had ever skated before, but Geoff and Reggie were patient and long-suffering since at first both girls fell over frequently, dragging their instructors down with them. By the end of the day, however, they had got the knack and were able to circle the pond with a degree of skill. In fact, at one point they formed a human chain across the ice with the girls, in their shoes, forming a centre pivot while the boys, using the skates, whizzed round the perimeter faster and faster, until Reggie lost his grip on Geoff's hand, allowing him to career off by himself, ending up in a tangled heap amongst the bulrushes which grew against the bank. By then, it had been growing dusk, and when they had rescued Geoff and made sure he was unhurt they had judged it time to make for the city once more, and went home in great good fellowship, almost falling asleep on the back seat of the bus.

Right now Lizzie and Sally turned into Burlington Street. With Christmas only a couple of days away the dances grew livelier and more festive, and because the girls were popular with their fellow workers neither had lacked for a partner all evening. None of them, Sally assured her friend, were as nice or amusing as Geoff and Reggie, though.

'I'm surprised you didn't click, Lizzie,' she remarked as they entered the court. 'Sometimes I wonder whether you even *try* to gerra feller, and it ain't as if you're serious wi' that Geoff because you told me weeks ago you weren't. Wharrabout the feller who wore that little knitted cap? He were keen, I could tell.'

'I'm not really interested in anyone right now,' Lizzie said evasively. 'Night, Sal. See you tomorrow.' She headed for the front door of number nine and was actually beginning to ascend the steps when she stopped short. 'Damn and damn and damn!' She had promised Aunt Annie that she would nip along to Paddy's Market before the stalls closed and pick up a chamber pot from the man who sold such things, Aunt Annie having mysteriously broken her own utensil the previous day. Lizzie had done just that, but had left the pot at the home of a friend who lived above a bicycle shop on the Scottie, meaning to get off the tram a few stops early to reclaim her property. The trouble was, the dance had been such a success and such fun that her errand had clean gone from her mind. She now hesitated on the step, wondering whether to go back and collect the Jeremiah or whether to leave it for tonight and fetch it in the morning, before she went to work.

It was very dark and quiet in the court, the paving stones gleaming silver with frost and not a soul about to help her solve her dilemma. Undecided, she began to walk slowly towards the arch and was just about to re-enter Burlington Street when she heard a door open very softly behind her. Glancing back, she saw a large male figure – undoubtedly Uncle Perce –

emerging from number nine. He went carefully down the steps and set off in the direction of the two lavatories which stood at the end of the court, with the drinking water tap between them. Feeling horribly guilty, for she knew her uncle would not normally have visited the lavatory in the middle of the night but would have made use of his chamber pot, Lizzie shrank back into the deep shadow of the arch. To her surprise, however, her uncle did not go into either lavatory, but merely bent over the tap for a moment. She heard the slow trickle of water and then he was walking back towards her, half crouching, in a very peculiar way.

He must have got awful stomach ache – but why didn't he go into the lavvy? Lizzie asked herself. Then her uncle turned abruptly about, almost running to the nearest lavatory, going inside and shutting the door softly. Lizzie frowned. This was very odd. Moving as noiselessly as she could, she tiptoed towards the privies, taking a diagonal line rather than following the path, so that she might dodge into the shadow of the nearest house should her uncle suddenly emerge. She was wearing her thick, dark winter coat, with her golden head swathed in a navy blue headscarf. If she kept the pale oval of her face turned away from him, she should be invisible amongst the deep shadows.

She had almost reached the door of the privy into which her uncle had dived when she heard the soft and breathy mumble of a voice. For a moment she thought that Uncle Perce must be singing to himself, then realised there were two voices, one deeper than the other. She frowned, listening hard, but could not make out so much as a word and finally concluded that someone else had occupied the left-hand privy and the two of them were conversing, as they did . . . well, whatever they had gone into the privy to do.

She was about to turn away when a horrid thought occurred to her. Suppose it was Flossie in the left-hand privy? The cold was biting into her face now, making her aware that though her boots were stout enough, her feet would soon be thoroughly chilled and there was nothing worse than having cold feet in bed. But having begun to suspect who her uncle's companion was, she knew she could not go quietly off indoors. She would have to wait and see who emerged – and where they went furthermore.

She had a long wait, or at least it seemed a long wait to Lizzie for she had no watch on which to check the time passing. She guessed it was a good ten or fifteen minutes before her uncle came out, closing the privy door quickly behind him and, to Lizzie's horror, not taking the normal path away from the privies but doing as she had done, walking close to the houses on the left-hand side and then cutting across to his own front door. Lizzie had held her breath as her uncle passed within six inches of her, but he was clearly concentrating on making as little noise as possible and had not so much as glanced in her direction. Lizzie waited for a moment, wondering whether to go over to the privies and see whether one, or both were locked, but finally decided against it. She was terribly cold and reasoned that if her uncle was so mad about Flossie Sharpe that he was prepared to meet her in a privy, of all places, then there was little she could do.

Lizzie waited until she was sure that her uncle would be back in bed and then set off across the court and slid her key into the lock of number nine. But to her surprise it would not turn and then she realised that Uncle Perce had not bothered to lock the door behind him. I believe that second voice was just a sort of echo, Lizzie concluded, opening the door noiselessly and slipping inside. I've wronged the old devil, that's what I've done. It's clear as daylight: he's got a bad stomach upset so he left the door unlocked for his next trip out to the privy. Oh, if only I'd remembered that chamber pot!

As she climbed the stairs, a clock began to strike the half-hour and she was glad she had not returned to her friend's house to pick up the chamber pot. She had not realised how late it had grown and even if Mrs Batchelor had not already gone to bed, she would not have welcomed a visitor at past midnight. Lizzie sat down on her bed and began to tug off her boots, then stopped short as she became aware that there were sounds coming from the room beneath hers. She could hear Aunt Annie's voice, peevish and complaining, and Uncle Perce's too, apparently telling her aunt to stop moaning and go back to sleep. Which is all the sympathy she'll get from him, Lizzie thought crossly. Oh, hell and damnation! I suppose they've both ate something bad and Aunt Annie's got a stomach ache as well and their chamber pot's bust so they're having to go down to the lav in the court. Lord, shan't I be in trouble tomorrow!

Presently, her guess was proved right; she heard Aunt Annie's feet thump on to the floor of the bedroom, heard her aunt stumbling down the stairs and struggling with the front door. Uncle Perce had left it unlocked but poor Aunt Annie did not know this and was trying to undo an already unlocked door before she could reach her objective.

Guiltily, Lizzie tiptoed over to the window. She knelt by the sill, looking out at the scene below her, dimly illumined by the court's one gas lamp. She

324

noticed, with some surprise, that someone had put what appeared to be a pile of bricks, close by the route to the lavatories, and wondered why she had not noticed it earlier. Then her attention was caught by her aunt emerging from the house, descending the steps and setting off at a stumbling run across the paving stones. She was level with the pile of bricks when her feet suddenly seemed to go from under her. She made desperate attempts to keep her balance, arms flailing, and then went down heavily, her head striking the pile of bricks with a thud which Lizzie could hear even through the glass of the window pane.

She gave a stifled shriek and leapt to her feet. She ran across to her bedroom door when something stopped her. She stood for a moment, one hand to her hammering heart, and listened. Uncle Perce was descending the stairs, wheezing and muttering. He too must have been watching her aunt's progress through his bedroom window on the floor below her own.

For one awful moment, Lizzie wished herself any-where but here. But her body, it seemed, had already made up its mind to go and do what it could for her aunt. She found herself wrenching open the door and running down the stairs, only moments after her uncle had crashed out through the front door. He went straight across to where his wife lay and bent over her. Lizzie heard another thump and before she could stop herself had run across the court and was grabbing Uncle Perce by the arm. He turned and stared up at her, his congested face looking almost black in the gas light. He still had a hand on either side of her aunt's head and Lizzie, dropping to her knees beside him and grabbing her uncle's arm, put a hand out towards the still figure, saying in a hissing whisper: 'What have you done, Uncle Perce? Oh, what have you done to me poor aunt?'

Uncle Perce stared at her as though he could not believe his eyes. 'What do you mean, what have I done?' he said truculently. 'I ain't done nothin' . . . Don't you have no eyes in your head? She slipped on the ice and crashed into them bleedin' bricks what some idiot's left right agin the pathway to the lavvies. I were in me room when it happened but I heard the crash and come runnin' to see what were up.'

Lizzie took her hand from her uncle's arm and looked uncertainly at him. 'Is – is she dead?' she quavered. She knew what she had seen – and heard – but suddenly realised that she was in a horribly dangerous position. Uncle Perce was a big, strong man, and could easily wring her neck with one twist of his huge docker's hands. She must pretend to accept his explanation until she could get away from him and tell someone in authority what had really happened.

'I dunno if she's dead or not, I'm not a bleedin' doctor . . .' Uncle Perce was beginning, when another voice broke across his. A woman had approached them so quietly that neither Uncle Perce, nor Lizzie noticed her until she spoke, and Lizzie realised that she was hidden from the newcomer by her uncle's bulk.

'It worked like a dream, me love,' Flossie Sharpe said exultantly. 'If she ain't dead yet she'll freeze to death afore mornin', so we might as well . . .'

'Shut your bleedin' gob, Floss,' Uncle Perce said urgently, but it was too late. Lizzie was already turning away, prepared to run, when her uncle grabbed at her leg. 'If you say a word to a livin' soul about tonight's work, your life ain't worth a groat,' he hissed, the words more frightening for the calm and matter of fact way in which he spoke. 'Since you know so much, you'll have to go,' he chuckled ominously. 'I'll tell folk you ran down the stairs too fast when you heard me shout for help 'cos your aunt were hurt, shot through the front door and broke your neck on the paving. Yes, that'll do nicely. Or you could be found floatin' in the Mersey . . .'

He shifted his grip on Lizzie's ankle, clearly intending to bring her down with a crash on the paving stones, but she was too quick for him. She wrenched herself out of his grasp and ran towards the arch of the court with no other thought in her mind than to escape. Where she would go and how she would behave, she had not the foggiest notion; all she wanted to do was to put as much distance between herself and Uncle Perce as possible. She felt terribly guilty that she had not remained to make sure Aunt Annie really was dead, but she had little choice. Percy and his paramour would think nothing of killing both her aunt and herself if their own lives were at stake, as indeed they must be while Lizzie lived to tell what she knew.

As she darted into Burlington Street, instinctively turning left and seeing, out of the corner of her eye, that both Flossie and Uncle Perce were hot on her heels, she thanked God she had had no time to undress and was still warmly and darkly clad in winter coat, headscarf and boots, to say nothing of her black woollen gloves. If she could find a bolthole and stay very still, she would be invisible to her pursuers. Fear and exertion were warming her now, but how long could this last? If she did not find help soon, or if her pursuers caught her, then she was in an unhappy situation indeed.

She had passed the entrances to two courts as she ran, glancing sideways into both but not daring to enter them. There might be a light on, someone might still be awake, but there was no guarantee she would not simply find herself trapped with Uncle Perce and Flossie barring the exit and she herself perhaps knocked unconscious before she could even scream. The courts were no use then. She reached Vauxhall Road and hesitated for a second . . . which way, which way . . . then glanced back. Flossie was twenty yards behind her, though Uncle Perce had dropped well back, one hand to his side. Lizzie prayed that he had a stitch like a spear stabbing him and ran on, heading like an arrow now for the Houghton Bridge and the canal.

She could see the bulk of the sugar refinery against the clear, star-spangled sky and ran on, feeling the first surge of real hope. Out in the street, with the gas lamp's glow revealing her every movement, Flossie did not have to tackle her but merely to follow. If she could reach the unlit towpath beside the canal, however, she might well find either help or a hiding place. She knew enough about the canal barges from talking to Clem to know that, should an intruder step aboard a boat, the crew would be instantly awake. Explanations would be difficult but by no means impossible. In fact, once she roused people who would listen to her story, she imagined Flossie and Uncle Perce would make themselves scarce. In the light of day, they could put forward lies about Aunt Annie's death, say that Lizzie had been dreaming, was over-imaginative and disliked her uncle, but in the pitch dark, with Lizzie so clearly distressed, no one was likely to hand her over to a man claiming to be her uncle. Flossie would simply disappear because it would not do for her presence at the scene of Aunt Annie's 'accident' to be made public.

She reached Houghton Bridge some way ahead of Flossie who had stopped for a moment to disentangle her heel from the tram lines in Vauxhall Road, and dived down the steep bank on to the towpath. As Lizzie had hoped, all was quiet and dark around here, with three canal boats moored to the bank, all of them looking alike in the faint starlight. Lizzie realised she did not want the tangle of explanations, lies and excuses which would be inevitable if she climbed aboard an inhabited boat and was accused of theft, or at least the intention of thieving. Accordingly she ran to a butty boat, moored behind the nearest craft, and with fingers crossed and a fervent prayer on her lips, lifted the canvas cover over the cargo. It was fleeces, bales of them. There hadn't been the stirring of a sleeper as she climbed aboard. This was an unmanned butty boat, and what better place to hide than amongst such a quantity of warm and cosy fleeces?

With a little mutter of relief, Lizzie rolled herself inside a fleece, so that she was completely hidden. She lay there for a long time, listening intently, but so far as she could tell there were no footsteps on the towpath, neither the click-click of Flossie's heels nor the heavier ones of Uncle Perce's boots, and presently, to her own surprise, she found that she was sleepy . . . was going to sleep . . . was asleep.

Packed into the fleece as tightly as a needle in a haystack, Lizzie temporarily forgot her troubles in dreams.

Lizzie awoke. She did not open her eyes but was conscious that a little light filtered through her lids and that she was being soothed by a pleasant rocking motion. I'm a little baby in a cradle, she told herself drowsily and tried to turn, but movement was hampered by something gloriously warm and springy in which, it appeared, she was closely wrapped. Swaddling clothes! Lizzie told herself. I'm a baby, wrapped in swaddling clothes, and lying in a manger. But that sounded wrong, pleasant but wrong. Mangers, she knew, were filled with hay, not with fleeces, and furthermore . . .

Lizzie's eyes flew open. She was neither wrapped in swaddling clothes, nor lying in a manger, nor was she a baby, pleasant though that might have been. She was Lizzie Devlin and she was wedged into the cargo of fleece carried by an unknown butty boat. For one blissful moment she could not remember why she was here, and then everything came flooding back. Uncle Perce had murdered Aunt Annie in cold blood, assisted by Flossie Sharpe, and she, Lizzie, had run for her life and escaped them by hiding in the butty boat.

Her next thought was less a thought than a realisation that the boat was moving, being towed along the canal by the mother craft, and this, when she came to think about it, was the ideal solution to her problem. She could remain snug and warm among the cargo until they were well clear of Liverpool. Then, when the boat's owners realised they had a stowaway aboard, she would have plenty of time to explain for they were unlikely to drag her off to the scuffers if she chose a lonely stretch of countryside in which to declare herself.

The more she thought about it, the better this plan seemed to be. She knew the canal wound for some considerable way through built-up areas of warehouses, factories, coal yards and grain silos, so she would have to stay where she was possibly for a day and a night. She had no idea whether the butty boat was being towed by a fly boat or by a company-owned craft or a bye-trader like Jake. Not that it mattered. Provided she kept out of sight for at least twenty-four hours, she should be in the clear.

Lying comfortably cocooned in fleeces, Lizzie considered her options. She could try and escape unseen from the butty boat and make her way to the nearest village, but if she did that she might be pursued by the boat's owners who would think her a sneak thief. No, on the whole, it seemed safer to throw herself on their mercy, tell them the whole dreadful story and appeal for their help.

Lizzie felt the slow tears begin to form in her eyes and trickle down her cheeks, but she told herself sternly that it was no use crying for Aunt Annie now and rubbed her eyes with the palm of her hands. She loved her aunt – had loved her, rather – but this was not the time to weep. She must sort out in her own mind exactly what had happened so that when she had to tell her story to strangers, it would sound both logical and possible and not merely a tangle of half digested guesses.

Finally, having decided to take her own advice, she began to try to piece together just exactly what had gone on the previous night. She realised now, of course, that her uncle had gone to the tap in the yard with a bowl or basin which he had filled. He had retraced his steps along the route to the privy, carefully wetting the paving stones as he went. Then he had returned to the relative warmth of the privy and waited there until the water had frozen hard before going back indoors.

He must have known that the chamber pot was broken, Lizzie reasoned, and must have given her aunt something to eat which he knew would drive her to the privy during the night. In fact, he had probably broken the chamber pot himself and had not told her aunt, hoping that she would not discover the loss until too late. He could not have known that she had discovered the broken utensil and asked her niece to buy another one. If only I'd taken the wretched thing home before the dance, then Aunt Annie might still be alive, Lizzie mourned to herself now. Although, on thinking it over, she realised that Uncle Perce would simply have smashed the new one under some pretext or other. Having planned the 'accident' so carefully, he would not let a little thing like a new chamber pot hinder his dark design.

Next, Lizzie wondered about the pile of bricks. They must have been there all the time, piled up against the nearest house; Flossie had merely moved them so that they became a dangerous obstacle to anyone using the slippery path. She wondered what her uncle would have done had someone else walked into the trap, but realised this was highly unlikely to happen. The icy weather kept everyone indoors, particularly at night, and most households used chamber pots and slop buckets when people needed to relieve themselves during the hours of darkness. No, Uncle Perce had been safe enough in assuming that Aunt Annie, and only she, would hurry down that slippery slope.

Everything was beginning to fall into place. She no longer wondered why Uncle Perce had not taken the direct route from the privies to his front door but had walked along in the shadow of the houses on the left-hand side of the court. He had had no desire to go arse over tip on his own murderous pathway and had doubtless been eager to get back to the house so that he might hurry Aunt Annie to her doom. He would have pretended that his own visit to the privy had been caused by the same pains which wracked Aunt Annie, and would have urged her to hurry down as he himself had done before an accident happened.

If they didn't eat something bad, Lizzie's thoughts continued, he must have given her something. Something which didn't taste . . . no, something whose taste would be masked by a stronger taste. She knew that Uncle Perce had taken to bringing in a jug of Guinness, saying that it would do Aunt Annie good. Her aunt always wrinkled her nose and complained, 'It's as bitter as any gall and thick as syrup,' but she drank it to please her husband. I bet he added half a bottle of syrup of figs to her Guinness, Lizzie told herself. What a wicked old bugger he is. It's plain as the nose on my face he never gave Flossie up at all, they simply went underground like Geoff said. But why kill Aunt Annie? Why not just move out, find another house for rent somewhere, and live in it with Flossie? Of course they couldn't marry, but Lizzie judged that neither of them would care much about that.

She was still puzzling over it when the solution popped into her mind. Aunt Annie was a woman of means now, with the nice little nest egg her elderly relative had left her. Aunt Annie would not dream of making a will leaving anything to anyone but her husband. So with his wife dead, Uncle Perce was now a man of substance, someone who could legally marry Flossie Sharpe and give her at least some of the better things of life to which she had become accustomed. Provided, of course, that Lizzie did not surface and tell her story. Lying back amongst the bundles of fleece, she began to cry in earnest at the thought of her aunt's untimely death and her Uncle Perce's treachery, and it had been partly her fault. If *only* she had not gone to the dance. If only she had brought the chamber pot back with her, as she should have done. If only . . . if only . . .

But useless regrets would not bring Aunt Annie back nor save Lizzie from danger for there was no doubt that if Uncle Perce could lay his hands on her, her life would be snuffed out as easily as a candle.

It was a grim prospect, but one which had to be faced. She must either flee from Liverpool, never to return, or find someone in whom she could confide. On that thought, Lizzie snuggled down into the fleece once more, and presently slept though her dreams were troubled and her cheeks wet with tears, for Aunt Annie had been like a mother to her and her heart ached for her loss.

Chapter Nine

Despite her unhappiness and the worries which should have beset her, Lizzie slept deeply and almost dreamlessly for the rest of the day, worn out by the terrors of the previous night. She finally woke to find the butty boat in darkness and obviously moored to the bank once more, for the slap and gurgle of water against the hull and the soft rocking motion had ceased.

Listening hard, she could just about make out the sound of voices coming from the towing boat, and then she heard a horse being led along the towpath and guessed that one of the boat's crew was stabling the beast for the night. She wondered how she would manage, how she would contain her hunger if delicious smells of cooking came wafting from the lead boat's cabin, and was astonished to realise that the only sound she could hear was that of receding footsteps; the crew were clearly taking themselves off, possibly to a local alehouse where she assumed they would have their evening meal.

When there was complete silence once more, Lizzie wriggled out of her nest and stood up gingerly on the small stern deck, looking around her cautiously. The boat had not been moored in open country but close by a small village; she could see the lighted windows of several cottages and, in the distance, what looked like an inn for its many windows were brightly lit and, despite the bitter cold, its door stood open. By peering hard ahead, she could see what looked like bright colours in some of the windows and remembered that Christmas was fast approaching. These must be paper chains and other decorations put up ready for the holiday. It was still extremely cold but the icy wind which blew against her face was welcome after the stuffiness of the fleeces. Looking along the canal, she saw that the ice was still thick although someone had cleared a pathway wide enough for two boats to pass so that the lights of the inn were dancing on moving water.

Lizzie looked around her but could see no living soul. She jumped down on to the towpath and went cautiously along to the lead boat. It was called *The Singing Lark* – she could just about read it by peering closely through the dark, for it was painted in yellow letters on a red background – and she thought it was a nice name and hoped the owners would be pleasant people. Having scanned the boat, Lizzie stepped aboard, her stomach churning at the sudden thought that a dog might leap from the cabin fangs bared and hackles bristling. No such thing happened, however, and to Lizzie's surprise, when she put her hand on the cabin door, it swung gently open, revealing a pleasant, firelit room, empty of any living thing.

Feeling a little like Goldilocks, and watching apprehensively for the return of the three bears, Lizzie stole into the cabin. She was desperately thirsty as well as hungry and was pleased to see a kettle pushed to one side of the fire and a line of mugs hanging from the hooks above the food cupboard. Working quickly, she put a pinch of tea in one of the mugs, added hot water and a spoonful of sugar from the large jar on the sideboard, stirred briskly and then drank every drop. She then repeated the whole exercise, finishing the second mug with as much alacrity as she had the first. Then she opened the food cupboard. She had half expected to see piles of Christmas goodies but possibly this boat was not arranged as Priddy's was for all she found was some poor-looking apples, half a rather stale loaf, a chunk of farmhouse cheese and a tin box full of ginger nuts. She cut herself a good hunk of bread and another of cheese, shoving them into the pockets of her coat, then glanced round her for a jug or bottle in which she could carry away water to last her for a while for she had decided to lie low until they were further from civilisation. By her calculations tomorrow was Christmas Eve so she would have to stay in hiding for a while yet. She had decided that Christmas Day would be a good time to cast herself on the mercy of the boat's crew. Surely they would realise that no one would stow away aboard a butty boat and miss their family Christmas save someone in desperate trouble?

There were a couple of jugs but she realised that they might be missed at once, and this would scarcely make her presence more welcome to the crew when she was found, or rather when she revealed herself. No, it would be better to go without a drink rather than risk discovery and subsequent disgrace, but there were the withered apples and she pocketed four or five of them; they were better than nothing, she decided, and would help to quench her thirst. The piece she had cut off the loaf, and the cheese, were scarcely likely to be missed.

She took one last look around the cabin, checking that everything was as she had found it, then opened the door and glanced out. After the fire-glow the darkness outside seemed complete but it was only for a moment and presently she got her night-eyes and climbed up on deck, jumped cautiously on to the tow-path, and made her way back to her nest in the stern of the butty boat. She would have said she could not possibly still be tired, after almost twenty-four hours, so far as she could judge, of sleep, but events soon proved otherwise. She settled back into the fleece and lay there for a while, listening for the approach of the crew. But she fell asleep to silence save for the occasional creaks as the boat moved on the water and the soft lowing of cattle on the further bank.

'Thanks very much, Mrs Goudge, good morning to you. Who is next, please?' Geoff looked into the face opposite and smiled delightedly. It had been an exhausting morning with the queue of customers on the other side of the counter seeming never-ending. It was grand to see a friendly face. 'Sally! Nice to see you. But why aren't you in work? Where's Lizzie?'

'I've sagged off work today because I don't *know* where Lizzie is, nor don't nobody else,' Sally wailed. 'In fact, I thought she might have run to you. Oh, Geoff, you would tell me if she had, wouldn't you?'

'I've not seen Lizzie since we went skating,' he said at once. He looked more closely at Sally's face and saw it seemed white and blotchy; it was clear she had been crying. 'Why should Lizzie run anywhere, queen? What's been happening?'

Sally leaned across the counter, resting her head on the grille which separated the bank employees from the general public. Lowering her voice, she said: 'Oh, Geoff, dreadful things have happened and I've got to speak to you. When's your dinner hour? Can I wait somewhere outside so's we can meet? It's desperate that we find Lizzie as soon as we can. If we don't . . .'

Geoff glanced at the clock which hung on the wall

to his right. 'It's me dinner hour in ten minutes,' he said, keeping his voice low. 'Make out as if you were a customer, queen, or sure as eggs is eggs someone will complain that I'm talking to a pal instead of attending to business. Look, I reckon it's jolly cold outside so how about meeting me in a quarter of an hour, outside Cottles's? We can get a cup of tea and a sandwich there and talk while we eat.'

'Cottles's in fifteen minutes, right.' Sally said, turning briskly away and hurrying out of the bank. She left Geoff with his mind in a whirl, wondering what on earth could have happened, but the next customer soon brought his mind back to his work and in fact the ten minutes until he was relieved by another bank clerk passed quickly though the worry never quite left his mind. By the time he reached Cottles's, in fact, he was running and as he stopped beside Sally so breathless that he could hardly get the words out.

'What the devil's been happening? You're real upset, I can tell. Oh, we'd best not stand here on the pavement chatting, let's go and grab a table.'

They managed to get a corner table and when their tea and sandwiches arrived, Sally began her tale. 'I'll start at the beginning,' she said, 'otherwise you're not going to understand why I'm so worried. As you know, Lizzie and I went to the works Christmas do last night, the way we told you we would, and came home on the tram around half-eleven, I suppose. We'd had a grand time and Lizzie was as cheerful as anything, talking about Christmas and what we'd do if there was snow, 'cos when we were kids, we used to sledge down Everton Brow on wooden tea trays and have all sorts of fun. We parted outside our doors and I went in. I made meself a cup of cocoa and went upstairs to get ready for bed, though it were such a cold night I didn't take an awful lot off. I don't know what made me think of it, but just before I got into bed I remembered something.' She glanced rather shyly at Geoff across the white-clothed table which separated them. 'Lizzie's aunt had bust her guzunder – her chamber pot, you know – and Lizzie had bought her a new one from Paddy's Market earlier in the evening. Only no one would want to walk into a dance hall wi' a jerry under her arm, would they? So she left it with old Mrs Batchelor who lives not far from the hall. We meant to pick it up on our way home, but as we came out of the hall, a tram drew up right alongside and we hopped aboard without giving the matter another thought.'

'I'm glad you had a good time despite me and Reggie not being with you and I can understand you forgetting the jerry,' Geoff said, grinning. 'It ain't the sort of thing you have on your mind when you've spent the evening dancing. Go on, then.'

'Well, I got to wondering whether Lizzie had gone back to fetch the thing by herself, and that worried me. There's a lot of drunkenness about, so near Christmas, and she could have run into trouble. Even so, there weren't much I could do about it, but something made me gerrout of bed and go over to me window. I looked across at number nine and the door were open which really did strike me as queer. I mean, our houses is cold enough wi'out leaving your front door ajar! I were just wonderin' whether I ought to nip out and close it when a movement caught my eye and I looked sideways, up towards the end of the court where the – the tap is, you know. There were two or three people in a group, lookin' down at somethin', and suddenly one of them broke away from the others and went tearing out of the court with the others close on her heels. It were Lizzie, I'd know her anywhere, even though she had a dark headscarf on which covered most of her hair. And the feller were her Uncle Perce. I dunno who the other one was, but I'd put money on it bein' that bleedin' Flossie.'

'What the devil were they doing?' Geoff asked, seriously worried now. If Lizzie had caught Uncle Perce and Flossie in a compromising position, he thought it very likely that Uncle Perce might take a terrible revenge. 'Dear God, that man was violent!'

'I dunno what they were doing, but before I'd really thought, I was jamming on my boots and getting dressed. I swear it didn't take me more than two minutes, but even so I were well behind them when I burst on to Burlington Street. Lizzie were already out of sight, but Mr Grey were still stumbling on under the lamps, clutching his side as though someone had knifed him. I began to foller but when he reached Vauxhall Road, he met someone – couldn't see who – and while they stood there talkin', Mr Grey glanced back up Burlie, and – and I took fright. I knew Lizzie had got away, but I didn't know where she'd gone and I'm real scared of Mr Grey – bash you as soon as look at you, he would – so I went home.'

'And you *still* don't know where Lizzie is?' Geoff asked. 'Surely you went round this morning to call for her, when it was time for work?'

'Well, I would have,' Sally explained. 'Only this morning the place were full of scuffers and under-takers and all sorts. It seems poor Aunt Annie gorrout of bed during the night to go to the privy and slipped on the ice. She cracked her head open on a pile of bricks – the scuffers said a dog or cat must have knocked them over – and she were dead by the time Mr Grey realised she'd been gone too long and went down to see if she were all right. Though if you believe that, you'll believe anything,' she added viciously. 'I dunno how he done it, Geoff, but I reckon he must of give her a shove or something, and Lizzie saw and ran for her life. Only – only where *is* she?'

'Did they turn left or right along Burlie?' Geoff asked. 'I bet it was left.'

'Aye, it were left,' Sally said immediately.

'If she went to the left then she'd have gone to the canal,' he said positively. 'Best thing she could do, 'cos it's a long run to Shaw Street and she couldn't be sure anyone would be awake, even if she'd made it to the YM. But there's always boats moored alongside the towpath and plenty of places to hide. Look, this is an emergency. I'll nip back to the bank and tell the fellers to cover for me while I go and have a chat to Clem – if he's in the 'Pool, that is.'

'I'll come with you,' Sally said eagerly. 'Oh, I'm so glad I came to you, Geoff. I were so worried, I've not been able to think logically at all.'

And presently, having arranged matters with the bank, he and Sally set off for the canal.

Clem was hurrying. *The Liverpool Rose* had docked alongside the wharf earlier that morning and unloaded her cargo almost immediately. Because it was so near Christmas, they were taking grain up to Leeds, rather than the more perishable cargoes which Jake usually favoured, and this meant a straight run through, not having to stop at canalside villages and towns to unload small quantities of fruit, groceries or even sugar.

'Have you give that girl her woolly jumper, yet?'

Priddy had demanded that morning as they ate bacon sandwiches and drank mugs of tea. 'For the lord's sake, boy, stop shilly-shallying! Tomorrow's Christmas Eve and there ain't no better time to hand over a present than at Christmas. Gettin' grain aboard ain't no big deal – there's plenty of loafers hanging round the wharves, eager to earn a few bob humpin' sacks at Christmas time – so you go off and find your pal. You can kiss an' make up that silly quarrel first, then give her the present and ask her to come along here for a taste o' my home-made mince pies and a drink of cowslip wine. What do you say?'

'Thanks, Priddy,' he had said gratefully. 'I've been a fool not to have contacted her before, but the truth is her aunt made me feel so uncomfortable that it put me off visitin'. I kept hopin' Lizzie'd come down by the canal to search for me but I suppose it was askin' a bit much. She would have had no idea when we were due in or how long we'd be here. But before I go, I'll see the butty boat is laden properly – you and Jake will have your hands full with *The Liverpool Rose* and I don't want to find myself tipped into the canal because the grain hasn't been loaded evenly.'

So here he was, directing operations and trying not to think about the ordeal ahead, for it would be an ordeal, Clem was sure of it. Yet even as he thought this, he could feel a warm and pleasant glow of anticipation at the prospect of seeing Lizzie again and making friends with her once more.

Finally, the butty boat was loaded. Wiping sweat off his brow with a large spotted handkerchief, Clem was about to return to the cabin to fetch Lizzie's present when he heard the clatter of approaching footsteps along the towpath and saw Sally and Geoff approaching at a run. He went towards them but before he could so much as open his mouth, Sally was shooting questions at him. 'Where's Lizzie? Have you seen her? Oh, Clem, if you know where she is, for God's sake tell us 'cos we're mad with worry, me and Geoff here.'

'I've not set eyes on her for three months,' he said briefly. 'What's up? Don't tell me Lizzie's in trouble?'

It was like unleashing a dam. With interruptions from Geoff when Sally's tale grew confused, Clem soon knew as much as they did about the strange events of the previous night. When the story was finished, he looked grim. 'So you're fairly sure she came to the canal?' he said thoughtfully. 'If only we'd not moored up after going through the last locks . . . but there it is, we did, so I weren't around when I were needed. Are you *sure* she came to the canal?'

Sally shrugged helplessly. 'We aren't sure of anything,' she confessed. 'It just seems the likeliest place for her to make for, don't you think? The streets round here are fairly well lit – it would have been difficult for Lizzie to hide with the others so close – but the towpath would have been in darkness and I'm sure she felt the canal folk would stand her friends, even if *The Liverpool Rose* wasn't moored up here. Come to that, she might have hidden aboard one of the boats and got clean away. If she had hidden ashore, I guess she'd have gone searchin' for me or Geoff as soon as it was light, to tell us what had happened. But we've neither of us seen her so I'd take a bet she went off on one of the boats as soon as it loosed its moorings.'

Clem nodded, but inside his head, a terrible picture was forming; one of Lizzie, with her blonde hair streaming around her, floating face down in the canal. If her Uncle Perce had caught her up on the towpath,

344

what easier way to dispose of an unwanted witness to whatever dark deed had been done than to tip her into the icy water? She would be dead in a couple of minutes and since there had been no onlookers, folk would think that in running away from the horror of her aunt's death, she had missed her footing and plunged into the canal.

He did not say this to Sally, however. 'Have you spoken to the scuffers or told your mam and dad what you saw?' he asked her. 'I think you should, honest to God I do. They'll mebbe not believe you but it will make them think.'

'Aye, he's right, Sal,' Geoff said. He turned back to Clem. 'What else should we do, mate? I'm really worried about Lizzie. Anything could have happened to her.' Over Sally's head, the eyes of the two lads met and locked. Clem realised that Geoff, too, feared the worst, but would not say so before the girl.

'Tell you what, Geoff,' Clem said, 'you go with Sally and back up her story as best you can. I'm going to have a word with every boat crew moored along this bank – and further, if need be. Someone must have heard something, or if they didn't, at least they'll know the names of the boats which were moored up here last evening. That'll mean we'll be searching for a fugitive on half a dozen boats and not a couple of hundred.'

Geoff and Sally agreed with this and they parted; Clem first went aboard *The Liverpool Rose* to explain to Priddy and Geoff why he wasn't going to visit Lizzie at her home in the court. When he had explained, the old couple agreed that he must question the crews of the boats still moored alongside about the events of the previous evening, while they would get ready to depart.

'And don't think I can't guess you're worryin' young Lizzie might have ended up in the canal rather'n on it,' Jake said quietly to Clem as the two of them left the cabin. But remember, lad, a body fallin' in the water makes the most almighty splash. I'm tellin' you, every boat owner, every member of every crew, would have come shootin' out of their cabins to see what were up and that gel would have been fished out of the water before you could say knife. So there's one worry you can put *right* out of your head.'

Despite his long experience on the canal, Clem had not thought of this and felt a considerable degree of relief to hear it now. Of course, it was no guarantee that Lizzie was not hurt or even a prisoner, but at least he need no longer worry that she had been drowned. So it was with a much calmer mind that he set out along the bank to question the crews of the boats still moored there.

Geoff and Sally came out of the police station on Rose Hill and without exchanging a word made for Burlington Street once more. But when they drew level with Agnes Thorn's tea-room, Geoff caught Sally's arm. It was an extremely cold day, though the frost had given way to sleety rain, and it had been none too warm in the police station. In fact, he thought, the air in there had been almost as cold as the authority's attitude to their story.

'It's awful cold and there's no use going back to the canal yet, queen,' he said. 'It'll take Clem a fair while to explain to every one of them boat people what happened last night and the information he wants. By my reckonin', they'll have to consult each other and search their memories to find out who were moored up alongside the towpath last night. We'll have a cup of tea and a warm-up first and then go down to the canal when Clem's had a chance to get some facts together. Once we know what they heard on the canal last night, we'll be able to make up our minds what to do next.'

The tea-room was not crowded and Geoff ordered two cups of tea and a pile of hot buttered toast. Moments later, the two of them were attacking the food and drink with gusto. 'What do you think the scuffers thought?' Geoff said, when the worst of his hunger had been appeased. 'That chap on the desk were a bit cautious, weren't he?'

Sally, wiping melted butter from her chin, grinned. 'It's a lot to swallow, I suppose,' she said, 'and I'm not referring to the buttered toast! I don't suppose anyone's reported Lizzie missing – why should they? Mr Grey will just say she's at work – may even say she weren't in at all last night 'cos she were stayin' with friends. Come to that, Geoff, I don't see any reason for him to mention her at all. So far as anyone knows, Lizzie weren't involved in any way in Mrs Grey's death.'

'I dunno,' he said. 'Surely Mr Grey would have said something about a niece what lived in the same house? Won't he have said he ran in to get help? If only the scuffer on the desk had *known* something about the case, but he didn't seem to know a thing, did he? I mean, he knew an old woman had slipped on the ice and broke her neck, but it seems as if there were no suspicion of foul play and hearing that the accident could have been engineered were real bad news and something he didn't want to have to take on board, especially just before Christmas.'

'Well, I don't suppose you can blame him,' Sally said fair-mindedly, crunching her toast. 'That was prime, Geoff. I were in such a state this morning I didn't even grab a bit of bread and jam before hurrying out of the house. Do you suppose we could order some more?'

He obligingly ordered more toast and a refill of tea and the two of them discussed the possibility of seeing some more senior member of the force than the constable on desk duty, who had seemed to regard their story as either unimportant or untrue. 'The trouble is,' Geoff said gloomily, 'it's all guesswork from you and second hand from me, if you see what I mean. What we want is Lizzie to stand up and tell the scuffers what she knows.'

'Well, when we catch up wi' her, I'm sure she'll do just that,' Sally said comfortably. By now they had finished the toast, so Geoff drained his cup and the two of them got to their feet and began to put on their outer clothing once more.

'Missing girls,' Geoff said thoughtfully as they left Thorn's tea-rooms. 'Just lately, me life's been full of missing girls. Did I ever tell you about young Evie Evans . . .'

'Yes, Lizzie told me all about her,' Sally said, and looked at Geoff with considerable respect. 'And you've been searchin' for her all this while when you only met her the once? She must have made a real impression on you, Geoff. And I always thought you were sweet on our Lizzie!'

'I've been sweet on Lizzie since she were about ten,' he admitted briefly. 'But in a way, I believe I always thought of her like a sister. Evie Evans . . . I don't know, she seemed so – so vulnerable, and that Sid Ryder's a nasty piece of work. I wouldn't want any girl I was fond of involved with him. So, right from the start, I felt Evie needed help. Now Lizzie's a different kettle of fish. She's strong, is Lizzie, and independent, too. She fights her own battles and she'll take on anyone. For all she seemed so smart and knowing, I didn't think Evie was like that. I've wondered since meeting her whether she was a kid from an orphan asylum, like what I am. Of course, she's a working woman now, but I reckon being brought up in an asylum makes you a bit different. They do so much for you that when you have to go it alone, it's awful hard.'

'I expect you're right,' Sally acknowledged. 'But it sounds to me as though she's left Liverpool altogether. She's obviously so striking and beautiful that if she'd been around, surely either you or Lizzie would have come across her by now? I suppose she couldn't have gone with Sid, when he left?'

'No, I'm sure not,' Geoff said positively. 'I met him with all his luggage on Lime Street Station, remember. He was heading for pastures new and there was no sign of Evie anywhere.' He heaved a sigh. 'Oh, well, it's one of life's mysteries that I'll probably never solve, so I might as well stop trying.'

As he spoke, they reached the entrance to Cranberry Court and both glanced sideways into its dinginess, but nothing stirred. They continued on their way and presently descended the side of the Houghton Bridge and back on to the towpath.

But here a surprise awaited them. There were a great many boats loading and unloading, and a great many people bustling to and fro, but of *The Liverpool Rose* there was no sign.

'What the devil . . .?' Geoff gasped. 'They can't have gone – Clem told us he'd find out what had happened and let us know. Perhaps they've just gone along to a wharf somewhere to get – to get – oh, I don't know, but there has to be a reason. Clem wouldn't just make off without a word to us.'

And presently he was proved right. A round-faced, cheerful girl with a scarlet headscarf wrapped around her lank, brown locks, and a black frieze coat closely buttoned to the neck, approached them, holding out a piece of paper. 'You Geoff and Sally?' she asked.

'That's us,' he said eagerly, taking the paper from her. 'What happened? Clem said *The Liverpool Rose* wouldn't be leaving until we got back.'

'I dunno really,' the girl admitted. 'He went all along the bank, askin' everyone who was moored up here last night whether any of 'em had heard a commotion or knew of any boat which had moved on earlier. Most of us don't take no notice of noise which don't concern us, but last night there weren't no noise. We were moored up and didn't hear a dicky-bird – mind you, it were so bleedin' cold only an idiot would have been out in it, if you ask me. So, anyway, Clem had done about half the boats and had barely got aboard the Johnsons' craft – she's the *Mary Ellen* from Burscough – when he came haring out o' the cabin and made straight for *The Liverpool Rose*. I heered him yell suffin' at Jake – couldn't hear wharrit was – and next thing I knew they was castin' off and he were thrustin' a bit of paper at me and telling me to give it to you jest as soon as you appeared.' She stared curiously at the paper. 'Why don't you read it?'

Her curiosity was plain but since the paper was not even folded, Geoff assumed she already knew what was on it and said, rather impatiently: 'Oh, come on, you must know already! It can't be a secret from you since Clem didn't even fold it in two!'

The girl gave him a glance which somehow managed to combine shyness and amusement. 'I'm

Jenny Finnigan. I were born and bred on the canal an' I can't read nor write, like me mam and dad afore me. Go on, tell us what it says!'

Geoff spread out the note while both girls watched him eagerly. '"Geoff and Sally",' he read, 'Can't stay, but I got the information I wanted and we're hot on the trail. As soon as we catch up with Lizzie, we'll bring her back but keep her in the cabin while Jake or myself come ashore in search of one of you. Sorry we couldn't wait, but it's vital we find her soon. Clem".'

'Well, that seems straightforward enough,' he said, folding the note and shoving it into his pocket. 'Thanks, Jenny.' He took Sally's arm and the two of them headed for the Houghton Bridge. As soon as they were out of earshot, Geoff turned towards his companion, lowering his voice. 'Doesn't that seem odd to you, Sal? Why was it so urgent that *The Liverpool Rose* set off at once? Clem must have learned something he couldn't put down on paper – he never even said Lizzie was safe and well.'

'I reckon the fact he didn't say it means we can take it for granted,' Sally said comfortably. 'He said he were hot on the trail after all. I feel ever so much better about Lizzie now. I'm sure she must be all right and will soon be back with us and tellin' her story to the scuffers. It'll be a great weight off me mind when she does, 'cos I shouldn't think her life would be worth tuppence if that there Uncle Perce of hers thinks she knows too much.'

'Come to that, you'll have to watch your step, young Sally,' Geoff remarked as they made their way along Burlington Street. 'I know you're not alone in the world like Lizzie is now – you've gorra good mum and dad to look after you. But if Mr Grey knew that you knew things, you'd be in deep trouble, I'm tellin' you straight. He'd look for some way to stop your mouth, and that could be as dangerous for you as it is for poor Lizzie. Because I'm sure as sure that's why she ran and hasn't come back. She'll know she's the only person who could send him to the gallows, right enough – she's no fool, our Lizzie, and she's no friend to Percy Grey either.'

Sally sighed. 'I'm sure you're right, chuck, but don't it sound sort of – of – melodramatic? It's more like a play than real life – ole Uncle Perce searching the streets so that he can bump off anyone who suspects what he's been doin'.'

'It may sound a bit like a play, but don't forget, queen, he's already bumped off Aunt Annie, though I don't understand why he should have done such a thing. I mean, his bit o' stuff – Flossie Sharpe – has been happy enough to go with him without expectin' marriage. Indeed, I should think she's had enough of marriage, what wi' missin' out on old Sharpe's will an' all, to say nothing of being made to look pretty small at the will-readin', from what your pal told you.'

'Yes, I know what you mean,' Sally acknowledged. 'Where's the advantage to him of poor Aunt Annie being dead? Oh, he'll have the house, but it's only rented, same as ours is, and he must know that Flossie wouldn't be welcomed as a neighbour in the court, not after Aunt Annie. She were such a good woman, Geoff, did all sorts for others who lived in the court. She'd baby-sit, or cook, or give a hand when someone were ill . . . she'll be sadly missed.'

'I wonder what'll happen to Sausage and Mash?' Geoff asked idly as the two of them reached the entrance to the court once more and paused on the pavement outside. 'I remember Lizzie saying that her uncle hated the hens at first, though latterly he put up wi' them, partly for the eggs but mostly for a quiet life, 'cos Aunt Annie fair doted on the pair o' them.'

'If he's in I'll nip over and ask whether he'd like me to take care o' them for him. I could ask him at the same time if he's seen Lizzie since she wasn't in work this morning,' Sally said glibly, but Geoff shook his head at her.

'No, don't do that. It's too dangerous right now. Wait until tomorrow morning, then if there's still no sign of her, get your mam to go over with you. He won't dare do nothin' if there's two of you. Well, I'm for the bank. Will you come round tomorrow after work and tell me what happened and whether Lizzie's turned up?'

'Yes, of course I will, although I doubt there'll be any news. But why don't you come round to our place on Christmas Day and have your dinner wi' us? You'd be ever so welcome, and Mam was saying that Lizzie must come to us now her auntie's gone . . . so there'll be plenty of food. Go on, say you will!'

'That's kind of you, and I'll be glad to come,' Geoff said at once. He knew that the YMCA would do their best to make sure everyone had as good a time as possible, but he had had too many institutional Christmases to think that they might succeed. 'A real Christmas would be a treat,' he concluded. 'Tell you what, Uncle Perce knows I'm a pal of Lizzie's so the pair of us will beard the old devil in his den and ask for news of her. You can say you went into the factory this morning and she wasn't there – which she wasn't, of course – and you want to know what she's planned to do tomorrow now that her aunt's died. You thought she might be taking a day off to arrange the funeral.'

'All right. Just let's hope that ole Perce doesn't say that he's planning to have Sausage and Mash for his Christmas dinner, though,' Sally said with a shiver. 'If he thinks of it, he's likely already stretched their necks for 'em.'

'Like he's probably scared stiff they'll stretch his if Lizzie opens her mouth,' Geoff muttered ghoulishly as they climbed the steps to the door of number nine. 'You'd better let me do the talkin', queen, because he'll know – or think he knows – that I don't know nothing.'

Sally gave a wild giggle, clapping her hand over her mouth to stifle the sound as Geoff lifted the knocker and brought it down hard on the blistered paint of the front door. 'You and your. . . if he knew what you knew and he thinks he knows,' she spluttered, then stopped short as Geoff gave her a glare and a hard nudge. 'Sorry, sorry, I'll keep me gob shut, I promise.'

But the promise was not needed, for though they knocked several more times no one answered the door; within all was silent, not even the hens clucked or scratched, and when, highly daring, Geoff pressed his nose against the glass and stared into the kitchen, he was only able to report that the fire was out, the hens apparently gone and the place deserted.

'There! If the hens have gone he'll have wrung their poor necks for them, Sally said with a little catch in her voice. 'Oh, Geoff, they weren't really like hens at all, they were more like pets. Annie were ever so fond of them and they trusted people, thought all folk were their friends. They'd have gone to Mr Grey without a qualm. Well, I just hope he gets his comeuppance, that's all.'

The two of them descended the steps and were

about to cross the court once more when Mrs Figgett, who lived at number ten, came out of her door and called them across. 'If you're wonderin' about them hens then I've gorrem safe,' she said in a conspiratorial tone. 'I were up early on Tuesday morning, hearin' all the fuss and fluster when the scuffers and the ambliance an' that come callin', an' I see Mr Grey go off, leavin' the front door a bit ajar. So, I nips in, don't I, to see whether he fed them hens. Poor old Annie thought a deal of them hens – they was like children to her and she were a good pal to me, so I knew where she kept their corn and I give 'em some and some odds and ends of scraps. Then I began to worry what 'ud happen when Annie's old feller came back 'cos he's got a nasty temper on him and very little patience. So later in the day I went and fetched the hens and their corn an' that over to my place, an' they've bin there ever since, happy as pigs in muck.' She looked anxiously at Sally. 'Were that all right, d'you think, queen? I reckon Percy come back at dead o' night on the Tuesday, but he went off again wi'out doin' the hens no harm, thank Gawd.'

'I think you did exactly right, Mrs Figgett,' Sally said earnestly. 'Lizzie will be ever so grateful to you for saving Sausage and Mash. In fact, I sure she'd happily give you the hens to keep for your own, because she'll have nowhere to put them.'

'Well, that's what I thought,' the little woman said, looking vastly relieved. 'They won't be no one's Christmas dinner while they're under my roof!' And with that she waddled back into her own house.

'Well, I'm real glad the hens are safe,' Sally said frankly as she accompanied Geoff to Burlington Street. 'But it fair gives me the willies, knowin' the old devil's livin' right opposite me. I suppose he's searchin' the city for Lizzie.' She shuddered. 'I pray to God he don't find her!'

Clem, trudging along the towpath with a hand hooked into the ring of Hal's bit and Brutus walking so close that he could feel the dog's warmth against his knee, was scarcely conscious that it would soon be Christmas, nor that the rain had started once more and was driving coldly against his face. All he could think of was the need to hurry, hurry, hurry. He knew that Hal was doing his best to keep the barge moving, even though there were still considerable areas of the canal iced over, so that the craft could not round the corners as neatly as usual, though the locks, he thanked God, were clear.

On board *The Liverpool Rose*, Jake was as aware as Clem himself of the need to move swiftly, though Priddy, now in charge of the butty boat, had told him that he was probably worrying unduly.

'You said yourself that of the dozen or so boats moored alongside the canal last night, she could have sneaked aboard any one,' she had reminded him when she had tried to persuade him to call a halt while they had a bite of dinner. 'You're lookin' on the black side, Clem, and no good ever came of that. After all, most folk on the canal would give a hand to a gal in trouble. In fact there's only one crew what moored up in the 'Pool last night that I'd not trust to take care of *The Liverpool Rose*, even fully loaded.'

'But Prid, canal folk is law-abiding, I've heard you say so a hundred times. I think most of 'em would have took Lizzie's side, gone to the scuffers with her, done something positive to help. There's only one lot who would have shove her on board and taken her away for their own ends, though heaven knows what those might be. That's why I don't want to stop, not a moment longer than we have to.'

So they had eaten bacon sandwiches followed by chunks of bread and honey as they travelled, never neglecting to ask every craft that passed whether they had seen a young girl with a long, blonde plait aboard a vessel heading towards Leeds. All the replies had been in the negative, but that did not stop the Pridmores and Clem from asking, though as the day wore on there were fewer and fewer boats actually traversing the canal. Most of them were getting a good mooring so that they could enjoy Christmas amongst friends with the possibility of a jolly evening spent at the nearest public house before the holiday closed down the inns and alehouses.

Clem knew that they would have to moor up for the night since it would not be fair on Hal, Jake and Priddy to try to press on during the hours of darkness. Besides, doing so might well mean that they missed seeing the very craft Lizzie was on, for they could scarcely wake the crew of every boat they passed to enquire whether they had a passenger aboard. And tomorrow, Clem reflected, the chances were that no boat would be stirring which would make their search considerably easier. On Christmas Day, the boat people would welcome friends dropping in to exchange the compliments of the season and to share a glass or two and a chat. Yes, tomorrow would be a good day to continue their search.

They had passed through Burscough earlier in the day, without stopping, Clem having ascertained as he led Hal past the Farmer's Arms, by the New Lane Swing Bridge, that none of the boats moored alongside were those for which he searched. As they passed the cottages on New Lane, he glanced sideways, as he always did, at Priddy's little place. For some months now it had been empty, the old couple who had rented it from her having moved further along the canal to Appersley Bridge to live with their married daughter. Priddy had talked vaguely of the possibility of re-letting it, but Clem did not think she would do so. He did not imagine that the Pridmores meant to retire while they were still hale and hearty, but he knew that Priddy looked forward to furnishing the place so that when they finally did, they could simply move into the premises which had housed members of the Pridmore family for many years.

However, Burscough having passed by in the grey afternoon, the long run to the Wigan locks and swing bridges lay ahead, and Clem could only hope that the Wigan Wolves would be in their own homes rather than haunting the canal. After all, there was little traffic for them to prey upon and the rain, which had turned into a steady and unrelenting downpour, was surely enough to put off the most determined thief.

Events soon proved him right. They passed through the area in deepening dusk, having to light all their lanterns to see their way, and it was with considerable relief that Clem heard Jake shout to him to moor up under the big clump of willows which edged the water meadows, some way past the last bridge. He was eager to get on, and knew that Jake and Priddy sympathised, but he could tell by Hal's lowered head and slowing gait that the big horse was nearly done and must have rest and decent stabling on such a night. So they moored *The Liverpool Rose* up against the bank and Clem unfastened the tow rope and led the big horse across to the farmer's barn which they used when in the area and which was no more than ten minutes' walk from the canal. Once inside and out of the rain, Clem shed his jacket and cap and began the serious work of rubbing Hal down until the horse's rain-darkened coat was no more than damp and he could tell from the feel of it that blood, sluggish from the cold, was beginning to circulate freely once more. Brutus, who had been rolling in the hay to get some of the rain off his own shaggy coat, sat up and looked hopeful as Clem tipped oats, chopped straw, clover, beans and dried pea fodder into the manger. The big dog adored oats and would happily crunch up a mouthful of them if given the opportunity. He was also very fond of chopped sugar beet, so Clem fished around in the sack of food, found a few withered little squares, and let the dog pick them daintily out of his palm, enjoying the warmth of Brutus's soft tongue as he finished every last fragment.

Once or twice he had wondered whether the dog might be more comfortable sharing the horse's stabling for the night but Brutus, so close to Clem that he could feel every movement of the dog's big body, always left the stable when he did and accompanied him back to the boat. Tonight was no exception. Soon the whole family, including the dog, settled down in the brightly lit cabin to enjoy their evening meal and then get ready for the night.

'There's more rain on the wind,' Jake said later as he stepped on to the moonlit deck, the downpour having ceased for the moment. 'But there's some bitter cold ahead, if you ask me. It's clear enough now but it'll change during the hours of darkness, you mark my words. We'll move on as soon as there's enough light to steer by.'

Clem and Brutus went to their tiny sleeping cabin and despite Clem's worries and fears – or perhaps because of them – he slept almost immediately, dropping into a deep, though troubled sleep which was enlivened the night long by hideous dreams in which he was constantly just missing Lizzie and watching in helpless horror, as she fell deeper and deeper into trouble. Indeed, so bad were the dreams that he was glad to get up and begin to prepare for the day ahead, well before the sky had begun to grey in the east. Walking to the stable to fetch Hal, he thought that Jake had been wrong in his weather forecast. After the extreme cold of the past few weeks, the air on his face felt almost balmy. Abruptly, and for no good reason, he suddenly felt full of hope. 'We're goin' to find her, old feller,' he said to the dog trotting at his side. 'And she'll be all right and we'll all share a grand Christmas in the good old *Liverpool Rose*.' And with these words, he entered the barn and the day's work began.

Lizzie woke late on Christmas morning. She had expected to be bored by having to spend the whole of Christmas Eve hiding away in the fleeces but in fact had quite enjoyed the enforced rest. She managed to wriggle her way through the cargo until she could lie with her gaze on a level with one of the eyelets through which she got an excellent view of the passing scene. Being winter, and still extremely cold, the view might have seemed restricted to some, fringed as it was by frozen reeds and grass starched with frost, but to Lizzie it had the charm of novelty and what with passing craft and little villages, fields of sheep and woods and valleys, she managed to enjoy the day.

When night time came she waited for the gentle rocking motion to stop and indeed it had done so at a small village. But the stop had been a short one only and after no more than twenty minutes they had set off again and the boat continued to move forward, hour after hour, until at last in sheer weariness she had fallen asleep.

Now, she was surprised to find that the boat was motionless and that silence reigned. The crew had decided not to travel right through the night, she supposed, but had merely pressed on to some pre-selected destination. However, she had expected them to be up by now since she felt sure the morning was well advanced. She had thought they'd be making preparations for their Christmas dinner and probably cooking – and eating – a hearty breakfast, but clearly this was not the case. She lay for a little while, gazing up at the green canvas above her head, and then realised that there was something odd about the light which filtered through to her. It was suffused by a darker shade, as though someone had laid another covering over the canvas one she was growing to know so well, and presently, curiosity got her out of her nest in the fleeces and brought her to the fastenings at the end of the butty boat. Peering through the eyelets, she beheld a white world. As far as the eye could see, the country was completely blanketed with snow. Half horrified, half entranced, Lizzie unlaced the fastenings and slid out on to the tiny deck. She got carefully down on to the towpath and saw at once that they were in wild and uninhabited country, though there was a small stable-like building made from bales of straw piled one upon the other and roofed with canvas where, she supposed, the horse must be spending the night.

Looking around at the bleakness of moors and hills, Lizzie shivered. She had been half tempted to slip quietly away and find help in some hamlet close to the canal, but clearly this was not an option. She would simply have to throw herself on the mercy of the canal boat's crew and hope they would understand her predicament and allow her to remain on board until they reached a town or village where she might go to the authorities and explain what had happened.

Accordingly, she walked alongside *The Singing Lark*, climbed on to the deck and rapped, as hard as she dared, on the wooden doors of the cabin. This elicited no response at first, but upon her repeating her knock, a long moan issued forth, followed by a grumbling masculine voice complaining that his head was sore as a bear's, and that he was sure it waren't mornin' yet, not by a long chalk it waren't.

'It is morning,' Lizzie called in a small, apologetic voice. 'I dunno what time it is but it's broad daylight and there's snow.' Even as she spoke, big, feathery flakes began to descend once more, looking grey against the whiteness of the sky overhead, and the voice from within the cabin could be heard adjuring his companion to 'gerrout of his bleedin' pit and set a match to the fire afore they all fruz to death'.

Lizzie, listening, felt half inclined to scoot for the hills, despite the cold, but then the owner of the voice thrust the cabin door open and appeared on the deck. He was a jovial, red-faced man, probably in his mid-thirties, clad in the boatmen's usual rig-out and with a broad smile bisecting his face. 'Well, if we ain't in luck, Reuben,' he called over his shoulder. 'Here's a beautiful young gal, come a-callin' to wish us the compliments o' the season and offer us a nice hot breakfast.' He winked at Lizzie as he said this. 'I've gorra gerrim out o' that bed so's I can light the fire and begin to fry bacon,' he confided, lowering his voice. He jerked his thumb at the cabin behind him. 'Yon slug-a-bed is me brother, Reuben, and I'm Abe, short for Abraham.' He chuckled. 'Our mam were a good Christian so all of us kids had biblical names.'

'I'm Lizzie Devlin,' she said. 'How d'you do, Mr...?'

'Call me Abe, like everyone else does,' the man said. He glanced up at the now swiftly falling flakes. 'By Jupiter, a white Christmas, eh? Now where's your craft, lass? 'Cos there ain't a farm for miles, as I know on, and you can't 'ave sprung out o' the canal like some perishin' mermaid!'

'Oh! To tell you the truth, I came aboard your butty boat,' Lizzie mumbled, half afraid that the man's friendly attitude would change upon hearing this revelation, but if anything, his smile broadened.

'Well, I'll be dommed! We gorra stowaway,' he said gleefully, throwing the words back over his shoulder towards where his brother was slowly unwinding himself from his cocoon of blankets. 'But why, lass?' His eyes sharpened suddenly, looking less friendly. 'You ain't escapin' from the law, are you?'

'No, no,' Lizzie said hastily. She realised that it was not necessary, or not now at any rate, to go into the whole story of her flight from home. It would probably be wisest, at this stage, to prevaricate a little. 'My uncle's gorrin' a great rage with me because I were late comin' in from a dance, so I lit out before he could beat the living daylights out o' me. He chased me down to the canal and – and – I've a friend with a butty boat . . . I got aboard and snuggled down in the fleeces, thinkin' it was me pal's boat, only – only – this morning I saw the name and realised . . .'

'. . . realised you'd made a mistake,' a voice interpolated from the cabin as another man emerged on to the tiny deck. 'Well, lass, you couldn't have come at a better time, I'll say that for you. We're a three-man crew as a rule – you need three to see a barge and a butty boat through the locks – but our younger brother's in 'ospital. He fell on the ice and broke his thigh bone – too much Guinness, I reckon – so we're muddlin' along wi' just the two of us. If you've a mind to work your passage, then you're welcome as water in a desert. What do you say?'

The speaker was as ruddy-faced as his brother and Lizzie could see a strong family likeness, though Abe was brown-haired and brown-eyed whereas Reuben was so fair that his hair seemed almost white, and his eyes such a pale blue that they appeared at first sight to be colourless. However, both men seemed well disposed towards her and Lizzie, having looked around the bleak countryside surrounding the canal, was happy to agree to this.

'Are you taking the fleeces right through to Leeds?' she asked. 'Will there be someone to receive them? Only tomorrow's Boxing Day and I daresay the mills will still be closed.'

Abe guffawed. 'Yes, we're goin' right through to Leeds, but we ain't a fly boat, chuck,' he reminded her. 'We don't travel by night and old Boxer – that's our horse – ain't in the first flush of youth, either. We shan't be in Leeds till well after the holiday. Now how about a bite o' breakfast?'

'The bloody fire's gone out,' Reuben grumbled, then shot a guilty glance at Lizzie. 'Sorry, young 'un, I were forgettin' the company. Still an' all . . . can you make a fire? If so, I'll go and fettle up the horse while you get the fire goin' and make us a bite of breakfast.'

Lizzie opened her mouth to remark that there was only bread and cheese in their cupboard, then remembered that it would not do to admit she had stolen some of their food. Instead, she said she had made many a fire in her time and doubted that this would be much different from the rest. Having been shown over *The Liverpool Rose* by Clem and having watched Priddy closely as she went about her work, Lizzie knew where dry wood and coal would be kept and soon had a good fire blazing in the closed stove. She went to the cupboard and opened it, thinking that only bread and cheese would meet her eyes, and was surprised and gratified to find some bacon, a bowl containing a dozen or so brown eggs and a freshly baked loaf. On the shelf below, she saw the still-feathered form of a goose and a small sack which she guessed would contain potatoes or some similar vegetable. Wherever they had called last night, they had clearly stocked up for Christmas.

An hour later, Lizzie, Reuben and Abe were sitting round the table, having eaten an excellent breakfast and drunk a great deal of strong tea. Lizzie had noticed Reuben glancing wistfully towards a large enamel jug, but when he had put out a hand towards it, his brother had reproved him instantly. 'No decent body has porter for breakfast,' Abe had said. 'What'll our new mate think of us if we start boozin' when there's work to be done? Besides, that there porter's for to drink wi' our Christmas dinner.'

Reuben had sighed but drunk his tea and now, with the meal completed, was getting to his feet and shrugging himself into his jacket. 'I'll lead the horse while the young missy clears away and does wharrever she needs to do down here,' he said gruffly. 'We'd better all take a turn at leadin' Boxer because it'll be hard work sloggin' along the towpath in weather like this.'

The three of them set about their various tasks and well before Lizzie had finished clearing down the cabin, putting the beds away and making up the fire, *The Singing Lark* was on the move. When she opened the cabin door, she could see Abe at the tiller, completely covered with snow so that even his lashes wore a rim of the stuff. Ahead of them, she could just about make out Boxer's huge, rounded rump, almost dwarfing Reuben's well-swathed figure at his head.

'In another mile or so we'll change places,' Abe shouted to her, for the wind was howling loudly enough to make normal conversation impossible. 'This is no ordinary snow storm, queen, it's a blizzard. I dunno as we can keep goin' for the whole of the day. Still, if we tie up early and get movin' as soon as the weather clears, we shouldn't be too late arrivin' at the wharf. We're on a promise to get this lot', he jerked his head at the cargo, 'to a pal o' mine in good time, and I wouldn't want to let him down.' He lowered his snow-covered head and peered at her 'You're sure there won't be no scuffers lookin' out for you? Only me and Reuben's never had no trouble wi' the law and we don't need it now.'

Lizzie was a little startled by the unexpected question, but shook her head and grinned at him. 'I told you I wasn't in any trouble, 'cept wi' me uncle,' she reminded him. 'But if you're worried about it, just you drop me off at the first village we pass and I'll either make me way back home or sign on with another boat's crew, if they'll have me.'

Abe grinned back at her, shaking his head until the snow flew. 'Don't take offence, queen. But you must admit it were a strange thing, you turnin' up out o' nowhere in the middle of a blizzard. Why, I never even asked you where you got aboard. Still an' all, you're a grand little worker and me and Reuben's glad to have you to help out. I can't promise to pay you, but you'll be well fed and you can sleep in the fleeces, warm as a bug in a rug and safe as houses. Will that do?'

'It'll be grand,' Lizzie shouted above the howl of the wind. 'Are you going to spell Reuben now? If so, I'll take the tiller for a bit, so's he can have a warm, get his circulation moving again, like.'

'If you'll take the tiller, I'll nip below meself and mebbe have a mouthful of somethin',' Abe said briskly. 'Then I'll send Reuben back for a warm after that.'

For the rest of the day, the three of them worked a sort of rota, each taking a turn with the horse and the tiller, though when they reached a lock, it took the united efforts of all three to get *The Singing Lark* and her butty boat through unscathed. Abe had told Lizzie that they would cook the goose when they tied up for the night since, because of the storm and the short December days, this would be earlier than he would have liked. 'Normally we'd allow ourselves a decent rest time over Christmas – mebbe attend a church service – like other canal folk will be doin',' he said piously. 'But this cargo's kind o' special. I give me word to me pal to get it through in good time and I'm a man of me word, even when weather conditions are agin me. So we'll press on till darkness forces us to moor up and then we'll have a real merry Christmas, just the three of us.' He chuckled fatly. 'Just the three of us and the goose,' he amended.

Clem had been dismayed, upon waking on Christmas morning, to discover that the snow was whirling briskly past the boat and covering the countryside in a soft, white blanket. He guessed this would make his task a good deal harder and besides worrying that Lizzie might have got into bad company, became even more worried that she might have decided to set off into the countryside and even now be lying dead in a ditch, frozen as solid as ice. He voiced his fears over breakfast, but Priddy and Jake shook their heads at him, Jake going so far as to lean across the table and buffet his shoulder. 'From what you've told us, young Lizzie's a gal with a deal of common sense, not some silly little ninny who's been reared in cotton,' he said robustly. 'I know you think she might have been enticed aboard the Trelawney boat – or might have stowed away aboard it, I suppose – but remember, there were a dozen others she could have chose. And not even the Trelawneys would kick her off their craft in weather like this.'

Clem heard Priddy mutter something, but when he asked her to repeat it, she simply smiled grimly and recommended him to, 'Stop fussin' and get a move on, so's we can fetch Hal and get goin' once more. The Trelawneys are a bad lot, but they ain't never done no murders as I've heard of and turnin' a girl out on a day like this would be murder, or as good as. We'll go straight through wi'out stoppin' and whenever we pass a moored craft we'll check the name, and unless it was one of the boats moored at Tate's that night we'll not bother to question the crew. We wasted time doing that yesterday. Today we'll cover more ground.'

Clem agreed with this eminently sensible suggestion and very soon he was trudging along the towpath at Hal's head, keeping as close to the massive horse as he could, for Hal's sturdy form kept the worst of the snow off him as well as exuding a very pleasant warmth. On his other side, Brutus pressed close, seeming almost to relish the awful conditions, or at any rate ignoring Clem's frequent suggestions that the dog might return to the boat for a warm. Even when they changed over, so that Jake could lead while Clem steered, the dog did not go below into the cabin but remained against Clem's side, staring ahead through narrowed eyes as the snowflakes whirled down ever faster.

At some time during the day, Priddy supplied them with hot cocoa and cheese sandwiches and remarked, as she handed the thick doorstep to Clem, that they had only passed two moored up craft. 'What with Christmas Day and the weather, everyone will have taken to towns or villages where they can meet up for a bit of a jolly,' she shouted. 'For all we know, whatever boat Lizzie's on may have done just that. If so, we'll mebbe find it moored alongside the next village we reach.'

'Oh, Priddy, I've ruined your Christmas Day,' he said suddenly, realising for the first time he had completely disrupted the Pridmores' plans. They had meant to moor up in Liverpool for the holiday and had actually invited a retired couple they knew to share their Christmas dinner. 'What'll Mr and Mrs Routledge do when they find *The Liverpool Rose* has gone missing?'

'I left them a message,' Priddy shrieked against the wind. 'I told Jenny Finnigan to say as how we were real sorry but we'd been called away on important business. As for ruinin' Christmas, can't you smell roastin' goose? I've had 'un in the oven for the past two hours. She'll be nicely cooked when it's too dark to go no further.'

Clem could not smell the roasting meat through

the muffler wound round his face but he was glad that the Pridmores would have some sort of Christmas cheer, despite his quest. Though when eventually they sat down in the cosy cabin, with the snow still whirling down from the black sky, the goose might have been bread and cheese – or indeed sawdust – for all he noticed. He could not help it, his concern for Lizzie grew apace with every moment that passed and when he went to Hal's stable to check that the horse was comfortable before seeking his own bed, the ferocity of the weather was such that he was unable to get a wink of sleep for some consider-able while. He lay in the dark, a prey to increasingly horrid worries, until at last sheer exhaustion dragged him down into sleep.

Clem was awoken some hours later, by the sound of Brutus growling softly. Listening, he realised that he could hear voices. He lay for a moment, still dazed with sleep, and then became aware that it was not only voices he could hear, but the rattle and scrape of a craft being brought alongside and then the even more definite rattle as someone knocked loudly on the cabin doors of *The Liverpool Rose*. Brutus barked sharply and he and Clem emerged into the whirling snow and dark on the little deck together. A tug was drawn up ahead of *The Liverpool Rose* and its crew, two sturdy-looking men in jackets and flat corduroy caps, were standing on the towpath, holding a lantern by whose light they could see to knock on the cabin door with a boat hook. Brutus immediately took exception to this and leapt ashore, growling ominously as he ran along the path. Clem shouted to the dog who skidded to a halt and sat back on his haunches, though he continued to growl, hackles raised, even after the two men had stepped hastily away from *The Liverpool Rose* and turned back towards Clem. 'Sorry to wake you so early, la',' the older of the two said apologetically, pushing back his cap to scratch his forehead. 'The thing is, we's desperate for some information and there's precious few craft around whose crews we can ask. But we saw you'd been moored snugly here overnight – the depth of the snow on your fore-deck told us that – so we thought we'd stop and ask if you'd seen or heard owt of any other craft headin' for Leeds?'

'No, but I've slept like the dead all night,' Clem said. 'I dunno about Priddy and Jake, though. Jake always says he sleeps with one eye and one ear open so mebbe, if a fly boat passed . . . not that I can imagine any fly boat being foolish enough to work through the night over Christmas and in this sort of weather . . . he may have heard it.'

At this point, the door of the cabin creaked open and Jake's head appeared. 'There's nowt been past this night,' he said authoritatively. 'A fly boat makes a deal of motion in the water and I'd have known of its passing even if I didn't wake.' He peered curiously at the two men in the lamplight, screwing up his eyes as though to see better. 'It's Alf Hitchin, ain't it? Wharra you doin' out at this hour, Alf? It can't be more 'an six o'clock.'

'Mornin', Jake,' the older of the two men said. 'I'm almost ashamed to tell you 'cos I've been made a right fool of, that's what. A couple o' days ago we brung a load of fleeces down from Leeds to the Liverpool docks in *The Pride of the 'Pool*. We unloaded Christmas Eve but the ship what was meant to take them aboard was late dockin', so we left them under canvas on the wharf. Never gave a thought to trouble, believin' the ship would dock that night. Only next mornin', when she did dock and we went to help load, there weren't a fleece in sight. We axed around, but at first no one had any idea what had happened to them. Then someone said they'd seen the Trelawneys in one of the dockside pubs – you know what their reputation is, Jake – and the brothers had said they were spending Christmas in the 'Pool, 'cos the youngest lad, Job, had broke a leg slipping on the ice, and it takes three of them to manage the two boats.

'So me and Bill here went along to where the Trelawney boat should ha' been only she'd slipped moorings and made off during the hours of darkness. And if that ain't a sure sign that them buggers have burgled our fleeces, I don't know what is,' he finished.

'If they left when you say they did, then they'll be well ahead of here by now,' Jake observed. 'They won't stop for darkness, not wi' a stolen load aboard, they'll keep goin' night and day until they reach Leeds – unless they know someone in a canalside town or village who'll handle stolen goods, that is – and you won't catch up with 'em unless you do the same.'

'You're wrong there, 'cos for one thing *The Singing Lark* is horse-drawn and horses need a rest, particularly in weather like this, and for another there's only two of 'em doin' the work of three, so navigatin' through the locks is liable to be a perilous slow business,' Alf's companion observed. Freddie was about Clem's age with a thin, cheerful face, although right now he was scowling. 'What worries me is that they might have taken t'other route to Leeds, goin' via Leigh, across the Barton Aqueduct and up to the Rochdale. Come to that, they could take any number of other routes because although they're usually on the Leeds and Liverpool, there's nowt to stop 'em switchin', particularly if they think we're hot on their trail. What'll concern them most is selling the fleeces before we've got word out that it's a stolen cargo – if only it weren't Christmas and the weather so foul!'

It was at this point that Clem broke in. 'We're searchin' for a pal of mine who might well be aboard the Trelawneys' boat,' he said, trying to keep his voice steady and matter-of-fact though the information the two men had given had struck yet another chill into his heart. 'That's why we're on the canal making for Leeds and not enjoying our Christmas back at the 'Pool. We're wanting to get my pal away from those Trelawneys before they get her involved as deeply as themselves.'

'Her? D'ya mean it's a gal?' Freddie said, his eyes widening. 'Dear God, you want to get a move on, 'cos their reputation wi' women is as bad as their reputation for stealin' other men's goods. What's a gal doin' wi' the likes of them anyroad?'

'She may not even be with 'em,' Jake struck in. 'But the more I hear, the more I suspicion the lad's right. Look, we're goin' to stick to the Leeds and Liverpool 'cos it's what we know, but we'll set off right now, 'stead o' waitin' for the light. If they're headin' for Leeds, they'll be slower than us at locks and swing bridges 'cos Lizzie's norra canal woman and she won't be as fast as an experienced gal would be. What's more, their old Boxer ain't a patch on our Hal where pullin' and endurance is concerned. So seein' as a tug is a good deal faster than horse-drawn, perhaps it might pay us to join forces, with us stickin' to the Leeds and Liverpool and you tryin' all the cuts and side canals along the way. If we do that, one of us is bound to catch up with them. You'll take Lizzie aboard the tug and bring her to us, if she's with them?'

'Aye, surely we will,' agreed Alf. 'Well, if we're going to retrace our steps and search the side canals, young Freddie, we'd best get a move on.'

At this point, Priddy joined Jake on the deck of *The Liverpool Rose*. She had clearly been listening to their conversation as she dressed herself in her outdoor gear for she said briskly: 'But how's we to keep in touch, so's we know if one or other of us finds *The Singing Lark*? And we can't arrest them two big blokes, 'cos we ain't the scuffers, and besides we'd be no match for Abe and Reuben.'

'You've gorra point, Mrs Pridmore,' Alf admitted. 'Tell you what, if you catch up with 'em first, get your gal off and then make for the nearest police station. We'll do the same. The scuffers will ring around and we'll check as we go along. When we reach Leeds we'll wait for you down by the wool wharf, so's we know where we stand.'

It wasn't the best plan in the world but it seemed to cover most eventualities, Clem thought as he waved goodbye to the tug and went to fetch Hal from his stable. With the two boats searching, he was actually beginning to feel that one or other of them might catch up with the Trelawneys before the worst – whatever that might be – had occurred. He realised, of course, that there was no guarantee Lizzie would be aboard – indeed, he prayed she was not – but he was becoming more and more convinced that there could be no other explanation.

By the time he returned to the canalside with Hal geared up for pulling, Priddy was handing out steaming mugs of cocoa and great doorsteps of bread with fried egg and bacon sandwiched between them.

'We won't stop for our midday,' she said grimly, handing out the food. 'It were a good idea to send the tug to search other routes, but it's my belief we'll catch up with them first, either today or tomorrer. I don't believe those two fools will be able to keep their noses out of the ale jug for longer'n a couple o' days, and once they get to drinkin' they'll want to moor up so's they can do the job proper. So come along, young Clem, get Hal moving and we'll be on our way.'

'If only the bleedin' snow would stop and we get along faster,' he muttered as he took his place beside Hal's head. 'Still, what's bad for us is worse for them. Poor old Lizzie, though. I reckon this will put her off canals for life!'

Chapter Ten

'Are you goin' to be long in there?'

Geoff was shaving, half his face still thickly covered in lather, the other half clean and smooth. He grinned as Reggie popped his head round the door, replying soothingly: 'No, I shan't be two ticks. I'm meeting Sally after breakfast and we're going down to the canal to see if there's been any news from Clem. Why?'

'Because it's bacon and egg for breakfast and I thought we might do something together, if you'd nothing better planned,' Reggie said, a trifle disconsolately. 'Boxing Day's always a bit flat, somehow, but there's the panto at the Empire Theatre – we could go along there, see if there's any seats still unsold.'

'I think you'd better count me out, old feller,' Geoff said, trying to sound regretful. 'As you know, I had me Christmas dinner with Mr and Mrs Bradshaw and they've invited me back to finish up the cold meat today.'

'For a feller who started off sweet on Lizzie and then swapped to Evie Evans, you're showin' a remarkable interest in Sally Bradshaw,' Reggie grumbled. 'Ain't one girl enough for you?'

'Sally and me's very worried about Lizzie,' Geoff replied with dignity. 'Well, we're not as worried as we were, truth to tell. Clem's a trustable sort of feller and he was sure enough that she's aboard a canal boat to go chasing off in pursuit of her, so Sally and I reckon she'll be safe and sound aboard *The Liverpool Rose* by now and probably tucking into as good a dinner as you'll get anywhere. One of the canal people – a gal called Jenny Finnigan – told us that, since they're laden, they'll pick Lizzie up and continue on to Leeds. They'll probably send a telegram tomorrow, when the Post Office is open again, letting us know all's well.'

'And what about Evie Evans?' Reggie asked suspiciously. 'You've forgot all about her, I daresay?'

Geoff, who did feel rather guilty about Evie, drew his razor so sharply down the side of his face that he nicked the skin and yelped as blood began to pump out. 'Now look what you've done!' he said crossly, pressing a tuft of cotton wool to the wound, then snatching if off again and splashing off the last of the shaving soap with handfuls of cold water. 'You'd best go and find yourself someone else to play with because I'm going to be busy all day. And furthermore,' he added frostily, 'I *haven't* forgotten Evie Evans, whatever you may think. Sally says she reckons I've been searching in the wrong places, so this afternoon we're going to take a look round an area I've not searched.'

Reggie sighed, but agreed he'd best go and find Steve Jones, who was also at a loose end, and presently Geoff, dressed in his best, set off for Burlington Street and Cranberry Court.

As soon as Geoff arrived in Cranberry Court he asked Sally whether Uncle Perce had yet put in an appearance, but she shook her head. 'The house is quiet as a grave. No one's visited, no one's gone in or out – unless they did it in the middle of the night – since the day Aunt Annie died,' she said positively.

'Mr Grey's never been popular – in fact he were well hated – and there's more than one who's suspicious about how Aunt Annie came to slip on ice when everyone had been so careful not to tip water when they carried it back from the tap. The trouble is, everything stops for Christmas so I suppose the scuffers are leavin' their investigations until the holiday's over. Of course, when Lizzie comes home . . .'

But at this point Mrs Bradshaw announced that dinner was on the table and very soon the family were tucking in to cold goose, ham and baked potatoes, and the subject of Uncle Perce and his whereabouts was dropped, for the time being at least.

Later that afternoon, Sally and Geoff set off through the whirling snow which still continued to fall for a wander around the places of entertainment which were open on Boxing Day. 'You tried all the dance halls, picture houses and big stores when you were looking for Evie,' Sally had observed earlier. 'I know you said she was smartly dressed and seemed to know her way around, and I imagine Sid would go for a sophisticated sort of girl rather than a quiet, studious one. So this afternoon we'll go to the theatres and concert halls, and see whether we can run her to earth there.'

Geoff was doubtful, but did not say so. The more he got to know Sally, the more he liked her, and the more reliance he placed on her practical common sense and knowledge of people. She had not seen Evie, however, with her smart little hat perched at an angle on her glossy black hair, those tottering high-heeled shoes and that straight tight black skirt. She had not looked the sort of girl to waste her time on either carol services or concerts, but Geoff had to agree that these were the sort of places he had never previously considered, and they were worth a try at least.

Accordingly, they visited some theatres where the crowds were gathering before a performance, then went to St George's Hall where 'The Christmas Oratorio' was being performed. They saw a great many smartly dressed men and women, but though Geoff scanned their faces eagerly he saw no sign of Evie Evans.

They were about to turn away, Geoff actually suggesting that they might try the Philharmonic Hall, when a crocodile of school children, all dressed alike in navy overcoats, with felt hats pulled well down over their brows, began to file past. Geoff was not looking at them, but suddenly got the feeling that someone was looking at him. Glancing at the nearest girl, he saw that she was smiling at him. She looked vaguely familiar and he supposed she must have come into the bank at sometime or possibly have lived near him when he was at the Branny. In fact, he was about to turn away when something in those dark, almond-shaped eyes touched a chord in his memory and he realised that, incredibly, this was Evie Evans!

There was no opportunity to speak to her, of course. One girl in a long line can scarcely be winkled out for private conversation with a young man, no matter how respectable, and Geoff had enough sense to realise that to try would put him in a bad light and probably get Evie into awful trouble. Sally, however, was a different kettle of fish. Geoff seized her arm and muttered in her ear: 'Sally! That girl, the one with the long black plait, it's her! Pretend you recognised her and go and have a word. Try to arrange a meeting – I've gorra know what's being going on. See if the school will let her out to have tea . . . say anything, but don't let her go and disappear again!'

Sally was nothing if not quick off the mark. She

took in Geoff's words and without waiting to argue or question him further dashed across to the girl with the long plait and caught her by the arm. Geoff could not hear what passed between them, but he saw an older woman in a nun's flowing habit, who had been at the back of the line, walk briskly forward and fall into step with Sally who was walking alongside Evie, talking earnestly. The nun clearly asked her what was happening, but Sally's answer seemed to satisfy her for the three of them continued to talk for a further five minutes while he kept well back, wondering anxiously what was going on.

Presently Sally broke away from the line, bobbing a little curtsey to the nun, and came towards Geoff, not rejoining him, however, until the crocodile of school children was out of sight. Then she grabbed his arm and began to hurry him towards St John's Gardens. 'I'm not sayin' nothing till we're somewhere quiet,' she hissed. 'I tell you what, though, it's a good thing that Evie's quick on the uptake or I could have been in an awful mess.'

Geoff longed to ask her why but did not say a word until they were brushing the snow off one of the slatted wooden seats under the bare-branched trees in the Gardens. Only then did he turn to Sally, agog to hear what had happened.

She took a deep breath and began to speak. 'Evie's in the top form at that Convent school and talking about taking up a musical career. Apparently she's an awfully good pianist,' she said bluntly. 'She remembers you, all right, and your pal from the YMCA, but she said she'd been in such trouble over Sid Ryder that she'd nearly been slung out. I asked her what happened that night – the one you met her – but the nun came up before she could tell me. Anyway, I did what you said and suggested a meeting – oh, I forgot to say I pretended to recognise her from when she lived in the courts – but she didn't think it could be arranged. I dunno what happened that night, but it were pretty clear the nun didn't trust her and were keeping a close watch on her. In the end, she said I could go round to the orphanage and Evie and I could have a bit of a crack about old times in the common room.' She smiled up at Geoff. 'Sorry, la', but it were the best I could do.'

'I think you did marvels,' he said frankly. 'D'you mind going round there for me, Sally, and seeing what you can find out? I don't suppose there's anything I can do to tell help her, and having seen her again . . . well, she's only a kid, isn't she? And from what you say, that evening at Sid's place was a one off. I reckon she's learnt her lesson and won't want to meet up with fellers again.' He thought back to that evening in Sid's flat, to the sophisticated and beautiful girl in her smart clothes and high-heeled shoes. 'Little Evie, a nun!' he said wonderingly. 'What kind of life is that for a beautiful, lively gal, though, Sally?'

'If it's what she wants, then it's what she wants,' Sally said baldly. 'Look, Geoff, there's no point talking about it. I'll go up to the orphanage around teatime – you can walk me up if you want and hang about until I come out. I shan't be long. Then we'll know what's what, okay?'

He thought her voice a trifle tart, her glance a little chilly, but realising that he was asking a lot of her, said humbly that he would be glad to go with her and keep out of sight until she emerged. Having made their arrangements the two of them went into Lime Street Station and killed time in the railway buffet while wondering aloud whether Clem had yet caught up with the other runaway.

'But he and the Pridmores know the canal and the folk who work on it like you know your own family,' Geoff told Sally confidently. 'He's sweet on Lizzie and always has been so I reckon he'll take better care of her than you or I could. We'll sort this Evie out and then see whether we can get any news from the canal people.'

Lizzie's Christmas Day was different from any she had ever imagined for most of it consisted of either leading Boxer along towpaths so thick with snow that several times one or other of the brothers had to dig his way through a particularly deep drift, or steering the boat in the teeth of a howling gale which blew the whirling flakes so thickly against her face that a wall of it built up on her muffler, making it almost impossible to see more than a few yards ahead. Despite this, however, she actually managed to enjoy the work, and since the brothers insisted that she had regular tots of what they called 'our Christmas spirit', she soon felt quite jolly and warm from the top of her head to the tips of her toes.

As darkness began to descend, she was sent below by the brothers to cook the goose, which Abe had plucked and drawn earlier in the day, and the accompanying vegetables. When they finally moored up for the night they had an excellent meal, though Lizzie felt it prudent to turn down any more of the 'Christmas spirit'. She thought the brothers were growing a trifle too merry, for some of their remarks seemed in very poor taste, but once the horse was stabled and the goose reduced to a pile of bones, she went to her bed amongst the fleeces, well satisfied with her day.

She awoke on Boxing Day morning to find the storm still raging and her two companions nursing sore heads. Abe was still eager to push on, fretting that they would let their pal down; but Reuben said frankly that he did not care who he let down, in weather like this they should lie up for a day until he felt more like himself. 'The poor bloody horse will be on his knees if we try to force him to go on with the canal path shoulder-deep,' he said angrily. 'You may not value Boxer but I does. A strong horse is worth its weight in gold, and don't you forget it.'

Lizzie was surprised at this, since she had thought several times that Reuben had little or no sympathy for Boxer, grumbling mightily when his brother commanded him to put more oats in the animal's nose-bag or to give him a good rub down and a hot mash when they reached stabling. But it was clear that neither man was relishing the fearful conditions and she supposed that this – plus the drink they had taken – made them argumentative.

Having once realised that the men were supplied with spirits, she began to notice that every time one of them went below they were clearly taking drink for she could smell it on their breaths as they passed her to go about their various tasks. By afternoon, in fact, they had progressed very little further and when Reuben grumbled again that both he and the horse had had enough, Abe reluctantly agreed and they moored the boat close under a group of willows whose branches were so laden with snow that they bent right down across the water, giving at least some shelter from the wind.

Lizzie volunteered to take the horse to a nearby barn and see him comfortably settled and Abe agreed that he and Reuben would prepare a meal. So she went off to the barn, Boxer trudgingly patiently beside her and a lantern in one hand. Once inside she took off the horse's gear, rubbed him down, picked the snow out of his hoofs and fetlocks. She had done this before, under Abe's guidance, but tonight she worked quickly and was on her way back to the boat faster than she'd expected. Knowing that the meal would still be in preparation, she was about to step aboard *The Singing Lark* and ask if she might give a hand when from within the cabin the sound of her own name stopped her in her tracks. 'I say Lizzie's done well be us an' we's in enough trouble wi'out givin' her cause to split on us to the scuffers,' Abe's voice said firmly. 'I know you're bored wi'out no women, nor no pubs where you might meet a pal or two, but that don't give you cause to go startin' on a young girl like her. We's a long way from Nat Shipley's yard yet, so don't you forget it.'

'I don't see why you think the gal would object,' Reuben said, his voice thick and slurred. 'I'll wait till she's tucked up in the fleeces and then I'll join her. I reckon she'll be grateful to have a feller like me tek an interest in her, give her a cuddle an' that.'

'I think she likes me a good deal better 'an she likes you,' Abe said in a grumbling voice, and Lizzie realised that both the brothers were what her Aunt Annie would have called, 'ugly drunk', and were therefore best avoided.

'I tell you, she's mine, 'cos I thought of it first,' Reuben said aggressively. 'You're an old man compared with me, Abe Trelawney, I'm tellin' you . . .'

But Lizzie had stopped listening. So these were the Trelawney brothers of whom she had heard Clem speak as the only really bad and dishonest family working the canals. Sick with self-disgust, because she had not even suspected it, Lizzie realised that if she returned to the boat, she would be in deep trouble. She glanced around her. She must run – but to where? Beyond the stable in which she had just left Boxer, the hills reared, wild and lonely, without so much as a shape or light of a house to which she could run. Perhaps if she went to the stable . . . but that would be the first place the brothers would look when she failed to turn up to share their evening meal. Lizzie wondered whether she could creep into the fleeces, right along to the far end, and remain undiscovered but she knew this would be madness. Surrounded by fleeces and with two men intent on her capture, she would be in a worse position even than if she sought shelter in the stable.

Desperately, Lizzie tried to remember whether they had recently passed through a village, or whether either brother had mentioned any sort of habitation ahead. The trouble was, what with the snow and the difficulty of their journey, she had scarcely noticed anything apart from the path ahead. Standing on the towpath in an agony of indecision, however, her mind was suddenly made up for her.

'She's takin' her time,' Reuben observed suddenly. 'I think I'll tek a stroll up to the stables, mebbe give her a hand wi' the horse.'

'That you won't,' Abe cut in roughly. 'If she needs to show gratitude to anyone, that'll be to me! I'm the older, it were my idea to bring her aboard, so *I'll* walk up to the stable and see if I . . .'.

But Lizzie waited to hear no more. She set off as fast as she could in the direction of the wild and lonely hills.

As soon as she left the towpath, however, the depth of the snow almost defeated her. It was well above her knees and difficult to wade through. But she could see the dimpled line of a stone wall, running away to her right, and reasoned that, since the wind was blowing into her face, walking would be easier if she scrambled over the wall on to its more sheltered side. She struggled towards it. After a moment, she turned to look behind her and saw one of the brothers – she could not, at this distance, tell which – emerging from the cabin, closely followed by the second man. Fortunately for Lizzie, both men set off along the towpath in the direction of the stable without glancing around them so she hurried on, making the best speed she could and heading always uphill. The snow, which had not ceased to fall all day, was falling still, but Lizzie fancied that it was beginning to ease off, though the wind still blew the drifts into vast caverns and crevices, making progress as difficult as though the storm had been still at its height.

It must have been ten minutes later when she heard a halloo from behind her and, turning as she topped a small rise, saw the brothers returning from the stable. The larger of the two, Abe, was shambling along with head down, but Reuben was staring up at her and Lizzie realised that even in the darkness she must stand out against all this whiteness, like an ink blot on a page. However, she was not given long to worry for the brothers immediately veered from the path and came charging up the slope, Reuben uttering blood-curdling threats while Abe moaned that she was an ungrateful critter and all they wanted to do was help her on her way and let her lie warm and snug in the fleeces till morning.

Lizzie had no breath to spare for the sharp – and rude – retort she longed to make, but tightened her lips and ploughed ahead. She soon realised that what with drink and their considerable weight, the two men were unlikely to catch up with her unless she foundered. What was more, the hills which looked so white and smooth from the canal were in fact full of hiding places. There were ravines, in the bottom of which, despite the snow, she could see the dark line of streams, and there were huge, rocky boulders, some as big as a house, which offered both a temporary respite from the howling wind and also the possibility of a hiding place. But the men were still coming on steadily. She realised she must begin to use the lie of the land to help her, otherwise all the Trelawneys had to do was to follow her tracks. While she remained in sight, they need not even bother following her footprints. If she could just get well ahead of them and out of their view, and if she could find shelter, then she thought she would probably be all right. She imagined that when the heat of the chase and their drunkenness both subsided, they would return to *The Singing Lark* and to their beds. In the morning she was sure good sense would prevail. But since she intended to steer well clear of the canal next day, the goings-on of the Trelawneys need no longer concern her. After all, they had been good to her until the drink had got into their blood; she would forget tonight and concentrate on getting back to Liverpool and telling the scuffers what she knew.

But right now, the danger was from the Trelawneys so she kept on, doggedly climbing the hill, even when she gathered, from the gradually fading voices of the brothers, that their pursuit had ended and they were returning to *The Singing Lark*. She topped a small rise and slithered into the hollow beyond and then, suddenly, the ground seemed to give way beneath her feet and she found herself falling . . . falling . . .

There was a moment when she was aware of the snow and the sky being blotted out by darkness and an uprush of what felt like warm air, and then something hard crashed against her forehead and she was plunged into unconsciousness.

The snow which had continued throughout the day seemed to Clem to be falling as fast as ever when darkness descended. He fully expected Priddy and Jake to pull over and begin preparations for their night's mooring, but although Jake seemed to be calculating the distance to the nearest stable, Priddy said that they must press on. 'We've gorra catch them Trelawneys up in the next few hours or they'll mebbe start trouble with the gal,' she said bluntly. 'I haven't said too much till now, Clem, but them boys have an evil reputation with women and though your Lizzie's only a slip of a thing, she'll be in mortal danger once they get fightin' drunk. I'm sorry for our dear old Hal, but he's a strong horse and can go a few miles yet, so we'll keep on all night, if need be, wi' a bit of a rest at locks or swing bridges so's the poor old feller don't founder. Agreed?'

Clem felt the hot blood rush to his face at the thought of his Lizzie in such danger. He had been afraid that they might bully her or turn her out to fend for herself but it had never occurred to him that the men might try to take advantage of her. Now he curled his hands into fists and told himself that if either brother harmed a hair of Lizzie's head, he would kill them without compunction.

Jake, looking startled, muttered that surely, not even the Trelawneys . . . she were only a young girl and defenceless at that . . . but Priddy cut him short. 'She's a woman and that'll be enough for Reuben even if Abe were to hold back,' she said brusquely. 'I'll not have it on me conscience that I let a bit o' weather put me off doin' me duty.'

Clem, looking round at what he could see of the snow-covered country through the still-descending flakes, marvelled at this understatement but agreed fervently that they must push on and went once more to Hal's head.

As it grew darker, he was immensely cheered, however, to realise that someone had been along this path before them, and fairly recently too. Though he had carried a shovel so that he might dig his way through drifts, it was no longer necessary, for someone had cleared the path before him and now he was looking for it, he could see, by the light of his lantern, that a very large horse, led by someone both small and light, had passed this way only a couple of hours before.

As soon as he was able, Clem passed this heartening news back to the Pridmores and continued to advance as fast as he could. Hal might have been tiring – must have been tiring – but showed no signs of giving up and kept *The Liverpool Rose* moving through the water at a good pace. Presently, Clem began to lead the horse through a tunnel of mighty willows which overhung the water – and suddenly realised there were two boats moored just ahead. These were the first craft he had seen for many hours and immediately his suspicions were roused. It was such a lonely and desolate spot, no one would have chosen to moor here over the Christmas holiday unless they had a good reason for keeping out of sight of other canal dwellers. Indeed, had the Pridmores owned a powered boat, they might well have passed by without noticing the moored craft since no one would have been walking the towpath.

As he neared the two boats, Clem swung his lantern cautiously and felt his heart lift as he saw the legend on the stern. *The Singing Lark*, it read.

They had found their quarry at last.

Clem pulled Hal to a halt and glanced towards the *Lark*'s cabin from which a line of light emerged. Now that he was near enough, he could hear the mumble of a muted conversation; so they were not yet abed, despite the lateness of the hour. He slid a hand along Brutus's ruff, turning him back in the direction of *The Liverpool Rose*. He felt he needed the support of Priddy and Jake before he tackled the Trelawney brothers. He and Brutus climbed quietly aboard and Clem explained the situation in a whisper.

Priddy was all for tackling the men at once, but Jake was more cautious. 'When they fellers has the drink upon them, they can be real mean. I've known Abe, when he was younger, lift a burly drayman above his head and hurl him clean across the pub. And Reuben used to box bare-knuckled. They say he'll fight wi' fists, feet and a broken bottle, too, when the drink's on 'im. If we can get Lizzie away from there wi'out trouble, ain't that best?'

'Ye – es,' Clem agreed doubtfully. 'If she's in the butty boat . . . but if they're having a meal, she'll be in the cabin, won't she? And there's no saying the Trelawneys are still drunk now, even if they were on Christmas Day. I think the best thing to do is to give them a knock and ask them, all friendly like and unsuspicious, if they've seen owt of a young girl with a long golden plait? That way they'll not be uneasy because o' the fleeces and we may get a straight answer out of them.'

So a few moments later the three of them walked

boldly along the towpath, not attempting to lower their voices or muffle their footsteps. Jake leaned over and banged on the cabin door and the three of them climbed aboard. From within the cabin there came a sharp exclamation and a voice said, 'She's come back! Well, I thank God, Reuben, and so should you, because . . .'

Another voice cut across the first. 'That ain't her,' it mumbled thickly. 'She'd have no need to knock, she'd just . . .'

The cabin door shot open and Clem saw two men's faces, dark against the light. One, the older of the two, had thick brown hair falling across his forehead and the beginnings of a beard on his square and jutting chin; the other had hair so fair it was almost white, pale blue eyes and a thin, angular face. Without knowing which was which, Clem guessed the dark one to be Abe and the other Reuben. But Jake was speaking now, his voice level and friendly. 'Evenin', fellers! Had a good Christmas?'

There was a short, astonished silence before Abe said reluctantly: 'Oh, aye, it weren't so bad. Is that you, Jake? It's difficult to see who's who on a night like this. What's you doin' in this godforsaken spot, anyroad?'

'We're searchin' for a pal of our 'n, or rather a pal of young Clem's here,' he said. 'She's called Lizzie Devlin and we know she got aboard a canal boat some time on Christmas Eve. She were runnin' away from a – a family row.'

Abe opened his mouth to reply, but Reuben cut in before he could do so. 'We ha' n't seen no girl,' he said thickly. 'What'd we do wi' a girl anyroad? Now clear orff, the lorrof you!'

Jake, looking baffled, took a step backwards, but

Clem leaned forward until his nose was no more than an inch from Reuben's and said threateningly, 'So what were you sayin' just before Jake here knocked on your cabin door, eh? You said something about a girl, we all heard you.'

Reuben began to reply, blustering that they must have misheard, and for the first time Clem smelt the rum on his breath and realised that the younger Trelawney, at any rate, was still drunk as a skunk. But at this point Priddy took a hand.

'If it's all the same to you, we'll take a look in your butty boat,' she said firmly. 'I'm not a one to call names or make accusations but the girl could easily have hid away in the butty boat wi'out either of you knowin'. If she's been there she'll have left traces, and if she ain't we'll say goodnight and continue on our way. What're you carryin'?'

Clem had to bite back the words, *It's fleeces, you know it is*, but Abe answered reluctantly: 'We're carryin' fleeces, Missus, but I don't know as it's necessary for you to go pokin' round in our cargo. We've done nothin' wrong. You heered what me brother said, there's been no girl . . .' He stopped short as Clem bent and picked something up from the deck by his boots. It was a small scarlet bow of ribbon.

For a moment no one spoke; every eye was focussed on the scrap of ribbon in his hand. Then Priddy said in a tone of voice which Clem had never heard her use before: 'Where is she? What in God's name have you done with her? If you've hurt a hair of her head . . .'

'. . . I'll kill the pair of you, and I'll kill you slow,' Clem finished for her. 'What's more, we know all about your thievin' ways and we'll make sure . . .'

At this point Reuben clearly decided that actions

spoke louder than words. He turned back into the cabin, grabbed a heavy iron pan from by the stove, and swung it at Clem's head. If it had connected, he would have been splattered all over the deck but, what with the drink spoiling Reuben's aim and Clem's quick evasive action, all that happened was that the pan bashed against the gunwhale, making Reuben howl and drop it. Fortunately it landed on his own foot. Almost gibbering with pain and rage, Reuben looked round for another weapon, but his brother grabbed him, threw him roughly into the cabin and slammed the doors shut, then turned to the three intruders. 'There were a girl aboard. She were a good girl, I'll grant you that,' he said grudgingly. 'She led the horse, took a turn at the tiller, even cooked the odd meal. But she left us a while back . . . dunno where she went. I reckon she thought she'd do better ashore with the weather so fierce.' As he spoke, Clem noticed the other man's eyes slide sideways and, following the direction of his eyes, he realised that a great many tracks led across the towpath towards open country.

'You're a liar, same as your brother,' he said harshly. 'She left the boat here for good reason and now she's gone off into that wilderness to gerraway from the pair of you. You think that if she's found tomorrow, frozen to death, she won't be able to tell on you, but it ain't goin' to happen. We'll find her and you'll bleedin' well help us!' He grabbed the huge man by both ears and shouted to Brutus, who leapt aboard and stood with bared teeth, growling ferociously at Abe. 'If you don't, I'll set him on you and in five minutes you'll be dog meat. Understand?'

Abe was beginning to reply, in a mumble, that they had meant no harm, that they did not mean the girl to die, when the cabin doors burst open and Reuben emerged on deck, this time gripping a wooden rolling pin. 'Gerroff this boat,' he screamed, 'and leave my brother alone or it'll be the worse for you. Go on, clear orff.'

Clem had grabbed the big dog's collar as soon as Reuben appeared but Abe, clearly already terrifed of Brutus, turned and disarmed his brother in one swift movement, then pushed him back into the cabin and followed him, slamming both doors shut. 'It's all right, Jake, Priddy,' his voice came to them, only slightly muffled by the closed doors. 'It's just the drink speakin'. Reuben's a good feller really, he don't wish the girl harm no more 'an I do. She lit off for the nearest village, I reckon, so you'll probably find her, no trouble. I'd give a hand but I think I should stay here wi' Reuben till he's sobered up else he'll make more trouble for you. As for that dawg, you keep a hold on him, young feller, 'cos if he attacks us it'll be murder, no less.'

Jake picked up a couple of stout staves and began to fix them across the cabin doors. Very soon the two men were imprisoned. Then he turned to Clem. 'Tell Brutus to guard 'em and tear 'em limb from limb if they so much as shows a nose outside,' he said grimly. Then with raised voice, 'Brutus already knows what sort of men they are, so he won't hesitate to maul 'em pretty bad if they tries to escape.' He gestured to the other two to leave *The Singing Lark* and, as soon as they were some way from her, lowered his voice and spoke again: 'There's tracks a plenty leading away from the canal at this point. All we need do is identify which were made by the girl. Then we can follow easy enough.'

'But first we'd best get back to *The Liverpool Rose*

and fetch a lantern each,' Priddy said with her usual good sense. 'What's more, we'd best carry a blanket and a bottle o' my brandy wine because that poor girl has been out in this wicked weather for a while judgin' by the snow settling into the footprints.'

'You go back to the boat then, and I'll take the lantern and start ahead of you,' Clem said.

Lizzie came to herself and, for a moment, thought she was back in the butty boat, cuddled down amongst the fleeces. There was something warm and woolly against her face. But when she moved, every bone in her body seemed to shriek a protest and the darkness before her eyes became filled with stars which owed nothing to the firmament above. Hastily, Lizzie stopped moving and with infinite caution opened first one eye then the other. It was no longer dark but the light was very peculiar, not in the least like the faded green glow to which she had grown accustomed while aboard the butty boat. The light here was yellowy-grey, a very odd colour indeed, and seemed to be coming from above her, but when she tried to move her eyes to look up, such an appalling pain arrowed through her head that she quickly closed her lids once more, deciding to give herself a few moments before further exploring her surroundings. She lay where she was for some time, she could not have said for how long, before daring to move again, and during this time, forced her mind to go back, to the chase on the hillside, her slide down into the gulley, and the manner in which what had seemed to be a snowy bank had simply given way beneath her feet.

She had no idea how long she had lain here, nor where the pursuit had gone, but she was quite sure she was alone so that when she distinctly heard someone breathing, followed by a little cough, she was so frightened that she nearly screamed out loud. However, instead of screaming, she opened her eyes and began to peer around her. She was careful not to swivel her eyes, but moved her whole head and was at last able to see, dimly, where she lay.

She was lying among a flock of sheep, all of whom were huddled into a cave-like structure, roofed by what appeared to be yellowing ice, through which came the light which illuminated her surroundings. A small stream nearby flowed between ragged banks and she realised, with some surprise, that the place was pretty well snow-free. The body heat from the sheep obviously kept the place sufficiently warm to melt it and she supposed, vaguely, that both sheep and shepherds knew this, which meant the shepherd would not search for his flock with too much anxiety, guessing that they were safe. As she watched, one of the sheep coughed again, sounding so human that, had she not seen it, Lizzie would still have looked for the shepherd. Now that she looked more closely about her, she could see the hole through which she had entered the sheep cave – if cave it could be called; it was quite small and fringed with snow and she guessed it would soon ice over, for already snow was forming around the edges. Having seen the stream, Lizzie became aware that she was terribly thirsty and tried to get herself on to her knees so that she might crawl over to the water and have a drink. As she began to move, she looked down at her hands and saw the knuckles raw and bleeding and the fingers of her left hand swollen into purple suasages. What was more, as she moved, she felt something trickle across her brow and her exploring fingers found a nasty gash on her scalp which stretched down on to her forehead and had begun to bleed sluggishly as she moved.

The crawl down to the stream was slow and incredibly painful but she managed it at last and filled her hands with the icy water, cupping them to her face and drinking greedily until she had slaked her thirst. I'll just lie here quietly and wait to be rescued, Lizzie told herself, for the effort of reaching the stream had completely exhausted her.

The sheep, huddled together placidly chewing, glanced incuriously at her as she crawled past them back to her former nest amongst these living fleeces and Lizzie, aware that but for their warmth she would probaby be dead by now, smiled at them as she lay down once more. As she settled herself, she realised she had run away from *The Singing Lark* in darkness but while she had lain unconscious another day had dawned. A shiver of fear ran through her. How long would it be before someone came searching, either for her or for their sheep? How long could she survive on only water and with her hurts so many and various? Come to that, who knew she was missing? She felt certain the Trelawney brothers would not search for her, nor tell anyone she had run away from them and their boat the previous night.

But it was no use worrying. Lizzie took a deep steadying breath and reminded herself that sheep – if not runaway girls – were a valuable commodity for which someone would be searching. Then she began to pray.

Clem set off to follow the trail in hot blood and with considerable faith in his own ability to catch up with Lizzie before too long, but it proved much more difficult than he had expected. For a start, he had not realised there would be three trails; clearly, despite their words, Abe and Reuben had both been out on the hillside, presumably trying to find the girl. It was impossible, therefore, to tell one trail from the other because the snow was so deep – almost waist-high in places – that one could not see the footprints. What was more, the trails crossed and re-crossed each other and, in places, the wind had already blown enormous drifts over the marks in the snow, making his task incredibly difficult.

By the time Jake and Priddy joined him, Clem was beginning to despair. Had Abe been right? Had this foray up into the hills ended in Lizzie returning to the towpath in order to make her way along it, in comparative comfort, to the nearest village? After several hours of desperate searching in the dark, the three of them saw the dawn begin to grey the sky with considerable relief. '*Now* we'll have a chance to see what we're doin,' Jake said, with real satisfaction. 'D'you realise, Priddy, that it's been too dark to see a barn, even though we passed one by less than ten feet away? The gal could be shelterin' in such a place and us none the wiser, but now the light's come, we stand a good chance of catchin' up with her before . . .'

But despite their hopes, daylight was well advanced and they had still not discovered Lizzie, and what was worse the hillside was now a churned up mass of tracks where the three of them had been frantically searching.

Finally, they returned to the towpath, considerably chastened as well as exhausted by their unsuccessful search. 'We might as well make our way to the next village . . .' Clem was beginning, when Priddy gripped his arm. 'Brutus!' she said excitedly. 'The gal's hair ribbon! Dogs can follow a trail even after it's cold if they've got something to go on . . . to sniff at like, so's they know the right scent to follow.' She gestured to *The Singing Lark* and the dog still sitting patiently on the deck, eyes fixed on the cabin doors. 'Go and fetch him, Clem, and let him show us what he can do.'

'But if we takes the dog away, they'll be off, sure as eggs is eggs,' Jake said doubtfully. 'They're thieves as well as scoundrels don't forget, Priddy.'

'So far as I'm concerned, they can get off scot-free, if only we find Lizzie alive,' Clem put in grimly. 'But perhaps, now that it's light, they could lead us to her. We could rope their wrists and force them to walk ahead of us.'

But Priddy shook her head at him and gripped his arm. 'Let 'em go,' she said quietly. 'They'll be no manner o' use, they're more likely to hold us up. Let Brutus sniff that there ribbon and tell him to find Lizzie. He's an intelligent dog and scent's a wonderful thing. As for these fellers . . .' She jerked her head towards the cabin. 'They can't go far from the canal, so they ain't likely to escape justice, but we've got better things to do. Lerr'em go, then we can get Brutus on Lizzie's trail. Believe me, he'll be far more use to us than them idle, lyin' buggers.'

'I wonder if you and Jake should stay behind and keep an eye on the Trelawney lads, though,' Clem said, as the dog came bounding towards them at his whistle. 'Suppose they try to damage *The Liverpool Rose* so we can't follow them? If they do that, and we find Lizzie, we'll have no means of getting her to safety. Honestly, Jake, don't you think the two of you had best stay behind? You can get some porridge or something on the go, so when Brutus and me come back with Lizzie, there's summat hot to warm her up.'

Jake was reluctant because he said that Clem might need his help if he found Lizzie in a bad way, but

Clem assured him that he could cope with a slip of a thing like her on his own, so Jake consented to guard *The Liverpool Rose* and to keep an eye on *The Singing Lark* at the same time. 'It's a pity you whistled Brutus, because they may well guess the dog ain't there no more,' he remarked as he and Priddy turned back towards the canal boat. 'Still, what's done can't be undone, and they may think you only called him off for a moment.'

So, presently, Clem and Brutus set off together into the snow-covered hills.

Lizzie was dreaming. In her dream, she was a sheep, grazing happily on a great plain of grass and surrounded by other sheep, similarly employed. The sun was shining and the air was warm and sweet, the grass beneath her feet fresh and green. Suddenly, however, in the manner of dreams, the blue sky overhead took on a threatening aspect and Lizzie heard ominous sounds coming from the distant hills. The sheep around her raised their heads and began calling to one another, their unease evident even to Lizzie's unpractised eye.

The flock began to move off, bunching close, wild-eyed, but since Lizzie could see no danger she did not immediately follow their example and so was at the back of the flock when the frightened animals suddenly stampeded into terrified movement. Following them, Lizzie glanced back and saw, out of the corner of her eye, a lean and terrible grey shape. Wolves! Lizzie put everything into her running but already the thin, grey shapes of half a dozen enormous wolves were close on her heels, snapping at her thick wool, their white teeth and foetid breath horribly close.

She felt herself go down, felt the teeth close on the

wool around her neck ... and woke, a sheep no longer but a terrified girl, lying amongst sheep and prey, presumably, to their fears, for even as she sat up, wiping the sweat of terror from her brow, an enormous wolf came bounding towards her, across the broad backs of the sheep. It straddled her body but even as she drew in her breath to scream, it began to nuzzle and lick her face, uttering little whimpers of pleasure, and she recognised Brutus.

For one moment longer Lizzie's fears caused her to cringe back, then she flung both arms round the huge, shaggy neck and burst into tears of relief. If Brutus was with her, then Clem could not be far away, and she had no doubt he would take care of her and see her safe.

Clem had been keeping as close to Brutus as he could, fascinated by the fact that the dog was clearly following a trail across the deep snow, for he never took his eyes off the ground ahead, only pausing now and then to cast about where a drift was particularly churned up. He saw Brutus climb a small rise and then the huge dog appear to slip and disappeared into a gulley in a flurry of snow. Clem, following as fast as he could, gained the top of the rise and looked down. He saw what appeared to be a great hump of smooth, untrampled snow below him, and then spotted a jutting lip of rock with a semi-circular hole beneath it. Sighing to himself, he began to descend the slope; the big dog must have lost his footing and plunged down the ravine and through the snow covering into whatever lay beneath. During his time of living in a small village, Clem had heard all about sheep caves and guessed that this might be one of them – indeed, as he drew nearer, he could hear the faint shufflings and uneasy baaings of a flock of sheep into whose midst an enormous dog had just descended.

He reached the lip of rock and peered over. As he had suspected, he saw steam rising gently through a small hole in the thick carapace of ice formed when the sheep's warmth semi-melted the snow. It was not a large hole, but Clem decided that his own descent would probably enlarge it enough for him to drop through and, accordingly, scrambled from the rock, slid down the slope and entered the sheep cave, feet first, his body enlarging the hole as he did so, while the frightened sheep hastily backed away from him, so that he landed on wet, much poached grass.

For a moment, he took in only the sheep and Brutus turning to face him, gently waving his tail. Then he saw Lizzie, lying between the dog's forepaws. She was blood-streaked, battered and bruised, but she had one arm around Brutus's neck, her fingers clutching at his ruff . . . and she was smiling.

'Oh, Clem, ain't he just the bestest dog in the whole world?' she said in a small, croaking voice. 'I don't know how he found me, or if he were really searching for the sheep, but I reckon he's saved me life just about. I've never been so glad to see anyone, 'cos I thought I were a gonner when I fell in here last night.'

Clem approached her cautiously, then sat down beside her and gave her a loving squeeze, which made Lizzie draw in her breath sharply. 'Sorry, queen, I didn't mean to hurt you,' he apologised. 'I agree Brutus is a marvellous dog, 'cos all he had to go on was the ribbon off the end of your plait – it must have fallen off when you left *The Singing Lark* – yet he followed your trail through all that snow and didn't even let the sheep cave put him off. But Lizzie, old love, what on earth has happened to you? You look as though you've been run over by a bus, or mauled by a pack of wolves or some such.'

'I don't really know,' she confessed, leaning against his shoulder. 'I came to the top of a little hillock and went to go down – I were running away from the Trelawney brothers – then I must have slipped. I knocked myself unsconcious and when I came round, I was here, with the sheep all round me and a lot of aches and pains.' She looked anxiously up at him. 'How's we going to get out, Clem? I don't think I could climb up the way we came in.'

'No, I don't think I could either and I'm perishin' sure Brutus couldn't,' he agreed. 'But there must be another way out . . .' He looked round him. 'Ah, see that stream. If we follow it downhill, then we'll pretty soon find we're in open country once more. Are you game to try, love? Only the sooner we get you aboard *The Liverpool Rose*, the sooner Priddy can see to your hurts and get a good hot meal inside you.'

'I'll have a go,' Lizzie said at once, but as soon as she tried to put weight on her ankle, she gave a sharp cry and turned a scared, white face to his. 'Oh, Clem, there's something wrong with my leg. My ankle's agony, I can't possibly walk, even a step. Whatever will I do?'

'We can't stand up here anyway,' he said, 'the ice ceiling is too low. Can you crawl?'

'I think so,' Lizzie said doubtfully.

'I'll give you a fireman's lift when we're out in the open,' Clem said comfortingly. 'But until then, we'll just have to follow Brutus's example and go on all fours.' He kept a careful eye on Lizzie's slow, painful progress, wincing sympathetically every time he heard a sharp intake of breath, but there was little he could do to help, save for encouraging her to continue and promising that her ordeal would soon be over.

In fact, the sheep cave only continued for another five or six yards and then they were pushing through a wall of soft snow, which gave way as they thrust through it. With a sigh of relief, Clem stood up, brushed the snow from his face and bent to pick Lizzie up and prop her against a great, snow-covered boulder which stood beside the stream. As he had predicted, they were now on the downward slope of the great hill and below them they could actually see a part of the canal, though neither of the boats was in view from here. Clem turned back to Lizzie and put an arm around her waist. With her hair soaked and her face still bruised and blood-streaked, she looked a sorry sight, standing on one leg and breathing hard from her recent exertions. But when she saw him watching her, she conjured up a grin. 'Thank the Lord that part's over,' she said in a heartfelt tone. 'Suppose we try to get down together, like in a three-legged race, with me hopping? Would that work, do you think?'

Clem admired her pluck but shook his head firmly at the suggestion. 'No, it would be far too dangerous and painful for you,' he told her. 'I'm afraid you're going to get carried down that hill piggy-back style. Now, put your arms round my neck and keep as still as you can and we'll be down before you know it. Ready? Hold tight, here we go!'

It was a painful and perilous journey for both of them since Lizzie's grip tightened involuntarily every time Clem slipped – which was often – and he thought she might well strangle him before they ever attained the towpath, but they got there at last and, with an inward sigh of relief, Clem stood her down, supporting her with an arm about her waist once more. 'Now all we've got to do is get you aboard *The*

Rose,' he said cheerfully, if a trifle breathlessly. 'Then Priddy will clean you up and make you comfortable and we can turn and head for Liverpool once more.'

Lizzie, however, did not seem to be attending. She was staring at the canal as though she could not believe her eyes, then she turned to him. 'Where is she?' she asked wildly. 'Where's she gone, Clem?'

For a moment, he did not know what she was talking about. *The Liverpool Rose* was there, still moored to the bank and with smoke puffing gently out of her red chimney stack. Then he looked along the canal to where *The Singing Lark* had been moored beneath the willows and realised what Lizzie meant. The stretch of water was empty. *The Lark* and her butty boat had disappeared.

'What the devil's been happening?' Clem said breathlessly as he hauled Lizzie aboard the boat. 'Jake thought he had made the cabin fast but I suppose once Brutus had left to find you, the Trelawneys managed to break out somehow.'

'I don't care where they've gone . . .' Lizzie was beginning, when the cabin door opened and Priddy appeared. She was pale beneath her tan and began speaking even as she held the cabin door open for them to enter.

'Oh, Clem, you've found her – thank God!' she said fervently. 'But the fat's in the fire here. After you'd left, Abe asked Jake if they could have a bit of wood to start the cabin fire goin' because it were mortal cold in there. You know Jake, lad, he's soft as a brush, and besides, though he knows the Trelawneys are villains, he's always had a soft spot for Abe. Says he's not as black as he's painted and wouldn't hurt a fly, left to himself. So, anyroad, he fetches dry wood from the storage cabin, takes down the barricades and starts to feed the wood in, log by log, through a gap in the cabin door. I'm not too clear what happened next – though it might have been an accident – but Jake seems to have got knocked over the head and put out for the count. Then they chucked him ashore and, fair dos, Abe ran along the bank and told me there'd been an accident.' She snorted. 'I suppose he had to say that, and for all I know it could have been as he said. If Jake's head had been near the doors when that Reuben burst out of them, he could have taken a nasty knock, I suppose. So we'll lose no more time but get movin' towards Blackburn where a proper doctor can take a look at him and get a message to the police and the tug.'

Clem looked anxiously at Jake as he lay on his bed, his face paler than Priddy's and his mouth slightly open. He was making an odd snoring noise which filled Clem with foreboding, but he said bracingly: 'Yes, but in the meantime, Priddy, can you take a look at our Lizzie? I think she may have broke her ankle and there's a nasty cut clean across her scalp besides an awful lot of bruises and cuts. She tumbled into a ravine . . . but you'd best take a look for yourself while I get *The Liverpool Rose* ready to leave and harness Hal up.'

Priddy, immediately concerned, sat Lizzie down, poured hot water into a basin and began to bathe her head, saying over her shoulder as she did so: 'The Trelawneys took Hal, Clem. If you remember, we left him standing on the towpath with a couple of thick blankets over him and his nosebag full of oats while we searched for young Lizzie here – that's how they were able to gerraway so fast. But their old bag o' bones will still be in the stable, having had a good rest, and his tack will be with him. So you'd best bring him down and fasten him to the tow rope. This is a nasty

406

cut but not deep. I'll put some of me soothin' ointment on it and cover it with a piect of lint and it'll soon start to mend, though when we get to Blackburn it'll mebbe need a stitch or two. Now let's take a look at that ankle.' She left Lizzie for a moment, to pull down the bunk opposite the one on which Jake lay. 'Hop up here, love, let the dog see the rabbit,' she said cheerfully. 'We'll soon have you right. Which is more than I can say for my Jake here.'

The rest of that day passed in a blur of pain and puzzlement so far as Lizzie was concerned. Priddy's strong, clever fingers probed her ankle until she could not smother her screams, despite pushing her head into the duck-down pillow. But at last it was over. 'It weren't broken,' Priddy said breathlessly, with sweat running across her forehead and down the sides of her face. 'Somethin' had got dislocated, but I think I've put it right now. I'm goin' to strap it up tight so's it will bed down natural like, and as soon as he's able, I'll get young Clem to cut you a couple o' crutches because you mustn't put that foot to the ground for a few days. But once I'm sure it's knitted together, you'll be as spry as ever you was.'

Shortly after this, Lizzie had been wretchedly sick, vomiting up the lovely hot tea which Priddy had – perhaps unwisely – allowed her to drink before beginning to deal with her ankle. After this, the canal boat began to move as the Trelawneys' despised Boxer leaned his shoulders into the collar and began to pull.

The movement of the boat on the water should have been soothing and pleasant, Lizzie thought fretfully, but somehow it was not. Her head ached horribly and even the slight movement as the boat glided forward made her ankle stab with pain and increased her feeling of sickness. However, the cabin seemed a safe haven after the fear and horror she had endured in the sheep cave and she felt quite ashamed that she could not appreciate how much better her lot was than it might have been, and indeed, every time her eyes fell on Jake's still form, she realised the extent of her own good fortune. But for Clem and Brutus – and indeed, for Priddy and Jake – she might still be in the sheep cave or, worse, lying stiff and dead amongst the snow-covered hills.

That Jake was very ill, Priddy did not bother to deny. Had it been possible for her to treat him herself, she would undoubtedly have done so, but she told Lizzie, during the course of the morning, that she knew very little about concussion save that it was dangerous. She said she would feel very much happier when she was able to get Jake into hospital where they understood such things.

'How long will it take us to get to Blackburn?' Lizzie asked when dusk was falling and Clem had come down into the cabin to say they would soon moor up because they were near stabling where Boxer might spend the night. 'Do you think it might be wiser to try to get him a faster conveyance of some description? I know we're a long way from the city still.'

Priddy, however, was doubtful of the wisdom of such an action. 'I don't think he ought to be rattled around,' she said worriedly. 'Even though I wants him seen by a doctor, I don't think a journey on land could do anything but harm. He's best off in the old *Liverpool Rose*, where he's accustomed to the motion, like.'

And by evening she was proved right for when the corned beef hash was being served, with Lizzie sitting up in her bunk and Clem and Priddy perched on the two stools, Jake suddenly stirred. His eyelashes fluttered, though his eyes did not open completely, but he said in a slurred voice: 'Somethin' smells good,' before relapsing into seeming unconsciousness once more.

Priddy, delighted by this evidence that he was beginning to pull round, hastily heated a mug of beef tea and she and Clem supported the old man until he was more or less upright in his bunk. Then Priddy fed him the beef tea, spoonful by spoonful, and though the first attempts simply dribbled down his chin, he suddenly seemed to realise what was happening and his throat worked in regular swallows until half the mugful had disappeared. Only then did he give an inarticulate mumble and turn his head away, making it plain that he had taken enough nourishment for now at any rate.

Lizzie, Clem and Priddy were all immensely heartened by this, though Lizzie was worried that she was sleeping in Priddy's bunk and tried to insist that she would be quite comfortable on the cabin floor overnight. Clem said she might have his little cabin on the butty boat and he would curl up in the storage cabin aboard *The Liverpool Rose* but Priddy pooh-poohed this as being quite unnecessary. 'If you think I could sleep – aside from the odd cat-nap – with Jake so poorly, you must have a queer old opinion of me,' she said roundly. 'I'll sit in me old chair wi' a cushion behind me head and keep an eye on me invalids, so's if one of 'em were to stir, I'd know all about it. Now if you've stabled that dratted old horse and seen us moored up safe and sound, young Clem, you'd best be off to your bed 'cos I reckon we'll make an early start in the mornin'.

Chapter Eleven

Despite his brave words to Sally that Clem would be looking after Lizzie, Geoff found himself worrying more and more as his trips to the canal resulted in no good news, either of *The Liverpool Rose* or of Lizzie herself. In his worst moments, he imagined that Lizzie's Uncle Perce had somehow managed to get on her trail and was searching the canal vessels for her with murder in his heart, but at other times he was more sanguine. Canal folk stuck together, everyone said so, which surely meant they would protect Lizzie, who was Clem's good friend, from any evil which threatened her. What was more, the ferocity of the blizzard and the depth of the snow now covering the land was so great that many villages and towns were cut off, and common sense told Geoff that no matter how much Lizzie might wish to come back to Liverpool, she and *The Liverpool Rose* would almost certainly be unable to do so until the weather cleared. He spent a good deal of time over the Christmas holiday with Sally and her parents, though he and Sally tended to leave the court as soon as they could so they might talk over their various worries.

The court, of course, was full of gossip about Annie Grey's strange death and her husband's subsequent disappearance, but Sally had spoken seriously to Mrs Bradshaw and impressed upon her the importance of keeping her knowledge of Uncle Perce's liaison with Flossie to herself. Sally's mother had pooh-poohed this advice, reluctant to curb her desire to gossip, but fortunately Mr Bradshaw had backed Sally up and assured his wife that it was not only foolish but probably courting trouble to tell what she knew. 'A cornered rat is always dangerous,' he told her severely, 'and Percy's got a lot to lose if you go shootin' your mouth off. Do you want him comin' round here one dark night to shut your mouth for you, eh? If he's found guilty of murder then it's the noose for him, no question, so killin' one more woman isn't likely to worry him.'

Mrs Bradshaw might be a gossip – well, she was – but she had a strong sense of self-preservation and obviously decided that her husband's advice was worth following. At any rate, though she listened with interest to the tittle-tattle of her neighbours, she contributed nothing herself.

On the day following Boxing Day, which was a Saturday, Geoff returned to the bank though Sally's factory did not open until the Monday. She had agreed that she would go up to the orphan asylum of Our Lady of the Immaculate Heart today. So, after her dinner, Sally set off, her muffler well up over her face and her hands wedged into the pockets of her coat, for though it was no longer actually snowing it was still bitterly cold, and even in the city the snow was still piled in great drifts across many of the pavements.

She was a little nervous when she reached the convent, wondering how she would be greeted there, but the nun who opened the door to her and asked her name smiled very sweetly and led her inside, saying that she was expected and that Evie Evans could be with her in five minutes.

She indicated a chair upon which Sally could sit while she waited then disappeared down a long, flagstoned corridor, leaving the girl to glance, a trifle apprehensively, around her. The hall was oblong in shape and lit by a glass dome high above Sally's head. A broad staircase led to the upper floors. There were a number of holy pictures on the staircase wall and four small statues in the niches between various doorways, but other than that the place was completely bare. It was also extremely cold, the air seeming very little warmer than that outside. But Sally scarcely had time to wish she had not removed her muffler and gloves before Evie was crossing the hall towards her, throwing open one of the fine oak doors and ushering her into the small room beyond.

'I've got permish to use Sister Agatha's room because the common room's full of girls, all chattering away like magpies,' she said. 'Do sit down, Miss . . . er . . .'

'I'm Sally – Sally Bradshaw,' she said a trifle reproachfully. 'Don't you remember me from the old days, Chinky? Oh, I know I shouldn't call you that, you've turned respectable like what I have. You're Evie Evans now, but I thought you might remember me 'cos I remember you. At least,' she added honestly, 'I never would have known you, only Geoff told me that's who you were.'

'Yes, I do remember you, Sally,' Evie admitted. 'But you're a working girl now and I'm still at school. It makes a difference, doesn't it?'

'Yes, I suppose,' Sally said. 'But we've not met to discuss how much we've changed, queen. Geoff is desperate to know what happened to you after he and his pal left Sid's flat, and I'm pretty curious meself. You seemed to disappear off the face of the earth and we were real worried Sid might have harmed you in some way.'

'He did his best to,' Evie admitted, and sighed. 'It's a long story and if you're to make head or tail of it, I'd better start right at the beginning, when Sid first found out I was at the orphanage. It was like this . . .'

It was a long story, but one which Sally listened to with bated breath. She and Geoff had arranged to meet in Regan's dining rooms on Islington as soon as the bank closed. So it was over tea and cakes there that she repeated Evie's story with considerable relish.

She told Geoff how Evie had been picked up by the scuffer and accepted into the orphan asylum and how Sid had come across her as she made her way to a music lesson. At first, she had told Sally her meetings with him had been delightful interludes in her rather boring and restricted life, so when Sid had suggested that she might go out with him to concerts, films and so on, she had been both flattered and delighted. After all, she was a great deal younger than he and thought that he could have his pick of girls without having to work for their company the way he had to with Evie herself.

Sid had been very obliging, actually buying with his own money some black high-heeled shoes and a couple of cheeky, modern little hats, decorated with bunches of feathers and tiny half-veils. He had even invested in a long, straight skirt, so that she would not be picked out as the schoolgirl she was when they went around together, and the innocent Evie had taken this borrowed finery at face value. She had changed at Sid's aunt's house – or, at least, Sid had told Evie the woman was his aunt – and had felt very grown up and sophisticated at the cinema shows, theatre performances and concerts to which he had squired her. In fact, until the night he had taken her back to his flat, it had never occurred to her that Sid could have any reason other than sheer kindness for taking her about and spending money on her.

But on the evening in question, he had shown his hand for the first time. He had suggested, quite seriously, that Evie should leave the convent and go to work in one of the big stores. Had explained that with her unusual looks and slender figure, she could not only sell gowns but could model them for her customers and, consequently, be very much better paid than an ordinary shop girl. 'What's more, you'd meet the right kind of people, rich people – fellers as well as women – in a posh shop like that,' he had assured her. 'Then, of course, because you weren't stuck in that bleedin' convent of yours, I could take you to the races wi' me, introduce you to the fellers wi' *real* money, fellers who are longin' to meet a nice girl and give her a good time. Honest to God, Evie, you could have a grand life and make yourself a deal o' money, simply escortin' me rich clients to dances and so on. You could have a little flat in a smart part of town, a maid to keep things nice . . . I'm tellin' you, a girl like you could go anywhere,' he had said.

Sid clearly thought that Evie would leap at his offer but instead she had been unable to prevent herself from showing not only dismay but a good deal of annoyance. She had never pretended that she wanted a career as either a shopgirl or a 'friend' to rich race goers, and thought Sid was taking advantage of their friendship by making such suggestions. She was about to storm back to the orphanage when she and Sid bumped into Geoff and his pal.

The rest of the evening she genuinely enjoyed but

tried to leave the flat when the two lads did. Sid had prevented her from doing so and she had not demurred, believing he intended to take her home in style in a taxi. Once he had her alone, however, he had changed completely, and when she tried to leave, had beaten her into submission, actually saying he meant to keep her in the flat overnight so that even if she tried to return to the convent, the nuns would not take her back in.

Sally had been horrified by this dreadful story but soon realised that Evie was not the pushover Sid had taken her for. Beneath the veneer of a quiet and cultivated convent school girl lurked tough and self-reliant little Chinky who had fought her own battles for years. She had waited until Sid had gone into the kitchen to make a cup of tea, believing her to be too battered and bruised to resist, and then she had hidden behind the door, poker upraised. As Sid returned with two brimming cups, she had hit him behind his left ear and watched with considerable satisfaction as he fell senseless to the floor. 'I helped meself to the money out of his pockets so's I could get a taxi and went back to the convent,' she told Sally. 'I knew that the time for deceit was over if I wanted to continue with my musical career, so I went straight to the Mother Superior and told her everything. I told her that Sid's aunt was just a blind and I'd been a complete fool – and wicked as well – but that I'd learned my lesson and simply wanted to forget what had happened and remain a pupil here.'

'And she *forgave* you?' Sally had asked incredulously. 'Well, obviously she did, or you wouldn't be here today. I bet they punished you, didn't they?'

Evie chuckled. 'Not really,' she had assured the

other girl. 'Oh, I had to keep an eye on the little ones, and of course there were no more outings, but somehow it didn't seem like a punishment. I'm trying for a musical scholarship to the Royal College when I'm old enough, and in the meantime I'll do anything to help the nuns that I can because they've been so good to me.'

Sally had asked Evie whether the fact that she had left Sid lying unconscious on the floor of his flat, had worried her. 'After all, you might have killed him,' she had observed. But Evie, laughing, merely shook her head.

'I knew he weren't dead,' she had said breezily. 'He were beginning to stir as I let myself out. And anyway, he only got what he deserved. What's more, bad pennies like Sid don't die of a crack on the head. I reckon he'll be around, making life miserable for someone, for a good few years yet.'

Then Sally had told Evie about Geoff's meeting with him on Lime Street Station, and although Evie pretended to be indifferent she saw the younger girl's face brighten. 'So he's left the 'Pool?' she had said. 'Well, if he ever shows his face here again and tries anything on wi' me, I'll make sure he regrets it. Thanks for tellin' me though, Sally.'

By the time Sally had recounted Evie's story, she and Geoff had drunk a large pot of tea and eaten a plate of cakes, and he found himself suddenly smiling broadly and feeling . . . oh, feeling as if a weight had been lifted from his shoulders. He had liked Evie, had felt sorry for her, worried about her, but he realised now that he had never really known the girl and had been attracted to her simply because she was both beautiful and strange. He had also felt guilty for not making sure that she was all right, that Sid had not preyed upon her in some way.

Now, however, with the certainty that Evie was both all right and indeed happy, he realised he could turn his attention to Sally. He had been growing fonder and fonder of the other girl and hoped that, in her turn, she might be beginning to like him. Geoff did not usually feel at ease with girls, but he had been aware for some time that he was beginning to feel as though he had known Sally for years. Sitting opposite her at the table, he suddenly shot out both hands and seized hers. 'You're a grand girl, Sally, and you've relieved my mind no end. I felt responsible for Evie in a way, after leaving her with Sid that time. But I don't feel responsible any more – she's clearly happy – so now I can tell you . . . that . . .'

His words stuttered into silence but Sally was smiling at him, her expression understanding. 'I like you, too, Geoff,' she said softly. 'Ain't it odd how difficult it is to tell a feller – or a girl – that you like 'em? Is . . . is . . . that what you were goin' to say, chuck?'

'It was,' he said, mightily relieved to have the words said for him. 'So shall we go steady, queen? Only it seems to me we gerralong better than most. What do you say?'

'Well, wharrabout Lizzie?' Sally said cautiously, but her eyes were shining. 'I thought you and she . . .'

'We were just pals,' he said immediately. 'Besides, I reckon Clem's head over heels for our Lizzie. Come on, Sally, say you'll be me steady girl!'

She giggled. 'We'll give it a go then,' she said. 'Now let's visit the canal again and see if there's any more news of Lizzie or *The Liverpool Rose*.'

*

As soon as *The Liverpool Rose* reached Blackburn Clem took himself off ashore to persuade the police to telephone around to any officer stationed near the canal so they might keep a look-out for either *The Singing Lark* or *The Pride of the 'Pool*.

The policeman on the desk was eating sandwiches as Clem entered the station and hastily scooped up the greaseproof-wrapped package and shoved it out of sight under the counter. There was a slight pause while he chewed and swallowed frantically, then he spoke. 'Sorry, lad, just catchin' up on missing me breakfast. What can I do for 'ee?'

Clem took a deep breath before replying because he had so much to remember. Priddy had been firm on the point that, so far as he was able, he should not reveal that the Trelawneys were carrying stolen fleeces. 'Canal folk stick together,' she had said. 'If Alf Hitchin has already caught up with them, he'll have taken back his cargo and made them pay in some way for the theft. But none of us will want the police to go a-throwin' a boatman in the clink. It ain't natural, t'would just about kill the Trelawneys, I reckon, and besides, Abe isn't a bad feller. Why, even Reuben is only violent when he's drunk. No, no, we don't want the police interferin' with canal justice.'

'But what about Lizzie?' Clem had asked, rather scandalised by Priddy's attitude, though because of his close connection with the canal and its people, he could understand this reluctance to ask help from those ashore. Often enough, when he visited one of the larger towns in order to get supplies, he had been annoyed by the calm assumption that canal folk were really gypsies – water gypsies, to be sure, but even so, the term was abusive rather than complimentary. So now he chose his words carefully. 'I'd like to get a message to the crew of *The Pride of the 'Pool*,' he told the policeman. 'I can tell you more or less where they'll be, though they're a powered boat so they'll move a deal faster than us. We're the crew of *The Liverpool Rose* and we stick to the Leeds and Liverpool since we're horse-drawn. And I need to send a couple of telegrams to the wool wharf and to Nat Shipley's yard in Leeds, so perhaps you can tell me where the telegraph office is?'

The policeman pulled a pad of paper towards him and began to write. 'It's rare you canal folk ask for help from us,' he commented. 'So what's this all about?'

'A couple of nights ago we'd stabled our Clydesdale gelding in the Pennines alongside another barge horse. The other boat – *The Singing Lark* – left first, and I suppose, what with the darkness and one horse lookin' very like another, the crew of *The Singing Lark* tacked up our Hal instead of their Boxer,' Clem said. 'They'll have realised by now, of course, but I doubt they'll know whose horse they've got. We want them to hang fire in Leeds until we arrive so's we can swap the animals over again.'

The policeman was a large, ruddy-faced man who looked more like a farmer than a scuffer. He cocked a shrewd eye at Clem. 'I daresay Hal's a good deal better kept and fed than this 'ere Boxer, ain't he?' he asked, a grin lurking. 'Because, oddly enough, we haven't had no complaint from the crew of *The Singing Lark* that they've got the wrong animal!'

Clem grinned and nodded acknowledgement. 'Yes, Hal is in better condition than Boxer,' he agreed. 'But even if he weren't, we'd want the old feller back. You know how it is.'

'Aye, that I do,' the policeman said heartily. 'And is

419

it the same message for *The Pride of the 'Pool*?'

'No, not exactly. I want to let the crew of *The Pride of the 'Pool* know that *The Singing Lark* is still on the Leeds and Liverpool so they don't waste time searchin' for her all the way from the Mersey to the Aire and Calder Navigation. Oh, and I want them to know me pal Lizzie's aboard *The Liverpool Rose*.'

'Right,' the policeman said, turning the page and beginning to write. 'So what's the message, exactly?'

Clem thought for a moment, sorting out his ideas, then spoke. '"Lizzie is safe aboard *The Liverpool Rose*, though Jake has taken a nasty knock",' he said. ' "*The Singing Lark* is making her way to Leeds, pulled by Hal. We are following with Boxer." '

'Right. I'll see the messages get passed around to all the stations in the vicinity,' the policeman said. 'Anything else? You don't want to report your horse stolen, for instance?'

'No, no, it's just a simple case of mistaken identity,' Clem said hastily. He turned away and was halfway back to the door when the policeman's calm and steady voice stopped him dead in his tracks.

'This Lizzie,' the policeman said slowly. 'You wouldn't be referrin' to a young girl what's gone missin' from Liverpool, around the Burlington Street area, would you? Of course, Christmas is a difficult and confusing time sometimes, but when I come in this morning there were a message concernin' a young girl . . . I *think* Lizzie were her name . . . what someone suspicioned might have took to the canal to escape some unpleasantness.' He turned from the counter to root around amongst the papers on a large desk behind him, then turned back, flourishing a piece of paper in one hand. 'Yes, that's right. The missing girl's called Lizzie Devlin.' He must have been able to read the indecision in Clem's face, for he said chidingly: 'Don't you go keepin' information from the Law, young feller, or you really will be in trouble, stolen horse or no stolen horse. By the messages they've been sendin' out from the 'Pool, there's been nasty goings on up there. Mebbe even murder, readin' between the lines. Now tell me straight – have you got Lizzie Devlin aboard your boat or haven't you?'

Clem turned back, only half reluctantly, towards the counter. In fact, he realised, he felt considerably relieved. He had wondered how to get a message back to Sally that all was well with her friend, but since he did not know who else might be interested in the news had agreed with Lizzie's wish to reveal as little as possible of her whereabouts. However, if someone had reported Lizzie as a missing person then the sooner the whole thing was cleared up the better. It did occur to Clem, fleetingly, that Uncle Perce might have reported her as missing in order to try to shift the blame for Aunt Annie's death to his niece, but a little further thought banished this suspicion from his mind. The moment Lizzie reappeared she would tell the truth about that dreadful night and because of Uncle Perce's bad reputation, if nothing else, Clem was certain she would be believed before her uncle.

Accordingly, he grinned at the policeman and leaned his elbows on the counter. 'Yes, we've got Lizzie Devlin safe and sound aboard *The Liverpool Rose*,' he said at once. 'The reason I didn't tell you immediately, Constable, is because Lizzie is still in mortal fear of her Uncle Perce. She hid herself away on a canal boat because it was one place she thought he wouldn't search . . . She saw him trying to do in his wife, you see, and what's worse, he knew she'd seen. He and his fancy woman chased her a good way, but lost her on the canal bank. Now she's scared to return to Liverpool in case he's waitin' for her.'

The policeman turned and shouted, 'Andy!' and another man appeared. 'Take over the desk, will you?' the Constable said ponderously. He turned to unhook his cape from its place on a hat stand and clapped his helmet down over his bristly, brown hair. 'I'm just a-goin' down to the canal to interview someone as has been missin' since last Monday, so you'd best put the word around that Lizzie Devlin has been found, safe and sound, aboard *The Liverpool Rose*.'

'Safe but not altogether sound,' Clem interpolated, rather anxiously. 'She had a nasty fall in the snow and dislocated her ankle as well as cutting her head open, but Priddy – that's Mrs Pridmore, the Number One's wife – has strapped up the ankle and put a soothing ointment on her head. Mrs Pridmore says she'll soon be right as rain, as long as she doesn't overdo it. And I must say that Lizzie's gettin' on in prime style since I've made her a pair of crutches.'

The policeman's eyes had widened a little as Clem spoke. Now he shook his head slowly from side to side, looking a little like a baffled bull who knows he got into the field but cannot remember how to get out. 'I reckon there's a deal you ain't tellin' me,' he said accusingly. 'Did that uncle of hers beat her up before she got away, or did she try to stop someone a-takin' of the wrong horse? There's a mystery here and we're bound to get to the bottom of it in time, young feller, so why not come clean wi' me now? And what's a Number One when it's at home?'

Clem laughed. 'It's a feller who owns a canal boat,

422

rather than one who works for the company,' he explained. 'I know my story sounds bad when you put it like that but it's really quite straightforward. Lizzie was walking through the snow when she fell into a sheep cave . . . you've heard of sheep caves? . . . and did herself a deal of damage. She'll tell you herself when we reach *The Liverpool Rose*.'

Making his way through the snowy streets beside the policeman, Clem was heartily glad that Priddy had made them go over and over their story so that the whole crew knew precisely what to say when questioned.

Priddy had asked a doctor to come down to the boat. Having examined Jake, he had said that rest was the best treatment and advised them to continue with their journey but make sure Jake did not leave the cabin.

'Well, I think we was downright lucky,' Priddy said as Clem began to get the boat ready to leave. 'If that scuffer hadn't been an understandin' sort o' man, we could have been held up for half a day instead of half an hour. What's more, he might have insisted that Lizzie went back to Liverpool on the next bus, like it or not, some of 'ems that officious . . . so I reckon we were lucky.'

Jake, still lying in his bunk, agreed rather weakly that this was certainly the case. Priddy was still unhappy over his condition and had told Lizzie that if he did not improve a good deal over the next few days she would take him up to the Infirmary when they reached Leeds so that the doctors there could take a good look at him.

Now Lizzie was sitting at the table, preparing a quantity of vegetables for the stewpot. 'That constable were pretty nice, all things considered,' she said, scraping vigorously at the outer skin of an enormous carrot. 'But, of course, I know I've got to go back to Liverpool quite soon. Mind you, though the scuffer said Uncle Perce had disappeared, I'm still scared that he's hidin' away somewhere, waiting to get me. Once I open my mouth . . .'

'You've already opened it,' Priddy observed. 'You told Constable Rogers everything, just about. How the chamber pot were broke and how you saw your uncle deliberately spillin' water, and the syrup of figs your aunt always kept in the corner cupboard . . . you even told him how someone had moved the pile of bricks so that when your aunt fell she hit her head on them. Oh, the wicked old devil! I hope they catches up wi' him, so I do. And since he writ it all down, and you signed it and swore on the Bible it were true, they'll clap your uncle in the clink as soon as they lay hands to his collar.'

'That's certainly true, young 'un,' Jake said, from his bunk. 'I don't deny you'll have to go back to Liverpool when we've discharged our cargo and picked up a new one, but I don't see no hurry. After all, Priddy needs you to keep an eye on me when she's steerin'.'

'Which I'd better do right now,' Priddy said, getting to her feet and heading for the cabin door. 'We'd best get a move on, though, because I'm gettin' desperate worried about Hal. I know the Trelawneys feed Boxer the best they can and probably see he's stabled warm o' nights, but that's because they need him in good fettle to pull *The Singing Lark*. I wouldn't put it past them to keep Hal pulling day and night and forget all about stabling because they know very well we'll claim him back as soon as maybe.'

'Oh, the Trelawneys ain't that bad,' Jake said comfortably as his wife left the cabin. 'They've never had a name for cruelty to animals, though a good few company men ain't too particular how they treats their horses. I don't think they'd use Hal badly 'cos they know they'd have me to reckon with.'

'They were pretty good to the horse while I was with them,' Lizzie agreed. 'Tell you what, Jake, when I've done these vegetables I'd like to go and sit with Priddy for a bit so that I can take a turn at steering the boat. I know I'm not much use while I'm on crutches, but I'm sure I could steer, even if I had to take a stool out and sit down while I did it.'

Jake agreed that this should be perfectly possible and a great help. Lizzie tipped the prepared carrots, onions and turnip into the stewpot, added the chunks of mutton already floured and lightly fried, and pulled the pan over the fire. 'It'll be a while before it boils, so I'll nip out now and sit with Priddy for a bit,' she said. 'If you can give me a yell, Jake, when it starts to simmer, then I'll come in and bank the fire down so's it doesn't boil over.'

He said he would do so and very soon Lizzie was outside and making her way along the deck to the rear of the boat. She moved cautiously because of the crutches, but already she was able to rest the toe of her injured foot on the ground to give her a bit more stability, and hoped that in a few days she would be able to abandon the crutches and be really useful once more.

Priddy greeted her warmly and very soon the two of them were comfortably settled, taking turns to steer the boat. It was not a difficult job, provided one kept one's mind on the work. Presently, Lizzie remarked that when she had fed the hens earlier she had found two eggs in the straw and had taken them into the cabin. 'The trouble with feeding the hens is that it reminds me of Sausage and Mash, and that makes me think of poor Aunt Annie and how she loved them,' she admitted. 'I dare not think what Uncle Perce may have done to those hens without either me or Annie to protect them . . .'

'Likely they'll be all right,' Priddy said comfortably. 'That uncle of your'n is going to have other things on his mind than hens. After what he done to his wife he'll likely be on the run, and no one runs wi' a couple of squawkin' hens in their pockets.'

'I expect you're right,' Lizzie said with a sigh. 'But I'm goin' to miss Aunt Annie most dreadfully, Priddy. You never met her, did you? She was one of the kindest people I ever knew, and she treated me like a daughter. If only . . .'

'They say "if only" are the saddest words in the language but, meself, I think they're the daftest,' Priddy said with a sniff. 'When a thing's happened, it's happened. It's no use wishing it hadn't. Now just you think positive, queen. There'll be troubles ahead when we reach the Bingley Five Rise – that's five locks – it'll take the three of us all our time to get *The Liverpool Rose* and her butty boat safely through. I daresay the Trelawneys taught you to open and close the locks, but you weren't on crutches then. I wish I could say Clem and me could manage between us, but to be honest, wi' the two boats, it needs three pairs of hands.'

'If that's so, how will the Trelawneys cope?' Lizzie asked curiously. 'There's only two of them to get *The Singing Lark* and her butty boat through all the locks between here and Leeds.'

'I don't say it isn't possible,' Priddy admitted.

'Those two fellers were born and bred on the canal and they're both strong as oxes. Why, in the old days, when Jake and I were in our full strength, we never thought twice about tackling the locks wi' only the two of us, but now it's different. I ain't as spry as I was and Jake don't have the strength. Then there's climbin' in an' out o' the locks to move the beam – me knees fair cripple me if I try to get out when it's a steel ladder, and Jake ain't much better. Clem's been a godsend to us and I don't mind who knows it. He's that quick to pick up our ways . . . but I don't need to tell you that because you're another such. What's more, you like canal life, don't you?'

'A good few shore folk try for work aboard the boats but very few of 'em last for more 'an a trip or two. It's hard and lonely, I guess. We don't have no picture palaces, nor theatres, nor dance halls. There ain't no department stores, nor big shops, and you can't just pop round to a neighbour's house to borrow a cup of sugar or have a bit of a chat, like. Washin' a shirt's simple enough in fine weather, but when it's cold and rainy or snowy – like it is now – then you have either to put off launderin' until the weather improves, or do the best you can in a little bowl of water on the cabin table. Then you'll have wet washin' draped round your fire for days until you could scream with the irritation of it. Why, even cookin' a meal gets tedious when the weather's bad so you have to keep the cabin doors closed or your fire will blow out. But Jake an' me's been happy as the day's long on the boats, and I think Clem would tell you he's the same.'

'I haven't been aboard a canal boat all that long, but I think it's grand,' Lizzie agreed contentedly, looking around her at the snowy landscape. 'It's so peaceful,

Priddy, and it must be such beautiful countryside when it isn't all hidden by snow. I can't imagine ever being bored on the canal because there's so much to see and do. And so much to learn,' she added, peering ahead. 'What's that across the water, Priddy? It looks like a bridge . . . oh, yes, it's a swing bridge. Whose job is it to open that?'

'Clem will open it and it's quicker if one of us closes it after we've gone through. I'll do it, bein' as you're on crutches and not so nimble as you were. There's seven swing bridges ahead of us on this stretch, but none of 'em's too bad and won't hold us up. The locks at Bingley Five Rise is a different matter, though. You can't hurry goin' through a lock.'

'Nor can the Trelawney brothers,' Lizzie observed as they slid under the swing bridge and Priddy got stiffly to her feet. 'Oh, I wish I could do it for you, Priddy, but by the time we come this way again, surely my ankle will be better!'

Despite Priddy's words, the crew of *The Liverpool Rose* made pretty good time and were mooring up for the night in company with a couple of other boats, taking cargoes through to Leeds, when Clem remarked that the snow was beginning to thaw at last.

'That's good,' Lizzie said absently. She, Clem and Brutus were taking Boxer to the stabling. The able-bodied ones were ambling along in the dusk while Lizzie swung beside them on her crutches. With every day that passed, she was becoming more expert with them, but as is always the way, her need for them diminished as her leg strengthened and soon, she thought hopefully, she would not need them at all.

'The thaw will turn the towpath into a perishin' bog,' Clem observed, leading Boxer across the cobbled yard and into one of the stalls reserved for boat owners' horses. 'I've never seen the canal this high before but the water level will even out – it always does. When you look up at those hills, there's a devil of a lot of snow and it'll all have to go somewhere.'

That evening, sitting cosily in the cabin, they heard the first drops of rain drumming on the roof. Lizzie thought it made the cabin even cosier to know that outside rain was falling while they were snug and warm in *The Liverpool Rose*, but Priddy soon disillusioned her. 'Floods can be terrible things,' she said, looking worried. 'But we should be safe enough on the canal because the lock-keepers regulate the flow of water, opening the sluices to let the excess through so that a stretch of canal never – or almost never – floods. Of course it's been known for a bank to burst.' She turned to Jake, who was now sitting up in a chair most of the day. He was looking frail and Lizzie knew that Priddy was still worried about him. 'Ain't that so, Jake?'

'Aye, Priddy, you're right,' he said. 'There have been terrible troubles when a bank has burst – boats can be carried away and wrecked.'

'That's true,' she agreed. 'But it's been a long time since a bank has gone. The bank rangers are proud of the way each one keeps his own stretch of canal in good condition'.

Because of Lizzie's presence, they had opened up the small stern cabin for her use, shifting the various sacks and bundles to one end of the restricted accommodation so that she, her blanket and pillow and a small lantern, might occupy the remaining space. Lizzie, whose attitude to Brutus had changed dramatically since the incident in the sheep cave, had

429

begged to be allowed to have the dog in her cabin at nights. Though Clem had been agreeable, Brutus had made it clear he did not intend to leave his master's side, so Lizzie barricaded herself in each night. Sleeping as soon as her head hit the pillow, she slept like a baby nightly, usually having to be roused by Clem in order to help Priddy get their breakfast.

On this particular night, however, she found she could not sleep. She could actually feel the water in the canal rising as *The Liverpool Rose* tugged and strained at her mooring ropes and was not surprised when someone banged on her cabin door and Clem's voice said urgently: 'Better get up, Lizzie, I can't tell canal from towpath and the water's running like a river. I reckon we need to wake Priddy and Jake. They'll know best what to do.'

Lizzie joined him within moments, pulling on the wet weather gear which Priddy had lent her, and soon Priddy herself emerged from her cabin, though she would not let Jake come out into the windy darkness. 'We can manage,' she said briskly. 'So long as we're moored we'll be safe enough, though someone will have to go ashore if there's a danger of the ropes breakin'.'

All that night, the three of them took turns to check that the moorings were secure. Both before and behind them, other crews were also about, going on shore from time to time – if you could call it shore – to do the same. As dawn began to grey the eastern sky, Jake insisted upon leaving the cabin and brought them all mugs of steaming tea and enormous cheese sandwiches. 'It'll line your stomachs and warm you up,' he said, handing over the food and drink. He turned to Priddy. 'Do you think the worst is over? It's stopped raining but there's still a deal o' snow to melt.' He glanced out across the expanse of water which had, the previous day, been the towpath and a snow-covered meadow. 'I wonder if we ought to get movin' again once it's daylight? Only we're on the downward run now and we're liable to meet more floods, not fewer. What do you think, Priddy?'

'I think you ought to get back in that cabin and stop worryin' about what don't concern you,' she said severely. 'You're gettin' better, Jake, but if you was to fall ill again, you could put us all in danger. As for movin' on, I think we're best where we are, for a bit at any rate.'

However, as daylight advanced, it was clear that remaining moored up to a towpath which was several inches underwater was beginning to get on Priddy's nerves. She fretted that the Trelawneys might have pressed on regardless, and wondered aloud how Hal was faring in such appalling conditions, and presently she went to one of the other boats to discuss with its Number One the chances of moving on that day.

Clem and Lizzie, sitting glumly on the gunwhales and watching the water running down the sides of the hills until the little streams became more like rivers, felt equally frustrated. 'After what those Trelawney brothers put you through, I don't fancy seeing 'em get off scot-free,' Clem observed. 'Why, if it hadn't been for them, you wouldn't be needin' those perishin' crutches, and Jake would be out here with us, instead of cooped up in the cabin. And though Priddy doesn't say much, I know she's worried about him. He isn't eating properly – he says he isn't hungry because he's not working – and sometimes you have to speak to him two or three times to get his attention. That knock on the head did more damage than he'll admit, if you ask me.'

'I know,' Lizzie said at once. 'Priddy won't be satisfied until they've taken a look at him in the Infirmary. But Clem, how old *is* Jake? I suppose he's getting on. They say the older you are, the harder it is to recover from a bad fall or a blow on the head, and he must be past sixty.'

'I don't know for sure, but I believe he's in his mid-seventies,' Clem admitted. 'Though Priddy's ten years younger.'

'And they still work the canals and do as well or better than folk a lot younger,' Lizzie said wonderingly.

'It's what they've been doing all their lives, they're expert at it and know the best and easiest way around any problem,' Clem explained. 'But Priddy's been talking about retiring just lately. They own a cottage close by the canal at Burscough and when the present tenant left, they didn't relet. I daresay it was just talk, but this business is bound to make them think seriously about their future.'

'What would you do, Clem, if Jake and Priddy did decide to retire and sold *The Liverpool Rose* and her butty boat,' Lizzie said, almost shyly. She realised she could not imagine him wanting work ashore after the freedom of life on the canal, but you never knew. He might long to work on a farm or in a shop or factory, though this seemed unlikely. She had not known him long enough, nor did she know him well enough, to guess how he would react if life on the canal were no longer possible.

But Clem answered unhesitatingly. 'Why, I'd either work for the company or for one of the bye-traders – that's another way of saying a boat owner – and save up to buy my own boat in time,' he said. 'And that would be only the beginning. There's cargo vessels which ply regularly between Britain and Ireland. I might get a job aboard one and work my way up – take exams and that – until I were an officer. But most of all, I'd like to own a boat like the old *Rose* because that way you're your own master yet you can have your wife and family around you so you're never lonely. Look at Priddy and Jake. I don't think they would exchange their life for any other, do you? Even if they retire, it'll be to a cottage close to the canal where they're amongst canal folk, with the water only a few feet from their door and a little boat so's they can take a trip out whenever they've a mind.'

'I guess you're right, and I wish my life was so uncomplicated,' Lizzie said with a sigh. 'But what with Uncle Perce looking out for me so's he can stop me telling what I know, and with no home to go to now Aunt Annie's dead . . . and probably no job . . . it looks as though, when I get back to Liverpool, I'm going to have to start from scratch.'

'Well, I'm sure you're welcome to stay aboard *The Liverpool Rose* until you've got your life sorted out,' Clem said, after a thoughtful pause. 'I don't know how we'd have managed without you, Lizzie, with Jake so poorly. And now you're not scared of Brutus . . .'

At this point, he was interrupted. Priddy came out of the cabin and called to them across the top of the cargo. 'We're movin' on, you two, so you'd best get Boxer down from his stable and tack him up. I talked it over with the Number One from *Kittiwake* and he's pretty sure the towpath will be negotiable all the way to Leeds, even if we do have to wade through floods as we go lower. There's no point in us sittin' here when we've a cargo to unload so let's gerra move on!'

*

The rest of the journey to Leeds, though wet, was fairly uneventful and when they reached the wool wharf, they found that *The Pride of the 'Pool* was there before them and that at least one of their problems had been solved. Alf and Freddie had brought Hal down from the stabling as soon as they had seen *The Liverpool Rose* in the distance and, amidst much rejoicing, Clem and Lizzie had swapped the horses over, filling Hal's nosebag with good things, and making much of him, though it seemed that the Trelawney brothers had looked after the great horse as well as they were able. As soon as this was done, they begged Alf to tell them what had been happening, and he was glad to do so. It seemed that Reuben, ugly drunk after emptying a barrel of rum which he had swapped for a dozen good fleeces, had laid about him with a boat hook when Alf and Freddie had gone down to Nat Shipley's yard to reclaim their property. Someone had called the police, and though the crew of the *Pride of the 'Pool* had not wanted to lay information about the theft against the Trelawney brothers, they had been forced to do so. Alf, who now nursed a fractured wrist and had a huge bump on his head and a black eye from Reuben's attack, admitted that he was not as reluctant to see his fellow boatmen in clink as he had been before his injuries.

'I feel sorry for poor old Abe, but if he can't control his brother then he'll have to pay the price, even if it's six months in quod,' Alf said as the crew of *The Liverpool Rose* gathered round him. 'Where's Jake and Priddy? I'd have thought they'd have been as keen to know what was happening as you two youngsters.'

'Jake had a run in with the Trelawneys, same as

434

you did, and got a wicked blow on the head,' Clem told him. 'Priddy's taken him up to the Infirmary to have one of these here X-ray things. She says they can look inside his noddle and tell what's what, 'cos he's not been right since the fracas with the Trelawneys.'

'Is that why you're on crutches, lass?' Alf said, sounding much shocked. 'I'd not ha' thought even Reuben would attack a young gel.'

Lizzie, who had definitely thought Reuben meant to attack her, nevertheless assured him that her injuries were the result of an accident. 'Though if it hadn't been for Reuben, I wouldn't have been trying to escape into the hills,' she told him, and between them, she and Clem related the whole story, not forgetting Brutus's part in her rescue.

As they made their way back to *The Liverpool Rose*, Clem admitted that he felt a good deal happier knowing that the Trelawneys were both under lock and key and were going to have to pay for their crimes. 'It's all very well to say boat people should stick together,' he observed, 'but a feller who can't take his drink and gets violent, and another who will steal from a fellow boatman, shouldn't be protected by the people they rob and misuse. I'm downright glad they're paying the penalty because after a spell in clink I guess they'll think twice before stealing or beating people up again.'

Lizzie hoped he was right, but thought privately that leopards don't change their spots; a real bad 'un like Reuben would need more than some time behind bars to make him change his ways.

She said as much to Clem when they were aboard *The Liverpool Rose* once more but he said that you never knew. For a shore man, a spell in prison only curtailed his activity for a while; for someone used to the freedom and fresh air aboard a canal boat, it would be purgatory.

'But right now, I think we ought to leave a message for Priddy and Jake that we've taken the *Rose* along to the grain wharf to land our cargo,' he said. 'They're taking an awful long time, but you know what hospitals are like. I daresay they may be away all day and the feller who wants this grain won't thank us if we hang about here when we could be unloading.'

Accordingly, the two of them took both boats along to the grain wharf, duly saw their cargo unloaded and were paid by the manager of the granary, stowing the notes away in the little cupboard where Priddy kept all her paperwork. Clem wondered aloud whether they should look out for another cargo going to Liverpool, but Lizzie thought they would do better to wait for Priddy and Jake's return. 'You know how organised Priddy is,' she observed, 'she may well have arranged for a return load which we know nothing about. Honestly, Clem, they'll be back before nightfall and one day lost isn't going to hurt us.'

When Priddy did return later that evening, however, it was without Jake. She came heavily into the small cabin and sat herself down in her little cushioned chair by the fire, sniffing approvingly at the stewpot suspended over the embers. 'Smells good,' she remarked, but in so lugubrious a voice that she could have been complaining that the food had burned to a crisp. 'They've kept Jake in the Infirmary and want him to stay for a few days whiles they sort him out. Clem, lad, I doesn't know what to do for the best. The doctors up there say he needs rest and 'vestigations – wharrever that may mean – but I'd arranged for a return load of textiles to be taken straight down to Stanley Dock. They're to go aboard the *SS Ludovic*. She'll dock in ten or twelve days and I wouldn't want to let 'em down. Yet how can I abandon Jake in a strange city? I told the doctors he could rest as well aboard *The Liverpool Rose* as he could in any old Infirmary – better, probably – but it seems they didn't agree. It's these 'vestigations, I think. He's gorra be there so's they can 'vestigate properly.' She looked helplessly from Clem to Lizzie, and the girl saw that tears trembled in her eyes. 'I dunno what to do for the best,' she repeated.

Clem, however, appeared to have no such doubts. 'You must stay with him while Lizzie and meself work *The Liverpool Rose* through to the Stanley Dock,' he said firmly. 'Why, if they released Jake from the Infirmary and he was on his own in a strange city, things could go badly for him. But as it is, you can get a lodging where he can be comfortable until we – and the *Rose* – return in three weeks or so. It wouldn't do to keep the boat hanging about here because it's a lot easier to lose your good name than to regain it, and folk knows the Pridmores are reliable and never let anyone down.'

Priddy's face had lightened at these words. She nodded slowly. 'But can you do it?' she enquired. 'Lizzie's still on them sticks so Gawd knows how you'll manage wi' the two boats in the locks.'

'I can walk without me sticks, pretty well,' Lizzie said eagerly. 'Honest, Priddy, thanks to you my ankle's as good as ever it was. I know it'll be hard work, but I've never been afraid of *that*, and once the floods go down there'll be kids hanging round most of the long rises, eager to earn a few pence by giving a hand. So I think you can trust us to get the textiles safely to the Stanley Dock. Unloading won't be a problem, there's always fellers looking for work down at the docks.'

'If you can manage that, it'll be just grand,' Priddy was beginning, when another thought struck her. 'Oh, but . . . there'll be talk, just the two of you, a young feller and a gal wi'out no older person to see you don't . . .'

Lizzie looked baffled but Clem, who knew more about the strict morals of most of the canal folk than she did, nodded understandingly, though Lizzie saw his colour heighten. 'Yes, I know what you mean, though the last thing you need worry about is that I'd overstep the mark,' he mumbled. 'How about if I hired a little lad? He and me could sleep in the butty boat and Lizzie could have Brutus in the living cabin. Or I daresay we could hire a girl, only she wouldn't be so useful, I don't imagine.'

'Hey, I've had a thought,' Lizzie said suddenly. 'Why don't you ask the scuffers if you can live aboard *The Singing Lark* while Jake's in the Infirmary? And when he comes out, for that matter, instead of having to waste your money on lodgings? I should think the authorities would be glad enough to have someone living aboard to keep an eye on the boat, and it would save a deal of money, probably more than we'd have to pay a lad for his three weeks' stint.'

Priddy seized on this idea with enthusiasm and within a remarkably short space of time it was all arranged. A fourteen-year-old lad called Geordie was signed on for his keep and a few pence a day, Priddy settled herself aboard *The Singing Lark*, and *The Liverpool Rose* took her new cargo aboard and set out once more in the direction of Liverpool, with her young crew anxious to prove themselves to be as capable as the Pridmores had always been.

Despite knowing that she had already told her story, Lizzie could not help feeling a little apprehensive as *The Liverpool Rose* began the journey which would end in Liverpool. It would be painful to return to the courts where Aunt Annie no longer held sway, and she knew she would feel afraid every time she turned a corner, in case she came face to face with Uncle Perce. But she also realised that this had to be tackled sooner or later, and knew she would feel a good deal braver with Clem and Brutus beside her than she would have felt on her own. So she went about her many tasks as cheerfully as she could and tried not to let anyone see how she dreaded the moment when they reached Liverpool once more.

Chapter Twelve

May 1928

Lizzie walked up Burlington Street towards Cranberry Court, glancing round her at the familiar shops and houses as she did so. When she had left here at Christmas the weather had been terribly cold and though she had been back once or twice since then, this was the first time she had re-visited Burlington Street in bright sunshine.

As she turned into Cranberry Court, she felt a tiny clutch of fear, though she knew very well that she was not going to meet her uncle. When she had returned from her first voyage aboard *The Liverpool Rose*, no one had known what had happened to him or where he had gone, but Geoff, clever imaginative Geoff, had managed to find out. He had come across Flossie when working in another branch of his bank which had been short-handed due to sickness amongst the staff. Flossie had been working for a fishmonger in the St John's fish market and had popped in to get change for a pound note. She had not recognised Geoff, but he had known her at once.

'Morning, Mrs Sharpe,' he had said, genially. 'I wonder if you could help me? I'm interested in the whereabouts of a feller I believe you used to know, a Percy Grey?'

On the other side of the counter Flossie's eyes sharpened and she stepped back, but since Geoff had her pound note and had not yet handed over the change, she clearly could not bolt from the bank but stood her ground, saying truculently: 'What's it to you? I s'pose it were you what telled the scuffers I'd been seein' the feller so they thought I'd had some hand in bumpin' off his old woman?' She snorted derisively. 'As if I'd have had owt to do wi' a villain like that – why, a feller what'll kill one woman will kill another. Now gimme me money or I'll see the manager and tell him what sort o' bank clerks he's employin' . . . blackmailin', that's what's on your mind.'

Geoff had smiled pleasantly but retained his hold on both coins and note. 'All I did was ask a simple question, Mrs Sharpe,' he said reproachfully. 'I'm just anxious to know if Mr Grey is still in the country, though my own feeling is that he's fled abroad – at least, he has if he's got any sense. You see, I'm friendly with his niece and though she no longer lives in the city, she'd feel a deal safer if she knew her uncle was out of it.' Flossie made to turn away and Geoff raised his voice slightly, holding the note to his nose as he did so and sniffing. 'Well, well, well, Mrs Sharpe, since this note smells strongly of haddock, I reckon you're working at the St John's fish market! I suppose if you refuse to answer my question, I'll find you there any time?'

As he told Lizzie afterwards, Geoff had guessed this would make Flossie see the impracticability of just walking away, and he also guessed that she had not found it easy to get another job since she would have had only bad references from folk who knew her. He was soon proved right. Flossie turned back towards him, her face reddening angrily.

'Quite the little detective, aren't you?' she hissed malevolently through the grille which separated them. 'Well, since you're interested, I see no harm in tellin' you. He took off aboard the *SS Clarabella Maria*, bound for Brazil, and I doubt very much he'll be with her when she returns to Liverpool for her next cargo.'

With that, she had almost snatched the change from Geoff's hand and then turned and left the bank.

He had thought that Flossie was probably right in her guess that Perce Grey would not willingly return to Britain where, he must realise, he would have to stand trial for murder, but Flossie had been more right than she knew. That evening, when Geoff and Reggie had been walking back to the YMCA, Geoff told his pal the whole story, feeling very pleased with himself for discovering so much with so little effort. But it seemed he was to discover even more. For when he had finished telling the tale, Reggie gave a low whistle. 'The *SS Clarabella Maria* did you say?' he asked, incredulously. 'Don't that name ring a bell with you, old feller?'

'Well, no, but I ain't in shipping,' Geoff had said. Reggie now worked in the Liver Buildings for a company who specialised in shipping insurance. 'Why? What should it mean to me, then?'

'No, of course you wouldn't know, not being in marine insurance,' Reggie said. 'The *SS Clarabella Maria* sailed despite that terrible blizzard we had at Christmas. She foundered off the Irish coast . . . I think it were between Cape Clear and Mizen Head . . . and there were no survivors, but wreckage from the ship came ashore in Roaring Water Bay a couple o' days later.' He grinned at Geoff. 'So I think your guess that you won't be seein' Lizzie's Uncle Perce again were spot on, old feller.'

Geoff had duly relayed this information to Sally, who had passed it on to Lizzie. She had gone once more to the police, who were gratifyingly interested this time.

The policeman had said they would confirm the story and did so, assuring Lizzie that her uncle had indeed signed on, and had sailed – and sunk – with the ship.

So now Lizzie knew that the little clutch of terror she felt was completely illogical and was more a reminder of past unhappiness than of any fear for her present safety. She did glance towards number nine as she passed it, but it had been occupied by a cheerful family originating from Dublin for some time now and there seemed to be nothing left to remind her of the past. The paintwork was clean and fresh, the windows sparkled, the steps were whitenened, and even the curtains, blowing in the breeze from the open window were fresh and crisp.

The house has changed, Lizzie told herself as she approached Sally's front door, but then so have I. When I left the court that December night, I never dreamed that in five short months I'd only see Liverpool once every three weeks or so, and would be actually living aboard a canal boat and loving every minute of it. Isn't life strange? I was frightened of Uncle Perce, truly miserable over losing Aunt Annie and sure that I'd no real future with the chance of a home of my own. But that part of my life's over now and I'm all set to begin a totally new one.

As she crossed the court, she thought nostalgically of that first terrible journey when she, Geordie and Clem had set out from Leeds, leaving Jake in the Infirmary and Priddy aboard *The Singing Lark*. All had gone swimmingly to begin with, despite the flood water which stretched, lake-like, on either side of the canal. To be sure, they had lost two of Priddy's beautifully made coir fenders when Lizzie had forgotten to put them out until she heard the *Rose*'s hull scraping against the stonework of the lock. Then she had thrown the fenders over, without checking that they were secure, and had only discovered her mistake when they reached the next lock, to find they were two fenders short.

Then there had been trouble with Geordie. Brutus had taken one look at their new crew member and had decided he was a Wigan Wolf in disguise; at any rate, he gave the boy a wide berth and warned him off whenever Geordie tried to enter the little cabin where Brutus and Clem slept. In the end, Lizzie slept in the main cabin, Clem stayed in the butty boat, and Geordie in the cabin Lizzie had occupied before. Not that he stayed in it for long. Lizzie soon realised that the boy was both lazy and a grumbler. If it was possible to get out of a task which he had been set, he would do so; if it was not possible, he whined and moaned and complained until someone – either Lizzie herself or Clem – took over from him in sheer desperation.

When they awoke on the fourth day out, however, and Lizzie began to prepare breakfast, Clem popped his head around the cabin door to say, approvingly, that Geordie must be getting used to their ways. 'He's already gone up to the stable to bring Hal down for tacking up,' he told her. 'It's the first time he's done *anything* without being ordered or cajoled to do it. Perhaps he'll become a respectable member of the crew by the time we get back to Leeds and we'll be sorry to lose him.'

But by the time the breakfast was on the table, Clem was beginning to have his doubts. No Geordie – nor even Hal – had appeared. So Clem took himself off to the stable and returned, very flustered, with Hal fully tacked up by his side. 'He's gone, scarpered, vamoosed,' he said. 'Oh, Gawd, Lizzie love, I'm the Number One while Jake and Priddy aren't around and I've already lost a member of me crew! I reckon Brutus was right. He knew him for a wrong 'un from the start, but though he warned us we didn't take notice and now look what's happened! I wonder what he took with him?'

'He took the loose change from Priddy's needlework drawer, the bucket with the roses and castles painted all over it, two beautiful new pairs of thick winter socks, and all the little cakes I baked yesterday,' Lizzie said grimly. She had said nothing to Clem, but as soon as she knew that Geordie was not aboard, she had begun to check their belongings. And over the course of the next few days, they gradually realised that he had been a proper little thief and had probably meant to rob them from the moment he had come aboard. Small things like teaspoons, meat skewers, in fact anything he could carry in his pockets, had been salted away, and Lizzie, not being as familiar with the contents of the cabin as Priddy would have been, only noticed something was missing when she actually tried to use it.

'We're better off without him,' she had told Clem a couple of days later when *The Liverpool Rose* and her butty boat were ascending the Bingley Five Rise. 'You're a really good teacher, Clem, and I'm learning far quicker than I would have if Geordie had been aboard to do some of the running around. Why, I'm real handy at working the locks now, aren't I? I know how important it is not to waste water, and I know it's no use pushing the beam before the water level's dropped or risen, and not to turn the windlass too soon.'

'Aye, you're right. But remember the reason we had Geordie aboard the boat in the first place,' Clem said, a trifle reproachfully. 'They're a narrow-minded lot, these narrow boat folk.' He laughed at his own joke, then added: 'But mebbe they won't notice there's just the two of us aboard because we don't even sleep on the same craft. I stick to my butty boat and you're snug down in the main cabin, the whole length of the butty boat away from me. Personally, I think Priddy was worrying unduly, but anyway there's nothing we can do about it except make sure we deliver our cargo to the Stanley Dock and pick up the new one as soon as it's ready to load.'

And the rest of that voyage, though it could not be described as trouble-free, was certainly far more enjoyable than Lizzie had expected it to be. His new responsibility as Number One sat easily on Clem's broad shoulders, and though he frequently had to instruct her in the ways of the canal, he never made Lizzie feel ignorant or foolish and usually, in fact, made her aware that he admired the quickness with which she took on a whole new way of life.

'When I remember that the only other time you've worked the canal was with the Trelawney brothers it's even more amazing you've took to it the way you have,' he told her one evening when they were comfortably settled in the cabin, eating stewed mutton and potatoes which had been sold to them cheap as they were badly marked by frost and flood. 'Not many girls could work in a factory one week and on a canal boat the next!'

'If you'd ever worked in a factory, you'd know it don't take a lot of skill nor much thought neither,' Lizzie assured him. 'But this . . . well, it's exciting, different. I can't imagine you'd ever want to work ashore after this, Clem.'

'Nor I would,' he agreed. 'Pass us the bread, queen.' The conversation then turned to other things and Lizzie could not help noticing how Clem could take instant decisions without having to mull over the various alternatives. She remembered Geoff had been studying hard to get on in his own world but knew that, for him, a decision was always an agonising choice between various alternatives. She supposed this was partly due to his having been brought up in an orphan asylum where decisions, by and large, would have been taken for him. Clem, on the other hand, had had to fend for himself from the moment that his parents died. It was pretty plain that once the Pridmores had taken him aboard *The Liverpool Rose* and put him in charge of the butty boat, he had learned his new role. Even when Jake and Priddy were not around, he knew exactly what best to do and how to do it.

But right now she had reached the Bradshaws' front door and rapped smartly upon it. Sally must have been watching for her because before Lizzie had even let go of the knocker the door had opened sharply inwards, almost precipitating her into the hallway.

'Steady on, queen,' Sally gasped, giving Lizzie a hug and a kiss on the cheek. 'I've been longing to see you so's you can tell me all the news. I know Jake and Priddy have been back with *The Liverpool Rose* for a good few weeks now, but how's Jake getting on?'

He had been allowed out of the Infirmary after three weeks on the strict understanding that he was not to work the locks, carry water, use the windlass or tack up the horse; in other words, he was forbidden to do any sort of hard physical work. Since he had naturally rebelled over being, as he put it, demoted to the role of cabin boy when he was a bye-trader aboard his own craft, Priddy frequently found herself acting as gaoler, which meant that without Lizzie's help, Clem would have had his work cut out to get the various cargoes to their destinations in good time. However, of late Jake had begun to accept that his role of Number One aboard *The Liverpool Rose* was never really in question; the other three made it clear that they would not dream of ousting him, but were merely trying to see that he regained his former health and did not overtax his strength.

'Oh, Jake's getting on pretty well,' Lizzie said, following her friend into the kitchen. 'Once or twice he ignored the doctor's advice and insisted on leading Hal, though only for a short stretch, and found it exhausting. Then, when Clem and I had gone to a farm to fetch hay for Hal and fresh milk for us, he took two buckets to the Winterburn reservoir pipe line to top up the water barrel. Halfway back to the boat, he reckons he slipped. He lost the water in both buckets and strained a muscle in his calf. Clem didn't think he slipped, he thought he had collapsed, but anyway the old feller was laid up for a week. That was a month ago, just about, and since then he's been much more sensible. Why, I actually heard him telling the Number One aboard *The Jenny Wren* that if a feller had a good crew, it was only right and proper that the Number One should do the brainwork – go touting for business, see that the cargo was loaded correctly and that his charges were reasonable for both parties. He added that a Number One could tell his crew what to do, knowing that it would be done properly, without losing his authority over them.'

'So are you coming back to the factory then?' Sally asked. She had produced a large, light-looking sponge cake from the depths of the pantry and set it down in the middle of the table, then ferreted in the drawer for a knife and cut two generous slices. 'Wet the pot, will you, Lizzie? I keep telling the boss you'll only stay on the canal while they can't manage without you, but I don't know where you'll live when you *do* move back to the city because lodgings is awful expensive and you'll want to be in this area so's you won't need to catch a tram to go to and from work. I've telled you before, our mam would have you to stay like a shot but you didn't seem to want to live in the court again. Though why that should be when you know your uncle's safely drowned at sea, I can't understand,' she added in an injured tone.

Lizzie laughed. 'It isn't that I don't want to live in the court again, and you know I'd love to share your home, Sally,' she said. 'But the truth is, I've taken a real shine to life on the canal. I've not been lucky enough to live in the country before, but now that I've done it, I get the feeling I'd never settle to town life again. And to tell the truth, Sal, I've had a word with Priddy and she's very keen to start putting the cottage at Burscough to rights, so's she and Jake can move in before next winter. She's happy for them both to live aboard *The Liverpool Rose* in spring and summer, but she doesn't think it's right for Jake once the weather gets severe. The doctors say the bump on the head meant that he was unable to move around as he normally does, which has led to congestion on his lungs, and that'll have to be watched, especially if he gets cold or chilled.'

'So does that mean you'll be stayin' aboard the boat?' Sally asked rather dismally. 'Oh, Lizzie, I do miss you. I never realised how lucky I were having me best pal living opposite, and though you've said you wouldn't want to live in the court again, I've always thought you'd come back eventually. Still, you're here every three weeks or so, so we'll just have to arrange more regular meetings, I suppose.' She turned from the table and, taking two mugs from the dresser, poured a small amount of condensed milk into each, added the tea and stirred both mugs briskly before pushing one across to her friend. 'Help yourself to cake, it's fresh made this morning. I'm getting into practice, you might say.'

'I know you and Geoff have been going steady, but does cake-making mean you're getting married soon?' Lizzie asked. She took a big bite then spoke through her mouthful: 'This is good! Your mam's got one of these new-fangled, free-standing stoves, hasn't she? I suppose you and Geoff will be saving up for one of your own!'

Sally shrugged. 'We'd like to get married soon, of course, and we could do if we moved into one of the cheaper suburbs, but we're both city-reared and don't fancy a long journey into work each day. Besides, I'm not eighteen yet and me mam and dad think that's much too young to wed. But wharrabout you, queen?'

'Me? Since I'm the same age as you, I reckon I'm too young to marry as well,' Lizzie said, but she felt warmth rise in her cheeks. The fact was that unless Jake and Priddy decided to employ another worker during the winter months, she and Clem would be uncomfortably situated once more, with no one to chaperone them on their trips up and down the canal. She knew that Priddy would not want to leave Jake alone while she accompanied *The Liverpool Rose* on her winter voyages, and several times she had been aware that Clem was on the verge of saying something about the situation. By now, Lizzie knew that she was fonder of Clem than she had ever been of anyone else, but oddly enough, the very closeness of their lives together was inhibiting any display of affection. Clem had been careful, right from the start, to keep a certain distance between them, though sometimes Lizzie thought she detected a warm glow in his eyes and once or twice, as though he could not stop himself, he had reached out a hand to rumple her curls gently or pinch her cheek, and had then apologised gruffly, reddening to the roots of his hair and making an excuse to move swiftly away from her. 'The truth is, Sal, that the canal folk wouldn't approve if Clem and I worked the boats between us during the winter months. They'd think it not right for an unmarried couple, you see, and though I think Priddy would agree to taking on a young lad – mebbe just for his keep – it didn't work with Geordie and I'm afraid it might . . . might spoil things. You see, it's taken three or four months to train me to be a useful member of the crew, which would mean the lad wouldn't be much of a help until his time with us was up. What's more, it wouldn't be very fair on him.'

'I see that,' Sally said, taking a bite out of her own slice of cake. 'But you can't have it both ways, chuck. It seems to me you either take a lad aboard or you and Clem had better get spliced, and I don't see no objection to that. You like him, I can tell, and I always did reckon he was sweet on you, even when the pair of you was just kids, so why not tie the knot, eh? Or do you have doubts or someone else in your eye?'

Lizzie took a large swallow of tea and grimaced. Over the last few months she had grown used to the pleasures of tea made with fresh milk and found this strong brew, liberally laced with conny-onny, rather too sweet for her taste. Setting her elbows on the table, she tried to sort out her own feelings so that she could explain them to her friend. The trouble was, she thought resentfully, her feelings regarding Clem had somehow got themselves into an awful tangle. After some thought, however, she began tentatively to put these thoughts into words. 'The thing is, Sal, I don't want Clem to feel he's being pushed into asking me to marry him just so's we can both go on working *The Liverpool Rose*,' she explained at length. 'As things stand at the moment, if he *were* to ask me to marry him, I'd never know whether he'd done it for . . . for the wrong reasons.'

'What's wrong with asking you to marry him so's you can both stay aboard the boat . . .' Sally was beginning, when she stopped short, grinning at her friend. 'Oh, I see! You're thinking he might ask you out of pity, because he knows you love the life and don't want to come back to the factory. That's daft! No feller would risk mucking up his whole life just so a gal can work on a canal boat!'

'It isn't just that,' Lizzie mumbled, feeling her cheeks grow hotter than ever. 'Now Aunt Annie's dead – and Uncle Perce too, of course – I don't have any relatives except for me cousins and they've never been over-fond of me, and I've no home, no place of my own to go to if I did have to leave *The Liverpool Rose*.'

'I said you're daft, and daft you are,' Sally said decisively. 'Firstly, we've telled you and telled you, you can live with us. Secondly, there'd be a job for you in the factory if you really wanted it. And thirdly, and most important, is how you feel about Clem and how he feels about you. Stop beatin' about the bush,

Lizzie, and tell me straight: DO YOU LOVE HIM?'

She had almost bawled out the last four words which, Lizzie thought afterwards, tricked her into an immediate reply. 'YES, I DO!' she shouted angrily, then clapped her hands to her mouth. 'Oh, Gawd, Sally, I've been trying to tell myself for months and months he were just a good friend and the nicest feller I knew, 'cos if he doesn't love me, doesn't want to marry me, then it's best I move away and forget all about him. Only . . . only . . .'

'I can see I shall have to come down to the canal and have a word with that Clem,' Sally said darkly. 'The pair of you are acting like two silly kids, both frightened of making the first move in case the other one doesn't follow suit. Well, Lizzie, if you want to ruin your whole life, go on as you're doing now. Why, until this minute you've even denied to yourself you're in love with the feller. He won't ask you to marry him out of pity, nor because he wants an experienced boat crew, so start showin' the poor feller how you feel instead of being brisk and business-like.' Lizzie began to shake her head, but Sally wagged a reproving finger at her. 'Now don't you interrupt me, milady, because I'm talkin' sense and in your heart you know it. Have you ever let Clem see that you really like him, that you ain't indifferent at all? Let's have the truth now!'

Lizzie, beginning to answer, suddenly felt a lump rise in her throat and before she knew it, she was sobbing with a mixture of misery and relief, for it was indeed a relief to have spoken to Sally about her problem and to hear her friend's common-sense view of Lizzie's situation. On the other hand, she realised more than ever how desperate she was not to rock the boat. To lose her lovely life would be dreadful, but to

453

lose Clem, she suddenly realised, would be far, far worse. You idiot, she chided herself, trying to stifle her sobs, there's nothing to cry about; if Clem loves you then you're all set for happiness, because you love him and you've known it for weeks. If he doesn't . . . well, it will have to be faced. But at least now you've admitted what you really want – who you really want, rather – which has to be a move in the right direction. And with that, Lizzie dried her eyes and gave Sally a rather watery smile. 'Sorry about that,' she said apologetically, 'but you've done me a really good turn, our Sal. I'm thinking straight for the first time for weeks and weeks and I'm going to take your advice. Oh, don't worry that I'll throw myself at his head because that's not my style. But I'll stop pretending I don't care about him and give us both a chance to sort things out.'

Since Lizzie had gone off to visit her friend Sally, Clem had decided to clean down the cargo holds of both boats and was busily employed in so doing. It was a brilliantly sunny afternoon and he could not help thinking, wistfully, what fun it would have been had he and Lizzie been able to go around the town together, doing a bit of shopping and seeing the sights. But somehow he had not liked to suggest it, knowing that she had few opportunities to mix with girls of her own age since the young women on the other canal boats still held aloof from her, regarding her, he knew, as an interloper.

Clem had thought and thought about the situation between himself and Lizzie but had come to no firm conclusion. He had always liked her but love had come more gradually, over the many months they had known one another. He had first realised how he felt when Sally had told him Lizzie had disappeared, and had known then that without Lizzie in it his life would seem hollow. He loved his work, Brutus, Hal and the Pridmores, but just the sight of Lizzie sauntering along the towpath towards *The Liverpool Rose* was enough to quicken his heartbeat. Knowing her to be lost, therefore, had filled him with very real dismay and when he had seen her lying in the sheep cave, white-faced, bruised and blood-streaked, fear and relief had fought for supremacy, relief winning when he realised she was alive and not seriously hurt.

Then there had been the past few months on the canal. At first, while winter still gripped the land, it had been pretty grim, particularly trying to work the boat with only the two of them, but because it was Lizzie he was instructing, he had even enjoyed that. As soon as the weather began to improve, every day had been a fresh delight. Lizzie's love and appreciation of the beautiful countryside through which they passed had very soon equalled his own.

Oddly enough, it was this very love and appreciation of her surroundings which stopped Clem from suggesting to her that the two of them might get wed. He realised that he had no idea if she loved him, or indeed even liked him as anything other than a friend, and did not want her to have to consider marriage to him as an alternative to losing her place aboard *The Liverpool Rose*.

Had it not been for Jake's illness, of course, the question would not have arisen and Clem would have been able to take his time and begin to build up the sort of relationship which he assumed Geoff and Sally enjoyed. Indeed, he could do so now, for it was several months more before Priddy meant to take Jake ashore, but still he hesitated. What if Lizzie turned him down? It would make life aboard *The Liverpool Rose* very dificult for both of them. Almost worse was the fear that she might accept his advances rather than lose her place aboard. Clem could not bear to think of Lizzie marrying him merely for the sake of the life she loved, but she had never given any indication that he was anything but a friend. However, Priddy had told him earlier that same day that he really ought to take Lizzie about more.

'I know you're sweet on her and I'm pretty sure she's sweet on you,' she told him reprovingly. 'But the pair of you is too scared to show your feelings, afraid you'll make fools of yourselves, while all the time you must know in your hearts how you feel. 'Tarnation, boy, if I can see what's goin' on under me nose, why can't you?'

But despite Priddy's words, Clem was still unsure. He was just about to finish his work on the cargo hold and was eyeing the pale, clean decking with considerable satisfaction, when Priddy appeared on the towpath alongside him. 'Where's Lizzie?' she asked baldly, and when he told her that Lizzie was spending the afternoon with her friend, she cast her eyes up to the sky, heaved a deep sigh, and told him she had a good mind to wash her hands of him. 'You'll ruin your lives, and ours too, if I don't take a hand in this. And what's more, Jake and meself have been talkin' it over and we've made a decision. That is, it were Jake's idea and I agreed. Don't know why I didn't think of it myself because it's so obvious.'

Clem looked up from his work, pushing a strand of hair back from his eyes. 'What idea is this?' he demanded suspiciously. 'If you're thinking of employing a lad . . .'

'We ain't thinkin' no such thing,' Priddy assured

him. 'In fact, you could say we were thinking just the opposite. Jake says as how trade's always slower on the canal in winter time, and since me and hisself won't be aboard, your expenses – food and that – won't be as high as in summer, so we've decided we'll keep the butty boat moored up the cut near the cottage in the winter, which means you and Lizzie should be able to manage *The Liverpool Rose* just fine without having to employ a lad.'

After only a moment's thought, Clem had beamed at her, seeing at once the many advantages of such a scheme. 'You're right,' he said delightedly. 'Why, the time we'd save at locks alone would make it financially worthwhile to take the one boat. Even swing bridges would be much quicker negotiated with just one and Hal would be in his element. He wouldn't need the extra oats, either, though I wouldn't dream of stinting on his feed. Jake's a genius, ain't he, Priddy?'

'Aye, he's a genius all right,' she said, with a grim little smile playing about her mouth. 'Because one boat means one sleeping cabin and not the broadest minded family on the canal would approve of you and Lizzie livin' tally. So it's make your mind up time, lad!'

Clem sat back on his heels, knowing that his eyes were rounding and his mouth was dropping open, but before he could say a word, Priddy spoke once more. 'When Lizzie comes home, just you send her straight to me, boy, because I'm sick and tired of all this pussy-footin' around. I'm going to put things to her straight . . . see how you like that!' she declared robustly, turning as she spoke and heading back towards their living quarters.

Clem scrubbed the last foot of the cargo deck,

wiped it down with a cloth and threw both implements into his bucket. Then he stood up. He realised he had no desire to see Priddy taking his lovelife into her capable yet ruthless hands. She might easily do a great deal of harm to his tentative relationship with Lizzie and he decided suddenly that he would make a mess of things himself rather than see Priddy do it for him. I'll smarten myself up, put on a clean shirt and me best kecks, and go round to Sally Bradshaw's place, he decided. And when I get there I'll tell Lizzie I'm taking her dancing to that Grafton Rooms place.

When the knock sounded on the Bradshaws' front door, Sally immediately flew to her feet, her cheeks flushing. 'It'll be Geoff,' she said, her pleasure plain. 'I said you'd be comin' round, Lizzie, so I hoped he might turn up a bit early. He were playin' football for the YM on Shaw Street against the fellers in the one at Toxteth. I guess they must have started – and finished early.'

It was some while since Lizzie had seen Geoff and she hoped that her face was not still tear-stained nor her eyes red. She walked across to the sink and was about to splash her cheeks with cold water from the bucket beneath it when something in the tone of the voice which answered Sally's made her turn towards the doorway.

'Clem!' Lizzie exclaimed. 'I *thought* it was your voice! What's happened? Don't say Jake's took a turn for the worse?'

He came slowly into the kitchen. He was wearing his best things and held his peaked boatman's cap in one hand but, at her words, he shook his head reassuringly. 'No, no, don't worry, Jake's fine. Or at least he was when I left *The Liverpool Rose* ten minutes ago. The fact is, Liz, I finished cleaning out the cargo holds and thought you might like to go dancing this evening. Or – or anything else you might like to do,' he added hastily. 'It's such a fine evening, it's a shame to be shut away indoors when we could be outside.'

To say that Lizzie was astonished was putting it mildly; it was almost as though the thoughts which had been revolving in her own head had also been revolving in Clem's. Earlier in the week, before she had thought matters through, she would have been embarassed by his suggestion, would have thought he was making it for all the wrong reasons, but now she simply took it at face value and said eagerly: 'I'd like to go dancing, but I'm not really dressed for it. There's lots of other things we could do, though. There's cinemas, theatres, and some lovely parks we could visit, or, . . .'

'I'll lend you a dress, queen,' Sally cut in eagerly. 'I wonder what happened to your clothes, Lizzie? Remember that dress you bought just before . . . but anyway, you can borrow my blue taffeta. It'll suit you, go with them blue eyes.'

Lizzie glanced rather doubtfully at Clem. 'That'd be grand, Sally. What's you and Geoff thinking of doing this evening? We could all four go.'

'We were going dancing actually,' Sally said. 'Of course the halls don't open till seven, but Geoff usually comes here for his tea first – Mam's willing – and then we go on to the dance afterwards. You're very welcome to join us, the two of you. I can nip out right now and get another loaf of bread and some bits and pieces.'

This, however, Clem refused to allow her to do. 'I'll take our Lizzie along to the nearest dining rooms and we'll have a bite there,' he said. 'We've got a deal of talking to do, so we can get started over our tea.'

Lizzie looked at him a trifle doubtfully. Why should Clem suddenly seek her out at her friend's house? And, more surprising still, why should he want to talk to her so urgently? The two of them chatted away all the time when they were fetching water, stabling Hal, walking Brutus or simply eating a meal in the cabin of *The Liverpool Rose*. But she supposed that it was time they talked things through, so agreed that the two of them would go down to Lewis Cann's dining room by Victoria Square and return to Cranberry Court in time for her to change into Sally's dress, so that the four of them could catch a tram to the ballroom. 'You'll have to borrow me dancin' pumps as well,' Sally remarked, looking accusingly at her friend's feet in their sturdy, well-worn boots. 'Good thing I've got three pairs, but what size is your feet, Lizzie?'

'Oh, about the same size as yours,' she said airily, and presently she and Clem set off in the direction of the dining rooms.

The meal was an unqualified success but the conversation had not gone as Clem had planned. When it came to the point, he had simply been unable to tell Lizzie how he felt about her, which was ridiculous, considering how he had longed to do just that. What was more, she looked so deliciously pretty sitting opposite him at the small table, with her long, golden plait falling across one shoulder and her eyes sparkling every time they met his, that he should have had no difficulty in telling her how lovely she looked. Instead, unfortunately, he found himself telling her of the plans to leave the butty boat at Burscough so that the two of them could manage *The Liverpool Rose* unaided.

'It will be a good deal quicker and there'll be other advantages, such as a lighter load for Hal and less trouble getting through the locks,' he said enthusiastically. 'What's more, we shan't need to employ a lad and I was worrying about that, remembering how Geordie let us down.'

'Ye – es, but . . .' Lizzie began, then flushed to the roots of her hair and bent over her plate once more, allowing the sentence to finish in an embarrassed mumble.

Greatly daring, Clem reached across the table and took her hand in his. Then, as she continued to look downwards, he reached out the other hand and tilted her chin so that she was forced to look into his eyes. 'Lizzie, I know what you're thinking but . . . would it be so terrible, to be married to each other, I mean?' he said gently. 'It isn't that there's no alternative because I could tell Priddy and Jake that we weren't willing, that we'd rather take both boats and employ a young feller to help. I'll do that if it's the only way to keep you aboard,' he added, with a flash of such understanding that Lizzie actually tightened her grasp on his hand. 'Look, I'm not asking you to make up your mind right here and now, but I am suggesting that we stop thinking of each other as – as two crew members, and start thinking about being – oh, damn it, I don't want to upset you, but as something a bit closer, like. Will you try to see it my way, Liz?'

'I'll try,' she murmured. 'And I know how badly you want to stay aboard *The Liverpool Rose* so . . .'

'That *isn't* why I want us to marry,' Clem said angrily, feeling the hot colour flood his face. 'Damn it,

461

Lizzie, why do you make it so hard for me? All I want is . . .'

But at this point they were interrupted. 'Was it you asked for more tea?' a voice said, and the little waitress who had served them plonked a large hot water jug down on the table between them. Clem, hastily letting go of Lizzie's hand, glanced around him and realised that his raised voice had attracted a good deal more attention than he wanted. The couple at the adjoining table were listening unashamedly and so was the family group at the table beyond that. He sighed and gave Lizzie a reluctant grin. 'We can't talk here, with every bloody fool stretching their ears and goggling at us,' he muttered. 'Let's drink this bloody tea and get back to the court. Perhaps we can talk easier there.'

Sally had been right, Lizzie reflected, making her way down the stairs in her friend's blue taffeta dress later that evening. She thought it was extremely generous of Sally to have lent what was clearly a new dress, and the little satin slippers which went with it looked charming, though they were far too tight for Lizzie and caused her some pain. But it was worth every pang when she saw Clem's face as she entered the kitchen. She had combed out her long, blonde hair, gathering up the sides and securing them on the top of her head with a length of blue satin ribbon, and letting the rest ripple down her back, nearly as far as her waist. Clem's eyes told her she was looking her best.

In one way it was lovely to be looked at with such startled admiration, but when he took her arm as they left the house, she realised, with some dismay, that he was no longer treating her like his old friend Lizzie.

His gentle touch on her elbow seemed to imply that she was a fragile thing, to be treated with every care, and this might work against the new relationship which she was almost sure they both wanted.

Geoff and Sally had followed the two of them into the roadway and now the four young people stood at the tram stop, discussing the evening ahead, until, that was, Geoff began to describe the various moves by which his team had won the football match. It soon appeared that Clem had been a keen footballer before he joined *The Liverpool Rose* and the two young men began to discuss the game so enthusiastically that Sally and Lizzie were able to exchange a few words in undertones.

'Has he asked you yet?' Sally hissed. 'When you came back from having your tea, there was me mam, me dad and Geoff all listening to every word so I didn't like to ask. And when we was changing, Mam kept popping in and out with jugs o' water and clean towels . . . so tell me now, quick! Has he asked you?'

'Not exactly, but we did talk about getting married,' Lizzie murmured. 'It's awfully awkward because neither of us wants to push the other one into doing anything rash, but we're going to have to think about it because . . .'

But here the tram arrived and the four of them, and a great many other young people, all bound for the Grafton Rooms on West Derby Road, scrambled aboard. None of them managed to get a seat and Lizzie was glad she was not wearing the satin pumps but carrying them in a paper bag; as it was, her booted feet got trodden on several times as the crowd surged to the tram's motion and she was glad enough to leave the vehicle when Sally indicated they had reached their destination.

463

It was exciting, going to a dance after so long, and to her surprise and pleasure, Lizzie found that a number of girls she had known at school and in the factory were present. They greeted her enthusiastically, wanting to know what she was doing now, and were visibly impressed when she introduced them to Clem, making Lizzie realise afresh how very good-looking he was.

Making their way into the ballroom, the four of them managed to get a tiny table and chairs right against the dance floor and were soon watching as the evening commenced with an exhibition tango. The wonderful dresses and the exotic, swooping movements mesmerised Lizzie but she became aware that Clem was not similarly impressed. He was looking worried and, as the dance ended, leaned over and hissed urgently in her ear: 'I don't think I could do that, Lizzie. My God, I never realised dancing could be so . . . so . . .'

Lizzie giggled. She knew exactly what Clem meant and had herself felt quite embarrassed by the abandon with which the dancers had behaved, but she assured him that this was an exhibition dance, and would not be indulged in by ordinary people like themselves.

Clem looked relieved. When the tango dancers left the floor and the band struck up a waltz, Geoff got to his feet and held out a hand to Sally and soon they were whirling round the floor, Sally's feet following the movements of Geoff's effortlessly while the tassels on the hem of her dress flared out to show her silk-clad knees.

All around them, other couples had taken to the floor and Lizzie waited impatiently for Clem to follow suit. But he looked as though he was stuck to his chair by the seat of his trousers and made no attempt to rise. Then a young man in matelot uniform approached them, very stiff and correct, and asked Lizzie if he might have the pleasure of this dance. Lizzie cast an agonised look at Clem but realised that she could not refuse without seeming extremely rude and got reluctantly to her feet. So she found herself in the matelot's arms, being whirled expertly round the floor, while Clem, red-faced, sat and watched.

Clem had never felt quite so helpless because the truth was, from the moment the dancing had started, he had realised he simply dare not take Lizzie on to the floor. Having had no personal experience and going on what he had seen at the cinema, he had assumed, perhaps foolishly, that all a man had to do was hold a girl in his arms and walk slowly forward, while she walked slowly backwards. He had had no idea, until this very evening, that one's feet were supposed to perform complicated movements in unison while one's upper half remained relatively still.

The exhibition tango had not only frightened him, it had also shocked him. The way the man bent the woman backwards until they were both almost horizontal he thought downright immoral, and he had been mightily relieved when Lizzie assured him that ordinary people did not indulge in this intimate behaviour when dancing. However, as soon as Geoff and Sally had taken to the floor, Clem had seen, with horror, that he had had no idea of the intricacies which his feet would be asked to perform. Fortunately he was not wearing clogs, but not even his best shoes could help him in his present predicament. He was, in fact, completely stymied; if he asked Lizzie to dance, he would make a complete fool of both of them, and if he did not ask her, that bleeding, impudent matelot would undoubtedly annexe her for the rest of the evening because Lizzie was easily the prettiest girl present and the matelot – Clem ground his teeth – was a handsome chap and an expert performer of the waltz.

He sat there in an agony of indecision. Should he get up and simply leave? Or should he try desperately to practise his non-existent skills with one of the plain little wallflowers who sat around, clearly hoping for a dance? He could crush their toes with impunity, but suppose his victim simply abandoned him in mid-dance, having suffered enough at his hands – or rather – feet?

He was still pondering the matter when a hand descended on his shoulder and a voice said in his ear: 'Wharra you doin' here, eh, Clem? I ain't never seen you in a ballroom. I allus thought you had two left feet.'

Clem glanced instinctively down at his feet then up at the speaker. It was Jenny Finnigan and a group of friends, all of whom he recognised from the canal. Grinning sheepishly, he admitted that he had come here under false pretences since he had not realised that dancing was such a complicated matter. 'I dunno what Lizzie will think of me,' he ended gloomily, 'asking her to come dancing and then not liking to take to the floor. I reckon she'll probably never speak to me again. Still, there you are, if you can't dance, you can't.'

But Jenny Finnigan was not having any such defeatist talk. 'Rubbish!' she said roundly. 'Gerroff your bum, Clem Gilligan. I can teach you a waltz in ten minutes flat and a slow fox-trot in even less. As for the other dances, the modern ones, you'll pick them up easy as easy, just you see.'

Clem tried to resist but Jenny had not spent her life hefting cargoes and heaving on locks for nothing. She dragged him on to the floor, placed his left hand in her right, and his right arm about her waist, and began to show him how it was done. At first Clem was so nervous that he scarcely listened to her careful explanation of what his feet should be doing. Then, suddenly, it was as though they began to move in time to the music of their own accord and he was listening to Jenny's voice in his ear, obeying her instructions and enjoying – actually enjoying – moving around the floor in perfect rhythm with a pretty girl in his arms.

When the music ended, he would have returned to his table and Lizzie, but Jenny prevented him. 'They'll play a slow fox-trot next,' she said authoritatively. 'You've got a good sense of rhythm – I reckon balancing on the deck of a moving canal boat probably helps – so it won't take long for you to get the fox-trot by heart. But if you're so keen on Lizzie Devlin, why didn't you ask her to teach you?'

He was spared the task of answering her by the band striking up and the two of them moved away, much more slowly and languorously, and Clem found it easier to follow Jenny's footsteps this time. Once more he began to enjoy himself, and when she repeated the question answered honestly that he had not thought anything which looked so complicated could be taught so easily.

'Well, you know now,' Jenny said. 'I s'pose you and she is going to get hitched? There ain't a soul on the canal who don't think it's time you done the decent thing by her, Clem.'

Once he would have taken offence at this rather heavy-handed teasing, but now he just grinned. As soon as he and Jenny parted, he decided he would dance with his dear Lizzie and somehow turn the conversation back to marriage. With their arms about each other and their bodies so close, surely she would be more receptive to the idea?

But this time when the fox-trot ended the band began to play a quicker, livelier tune, which Jenny informed him was a Charleston. 'You might as well learn this while you are about it,' she said, and the two of them struck out on to the dance floor once more. Then Clem shook his head firmly.

'If looks could kill, we'd both be stretched out dead on the floor,' he said wryly. 'Remember, I asked Lizzie to this place and didn't have the courage to explain that I'd never danced in me life so she must be wondering what on earth I'm up to.' He patted Jenny's shoulder, smiling down at her. 'You've been a real pal. I shan't forget it, and I hope you'll dance at me wedding.' And with these brave words he went across to the little table where Lizzie, Sally and Geoff were just standing up, presumably to take part in the Charleston.

Geoff led Sally on to the floor but Clem went straight to Lizzie and took both her hands in his despite the fact that she was glaring at him in cold fury. 'I'm sorry, Liz. I should've explained that I'd never actually danced before,' he said frankly. 'I knew that if I asked you to have a waltz, I'd only trample on your toes and ruin Sally's satin slippers. Besides, there was the matelot . . . and then Jenny offered to show me the steps and. . . and . . .'

'Oh, I don't mind you dancing with Jenny Finnigan, that's your privilege,' Lizzie said airily.

'Only since you asked *me* to come with you tonight, I kind of expected that you'd dance with me as well.'

'I would have! I've explained . . .' he said wildly. 'I was a fool, I should have admittted I couldn't dance and asked *you* to teach me. Only I didn't think . . . I guess it would've made me feel small, asking you to show me dance steps. Oh, Lizzie, I'm really sorry, honest to God I am.' He gripped her hands harder than ever, gazing down into the brilliant blue of her eyes. 'Why do I always do things wrong? I seem born to put my foot in it. Can you forgive me?'

'I suppose you can't help not being able to dance,' Lizzie said. She spoke rather grudgingly, Clem thought. 'Still, it's not too late to start. Come on!'

On the floor couples were gyrating and whirling to the music of the Charleston; Clem saw feet twinkling, elbows waggling, fingertips flying and thought for an astonished moment that the dancers looked more like chickens when a fox has got into the hen run than human beings. He turned helplessly to Lizzie. 'I can't do this one! Honest to God, Lizzie, if you drag me on to the floor we'll both regret it. It's too . . . too . . . complicated. I couldn't possibly . . .'

'So you think I'm not capable of teaching a feller how to dance?' she said truculently, pulling her reluctant companion on to the floor. 'Anything Jenny Finnigan can do, I can do. Don't worry, I'll see you don't get trampled underfoot.'

'We'll regret it,' Clem muttered beneath his breath, but he followed Lizzie meekly enough. It was clear that her mind was made up and he did not want to quarrel with her in such a public place. Besides, it would have been useless. They were already on the dance floor and beginning to . . .

Even if Lizzie was not regretting it – and Clem guessed that she must have been – he himself very soon was. He did his best to keep out of the way of twinkling feet, kicking heels and snapping fingers, but this was not like the more conventional dances which Jenny had taught him. This was dangerous and when, after a particularly painful blow in the eye from a passing elbow, he made his way off the floor, Lizzie followed him. Breathing hard she said angrily: 'You didn't even try to follow me. Well, if that's how you feel . . .'

'I did my best,' Clem said doggedly, wiping the sweat out of his eyes. 'Look, Lizzie, why can't we make ourselves scarce? I don't want to quarrel with you, I want to talk and a dance hall's no place for conversation. I hadn't realised what a deal of noise the band makes, nor that everyone talks all the time and stamps and shrieks. Can't we go outside somewhere it's quiet?'

'We can't just desert Sally and Geoff,' Lizzie was beginning, but Clem interrupted her.

'Look, I've simply got to talk to you,' he said fiercely. 'It's no use aboard the *Rose* 'cos we're boat's crew then and Priddy and Jake are never far away. It's no use in this dance hall 'cos it's rowdy and hot and I don't mean to have to bellow when I'm asking the girl I love to marry me. So please, my darling Lizzie, let's gerrout of here. Sally and Geoff will understand.' He tugged at her hand and to his secret astonishment she followed him meekly out of the main hall and into the street beyond.

Standing under a street lamp, however, she suddenly turned back. 'I've left me jacket and me own boots in the cloakroom,' she said desperately. 'I must fetch 'em. Besides, Sally's slippers are crippling me –

I'd never get as far as the tram stop, let alone all the way to the canal.'

This made Clem remember that his own jacket and cap had been similarly abandoned and the two of them returned to claim their property, meeting outside on the pavement once more with a definite sense of anti-climax. Without speaking another word they headed for the nearest tram stop, but when they reached it Clem put his arm around her waist and led her firmly past. 'We won't catch the tram, 'cos I've already explained it's no use trying to talk aboard *The Liverpool Rose*,' he said. 'Lizzie, I want us to marry because I can't imagine ever being happy without you. If the only way I could get you was by going back to the pit then I'd do it. Will that convince you it's you I want and not just a crew member for the dear old *Rose*?'

Lizzie stopped short, pulling Clem to a halt beside her. She turned to face him then threw both arms round his neck, giving a stifled sob as she did so. 'Oh, Clem, why didn't you say that before?' she asked. 'If you'd said it before, I'd have understood. I wouldn't never have . . .'

'Said what?' he asked, bewildered. 'About going back to the pit, do you mean?'

Lizzie, her head tucked comfortably under his chin and her arms straining around him, gave a watery laugh. 'No, not that,' she murmured. 'The – the other bit. The bit you said in the dance hall about – about not havin' to bellow when you're asking the girl you love to marry you. You never said you loved me before, Clem.'

Clem's arms were already tightly around Lizzie but now he held her a little away from him. 'I never seemed to get the chance,' he admitted. 'But I *do* love you, Lizzie, more than I've ever loved anyone in my life before. And come to that,' he added in an injured tone, 'you *still* haven't said you love me, queen.'

'Oh, Clem, I love you ever so much,' Lizzie said raptly. She snuggled back into his arms as though it was the place she most wanted to be. 'Aren't we a couple of idiots, though? Both of us loving the other one and too perishing frightened to say it out loud. Oh, Clem, I'm so happy! And as for sendin' you back to that bleedin' awful pit when we could live out our lives on *The Liverpool Rose* . . . as if I would! We may never be rich, but we're going to be the happiest couple in the whole world!'

The **POCKET**Guide

NEW YORK

New York: Regions and Best places to see

 Best places to see 20–41

 Featured sight

Midtown Manhattan 45–56

Empire State Building to
Greenwich Village 73–82

Uptown and Central Park 57–72

Lower Manhattan 83–95

Written by Mick Sinclair
Updated by Andrea Scott

© AA Media Limited 2008
First published 2008. Reprinted May 2010

ISBN: 978-0-7495-5527-6

Published by AA Publishing, a trading name of AA Media Limited, whose registered office is Fanum House, Basing View, Basingstoke, Hampshire RG21 4EA. Registered number 06112600.

AA Media Limited retains the copyright in the original edition © 1998 and in all subsequent editions, reprints and amendments.

A CIP catalogue record for this book is available from the British Library.

Colour separation: Keenes, Andover
Printed and bound in Italy by Printer Trento S.r.l.

Front cover images: (t) AA/C Sawyer; (b) AA
Back cover image: AA/S McBride

A04460
Maps in this title produced from map data © Tele Atlas N.V. 2005   Tele Atlas
Transport map © Communicarta Ltd, UK

About this book

This book is divided into five sections.

Planning pages 6–19
Before you go; Getting there; Getting around; Being there

Best places to see pages 20–41
The unmissable highlights of any visit to New York

Exploring pages 42–95
The best places to visit in New York, organized by area

Excursions pages 96–111
Places to visit out of town

Maps pages 115–126
All map references are to the atlas section. For example, SoHo has the reference ✚ 122 A4 – indicating the page number and grid square in which it can be found

Contents

PLANNING

6 – 19

BEST PLACES TO SEE

20 – 41

EXPLORING

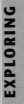

42 – 95

EXCURSIONS

96 – 111

INDEX & ACKNOWLEDGEMENTS

112 – 114

MAPS

115 – 126

Planning

Before you go   8–11

Getting there   12–13

Getting around   14–15

Being there   16–19

Before you go

WHEN TO GO

JAN	FEB	MAR	APR	MAY	JUN	JUL	AUG	SEP	OCT	NOV	DEC
4°C	5°C	8°C	16°C	21°C	27°C	29°C	28°C	25°C	19°C	12°C	4°C
39°F	41°F	46°F	61°F	70°F	80°F	84°F	82°F	77°F	66°F	54°F	39°F

🟤 High season ⬜ Low season

The temperatures given in the above chart are the average daily maximum for each month. Average minimum temperatures are typically 15–20°F (8–11°C) lower. The best times of the year for pleasant weather are May, early June, September and early to mid-October. In July and August the temperatures can soar to more than 86°F (30°C), sometimes reaching 95°F (35°C) or more. Humidity can be up to 90 percent.

Every few years the city has a **blizzard** during the winter but generally the total annual **snowfall** is less than 2ft (61cm). When snow does fall in quantity, life in the city is rarely disrupted.

For information and weather reports visit **www**.cnn.com/weather.

WHAT YOU NEED

●	Required	Some countries require a passport to
○	Suggested	remain valid for a minimum period (usually
▲	Not required	at least six months) beyond the date of
		entry—contact their consulate.

	UK	Germany	USA	Netherlands	Spain
Passport (or National Identity Card where applicable)	●	●	▲	●	●
Visa (regulations can change—check before you travel)	▲	▲	▲	▲	▲
Onward or Return Ticket	●	●	▲	●	●
Health Inoculations	▲	▲	▲	▲	▲
Health Documentation (► 9, Health Advice)	▲	▲	▲	▲	▲
Travel Insurance	●	●	▲	●	●
Driving License (national)	●	●	●	●	●
Car Insurance Certificate	○	○	●	○	○
Car Registration Document	●	●	●	●	●

ADVANCE PLANNING
WEBSITES
- NYC & Company
www.nycvisit.com
- Metropolitan TransitAuthority
www.mta.nyc.ny.us
- The Official New York City
Website: **www.**nyc.gov
- The Official New York State
Website: **www.**iloveny.com

TOURIST OFFICES AT HOME
In the U.S.A.
NYC & Company
810 Seventh Avenue
New York NY 10019
☎ 1-800 NYC-VISIT

In the U.K.
NYC & Company
36 Southwark Bridge Road,
London SE1 9EU
☎ (020) 7202 6368

In Canada
Consular Affairs Bureau
☎ (800) 267-6788 or
(613) 944 6788;
www.voyage.gc.ca

In Australia
Trade Advisory and Consular
Assistance
☎ (300) 139 281;
www.smartraveller.gov.au

HEALTH ADVICE
Call 911 for emergency assistance.
For medical aid that doesn't require
an ambulance, hospital emergency
rooms are open 24 hours daily.
There are also walk-in clinics
particularly in Midtown Manhattan.

Medical and dental insurance
Cover of at least $1,000,000 is
strongly recommended. If involved
in an accident in New York you will
receive treatment by medical
services and be charged later.
Dental cover is usually included.

TIME DIFFERENCES

GMT	New York	Germany	USA (LA)	Netherlands	Spain
12 noon	7AM	1PM	4AM	1PM	1PM

New York is on Eastern Standard
Time, which is five hours behind
Greenwich Mean Time (GMT-5).
Daylight Saving Time (GMT-4)
comes into operation from early
March (when clocks are advanced
by one hour) and runs through to
early November.

WHAT'S ON WHEN

January/February
Chinese New Year: Parades in and around Chinatown; actual date accords with the lunar cycle.
Winter Restaurant Week: New York's finest restaurants serve prix-fixe lunches and dinners at special low prices.

March/April
St Patrick's Day Parade: Massive march of Irish and would-be Irish along Fifth Avenue, with countless related events.
Easter Promenade: A parade of outrageous Easter bonnets along Fifth Avenue.
Cherry Blossom Festival: Centered on Central Park's Conservatory Garden and Brooklyn's Botanic Garden.

May
Opening day of the baseball season: At Yankee and Shea Stadiums.
Bike New York Five Boro Bike Tour: Thousands of cyclists of all levels ride through the city.

June
Lesbian and Gay Pride Day: Enormous march along Fifth Avenue from Midtown Manhattan to Washington Square; many related events throughout Greenwich Village.
National Puerto Rican Day: Parade along Fifth Avenue between 44th and 86th streets.
Shakespeare in the Park: Works of the Bard staged for free in Central Park's Delacorte Theater; continues into August.
Museum Mile Festival: Nine museums along Fifth Avenue stay open late for a mile-long block party.

July
Independence Day: Celebrated with special activities throughout the city and fireworks over the East River.

NATIONAL HOLIDAYS

JAN	FEB	MAR	APR	MAY	JUN	JUL	AUG	SEP	OCT	NOV	DEC
2	1	1(1)	(1)	1		1		1	1	2	1

Jan 1 New Year's Day
Jan (third Mon) Martin Luther King Day
Feb (third Mon) Presidents Day
Mar 17 St. Patrick's Day
Mar/Apr Easter (half day Good Friday, Easter Monday whole day)
May (last Mon) Memorial Day
Jul 4 Independence Day
Sep (first Mon) Labor Day
Oct (second Mon) Columbus Day

Nov 11 Veterans' Day
Late Nov Thanksgiving (4th Thu of month)
Dec 25 Christmas Day
Banks, businesses, museums and most shops are closed on these days.

Boxing Day (December 26) is not a national holiday in the U.S.

Lincoln Center Festival: Music, opera, dance and theater events for several weeks each summer.

August/September
Harlem Week: Special events marking Harlem's history and culture.
U.S. Open Tennis Tournament: The last of the grand slams, held in Queens.
Feast of St Gennaro: A 10-day festival based in Little Italy's Mulberry Street; stands dispense food and an image of the patron saint of Naples is showered with dollar bills.

October
Columbus Day Parade: Italians celebrate their heritage in a parade up Fifth Avenue.
Halloween Parade: Amazing costumes and masks worn in a parade through Greenwich Village.

November
New York Marathon: Begins in Staten Island and concludes in Central Park.
Macy's Thanksgiving Day Parade: Massive balloons paraded along Central Park West and Broadway.

December
Lighting of a tree at Rockefeller Center marks the start of the Christmas season.
New Year's Eve in Times Square: The ball drops and thousands dance in the streets.

Getting there

BY AIR

New York has three main airports:
John F. Kennedy Airport (☎ 718
244 4444), LaGuardia Airport
(☎ 718 533 3400) and Newark
Liberty International Airport (☎ 973
961-6000). International flights fly
into John F. Kennedy and Newark
airports and most domestic flights
are handled by LaGuardia. All are
part of the Port Authority of New
York and New Jersey
(www.panynj.gov). For driving and
transit information, call Air Ride
(800) 247 7433 or see the website.

John F. Kennedy International
Airport is 15 miles (24km) from
Manhattan (a 1-hour drive) and has
nine passenger terminals. Three
are dedicated to specific carriers;
British Airways operate from
Terminal 7, JetBlue from Terminal 6
and Delta Airlines from Terminals 2
and 3. The other terminals handle
all other major international carriers.

For transfers from the airport
head to a Transportation Center
booth where you will be able to
make transport bookings and be
given directions to public transit.
Transfers to and from the airport
can be taken in several ways.
Taxis from stands in front of the
terminals charge a flat rate of $45
plus tolls—expensive compared to
other modes for one person but not
for two or three. When traveling
back to the airport the fee is on
the meter.

The AirTrain is an inexpensive
way to travel and connects with
the A and other subway trains.
See www.panynj.gov for routes
and schedules.

The SuperShuttle Manhattan is a
shared-ride van service that
operates 24 hours (☎ 212/258
3826; www.supershuttle.com) and
is moderately priced. The vans fill
with passengers who are all
headed to the same part of the
city and serve the area between
Battery Park and 125th Street
(96th Street from Newark Airport).
Reserve seats on a SuperShuttle at
the Ground Transportation Center.

Alternatively, the New York
Airport Service Express Bus
(☎ 212/875 8200) operates a

service that stops at Penn Station, the Port Authority Bus Terminal and Grand Central Terminal.

LaGuardia Airport is 8 miles (13km) from Manhattan in Queens or approximately a 40-minute drive from Midtown.

A taxi will charge metered rates, typically $21–$30 plus tolls.

The SuperShuttle Manhattan, the New York Airport Service and the Express also operate from LaGuardia.

Alternatively there are buses (take note: no luggage racks) that connect with the subway to take you to town; the Q47 and the Q33 connect with the 7 subway train, which stops at Grand Central Terminal and Times Square.

Newark International Airport, New Jersey, is 16 miles (26km) from the city or a 40-minute drive.

Taxi transfers to Newark are expensive and will charge extra to

go to the Upper East Side than to get to Midtown.

The SuperShuttle Manhattan service also operates 24 hours from Newark.

Another transfer option is the Newark Liberty Airport Express Bus (☎ 877-8NEWARK) which makes stops at Penn Station, the Port Authority and Grand Central Terminal.

There is also an Air Train which links the airport with Amtrak or New Jersey commuter train. See **www.**panynj.gov for schedule.

TRAIN AND BUS STATIONS

New York's long-distance train and bus terminals are located on the West Side.

For trains there are Grand Central Terminal, Park Avenue at 42nd Street, Metro North (☎ 212/532 4900) and Pennsylvanian Station, 7th Avenue between 31st and 33rd streets (☎ 212/630 6400), where Long Island Railroad and New Jersey Transit trains stop and where you can connect with the subway system or catch a taxi.

For buses, go to the Port Authority Bus Terminal 8th Avenue between 40th and 42nd streets (☎ 212/564 8484), where buses from New Jersey and interstate and Canada serve the terminal.

Getting around

PUBLIC TRANSPORTATION

Public transit information (24 hour) ☎ 311; **www.**mta.com. Buy multi-trip MetroCards at the entrance to the stations and swipe them through the turnstile to access the subway platform or bus. The $7 Fun Pass allows travel on buses (not express routes) and

subways until 3am the next morning and is available from MetroCard vending machines and some MetroCard vendors (including Times Square Visitor Center) but not at subway station booths. Schedules and maps are available from the concourse of Grand Central Terminal.

TRAINS

The subway offers the fastest way to travel around New York. The five main services mainly run parallel along Manhattan's main avenues. PATH trains from Penn Station

serve New Jersey and MTA trains from Grand Central Terminal serve towns north of the city.

BUSES

The bus system is simpler but slower than the subway, but has the advantage of cross-town routes. There are more than 200 bus routes, with stops every two or three blocks. Buses are equipped with lifts for wheelchair access.

FERRIES

The Staten Island Ferry (☎ 311; **www.**siferry.com) runs a 24-hour service. Circle Line (☎ 212/563 3200; **www.**circleline.com) sightseeing cruises run tours from Pier 83 at 2nd Street and 12th Avenue that circle Manhattan Island and from Battery Park to Ellis Island and the Statue of Liberty.

TAXIS

Yellow Cabs display an illuminated sign on the roof when available for hire, and can then be hailed on the street. There are a few taxi ranks at high-traffic areas such as Grand Central Terminal. Drivers are legally bound to take you anywhere within the five New York Boroughs but will charge for bridge or tunnel tolls.

Drive on the right.
Speed limit on freeways:
55–65mph (88–105kph)
Speed limit on main roads:
50–55mph (80–88kph)
Speed limit on urban roads:
25–40mph (40–65kph), relevant to
the area.

Stretch limousines (with a driver)
can also be booked at competitive
rates if 8 to 10 people share.

CAR RENTAL

There are many car rental
companies and prices are
competitive, so shop around. You
must be over 25 and have a credit
card to rent a car. The main rental
companies have toll-free (800)
telephone numbers, and airports
and hotel lobbies will provide
details. Special weekend deals are
widely available, but a full valid E.U.
driving license is acceptable, or an
International Driving Permit.

DRIVING

Driving is not recommended in
Manhattan. Parking places are
costly and difficult to find. If you
break down with a rented car, call
the rental company, or the
breakdown number which should
be prominently displayed on or near
the dashboard. There are no right
turns on red lights within the New
York City limits.

Seat belts Compulsory for
everyone in the front seats and for
children in the back.
Drink driving Drivers can be
stopped at random for a
breathalyzer test (alcotest) by
police. Zero tolerance is now the
police code in New York.
Fuel Gas (petrol) is sold in
American gallons. Five American
gallons equal 18 liters. Most late-
night and 24-hour gas stations
require you to pay the cashier
before filling commences.

DISCOUNTS

Students/youths Students are
entitled to discounts on many
attractions. Show proof of age
and student status, with an
International Student Identity Card.
Seniors (senior citizens) Seniors
will find discounts on many
attractions and some restaurants.
Some variations in qualifying ages,
ranging from 50 to 65 apply, and
you will usually be asked to show
your passport.

Being there

New York City's Official Visitor Information Center
www.nycvisit.com
810 Seventh Avenue
NY 10019
☎ 1-800 NYC VISIT
City information (transit routes, tour reservations for city buildings, taxi complaints etc) ☎ 311.

KIOSKS
Downtown
NYC Heritage Tourism Center
City Hall Park at Park Row
Chinatown
Canal/Walker/Baxter streets
Harlem
163 West 125th Street and Adam Clayton Powell Junior Boulevard (Seventh Avenue)
Times Square Information Center
Embassy Movie Theater, Seventh Avenue between 46th and 47th streets. Operated by Times Square Alliance, a nonprofit organization that offers a free walking tour and sells souvenirs and memorabilia (☎ 212/768 1560; **www.**timessquarebid.org).

TKTS half-price ticket booths
Broadway and 47th Street and South Street Seaport's Pier 17 operated by Theater Development Fund, a nonprofit organization (☎ 212/221 0885; **www.**tdf.org).

EMBASSIES AND CONSULATES
UK ☎ 212/745 0200
Canada ☎ 212/596 1628
Germany ☎ 212/610 9700
Netherlands ☎ 212/246 429
Spain ☎ 212/355 4080
Australia ☎ 212/351 6500

EMERGENCY TELEPHONE NUMBER
Police, Fire, Ambulance 911

INTERNATIONAL DIALING CODES
Making overseas calls from hotel phones can be expensive. International phone cards can make calls more affordable.

OPENING HOURS

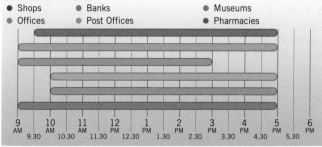

- Shops
- Offices
- Banks
- Post Offices
- Museums
- Pharmacies

9 AM	10 AM	11 AM	12 PM	1 PM	2 PM	3 PM	4 PM	5 PM	6 PM
	9.30	10.30	11.30	12.30	1.30	2.30	3.30	4.30	5.30

Shop hours vary greatly but open until 9pm on one day; some open Sunday noon–5. Some banks open until 3.30pm. Post offices open Saturday till 1pm.

There are over 2,500 places of worship in New York of every religious denomination—see Yellow Pages.

Opening times of museums vary, check with individual museums.

There is an all-night pharmacy at Duane Reade, 224 W 57th Street (☎ 212/541 9708).

Numerous internet cafés and other internet points offer email access at little cost.

Dial 011 followed by
UK: 44
Ireland: 353
Australia: 61
Germany: 49
Netherlands: 31

POSTAL SERVICES

The main branch of the U.S. Post Office is on Manhattan's West Side, at 421 Eighth Avenue/33rd Street,

NY 10001, ☎ 800/ASK-UPS. Open 24 hours.

Other post offices can be found in Yellow Pages. Most are open Mon–Fri 9–5, Sat 8–4.

Mail boxes are on street corners. Hotel desks provide many mail services.

ELECTRICITY

The power supply is 110/120 volts AC (60 cycles).

Sockets take two-prong, flat-pin plugs.

Visitors should bring adapters for their 2-round-pin and 3-pin plugs. European visitors will need either dual voltage facility or a transformer.

CURRENCY

An unlimited amount of American dollars can be imported or exported, but amounts of over £10,000 must be reported to U.S. customs, as should similar amounts of gold. U.S. dollar traveler's checks are accepted with photo ID in most places (not taxis), as are credit cards, (Amex, Visa, MasterCard, Diners Card). Bills (notes) come in denominations of 1, 5, 10, 20, 50 and 100 dollars. One dollar is 100 cents. Coins come in denominations of 1 cent (penny), 5 cent (nickel), 10 cent (dime), 25 cent (quarter), 50 cent and (rarely) 1 dollar.

HEALTH AND SAFETY

Sun advice New York can be very hot and humid in summer. It is wise to use a sunscreen and drink plenty of fluids.

Drugs Pharmacies dispensing prescription and over-the-counter treatments are on almost every block. If you need regular medication, take your own drugs and your prescription (for U.S. Customs). For out-of-hours

TIPS/GRATUITIES

Yes ✓   No ✗

It is useful to have plenty of small notes

Restaurants (waiters, waitresses)	✓	15%
Hotels (chambermaids, doormen etc)	✓	$1
Bar service	✓	15%
Taxis	✓	15%
Tour guides	✓	discretion
Porters	✓	$1 per bag
Hairdressers	✓	15%

CLOTHING SIZES

France	UK	Rest of Europe	USA	
46	36	46	36	
48	38	48	38	
50	40	50	40	
52	42	52	42	
54	44	54	44	**Suits**
56	46	56	46	
41	7	41	8	
42	7.5	42	8.5	
43	8.5	43	9.5	
44	9.5	44	10.5	
45	10.5	45	11.5	**Shoes**
46	11	46	12	
37	14.5	37	14.5	
38	15	38	15	
39/40	15.5	39/40	15.5	
41	16	41	16	
42	16.5	42	16.5	**Shirts**
43	17	43	17	
36	8	34	6	
38	10	36	8	
40	12	38	10	
42	14	40	12	
44	16	42	14	**Dresses**
46	18	44	16	
38	4.5	38	6	
38	5	38	6.5	
39	5.5	39	7	
39	6	39	7.5	
40	6.5	40	8	**Shoes**
41	7	41	8.5	

emergencies several branches of Duane Reade are open 24 hours, including 224 W 57th Street (☎ 212/541 9708).

Safe water Restaurants usually provide a glass of iced water. Drinking unboiled water from taps is safe. Mineral water is cheap and readily available.

Personal safety Crime levels in New York have fallen sharply over recent years. But it is still wise to take sensible precautions:
● Do not take the subway alone after midnight.
● Do not walk quiet streets or Central Park alone after dark.
● Carry only the cash you need, leave other cash and valuables in the hotel safe.
● Report theft or mugging to the nearest police station; this will provide a reference for your insurance company.

Best places to see

Central Park   22–23

Chrysler Building   24–25

Empire State Building   26–27

Grand Central Terminal   28–29

Greenwich Village   30–31

Guggenheim Museum   32–33

Metropolitan Museum of Art   34–35

Museum of Modern Art   36–37

Statue of Liberty   38–39

Times Square   40–41

1 Central Park

www.centralparknyc.org

Central Park, a mighty rectangle of green, is the soothing bucolic heart of Manhattan.

Filling 843 acres (341ha), Central Park evolved during the late 19th century as the visionary plans of Frederick Olmsted and Calvert Vaux—intended to turn a collection of pig farms and squatters' camps into a "specimen of God's handiwork"—took shape. Creating glades and rock outcrops, the landscaping also involved the planting of more than 4 million trees and the digging of the sunken roads that render traffic crossing the park invisible. Fifth Avenue became a fashionable address as the millionaires of the day erected handsome park-view mansions along the eastern side and crossed the park in carrriages. For New York's poor, the park provided a much-needed escape from sweatshops and filthy tenements.

The park continues to mirror the full range of New York life. Whether jogging, rollerblading, strolling or walking the dog, Manhattanites of all kinds relish its green spaces—though in several isolated sections lone visitors can be vulnerable to crime. Pick up a park map from the Visitor Center in the Dairy (mid-park at 65th Street), built in 1870 and first used as a place where traditionally attired milkmaids dispensed milk to mothers and

babies, and plot a route to the numerous points of interest in the park.

Cross the Sheep Meadow (which once really did hold sheep) for the Lake and the Ramble or stroll through the Mall, a formally laid-out promenade that continues towards Bethesda Terrace. Among the more recent additions to the park is Strawberry Fields, laid out as a tribute to British musician John Lennon and overlooked by the Dakota Building where he lived and was fatally shot.

➕ 116 F4 ✉ Between 59th and 110th streets, and Fifth Avenue and Central Park West ☎ 212/310 6600 ⊙ Always open; for safety, visit only during daylight ✋ Free 🍴 Tavern on the Green ($$$); snack stands 🚇 59th Street, 72nd Street, 81st Street, 96th Street, 103rd Street, 110th Street 🚌 1, 2, 3, 4, 5, 10, 30, 66, 72, 86, 104, Q32 ❓ Special events throughout the year

2 Chrysler Building

Even in a city packed with architecture of great merit, the Chrysler Building stands in a class of its own.

The definitive symbol of New York art deco and briefly the world's tallest building, the 1,048ft (320m) Chrysler Building was completed in 1930 and remains one of the most distinctive features on the Manhattan skyline. Reflecting the car manufacturing business of the building's owners and the era's enthusiasm for machine-inspired design, many features echo automobile design. Architect William Van Alen made the first large-scale use of stainless steel on a building exterior, employed hub caps as decoration on each setback and made the attention-grabbing spire resemble a car's radiator grille, complete with outward-leaping gargoyles.

Once partly used as a showroom for new Chrysler cars, the lobby underwent a comprehensive

restoration in the late 1970s. The work brought many features back to their original glory, notably the red-veined African marble walls and the elevators' plush laminated wood interiors. Although an observation level once existed at the base of the spire, there are now no public areas on the upper floors and visitors must content themselves with admiring Edward Trumbull's lobby mural depicting diverse images on themes of transportation.

The completion of the Empire State Building in 1931 robbed the Chrysler of its "world tallest" status, though the title was only acquired in the first place through some slightly devious behaviour by Van Alen. The needle-like spire that tops the Chrysler Building's 77 stories was secretly assembled inside the tower and pushed through the roof. In doing so, Van Alen outwitted his former partner, H. Craig Severance, whose Bank of Manhattan Building (40 Wall Street), completed at just about the same time, would otherwise have earned the accolade.

✛ 119 E6 ✉ 405 Lexington Avenue
☎ 212/682 3070 🕐 Mon–Fri 7am–6pm.
Closed holidays 🖐 Free 🚇 Grand Central
🚌 42, 98, 101, 102, 104

3 Empire State Building

www.esbnyc.com

Perhaps not the best or even the best loved, but the Empire State Building is certainly the world's best-known New York skyscraper.

Conceived in the booming 1920s but built in the gloom of the Depression, the Empire State Building rose at a rate of four-and-a-half stories a week and was completed in just 410 days. By the time it was finished, however, the Wall Street Crash had left few companies able to afford its rents, despite the prestige of being housed in the world's tallest building, at a height of 1,454ft (442m) to the top

of its lightning rod. Through its early years, the building's only source of income came from visitors paying to enjoy the panorama of 80 miles (130km) from its 86th-floor observation level.

The building is a major sight among New York's art deco constructions. From a base filling 2 acres/1ha (site of the original Astoria Hotel), the limestone and steel structure rises as a smooth-sided shaft with windows set flush with the wall. Inside, the three-story lobby boasts marble walls and aluminium decoration, including the panels added in the 1960s depicting the "eight" wonders of the world—the well-known seven plus the Empire State Building itself.

The building's 73 elevators include those designed to whisk sightseers to the observation levels at an astonishing rate of 1,200ft (365m) per minute, and can take just seconds from the lobby to the 80th floor. From there, two elevators lead up to the 86th floor, where there are outdoor promenades on all four sides of the building and a heated galssed-in area. Threre's also an observatory on the 102nd floor. The slower and much more arduous route, by foot up 1,576 steps, is no longer open to the public, but is undertaken annually in the Empire Step-Up race, completed by the speediest competitors in less than 10 minutes.

✚ 119 F5 ✉ 350 Fifth Avenue ☎ 212/736 3100 🕐 Daily 9.30–midnight 👢 Expensive 🍴 Snack bar ($) 🚇 34th Street 🚌 1, 2, 3, 4, 5, 6, 7, 16, 34, Q32 ❓ New York Skyride, a helicopter ride simulator on the second floor

4 Grand Central Terminal

www.grandcentralterminal.com

From an architectural viewpoint, there are few bigger, bolder or more beautiful places to buy a train ticket than Grand Central Terminal, built to house Cornelius Vanderbilt's railroad network in the early 20th century.

The halcyon years of American rail travel saw Grand Central Terminal labelled "the gateway to the nation" and a red carpet set along a platform for passengers boarding the evening service to Chicago. As if to cement the terminal's metaphorical place at the heart of the nation's life, its name was (inaccurately) used as the title of a popular radio soap opera, Grand Central Station, first broadcast in 1937. Now, it is mostly commuters to Conneticut's and New York's northern suburbs who can be found in lines at the ticket booths inside the Main Concourse.

Nearly demolished in 1968, the terminal was restored in the 1990s and now serves as the hub for dozens of shops and restaurants, including the Oyster Bar, which opened in 1913. The Main Concourse, 275ft by 120ft (84m by 37m), enjoys a *beaux-arts* form and a staircase modeled on one in the Paris Opera. Above, the vaulted ceiling, 125ft (38m) high, is decorated by artist Paul Helleu's interpretation of the zodiac constellations. Although architects Warren and Wetmore take credit for the Main Concourse, much of the terminal's design is thought to be the work of another architectural firm, Reed and Stem.

The southern facade, clad in limestone and modeled on a Roman triumphal arch, features Jules Coutane's sculpture of Mercury supported by Minerva and Hercules.

✚ 119 E5 ✉ 42nd Street and Lexington Avenue ⏰ Daily 5.30am–1.30am ⚕ Free 🍴 Various restaurants ($$–$$$), cafés and snack stands ($–$$) Ⓖ Grand Central 🚌 1, 2, 3, 4, 5, 42, 98, 101, 102, 104, Q32 ❓ Guided tours Wed 12.30 from Information booth on Main Concourse ☎ 212/935 3960

5 Greenwich Village

The cafés, restaurants and bars of culturally vibrant Greenwich Village are a major element in Manhattan social life.

Created as a wealthy residential neighborhood in the 1780s, Greenwich Village then marked the northern extent of Manhattan's settlement and served to keep the rich away from the diseases sweeping through the poorer social stratas to the south. As the rich moved on, their vacated brownstone townhouses became apartments for newly arrived migrants who swiftly established businesses. By the turn of the 20th century,

Greenwich Village was an ethnically diverse and socially tolerant area, with the low rents that helped attract the creative and unconventional members of what was later lauded as the first American Bohemia.

Henry James, Eugene O'Neill and Edward Hopper were among the locally based novelists, dramatists and artists who created Greenwich Village's cultural reputation. By the 1950s, Beat writers such as Allen Ginsberg and Jack Kerouac and abstract expressionist painters like Willem de Kooning were gathering in the area's cafés, and a decade on, the Greenwich Village folk clubs that launched Bob Dylan.

Gentrification raised rents through the 1970s and 1980s and Greenwich Village people today are more likely to be successful lawyers or publishers than striving creative types. The haphazard streets are a delight to stroll, packed with unusual stores and lined by well-tended brownstones, many sporting "stoops" (entrance steps, a style introduced by 17th-century Dutch settlers that was used to prevent flooding back in the Netherlands) attractively decorated by their occupants.

At the heart of the action are New York University and Washington Square Park—a domain of skateboarders, buskers and onlookers, above which stands the triumphal Memorial Arch.

🕂 120 D3 ✉ Bordered by 14th Street, Hudson Street, Broadway and Houston Street 🚇 W 14th Street or Christopher Street 🚌 1, 2, 3, 5, 8, 10

6 Guggenheim Museum

www.guggenheim.org

The architecture might overpower the art but fans of both will find plenty to thrill them at this landmark museum.

Frank Lloyd Wright's stunningly designed Guggenheim Museum is a daring addition to the Fifth Avenue landscape. Outside, its curves and horizontally accentuated form is at odds with the traditional architecture all around, and inside, the

THE THANNHAUSER COLLECTION

exhibits are arranged along a spiral ramp where visitors start at the top and make thier way down.

Solomon R. Guggenheim differed from other art investors by switching from Old Masters to invest his silver- and copper-mining wealth into the emerging European abstract scene of the 1920s. Guggenheim acquired works by the major exponents such as Léger and Gleizes, and a spectacular stash of paintings by Vasily Kandinsky. With these works and others hanging on the walls of his apartment at the smart Plaza Hotel, Guggenheim set up a foundation in 1937 to promote public appreciation of abstract art that eventually grew into the present-day museum, which opened in 1959, 10 years after Guggenheim's death.

Selections from the Guggenheim collections, which range from Klee and Mondrianto Kloons and Robert Mapplethorpe, are shown on rotation and share space with high-quality temporary exhibitions. A broader selection of art is displayed in the Thannhauser Tower, a 1992 addition with a permanent exhibit of the acquisitions of art collector and dealer Justin K. Thannhauser. These include important pieces by Gauguin, Picasso, Van Gogh, and Cézanne.

➕ 117 E5 ✉ 1071 Fifth Avenue ☎ 212/423 3500
🕐 Sat–Wed 10–5.45, Fri 10–8. Closed 25 Dec, 1 Jan
♿ Moderate 🍴 Café ($–$$) 🚇 86th Street
🚌 1, 2, 3, 4, 18 ❓ Lectures

7 Metropolitan Museum of Art

www.metmuseum.org

Founded in 1870, this mighty museum is a vast collection of anything and everything of artistic value ever produced anywhere in the world.

More than deserving of its reputation as one of the world's greatest museums, the Met's contents exhaust visitors long before visitors exhaust them. Make use of the information center at ground level to plan your explorations and be selective. Special exhibitions are often crowded; go early on a weekday if you can. Art lovers can meander through galleries that chart virtually the entire course of Western art. The Impressionist and Post-Impressionist galleries hold noted works by Cézanne, Gauguin, Renoir and Van Gogh.

The influential paintings of the Hudson River School and a series of period-furnished rooms highlight the increasing self-assurance of American art as the country evolved into an independent nation. Among the strong points are a dazzling stock of Tiffany glasswork and a special section devoted to architect Frank Lloyd Wright.

With 36,000 objects dating from pre-dynastic

times to the arrival of the Romans, the Met's Ancient Egyptian section begins with a walk-through reconstruction of the Tomb of Perneb and continues with case after case of immaculately preserved original exhibits. Major assemblages of Roman and Greek art, Chinese and Japanese ceramics, medieval European art (which continues at the Cloisters, ➤ 60), European arms and armor, the art of Africa, Oceania and the Americas, musical instruments, plus galleries of drawings, prints and photography, and modern art, consume only some of the rest of this vast museum.

The galleries of Islamic art are closed for several years for renovation. A selection from the collection of more than 10,000 objects is on view in a temporary installation.

✚ 117 E5 ⊠ 1000 Fifth Avenue ☎ 212/535 7710
🕐 Tue–Thu and Sun 9.30–5.30, Fri and Sat 9.30–9
🖐 Moderate 🍴 Restaurant ($$), cafeteria and cafés ($)
🚇 86th Street 🚌 1, 2, 3, 4, 18 (includes admission to the Cloisters on same day) ❓ Lectures, films

8 Museum of Modern Art

www.moma.org

Probably the world's best repository of modern painting and an excellent exhibitor of sculpture, film and video.

It is hard to credit today, but when the Museum of Modern Art (MoMA, as it is known) staged its first exhibition in 1929 the featured artists—Cézanne, Van Gogh, Gauguin and Seurat—were not represented anywhere else in the city and were considered too risky by the Met. Despite this, 47,000 people attended the exhibition over four months and, a decade later, the museum acquired its current site, a gift from the wealthy Rockefeller family.

As the new museum was being created, the outbreak of war in Europe caused many leading artists to leave Paris for New York, making the city the center of the art world and setting the scene for abstract expressionism, the U.S.'s first internationally influential art movement.

Abstract expressionism accounts for some of the most noted holdings: Pollock's immense and spellbinding *One*, Rothko's shimmering blocks of color, and works by De Kooning. European contributions include Van Gogh's much eulogized *Starry Night*, one of Monet's *Water Lilies*, Matisse's *Dance*, Picasso's *Three Women at the Spring*, Braque's *Man With A*

Guitar, and Mondrian's Broadway *Boogie-Woogie* revealing the impact of New York's jazz rhythms and grid-style streets on the Dutch artist.

A soaring remodeled building designed by Yoshio Taniguchi opened in 2004 with nearly twice the space. It preserves Philip Johnson's 1953 design of the beloved Abby Aldrich Rockefeller Sculpture Garden and allows works to be displayed in new juxtapositions. The most modern pieces are displayed on the second floor, with selections from the permanent collection on the fourth and fifth floors. That collection also includes some 22,000 films and videos, and there's a regular program of screenings. The department devoted to architecture and design includes the Mies van der Rohe archive and an eclectic range of objects.

➕ 119 C5 ✉ 11 W 53rd Street
☎ 212/708 9400 🕐 Sat–Mon, Thu 10.30–5.30, Fri 10.30–8 💲 Expensive (free Fri 4–8) 🍴 Restaurant ($$$) and cafés ($–$$) Ⓜ Fifth Avenue, 53rd Street 🚌 1, 2, 3, 4, 5 ❓ Films, lectures

9 Statue of Liberty

www.nps.gov/stli

The most potent and enduring symbol of the U.S. as the land of opportunity is the landmark Statue of Liberty.

Nowadays it is strange to think that an American emblem known worldwide was initially intended by its creator, Frenchman Frédéric-August Bartholdi, to stand in Egypt above the Suez Canal. The plans were rejected, but in 1871 on a visit to New York, the sculptor found the perfect site for his torch-carrying lady—at the entrance to the city's harbor. Equally surprising in retrospect is the antipathy towards the project on the American side following the decision for costs to be shared between France and the U.S. as a sign of friendship and shared democratic ideals.

As the lady, formally titled *Liberty Enlightening the World*, took shape in Bartholdi's Paris studio, the pedestal—the responsibility of the U.S.—made slow progress due to lack of funds, which prompted newspaper publisher Joseph Pulitzer to mount a campaign to raise money through small donations. The finished statue arrived in New York in June 1885 and Pulitzer announced that $100,000 had been collected. The lady was placed atop the pedestal and dedicated in October 1886.

Ferries to the statue, which is 152ft (46m) high, leave regularly from Battery Park, also stopping at Ellis Island. Access is limited, so order tickets in advance. Once ashore, visitors not only have an excellent view of the lower Manhattan skyline but can tour the Statue of Liberty museum on the 16-story-high pedestal level. Exhibits document the history and symbolism of the statue, while the interior of the statue itself can be glimpsed through a glass ceiling. Further access is not possible.

🚹 122 F3 (off map) ✉ Liberty Island ☎ 212/269 5755 (ferry information); 212/363 3200 (statue information) 🕐 Daily 9.30–5 ♿ Moderate 🍴 Cafeteria ($) 🚢 Battery Park ❓ Tours

10 Times Square

www. TimesSquarebid.org

If a single spot yells "this is New York" to the world at large, it is Times Square with its towering, animated neon signs.

A gathering place for hundreds of thousands celebrating each New Year's Eve and the heart of New York's theater district, Times Square is a frenetic, gaudy and until the late 1990s, rather seedy junction whose fame far outstrips its actual appeal. The immediate area fell into social decline after World War II, but a major campaign to rid the area of its prostitutes, drug dealers and street con artists, and to limit the numbers of porno cinemas and adult bookshops in its vicinity, met with considerable success.

Designated a Business Improvement District under a nationwide scheme financed by a tax on local businesses, the square steadily became safe for tourists and legitimate businesses with a major new development of hotels, shopping complexes, and office blocks, and the restoration of many historic theaters. Major retail franchises, a number of theme restaurants, and a never ending stream of sightseers now dominate the area, which is patrolled by an unarmed security force.

Times Square was originally Longacre Square, but acquired a new name in 1904 when the owner of the *New York Times* got permission to build the office tower (One Times Square) from which the

New Year's ball is still dropped. By the 1920s, the vibrant New York theater district had become established on nearby streets. Raised in the heyday of vaudeville, many of the plush theaters remain in varied states of restoration. Through the 1930s, the local section of Broadway became known as "the Great White Way" for its immense electrically lit marquees and advertising billboards.

➕ 118 E4 ✉ Between Broadway and Seventh Avenue, 42nd and 47th streets 🚇 Times Square 🚌 5, 6, 7, 10, 42, 104 ❓ Walking tours

Exploring

Midtown Manhattan	45–56
Uptown and Central Park	57–72
Empire State Building to Greenwich Village	73–82
Lower Manhattan	83–95

Manhattan may only be a part of New York City, but as far as the world is concerned Manhattan is New York. For visitors from near and far, this long slender island is everything they ever imagined New York to be. Times Square, Broadway, Central Park, the Empire State Building, the Museum of Modern Art and everything else that defines New York to the world at large has a Manhattan address and entices visitors to spend day after day tramping its streets with a sense of wonder.

Once acclimatized to the cruising yellow cabs, the street food vendors, legions of office workers crossing the road as one and the general commotion that fills many a Manhattan street, newcomers will find themselves steadily discovering another Manhattan: One of neighborhoods with a village-like insularity harboring undiscovered attractions on quiet residential streets.

Midtown Manhattan

With its skyscrapers, department stores, high-class hotels, hotdog vendors, bustling office workers and tourists, Midtown Manhattan is for many visitors what New York is all about. From Times Square to glossy Fifth Avenue you will encounter crowds of sightseers as well as busy New Yorkers rushing to work whilst grabbing a hot dog "to go" and talking into a mobile phone.

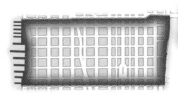

While the streets are teeming with humanity by day, after the evening rush hour much of the area is remarkably empty, save for areas such as the theater district around Times Square. Some of the city's best loved attractions lie between 8th Avenue and Lexington Avenue, with Fifth Avenue slicing through the middle to define the east and west.

The only deviation from Midtown's grid-style street layout is the

former Native American trail better known as Broadway, which cuts a diagonal path not only through midtown Manhattan but continues 140 miles (225km) to the state capital of Albany.

CARNEGIE HALL

Carnegie Hall was built with $2 million from the fortune of industrialist Andrew Carnegie and has been highly regarded ever since Tchaikovsky arrived from Russia to conduct on the opening night in 1891. Guided tours lead visitors around the horseshoe-shaped auditorium, with world-famous acoustics, its design modeled on an Italian opera house.

The adjoining museum remembers many of the great artists who have appeared here.

www.carnegiehall.org

🚩 118 C4 ✉ 57th Street and 7th Avenue ☎ 212/247 7800 🚻 Other than shows, interior only on guided tours 👐 Inexpensive; museum free 🚇 57th Street–7th Avenue ❓ Guided tours during the season ☎ 212/903 9765

CHRYSLER BUILDING

See pages 24–25.

DAILY NEWS BUILDING

Easy to imagine as the home of the *Daily Planet* and mild-mannered Clark Kent, alter ego of Superman, the Daily News Building was the base of the newspaper of the same name until 1995. In the lobby is an immense globe. The architect of the art deco building was Raymond Hood, also the designer of the GE Building in Rockefeller Center.

➕ 119 E6 ✉ 220 E 42nd Street 🕐 Lobby always open ♿ Free 🚇 42nd Street–Grand Central

GRAND CENTRAL TERMINAL

See pages 28–29.

INTREPID SEA-AIR-SPACE MUSEUM

Seeing service in World War II and the Vietnam conflict, the aircraft carrier U.S.S. *Intrepid* is now spending its retirement years as a museum. The workings and wartime exploits of the vessel itself are comprehensively detailed, and the many exhibits arranged around its decks explore the changing face of warfare and document the technological innovations spawned by it.

A former British Airways Concorde is among the civilian aviation exhibits. Temporary exhibitions cover related themes.

www.intrepidmuseum.org

➕ 118 D1 ✉ Pier 86, W 46th Street ☎ 212/245 0072
🕐 Apr–Sep Mon–Fri 10–5, Sat and Sun 10–6; Oct–Mar Tue–Sun 10–5 ♿ Expensive 🍴 Café ($) 🚇 42nd Street

LIPSTICK BUILDING

In a city that sometimes seems built entirely of towering rectangular blocks, the so-called Lipstick building dares to be different. Its nickname is earned by its elliptical shape, its telescoping tiers, and by its predominant colors of red, brown and pink. One of many buildings contributed to the New York skyline by veteran architect Philip Johnson and partner John Burgee, the Lipstick was completed in 1986.

➕ 119 C6 ✉ 885 Third Avenue ◷ Lobby always open ✋ Free 🍴 Café ($$)
🚇 Lexington–Third Avenue

MET LIFE BUILDING

Looming high above Grand Central Terminal and infamously blocking the view along Park Avenue, the Met Life Building (formerly the Pan Am Building) was completed in 1963 and became the largest commercial building in the world, rising 59 stories and offering 2.4 million sq ft (223,000sq m) of office space. Bauhaus mastermind Walter Gropius was among the architects that created the structure which has an angled face that many say resembles an aircraft's wing.

➕ 119 D5 ✉ 200 Park Avenue
✋ Free 🍴 Various restaurants ($$)
and cafés ($) on plaza level
🚇 42nd Street

MUSEUM OF ARTS AND DESIGN

Formerly the American Craft Museum, this collection features pottery, textiles, furnishings and sculpture. Compiled from loaned pieces and selections from the permanent holdings, exhibitions usually last several months. Due to relocate to 2 Columbus Circle.

www.americancraftmuseum.org

✚ 119 C5 ✉ 40 W 53rd Street ☎ 212/956 3535 ⏱ Daily 10–6, Thu until 8
✋ Inexpensive ⬤ Fifth Avenue

MUSEUM OF MODERN ART

See pages 36–37.

MUSEUM OF TELEVISION AND RADIO

The museum is actually an archive of U.S. television and radio, made available from a computerized cataloguing system. Selections from the 75,000 programs and commercials can be watched or listened to in private consoles, but most visitors will be content with the varied televisual selections screened each day.

➕ 119 C5 ✉ 25 W 52nd Street ☎ 212/621 6800 ◑ Tue–Sun noon–6 (Thu also 6–8) ✋ Moderate 🍴 Café ($$) Ⓜ Rockefeller Center

NEW YORK PUBLIC LIBRARY

The city's pre-eminent reference library and an architectural masterpiece, New York Public Library is guarded by a celebrated pair of stone lions, named Fortitude and Patience by Mayor Fiorello La Guardia in the 1930s. Inside, the splendors of the beaux arts design—such as the DeWitt Wallace Periodical Room and the wonderful mural lining the McGraw Rotunda on the third floor—are best discovered with the free guided tours. Various changing exhibitions in the side rooms, usually on themes of art and history, provide a further excuse to wander the magnificent corridors.

www.nypl.org
➕ 119 E5
✉ Fifth Avenue at 42nd Street
☎ 212/930 0830
◑ Tue and Wed 11–7.30, Thu–Sat 10–6
✋ Free
Ⓜ 42nd Street
❓ Free guided tours Tue–Sat at 11 and 2

ROCKEFELLER CENTER

Rockefeller Center arose through the 1930s to become a widely admired complex of streamlined limestone and aluminium buildings that form an aesthetically satisfying whole, despite being designed by different architects.

Intended to provide a welcoming environment where people could work, shop, eat and be entertained, structures such as Radio City Music Hall and the RCA Building (now the GE Building) became noted city landmarks. The labyrinthine walkways are filled with eye-catching art deco decoration while the Plaza provides a setting for outdoor dining during the summer and becomes a much-loved skating rink during the winter. Top of the Rock is an observation deck on the 70th floor, open (for a fee) 8.30am–midnight all year.

www.rockerfellercenter com

➕ 119 D5 ✉ Bordered by Fifth and Seventh avenues, 47th and 52nd streets ☎ Tours 212/664 7171
🕓 Always open 💲 Free 🍴 Various restaurants and cafés ($–$$$)
🚇 Rockefeller Center ❓ Tours (moderate/expensive)

ROOSEVELT ISLAND

Roosevelt Island is a long, thin strip of land between Manhattan and Queens and a curious piece of New York that few visitors ever become aware of. Take the short cable-car ride, the Roosevelt Island Tramway. The island once held hospitals providing for the terminally sick and mentally ill.

The ruins of the old hospitals (enhanced by avant-garde sculpture) stand on the island's southern end, while much of the rest has been developed since the 1970s as a car-free housing development by architects Philip Johnson and John Burgee. The 147-acre (60ha) island has five parks and interesting views of Manhattan and makes for an intriguing detour, if only to see Manhattan from a different angle.

🚻 119 A8 ✉ East River, between Manhattan and Queens
🚇 Roosevelt Island; also cable car from terminal 60th Street and Second Avenue

ST. PATRICK'S CATHEDRAL

Nowhere else in Midtown Manhattan is there a sense of peace and tranquility matching that found inside St. Patrick's Cathedral, at its best when its interior is illuminated by candlelight. In a loosely interpreted French Gothic style, the cathedral was completed in 1878 by celebrated architect James Renwick; the twin towers that rise to 330ft (100m) were unveiled 10 years later. Despite being enclosed by modern high rises, the Roman Catholic cathedral, the largest in the U.S., retains its sense of majesty.

www.ny-archdiocese.org

✚ 119 D5 ✉ Fifth and Seventh avenues, 50th and 51st streets
🕐 8am–8.45pm 👆 Free 🚇 Fifth Avenue–53rd Street

SEAGRAM BUILDING

Ground-breaking architecture is prevalent in Manhattan, but no single building is perhaps more influential than Mies Van Der Rohe's Seagram Building, completed in 1958 and widely regarded as the perfect expression of the International Style. Rising 38 stories in glass and bronze, the Seagram Building also gave New York its first plaza, a feature that subsequently became common with high-rise development, sometimes being enclosed to form atriums. Walk into the lobby to peek into the Philip Johnson-designed Four Seasons restaurant.

☩ 119 C6 ✉ 375 Park Avenue 🕐 Lobby always open 🎟 Free 🍴 Four Seasons restaurant ($$$) 🚇 51st Street–Lexington Avenue ❓ Tours Tue at 3 (☎ 212/572 7000)

TIMES SQUARE
See pages 40–41.

TRUMP TOWER
The New York of the 1980s was the domain of the yuppie, and perhaps no greater role model existed for the rapid creation of wealth than high-profile property developer Donald Trump. A heady mix of vulgarity, ingenuity, and flamboyance, Trump Tower is a symbol both of the man and the decade's economic boom. The upper levels hold luxury apartments while the lower floors include the famous pink stone atrium and a gathering of luxury retail outlets and restaurants. The interior atrium includes a seven-story waterfall.

✚ 119 C5 ✉ 725 Fifth Avenue
🕐 Mon–Sat 10–6, Sun 12–5
✋ Free 🍴 Numerous restaurants and cafés ($–$$$)
🚇 Fifth Avenue–53rd Street

UNITED NATIONS HEADQUARTERS

The United Nations has been based in New York since 1947, much of its administrative activity being carried out in the unmistakable Le Corbusier-designed Secretariat Building rising above the East River. Public admission is by guided tour, which provides an informative hour-long sweep through the U.N.'s interior, including the General Assembly building and the Security Council Chambers. Outside, the 18-acre (7ha) grounds hold parks, gardens, and abundant monuments.

www.un.org/tours

✚ 119 D7 ✉ First Avenue at 46th Street ☎ 212/963 8687 ◷ Guided tours daily. Closed Sat and Sun Jan and Feb ✋ Moderate 🍽 Restaurant ($$$), café ($) 🚇 42nd Street–Grand Central

Uptown and Central Park

During the 19th century many of New York's wealthy moved north and settled either side of the newly created Central Park, in what became the Upper East Side and the Upper West Side.

The Upper East Side became fashionable in the 1890s when the top families in New York sociey began erecting mock-European mansions along Fifth Avenue, facing Central Park. Comfortable brownstone townhouses sprouted on adjoining streets, now also dotted with smart apartment blocks.

The main shopping street of the Upper East Side is Madison Avenue, which provides locals with antique shops, art galleries, boutiques, restaurants and dog-grooming specialists.

The Dakota Building (➤ 64) set the tone for the Upper West Side and many more luxury apartment blocks through the late 1800s as residential development quickly filled the area between Central Park and the Hudson River. After years of decline in the mid-20th century, writers and professors and professionals with young families discovered the spacious "pre-war" apartments with views of the Hudson River, and the neighborhood became a liberal enclave to the East Side's blue-blooded conservatism. Away from the quiet side streets, the commercial arteries hold a mix of furniture retailers, gourmet delis and fashionable ethnic eateries. Zabar's gourmet food store on Broadway is at the heart of the West Side's shopping area.

AMERICAN MUSEUM OF NATURAL HISTORY

The American Museum of Natural History was founded in 1861 and, with roughly 36 million exhibits drawn from every corner of the globe, is now the world's largest museum.

The fossil and dinosaur halls are places to admire five-story-high dinosaur skeletons and to experience state-of-the-art exhibits exploring the origins of life on earth from the Jurassic period onwards. A 94ft (28m) model blue whale, the world's largest mammal, hangs above the other exhibits in the Hall of Ocean Life. A butterfly conservatory is open October to June. Dioramas trace humankind and displays on humankind include halls devoted to Native Americans and the peoples of Africa, Asia, and South and Central America.

Alongside the museum, a steel and glass cube provides a striking transparent exterior for the Rose Center for Earth and Space. Inside is the Hayden Planetarium, where the show The Search For Life: Are We Alone, is narrated by actor Harrison Ford. A series of walkways and galleries hold displays on astronomical subjects iand an IMAX theater shows films on natural topics.

www.amnh.org

✚ 116 F3 ✉ Central Park West and 79th Street
☎ 212/769 5100 🕐 Daily 10–5.45 ♿ Moderate
🍴 Cafeteria ($) and cafés ($$) Ⓜ 81st Street

ASIA SOCIETY

Founded by John D. Rockefeller III in 1956, the Asia Society holds an impressive collection of Asian art, including wonderful Edo-period Japanese prints, pre-Angkor Cambodian sculpture and 11th-century Chinese ceramics.

The broader purpose of the society, which has centers around the U.S. and the Pacific rim, is to promote greater understanding between Asia and the U.S. To this end, it hosts an on-going series of movies, concerts, lectures and workshops on Asian themes.
www.asiasociety.org

➕ 119 A6 ✉ 725 Park Avenue ☎ 212/517 ASIA ⊗ Tue–Sun 11–6, Fri until 9 ✋ Moderate 🍴 Café ($$) Ⓜ 68th Street–Hunter College

CATHEDRAL CHURCH OF ST. JOHN THE DIVINE

The seat of the Episcopal Diocese of New York, the largest Gothic-style cathedral in the world (it covers 11 acres/4.5ha), is still unfinished. The cornerstone was laid in 1892 but wars, the death of the architect, changes in design and shortages of finance have resulted in sporadic building work. The cathedral is now two-thirds complete, and no new construction is planned for the immediate future. Exhibitions fill the various nooks and crannies.

www.stjohndivine.org

✚ 116 B3 ✉ 1047 Amsterdam Avenue ☎ 212/316 7540 ⏰ Mon–Sat 7–6, Sun 7–7 💰 Inexpensive 🚇 Cathedral Parkway ❓ Tours Tue–Sat 11, Sun 1

CENTRAL PARK

See pages 22–23.

THE CLOISTERS

Medieval European monastic buildings might be the last thing anyone would expect to find in Manhattan, but the Cloisters are exactly that. Assembled on a site overlooking the Hudson River, these bits and pieces of five French monasteries collected in the early 1900s now showcase the Metropolitan Museum of Art's medieval holdings. The contents are a feast of 12th- to 15th-century creativity, but the show-stealer is the setting, with its splendid views.

www.metmuseum.org

✚ 116 A2 (off map) ✉ Fort Tryon Park, Washington Heights ☎ 212/923 3700 ⏰ Nov–Feb Tue–Sun 9.30–4.45; Mar–Oct Tue–Sun 9.30–5.15 💰 Moderate 🍴 Café ($) 🚇 190th Street

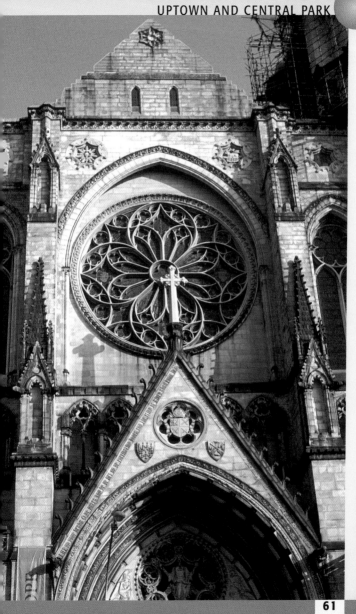

COOPER-HEWITT NATIONAL DESIGN MUSEUM

Part of the Smithsonian Institution, the museum, housed in the former mansion of steel mogul Andrew Carnegie, explores design and decorative arts from wall coverings and textiles to graphic arts and product design. The collection began with the oddments the three Hewitt sisters picked up on a visit to London in 1897. The fenced garden offers a tranquil oasis along Fifth Avenue.

www.si.edu/ndm

✚ 117 D5 ✉ 2 E 91st Street ☎ 212/849 8400 🕐 Tue 10–5, Wed–Fri 10–9, Sat 10–6, Sun noon–6 ✋ Moderate 🍴 Café ($) Ⓜ 86th Street

COLUMBIA UNIVERSITY

Founded by royal charter of British king George II in 1754, King's College, Columbia is the oldest institution of higher learning in the U.S. It has steadily moved northwards up Manhattan, arriving at its present site in 1897. The predominantly red-brick campus buildings, reflecting turn-of-the-20th-century American collegiate architecture, are grouped around

compact plazas on 32 acres (13ha). Inside the Low Library (based on Rome's Pantheon), at the heart of the complex, are displays tracing the history of the university.
www.columbia.edu

✚ 116 A2 ✉ 116th and Broadway ☎ 212/854 4900 🕐 Visit during daylight hours ✋ Free 🚇 116th Street ❓ Tours 11 and 2 weekdays
ℹ️ Visitor Center at 213 Low Memorial Library

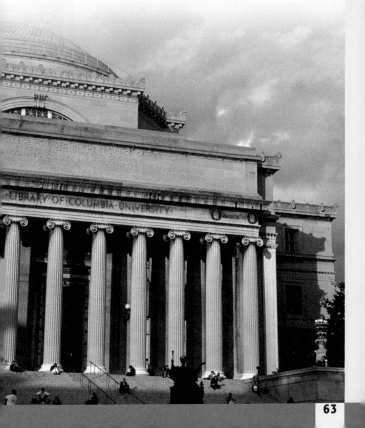

DAKOTA BUILDING

Destined to be remembered by the world as the place where ex-Beatle John Lennon was fatally shot in 1980, the Dakota Building had already earned a place in the annals of New York history by being one of the city's first purpose-built luxury apartment blocks. Raised in the 1880s, the Dakota steadily attracted the rich and famous to reside within its German Gothic/French Renaissance façade, and remains a prestigious address.

⊞ 118 A3 ⊠ 72nd Street and Central Park West ⓒ Private residence; view from street only ⓡ 72nd Street

EAST HARLEM

Once known as "Italian Harlem," East Harlem has been the main base of the New York's Puerto Rican population, known locally as "El Barrio," since the 1930s and 1940s. Although predominantly Puerto Rican, Mexicans and other Latin Americans also figure among the Spanish-speaking population, and the area is growing more diverse as real estates prices on the Upper East Side continue to rise. The center of activity is 115th Street and Park Avenue, where some 30 stalls of La Marqueta (the Market) proffer sugar cane, yams, and papaya, and other culinary delights of the island, while sounds of salsa reverberate in the air.

✠ 117 B6 ✉ First Avenue to Fifth Avenue, E 96th Street to E 125th Street 🚇 110th Street or 116th Street

EL MUSEO DEL BARRIO

With strong links to the local East Harlem community, El Museo del Barrio grew from a local school classroom into a museum devoted to the cultures of Latin America, particularly Puerto Rico. There is a small permanent collection of pre-Columbian objects, but greater prominence is accorded to many temporary exhibitions documenting facets of Latin American history and culture.

www.elmuseo.org

✠ 117 B5 ✉ 1230 Fifth Avenue ☎ 212/831 7272 🕐 Wed–Sun 11–5 (Thu until 8) ♿ Inexpensive 🚇 103rd Street

FRICK COLLECTION

Henry Clay Frick made his money in the late 19th century, and filled his mansion on Fifth Avenue with an outstanding art collection. The relative intimacy of the setting is as enjoyable as the

paintings, sculptures and decorative items. El Greco, Titian, Rembrandt and Turner are just a few of the painters represented by exceptional canvases, while two rococo delights—Fragonard's *Progress of Love* series and Boucher's *Arts and Science* series— each occupy a room of their own. Other highlights include Gainsborough's *The Mall in St James's Park* and Rembrandt's 1658 *Self-Portrait*.

www.frick.org

✚ 119 A5 ✉ 1 E 70th Street ☎ 212/288 0700 🕐 Tue–Sat 10–6 (Fri until 9), Sun 11–5 ✋ Moderate 🚇 68th Street–Hunter College

GRANT'S TOMB

Rising from obscurity to mastermind the battlefield strategies that helped the Union side triumph in the Civil War, General Ulysses S. Grant became one of the best-known Americans of his time and was president from 1869 to 1877. A million people lined the route of the parade and dedication ceremony in 1897 of what's the largest mausoleum in North America, and a resting place commensurate with his status. In addition to the 9-ton granite sarcophagi of Grant and his wife, exhibits depict Grant's life and accomplishments.

www.nps.gov/gear

✚ 116 A2 (off map) ✉ Riverside Drive at 122nd Street ☎ 212/666 1640 🕐 Daily 9–5 ✋ Free 🚇 125th Street

GRACIE MANSION

Standing deep in today's modern metropolis, it is difficult to imagine that, on its completion in 1799, Gracie Mansion served its owner, Scottish merchant Archibald Gracie, as a country retreat and that the 16-room house became familiar to many of the city's influential figures. But the War of 1812 decimated Gracie's trade and the house was sold in 1823. The Museum of the City of New York was among the subsequent occupants until 1942, when the house became the official residence of New York's mayor. It now houses a huge collection of American-made furniture and fixtures.

www.nyc.gov

➕ 117 E8 (off map) ✉ East End Avenue at 88th Street ☎ 212/570 4751
🕐 Guided tours only Wed 10–3 (pre-booked) ✋ Moderate 🚇 86th Street

GUGGENHEIM MUSEUM

See pages 32–33.

HARLEM

Many of the tens of thousands of African–Americans who arrived in New York in early 1900s settled in brownstone townhouses in what had been a German–Jewish neighborhood. By the 1920s the neighborhood had become the U.S.'s most culturally vibrant black urban area.

Partly dilapidated, partly gentrified, Harlem holds landmarks such as the Apollo Theater (253 125th Street) and Abyssinian Baptist Church (132 Odell Clark Place), one of hundreds of churches where gospel singing draws tourists along with neighborhood faithful.

🚩 116 A4 (off map) 🖂 North of Cathedral Parkway; west of Fifth Avenue 🚇 125th Street

JEWISH MUSEUM

An imitation French Gothic château erected in 1909 for banker Felix M. Warburg provides an impressive home for the largest collection of Jewish ceremonial art and historical objects in the U.S. Among the enormous collection are household objects, coins and religious pieces dating back to the Roman era that help create a picture of Jewish life from early times to the modern day. Special exhibits focus on Jewish history and art.

www.jewishmuseum.org

🚩 117 D5 🖂 1109 Fifth Avenue ☎ 212/423 3200 🕒 Sun–Wed 11–5.45, Thu 11–8, Fri 11–3. Closed public and Jewish holidays 🖐 Moderate 🍴 Kosher café ($) 🚇 92nd Street

LINCOLN CENTER FOR THE PERFORMING ARTS

Part of what was once known as Hell's Kitchen and the setting for the musical *West Side Story* is now the multi-building complex of Lincoln Center for the Performing Arts. Since its 1960s completion, the center has provided homes for a dozen resident cultural organizations, including the New York Philharmonic, the Metropolitan Opera, the New York State Theater, and the Juilliard School for the Performing Arts, all grouped on or close to a central plaza.

www.lincolncenter.org

✚ 118 B3 ✉ Broadway at 64th Street ☎ 212/875 5350 ⓘ Free to visit; charges for performances
🍴 Various restaurants and cafés ($–$$$)
Ⓜ 66th Street–Lincoln Center ❓ Daily tours; outdoor concerts in summer

METROPOLITAN MUSEUM OF ART

See pages 34–35.

MUSEUM OF THE CITY OF NEW YORK

This museum tells of the city's evolution from Colonial settlement to international metropolis. with photographs, costumes, maps and other objects from its collection. Among the permanent exhibits are a history of theater in New York and a collection of toys used by generations of New York children.

www.mcny.org

⊞ 117 C5 ✉ 1220 Fifth Avenue ☎ 212/534 1672 🕓 Tue–Sun 10–5
♿ Inexpensive 🚇 103rd Street

NEW-YORK HISTORICAL SOCIETY

The hyphen in its name dates from the society's founding in 1804, a time when the city was spelled that way and when no other museum existed to receive the many bequests of wealthy New Yorkers. Consequently the society acquired a tremendous batch of art, from amateurish though historically important portraits of rich city dwellers to seminal works by the Hudson River School painters and fine furniture from the Federal period. Highlights here include a substantial collection of Tiffany glasswork and the watercolors of John James Audubon's *Birds of America* series.

www.nyhistory.org

🕂 116 F3 ✉ 2 W 77th Street ☎ 212/873 3400 🕓 Tue–Sun 10–6
✋ Inexpensive 🚇 81st Street

RIVERSIDE CHURCH

Largely financed by John D. Rockefeller Jr., the French Gothic Riverside Church has loomed high alongside the Hudson River since 1930. Intended to serve its membership's recreational as well as religious needs, the church has at times held schoolrooms, a gym, a theater and even a bowling alley. Originally Baptist but now interdenominational, the church's tower, 392ft (120m) high, houses the world's largest carillon.

www.theriversidechurch.org

✚ 116 A2 (off map) ✉ 490 Riverside Drive ☎ 212/870 6700 🕐 Tue–Sun 9–5 ✋ Free 🚇 116th Street ❓ Sun carillon concerts; guided tours after Sun service

WHITNEY MUSEUM OF AMERICAN ART

When the Metropolitan Museum of Art rejected her collection of American painting and sculpture, Gertrude Vanderbilt Whitney responded by creating her own museum in 1931, and with it continued her long devotion to supporting new American art. The collection is now housed in marcel Breurer's "brutalist" inverted ziggurat of concrete and granite.

Often controversial and devoting much of its space to relatively unknown work, the Whitney has an incredible collection of works by major U.S. names such as Rothko, Johns and Warhol who are represented in the permanent collection. Three galleries are devoted to Calder, O'Keeffe and Hopper.

www.whitney.org

✚ 117 F5 ✉ 945 Madison Avenue ☎ 800/WHITNEY 🕐 Wed–Thu and Sat–Sun 11–6, Fri 1–9 ✋ Moderate 🍴 Café ($) 🚇 77th Street ❓ Lectures, films

Empire State Building to Greenwich Village

The Empire State Building and Greenwich Village epitomize the diverse attitudes of Manhattanites.

The Empire State Building stands between the Garment District and the Murray Hill neighborhood, once home to New York's best families. To the south are the Flatiron District, around the landmark building of that name (➤ 76) and New York's "Silicon Alley," Gramercy Park, a fashionable residential neighborhood on the east; and Chelsea, a village of tree-lined streets and art galleries on the west.

Originally "Greenwich Village" referred to the area bounded by the Hudson River and Fifth Avenue, 14th and Houston Streets. Today, "The Village" is generaly understood to extend from the Hudson all the way to the East River. The East Village, still gritty compared with the West Village, centers on Tompkins Square Park

in "Alphabet City"—Avenues A, B, C and D. New York University is headquartered in buildings around Washington Square Park, but the institution has spread into the East Village and north to Union Square.

CHELSEA

The heart of Chelsea is around the junction of 23rd Street and Eighth Avenue, busy with stores, restaurants, and art galleries since a 1990s regeneration made it one of Manhattan's most energetic neighborhoods. On Chelsea's western edge, in the former meat-packing district, many erstwhile warehouses were converted into galleries for the work of new artists, making the area a major showplace for emerging art. By the river, four early-1900s cruise-ship docks have been redeveloped as Chelsea Piers, offering sports activities, dining and shopping, beside the Hudson River.

✚ 120 C3 ✉ Sixth Avenue to the Hudson River, 14th Street to the upper 20s 🚇 Canal Street

CHELSEA HOTEL

The Chelsea Hotel has played a major role in New York cultural life, providing accommodations for artistic and literary notables from Mark Twain to William Burroughs since opening in 1905. Featured in Andy Warhol's movie *Chelsea Girls* in the 1960s, the hotel also earned a place in punk rock history as the place where Sid Vicious murdered his girlfriend. The lobby has artworks from former guests.

www.chelseahotel.com

✚ 120 B3 ✉ 222 W 23rd Street ☎ 212/243 3700 🕐 Lobby always open ✋ Free
🚇 23rd Street

EAST VILLAGE

After wealthy families like the Astors and the Vanderbilts moved north, immigrants from eastern Europe flooded into the East Village and the Lower East Side. Anarchist Emma Goldman published *Mother Earth* magazine on East 13th Street. Leon Trotsky ran a basement printing press on St. Mark's Place. The East Village was home to the beats in the 50s, hippies in the 60s, artists and and punk rockers in the 1970s. Gentrification arrived in the 1990s, though black leather, nose rings and tattoos are still far from unusual street attire.

Within the East Village are a host of ethnicities. One is the long-established ethnic pocket of Little Ukraine, and the section along East Sixth Street is called Little Bombay for its plethora of inexpensive Indian restaurants.

✚ 121 D5 ✉ Fifth Avenue to the East River, 14th and Houston streets 🚇 Astor Place

EMPIRE STATE BUILDING

See pages 26–27.

FLATIRON BUILDING

The obvious way to maximize the potential of a triangular plot of land at Broadway and Fifth Avenue was to raise a triangular building on it, and with the Flatiron Building architect Daniel Burnham did exactly that. Completed in 1902, the structure, 286ft (87m) high, became the world's tallest building and was among the first in New York to use a steel-frame construction. This was a crucial element in the evolution of the skyscraper pioneered by Burnham 20 years earlier in Chicago. *Beaux-arts* decoration on its limestone facade aids the building's lasting popularity.
➕ 120 B4 ✉ 175 Fifth Avenue 🌐 View from outside only 🚇 23rd Street

FORBES GALLERIES

Larger-than-life publisher Malcolm Forbes—his adventures included ballooning across the U.S. and riding his powerful motorcycle at full speed along Fifth Avenue—invested some of a fortune estimated to be worth $700 million on the eclectic collection of priceless objects and worthless curios that fill these galleries, within the building that houses *Forbes* magazine.

Forbes died in 1990 and the fabulous gem-encrusted Fabergé

eggs that once formed the centerpiece of the collection, have been sold. Still on show, however, are more than 10,000 model soldiers in battle-ready poses, and more than 500 model boats and submarines and other objects.

www.forbesgalleries.com

✚ 120 C4 ✉ 62 Fifth Avenue ☎ 212/206 5548 🕐 Tue, Wed, Fri, Sat 10–4
🖐 Free 🚇 14th Street–Union Square

GRACE CHURCH

The grey-stone suggests the European Middle Ages. Completed in 1846, the Episcopal church was designed by James Renwick, Jr. with a restrained Gothic Revival look, the earliest example of the style in New York. The success of Grace Church helped Renwick win the job of designing the more prestigious St. Patrick's Cathedral (➤ 53) and the first of the Smithsonian Institution buildings in Washington D.C. Peek inside to see the plaque installed in memory of the *Titanic* victims and restored stained-glass windows.

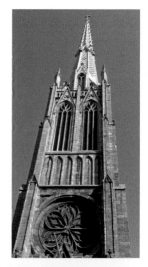

www.gracechurchnyc.org

✚ 121 D5 ✉ 802 Broadway
☎ 212/254 2000 🕐 Call for hours
🖐 Free 🚇 14th Street–NYU

GRAMERCY PARK

Enclosed by 19th-century brownstone townhouses intended to replicate some of the elegant squares of London, Gramercy Park is New York's only private park and entry is restricted to residents and guests of the Gramercy Park Hotel (52 Gramercy Park North).

A stroll of the park's perimeter passes several notable buildings: The National Arts Club (15 Gramercy Park South) was the home of state governor Samuel Tilden during his campaign against the notoriously corrupt Tweed ring in the 1870s before it became a club founded to support American artists. The Players Club (16 Gramercy Park South), marked by two ornamental theatrical masks designed by architect Stanford White, was a private club founded by actor Edwin Booth in what was his home. He is remembered by a statue in the park that depicts him immersed in the role of Shakespeare's *Hamlet*.

➕ 121 B5 ✉ Between Irving Place and Lexington Avenue, bordered by E 21st and 22nd streets ⏰ Only open to local residents and guests of Gramercy Park Hotel ✋ Free 🚇 23rd Street

GREENWICH VILLAGE

See pages 30–31.

LITTLE CHURCH AROUND THE CORNER

Formally known as the Church of the Transfiguration, this Episcopalian place of worship acquired its widely used epithet in 1870, when the pastor at a grander nearby church declined to conduct the funeral service of an actor and suggested that it be held instead at the "little church around the corner." New York thespians have looked kindly upon the daintily proportioned church ever since and several are remembered with their likeness in the stained-glass windows. The church sits behind a pretty and tranquil garden.

➕ 120 A4 ✉ 1 E 29th Street ☎ 212/684 6770 ⏰ Call for times ✋ Free 🚇 28th Street

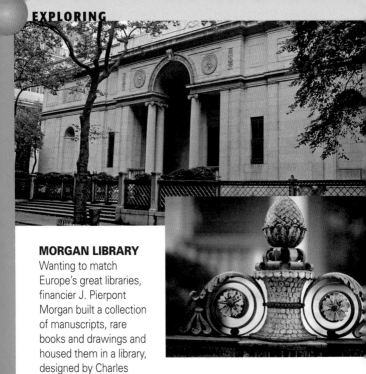

MORGAN LIBRARY

Wanting to match Europe's great libraries, financier J. Pierpont Morgan built a collection of manuscripts, rare books and drawings and housed them in a library, designed by Charles McKim, erected next to his residence between 1902 and 1906. Among the many treasures gathered here are Gutenburg Bibles, a Shakespeare first folio, the sole signed manuscript of Milton's *Paradise Lost*, and handwritten works by Brahms and Mozart.

No less imposing, however, is the setting. Morgan's study was once described as the "most beautiful room in America," but pales in comparison with the East Room, decorated by a mural-lined ceiling and a 16th-century Flemish tapestry above the fireplace.

www.morganlibrary.org

✚ 119 E5 ✉ 29 E 36th Street ☎ 212/685 0610 🖐 Moderate 🚇 33rd Street

ST. MARK'S-IN-THE-BOWERY

The Bowery was 17th-century Dutch governor Peter Atuyvesant's farm, and the Episcopalian Church of St. Mark's-in-the-Bowery was completed in 1799 on the site of what was probably Stuyvesant's chapel. Poets from Carl Sundburg to Allen Ginsberg have read here. It provides a useful local rendezvous for music and arts performances, as well as continuing its religious function. The now cobbled-over graveyard holds the bones of members of several generations of the Stuyvesant family.

➕ 121 D5 ✉ Second Avenue at E 10th Street ☎ 212/674 6377 ⏲ Call for times 👋 Free Ⓢ Astor Place ❓ Poetry, dance and alternative arts events

THEODORE ROOSEVELT BIRTHPLACE

Theodore Roosevelt, the only U.S. president to have been a native of New York City, was born to a prominent family at this address in 1858, now a national historic site. Although the building of that time was demolished, what stands now is a detailed reconstruction of the childhood home of the nation's 26th president and contains many of the family's furnishings. A detailed chronology of Roosevelt's life outlines his numerous achievements, not least of which his rise to popularity after leading the so-called Rough Riders during the 1898 Spanish-American War.

www.nps.gov/thrb

➕ 120 C4 ✉ 28 E 20th Street ☎ 212/260 1616 ⏲ Tue–Sat 9–5 👋 Inexpensive Ⓢ 23rd Street

UKRAINIAN MUSEUM

Though small, the museum in the area of East Village known as Little Ukraine stores several thousand items of Ukrainian art, craft and culture. Traditional regional dress, folk art such as the hand-painted eggs known as *pysansky* and contemporary painting and sculpture, along with changing exhibits, highlight various aspects of Ukrainian life past and present.

www.ukrainianmuseum.org

➕ 121 D5 ✉ 222 East Sixth Street ☎ 212/228 0110 ⏲ Wed–Sun 1–5 👋 Inexpensive Ⓢ Third Avenue

UNION SQUARE PARK

Renovated in the 1980s, Union Square Park holds a popular farmers' market four times a week where fruit, vegetables, cheese and bread are sold from stalls.

Created in the early 1800s, Union Square was originally at the heart of fashionable New York life but, as high society moved northwards, it became a focal point for political protest. By 1927, police had taken to mounting machine-gun posts on surrounding rooftops and, in 1930, no less than around 35,000 people protested here against unemployment. After the terrorist attack of September 11, 2001, it became a gathering place for memorial services.

Ringing the park are fashionable eateries and food markets, New York University dormitories and the final home of Tammany Hall (100–102 East 17th Street).

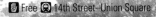 121 C5 ✉ Park Avenue and Broadway, 14th Street and 17th streets
Free 🚇 14th Street–Union Square

Lower Manhattan

Lower Manhattan is the oldest part of New York, with Dutch settlers arriving in the early 1600s. From the 1890s to the 1920s milllions of new immigrants were processed through Ellis Island and started their new lives in America.

There are many things to see and do in this area but an absolute must is to take a ferry ride out to the Statue of Liberty and Ellis Island. Wall Street, home of the New York Stock Exchange, is at the tip and nearby are the Civic Center and South Street Seaport Historic District, home to historic ships. The iconic Brooklyn Bridge was an example of pioneer engineering when it was built. Chinatown and SoHo lie north of the bridge and farther up is Lower East Side.

No part of Manhattan resonates with the immigrant experience more than that neighborhood. From the mid-19th century through the peak years of immigration into the U.S., its high-rise tenements became crowded with successive waves of arrivals: Irish, Germans, East Europeans, and Jewish settlers who made the Lower East Side the largest Jewish settlement in the world by the 1920s. Today, Orchard Street is noted for its discount clothing outlets and nearby Essex Street for its fruit and vegetable market.

The World Trade Center site remains unbuilt on, a huge hole in this part of the island. After the buildings were levelled in 2001, tightened security made touring in this part of Manhattan more difficult, and landmark sights and buildings such as the New York Stock Exchange and the Woolworth Building are no longer accessible to the public.

AMERICAN NUMISMATIC SOCIETY

Money through the ages and throughout the world is the main
subject of the exhibitions of the American Numismatic Society.
Displays include an assortment of maps, coins and paper currency
spanning 3,000 years from ancient Greece to the modern U.S.
Adjoining galleries showcase substantial numbers of medals and
other decorations.

➕ 122 D4 ✉ 96 Fulton Street ☎ 212/234 3130 🕐 Closed until 2008
🚇 Fulton Street

BATTERY PARK

Providing 22 acres (9ha) of welcome
greenery on the edge of the Financial
District, Battery Park also holds more
than its fair share of New York history,
some of the details of which are
supplied by the texts affixed to its
lampposts. Created in the 18th century,
the park's name stems from the
cannons that once lined State Street,
now framing the park but previously
marking the Manhattan shoreline.
The park's Castle Clinton National
Monument, site of the ticket booth
for Statue of Liberty ferries, was
completed in 1811. The Sphere, a sculpture damaged in the attack
on the World Trade Center, is on display at the east side of the park.

➕ 122 D4 ✉ Battery Place and State Street to New York Harbor 🕐 Always
open; visit during daylight 🎫 Free 🍴 Snack stands ($) 🚇 Bowling Green

BROOKLYN BRIDGE

Completed in May 1883, the Brooklyn Bridge provided the first
fixed link between Brooklyn and Manhattan and, with a total
length of 6,016ft (1,834m), it became the world's longest

suspension bridge. The twin Gothic stone arches that rise 272ft
(83m) give the bridge great aesthetic appeal, though the most
memorable aspect is the view of the Manhattan skyline as you
cross from the Brooklyn side. Walkers, roller-bladers, and joggers
regularly cross the bridge; in 1884 21 elephants did the crossing
in a stunt led by circus owner P. T. Barnum.

✚ 123 C6 ✉ Between Manhattan and Brooklyn ⏰ Always open ✋ Free
Ⓜ Brooklyn Bridge–City Hall

CHINATOWN

Around 150,000 people, mostly Chinese but also Vietnamese,
Cambodians and Laotians, live in Chinatown's tight-knit streets,
lined by restaurants, herbalists stores and stalls laden with exotic
foodstuffs. Chinatown became established during the 1890s but
began expanding beyond its traditional boundaries when the
easing of immigration restrictions in the 1960s brought a major
influx of settlers from Hong Kong and Taiwan. It's now the largest
Chinatown in the U.S., with Canal its main street.

✚ 123 B5 ✉ Broadway to Allen, Delaney to Worth Ⓜ Canal Street

CITY HALL

When designed in 1803, City Hall was intended to mark the northern edge of Manhattan, but nine years later at the time of its completion, it was already engulfed by fast-expanding New York. Raised in a mixture of Federal and French Renaissance styles, the dainty building retains its civic role, the oldest building in the nation that still functions as a city hall. Inside, the mayor and council members go about their business and temporary exhibitions document various aspects of city history.

🕂 122 C4 ✉ Broadway at Murray Street ☎ 212/NEW YORK ⏲ Tours by advance reservation ♿ Free 🚇 Brooklyn Bridge–City Hall

ELLIS ISLAND IMMIGRATION MUSEUM

Twelve million people from 120 ethnic groups became U.S. citizens after passing through Ellis Island, the country's major point of entry during the peak period of immigration from Europe that lasted from the 1890s to the 1920s. Examined for contagious diseases, signs of madness, and quizzed on their work skills, most arrivals found Ellis Island a bewildering and frightening experience, particularly after a long and uncomfortable sea voyage, and some were forced to spend time living in the cramped dormitories before being admitted to the U.S. (approximately 2 percent were denied entry altogether).

An excellent gathering of exhibits
and oral histories documents the
emotions of the immigrants and
goes some way to suggesting the
chaos that prevailed in the arrivals
hall, where 5,000 people a day once
entered carrying their possessions
and speaking little English but
looking forward to a new life.

🚻 122 F3 (off map) ✉ Ellis Island
☎ 212/269 5755 (ferry and ticket
information); 212/363 3200 (general
information) 🕐 Daily 8.30–5.15, longer in
summer ♿ Moderate 🍴 Café ($) 🚢 Ferry
from Battery Park, via Liberty Island

FEDERAL HALL NATIONAL MONUMENT

Federal Hall, in the heart of the
Financial District, was completed
in 1842 and is an accomplished
example of Greek Revival
architecture. Beneath an impressive
rotunda, the airy interior holds
assorted historical displays. One
exhibit remembers the inauguration
of George Washington as the
nation's first president in 1789, an
event which took place in the
previous Federal Hall which stood
on this site.

🚻 122 D4 ✉ 26 Wall Street ☎ 212/825
6888 🕐 Closed until 2008 ♿ Free
🚇 Wall Street

FINANCIAL DISTRICT

Wall Street is at the heart of New York's Financial District. Many of the high-rise towers of commerce that dot the neighborhood sit side-by-side with markers to a time when populated New York barely reached beyond today's Greenwich Village. Peek inside the 18th-century St. Paul's Chapel (on Broadway facing Fulton Street) to see George Washington's pew, and pay respects to Alexander Hamilton, the U.S.'s first treasurer, buried in the graveyard of Trinity Church (on Trinity Place, facing Wall Street).

Within the neoclassical facade that overpowers Broad Street is the high-tech money market of the New York Stock Exchange, where brokers, reporters and pagers stride purposefully around the 37,000sq ft (3,440sq m) of trading floor. Since September 11, 2001, visitors are no longer allowed inside.

➕ 123 D5 ✉ South of Chambers and Fulton streets 🚇 Bowling Green, Broad Street, Cortland Street, Fulton Street, Nassau Street, Rector Street, South Ferry, Wall Street or Whitehall Street

FRAUNCES TAVERN MUSEUM

A stately house built in 1719 and turned into a tavern in 1762, Fraunces Tavern was a hotbed of revolutionary activity until the Revolutionary War. At the end of the war, George Washington made a famously emotional farewell to his officers in an upstairs room, which is now the historical centerpiece of the present-day restored tavern.

www.fraucestavernmuseum.org

➕ 122 E4 ✉ 54 Pearl Street ☎ 212/425 1778 🕐 Tue–Fri 12–5, Sat 10–5 ✋ Inexpensive 🍴 Restaurant ($$–$$$) 🚇 Bowling Green, South Ferry, Wall Street or Whitehall Street

LITTLE ITALY

Today, only a few thousand Italians remain in Little Italy, an area that between 1890 and 1924 absorbed more than 100,000 immigrants from Sicily and southern Italy. Mulberry Street became awash with Italian restaurants and cafés.

Over subsequent decades, Italians from the area became ingrained in the social fabric of New York life. Italian–American New Yorkers that grew up in Little Italy still regard it as a spiritual home. Now, the neighborhood is being squeezed from two sides—Chinatown expanding from the east and gentrification from the fashionable Nolita (North of Little Italy).

Undoubtedly the best time to visit Little Italy is during the Feast of St. Gennaro in September, when the compact area regains something of its effervescent past.

➕ 123 A5 ✉ Bounded by Canal–Houston streets and Elizabeth–Lafayette streets 🚇 Canal Street

LOWER EAST SIDE TENEMENT MUSEUM

A cramped, rat-infested apartment shared with several other families was what awaited many arrivals to the Lower East Side in the 19th century—and for most it was far better than the conditions they had left behind in a troubled, oppressive Europe.

To get an inkling of early immigrant life in New York, visit this excellent museum which occupies an 1863 tenement building and is furnished to replicate the living conditions of the time. Companion exhibitions reveal diverse facets of local life and document the otherwise seldom acknowledged hardships faced by the Lower East Side's arrivals from Asia and Latin America.

www.tenement.org

➕ 123 A6 ✉ 108 Orchard Street ☎ 212/431 0233 🕐 Guided tours only: Tue–Fri every 40 mins from 1.20–4.45; Sat and Sun every half hour from 11.15–4.45 👆 Inexpensive Ⓜ Delancey Street ❓ Guided walks Apr–Dec Sat and Sun

MUSEUM OF CHINESE IN THE AMERICAS

A small but absorbing documentation of the settlement of Chinese in the U.S. The main exhibits are a mix of family photos, items from Chinese-run businesses, and objects of symbolic significance; temporary exhibitions examine aspects of the Chinese diaspora.

www.moca-nyc.org

➕ 123 B5 ✉ 70 Mulberry Street ☎ 212/619 4785 🕐 Tue–Sun 12–6 (Fri until 7) 👆 Inexpensive Ⓜ Canal Street

MUSEUM OF JEWISH HERITAGE

At the south end of Battery Park, this museum of the Holocaust occupies a granite building topped by a distinctive six-tiered roof. Displays trace Jewish life and history from persecution in Europe to the creation of Israel and the growth of Jewish communities.

➕ 122 E3 ✉ 36 Battery Place ☎ 646/437 4200 🕐 Sun–Tue, Thu 10–5.45, Wed 10–8, Fri 10–5 👆 Moderate Ⓜ Bowling Green ❓ Lectures, films

NATIONAL MUSEUM OF THE AMERICAN INDIAN

This collection of the Smithsonian Institution has largely moved to new quarters in Washingston, D.C., leaving the George Gustav Heye Center to display special exhibits in New York. The museum occupies an elegant 1907 *beaux arts* building designed by Cass Gilbert that formerly served as the U.S. Custom House, worth a visit in its own right. Inside are renowned murals of New York Harbor by Reginald Marsh.

www.nmai.si.edu

✚ 122 E4 ✉ 1 Bowling Green ☎ 212/514 3700 🕐 Mon–Wed, Fri–Sun 10–5, Thu 10–8 ✋ Free Ⓜ Bowling Green

NEW YORK CITY FIRE MUSEUM

Fires were the scourge of early New York and so too, in many cases, were the firefighters. Before the creation of a municipal fire service in 1865, fire crews were privately hired and usually

comprised members of rival gangs whose members fought each other before fighting the fire in anticipation of a reward.

The intriguing story of the city's fires and those who tried to put them out is told here over three floors with an entertaining collection of horse-drawn carriages, hosepipe nozzles, axes, ladders, dramatic photos, and New York's first fire bell.

www.nycfiremuseum.org

✚ 122 A3 ✉ 278 Spring Street ☎ 212/691 1303 🕐 Tue–Sat 10–5, Sun 10–4 ✋ Donation Ⓜ Spring Street

NEW YORK CITY POLICE MUSEUM

The fabled mean streets of New York have produced more than their share of notorious villains, and many of them are recorded here, as are the officers who brought them to justice. Displays include vintage motorcycles, historic badges and documents, and an exhibit chronicling the role of the NYPD on September 11.

www.nycpolicemuseum.org

✚ 123 D5 ✉ 100 Old Slip ☎ 212/480 3100 🕐 Tue–Sat 10–5, Sun 11–5 ✋ Inexpensive 🚇 Whitehall Street

OLD ST. PATRICK'S CATHEDRAL

Old St. Patrick's Cathedral, completed in 1815, served the spiritual needs of the Irish population that inhabited the immediate area before the ethnic turnaround that transformed the neighborhood into Little Italy. The Gothic-style cathedral lost its place as the city's Roman Catholic see with the consecration of its far grander namesake in Midtown Manhattan (➤ 53) in 1879. Though unspectacular, the intimate interior makes for a few welcome minutes of respite from the city frenzy.

www.oldsaintpatricks.com

✚ 121 E5 ✉ 263 Mulberry Street ☎ 212/226 8075 🕐 Call for times ✋ Free 🚇 Prince Street

SHRINE OF ELIZABETH ANN SETON

Elizabeth Ann Seton, who founded the Sisters of Charity, the first order of nuns in the U.S. in 1812, was canonized in 1975 for her philanthropic works, becoming the first American-born Roman Catholic saint. This simple but well-preserved Georgian and Federal-style house was her home from 1801 to 1803, prior to her conversion to Catholicism in 1805. It now serves as a church, where Mass is held daily.

www.setonshrine-ny.org

✚ 122 E4 ✉ 7 State Street ☎ 212/269 6865 🕐 Call for times ✋ Free 🚇 Whitehall Street

SOHO

In one of the transformations that regularly regenerate Manhattan neighborhoods, the previously derelict 19th-century factory buildings of SoHo, with cheap-to-rent loft studios, became the center of a vibrant art community in the 1960s and then of the world art market a few years later. The galleries remain on every street, alongside chic clothing and shoe stores and restaurants, but loft space is too expensive for up-and-coming artists. Most SoHo residents today are lawyers and other professionals.

✚ 122 A4 ✉ South of Houston Street, between Sixth Avenue and Broadway
🚇 Prince Street or Spring Street

SOUTH STREET SEAPORT HISTORIC DISTRICT

Through the 18th and 19th centuries, the center of Manhattan's thriving maritime trade was around the cobblestone area now the South Street Seaport Historic District on the East River. A mixture of mall stores and restaurants sits alongside a gathering of historic ships and nautically themed museums. The area and its numerous old ships—among them the 1911 *Peking*, a four-masted cargo vessel that can be boarded and toured—can enjoyably fill a few hours. The museum traces the history of the port of New York. Events takes place in and around the area during the year.

✚ 123 D5 ✉ Water and South streets; museum at 12 Fulton Street
☎ 212/748 8600 (museum) 🕐 Varies
✋ Varies 🍴 Numerous restaurants and cafés ($–$$) 🚇 Fulton Street or Broadway–Nassau

STATUE OF LIBERTY
See pages 38–39.

TRIBECA
Echoing the gentrification that transformed neighboring SoHo in the 1970s, TriBeCa was, during the early 1980s, steadily colonized by artists who created living and studio space in Federal-style residences and industrial buildings that once housed the city's food wholesalers. Soon, the area boasted a good elementary school and developers created chic loft apartments. TriBeCa's streets acquired fashionable restaurants and expensive boutiques, though it still has a community feel. It's now home to an annual

spring film festival started by Robert De Niro.

➕ 122 B3 ✉ South of Canal Street, between Broadway and the Hudson River 🚇 Chambers Street or Franklin Street

WOOLWORTH BUILDING
The world's tallest building for 16 years, the Woolworth Building—once headquarters of the retail organization—was opened in 1913 by president Woodrow Wilson who flicked a switch and bathed the building in the glow of 80,000 electric bulbs. Leering gargoyles decorate the tower, 792ft (241m) high. The lobby (closed to the public) has an elaborate interior and sculptured caricatures of the building's architect, and its original owner, F.W. Woolworth.

➕ 122 C4 ✉ 233 Broadway 🚇 City Hall or Park Place

WORLD TRADE CENTER SITE

Almost twice the height of the highest buildings around them, the twin towers of the World Trade Center became a symbol of New York and of a U.S.-driven global economy. On September 11, 2001, the destruction of the towers by hijacked passenger planes immediately claimed almost 3,000 lives. Following the attack, the site became a place of pilgrimage and neighboring St. Paul's Chapel was bedecked with handwritten tributes to, and mementos of, the dead. New commercial buildings nearby reflect the Financial District's determination to recover from the tragedy. Plans for redevelopment of the 16-acre (6.5ha) site and a permanent memorial are still in flux.

www.nycvisit.com

✠ 122 C3 ✉ Church, Barclay, Liberty and West streets; viewing area at Liberty Street ☎ 212/484 1222 Ⓜ Cortlandt Street

Excursions

The Bronx   99–100

Brooklyn   100–106

Queens   107

Staten Island   108–111

The Bronx, Brooklyn, Queens and Staten Island, sometimes dismissively called the "Outer Boroughs," have become more than dormitory accommodation for those who live and work in Manhattan.

As Manhattan real estate prices push out the young, the newly arrived and the artistic, new areas such as Astoria in Queens and DUMBO (Down Under Manhattan Bridge Overpass) in Brooklyn are growing vibrant. In addition, each of the boroughs has its own sense of identity, history and cultural worth and each, in its own way, has something special to offer the curious traveler. Certainly a visit to one or a number of them will provide a fuller picture of the real New York City.

The Bronx

Spanning rundown areas such as the South Bronx, and comfortable residential areas such as Riverdale, the Bronx tends to be neglected by visitors and New Yorkers alike. Nonetheless, with the Bronx Zoo and Yankee Stadium, the borough holds two of the city's major attractions as well as several minor ones. Two important gardens are in the Bronx: the New York Botanical Gardens (Bronx River Parkway and Fordham Road), with the largest conservatory in the U.S., and Wave Hill Gardens (West 249th Street and Independence Avenue), with stately beeches and views of the Hudson. Historical sites include the one-time home of author Edgar Allen Poe (East Kingsbridge Road) and the elegant 18th-century Van Cortlandt Mansion (Broadway at West 246th Street), built for a family prominent in politics and farming, now a showplace of English, Dutch and Colonial period furnishings.

BRONX ZOO

The largest city zoo in the U.S., the Bronx Zoo holds spacious replicated habitats inhabited by antelopes, rhinos, elephants, snow leopards, monkeys, gorillas, and many more creatures from around the world. Among the special attractions is the 6.5-acre (2.6ha) Gorilla Forest, with two troops of lowland gorillas.

www.bronxzoo.com

✚ 125 A6 ✉ Bronx River Parkway, Fordham Road ☎ 718/367 1010 🕐 Apr–Oct Mon–Fri 10–5, Sat–Sun 10–5.30; Nov–Mar daily 10–4.30 ♿ Moderate 🚇 Pelham Parkway

YANKEE STADIUM

Home of the New York Yankees baseball team since its 1923 completion, Yankee Stadium has seen tens of thousands of spectators thrilling to "the winningest team in baseball." Babe Ruth and Joe di Maggio played here, and Pope Paul conducted Mass at the stadium in 1965. It's often filled to its capacity of 57,000. Monument Park, beyond the outfield fence, is filled with memorials to Yankee greats. Construction of a new stadium next door is underway, expected to open for the 2009 season.

www.yankees.com

✚ 125 A5 ✉ Junction of 161st Street and River Avenue ☎ 718/293 4300
🕐 Baseball season Apr–Oct ✋ Variously priced match tickets
🚇 161st Street–Yankee Stadium

Brooklyn

Physically, only the East River divides Brooklyn from Manhattan but this borough retains a distinct identity, in part a legacy of its origins as a self-governing city separate from Manhattan. In a mood of regional unity that followed the opening of the Brooklyn Bridge, the people of Brooklyn voted by a narrow margin to give up their autonomy in 1898.

BRIGHTON BEACH

The decline of residential Brighton Beach more or less matched that of nearby Coney Island until the 1980s, when a Russian emigre community started building here. Now nicknamed Little Odessa, the area is filled with Cyrillic signs advertising caviar and vodka and scores of lively Russian restaurants.

✚ 125 E5 🚇 Brighton Beach

BROOKLYN MUSEUM OF ART

Among New York museums, the Brooklyn Museum of Art is second in size only to Manhattan's Metropolitan Museum of Art. Its exuberant *beaux arts* building was created by the revered New York firm of McKim, Mead and White between 1897 and the 1920s and only partially completed.

The Brooklyn Museum can easily consume several hours, if not a full day. The Egyptian collections are outstanding and include more than 500 items of stunningly decorated sarcophagi,

sculpture, and wall reliefs. Mosaics, ceramics and bronzes feature among the substantial horde of artifacts from ancient Greece and Rome, and 12 monumental reliefs from 9th-century BC Abyssinia form the core of the Middle East displays.

From more recent periods, a fine collection of paintings and period rooms highlight changing American tastes from Colonial times onward. Among the canvases are one of Gilbert Stuart's iconographic portraits of George Washington, painted in the 1790s. Impressive works from the Hudson River School artists culminate in Albert Bierdstadt's enormous evocation of nature in *Storm in the Rockies*. Its collection of American watercolors includes important works by John Singer Sargent, Winslow Homer and many 20th-century practitioners. The museum also mounts changing exhibits showcasing new and emerging artists.

www.brooklynmuseum.org

✠ 125 D5 ✉ 2000 Eastern Parkway at Prospect Park ☎ 718/638 5000
🕔 Wed–Fri 10–5, Sat and Sun 11–6; first Sat of month 11–11
♿ Inexpensive 🚇 Eastern Parkway

BROOKLYN BOTANIC GARDEN

Occupying a one-time waste dump, the Brooklyn Botanic Garden fills 52 acres (21ha) with 12,000 plant species. Passing magnolias and cherry trees, the footpaths weave through lushly landscaped surrounds linking the various sections. Perennial favorites are the Rose Garden, Herb Garden, and the exquisite 1914 Japanese Garden complete with pond, stone lanterns, and viewing pavilion.

Inside the three-part Steinhart Conservatory are plants from the world's deserts, rainforests, and warm temperate regions, while fans of bonsai will find much to admire in the C. V. Starr Bonsai Museum.

www.bbg.org

✚ 125 D5 ✉ 1000 Washington Avenue ☎ 718/623 7200

🕐 Apr–Sep Tue–Fri 8–6, Sat–Sun 10–6; Oct–Mar Tue–Fri 8–4.30, Sat–Sun 10–4.30

✋ Inexpensive (free Tue Oct–Mar) Ⓔ Eastern Parkway

BROOKLYN HISTORICAL SOCIETY

This elegant and spacious red-brick, Queen Anne-style building was purpose-built in 1881 to house the collection of the Society, founded in 1863, when Brooklyn was the commercial and cultural center of Long Island.

Exhibits focus on Brooklyn cultural themes such as the changing ethnic makeup of the city, the rise and fall of the naval dockyards, the opening of the Brooklyn Bridge, the creation of Coney Island, or the 1955 World Series-winning Brooklyn Dodgers.

www.brooklynhistory.org

➕ 123 E7 ✉ 128 Pierrepont Street
☎ 718/222 4111 🕐 Wed–Sun noon–5, Fri until 8 ♿ Inexpensive
🚇 Borough Hall or Court Street

CONEY ISLAND

Up until the 1940s, Coney Island not only promised New Yorkers a day by the sea for the price of a subway ride, but provided the additional allure of state-of-the-art fairground rides and assorted lowbrow theatrical events, from peepshows to freakshows. Up to a million people a day flocked here to be seduced by the roller-coasters and rifle ranges, or simply to stroll the coastal Boardwalk munching a hotdog from the celebrated Nathan's Famous.

After decades of neglect, Coney Island has been recognized as a living piece of Americana. Diverse exhibits from its glory days are displayed at the Coney Island Museum, which also organizes local walking tours. Nearby, the towering Cyclone roller-coaster continues to provide gravity-defying rides and forms part of the thrills and spills offered at the Astroland Amusement Park. More sedate ways to pass the time include the New York Aquarium, featuring performing dolphins and sea lions and a re-created Pacific coastal habitat complete with walruses, seals, penguins and sea otters.

✚ 125 E5 ✉ Surf Avenue between W 37th Street and Ocean Parkway ☎ 718/372 5158 (museum) Ⓠ Stillwell Avenue–Coney Island 🖐 Museum moderate, Astroland expensive

NEW YORK TRANSIT MUSEUM
Housed in a former subway station, the New York Transit Museum shows off the finely crafted art deco air vents and ceramic station nameplates indicative of the care that went into creating what became the world's second-largest mass transit system. Arranged alongside a platform, walk-through restored subway cars from 1904 to 1964 demonstrate stylistic changes and technological innovations. A simulated intersection is the scene for an interactive display of buses.
www.mta.info/museum
✚ 124 E4 ✉ Boerum Place and Schermerhorn Street
☎ 718/694 1600 ⏰ Mon–Fri 10–4, Sat–Sun noon–5
🖐 Inexpensive Ⓠ Boerum Place–Schemerhorn Street

PLYMOUTH CHURCH OF THE PILGRIMS

From its founding in 1850, a stop of the "Underground Railroad" that helped runaway slaves escape to Canada, the Plymouth Church of the Pilgrims became the best-known public meeting place in Brooklyn. The church was noted above all for the sermons of Henry Ward Beecher, resident clergyman for some 40 years until his death in 1887 and a popular speaker who promoted the abolition of slavery and women's suffrage, while his writings controversially supported Darwin's theory of evolution.

He's remembered by a statue that stands in the adjoining garden. Some of the windows in the church were designed by Louis Comfort Tiffany. The church is now of the Congregational denomination.

www.plymouthchurch.org

✚ 123 D7 ✉ Hicks and Orange streets ☎ 718/624 4743 🕐 By appointment ✋ Free 🚇 Clark Street

PROSPECT PARK

Manhattan's Central Park may be better known, but many Brooklynites regard it simply as a trial run for Prospect Park, laid out by the same design team of Frederick Law Olsted and Calvert Vaux and completed in the late 1880s. The 526-acre (213ha) park encompasses lawns, meadows, streams and ponds, and provides the community with a bucolic space for jogging, strolling, picnicking, plus many special events throughout the year. In 1892, the park's main entrance at Grand Army Plaza gained a Memorial Arch, a triumphal marker to the fallen of the Civil War. The Prospect Park Zoo is on the Flatbush Avenue side. A free trolley operates at weekends.

🕂 125 D5 ✉ Prospect Park West, Flatbush, Parkside and Ocean avenues ☎ 718/965 8999 (events) 🕐 Visit during daylight hours ✋ Free 🚇 Grand Army Plaza

Queens

With 2 million people spread across 112sq miles (290sq km), Queens is in part all-American suburbia, but also holds an ethnic mix of long-established Italians and Greeks alongside more recently arrived Koreans, Indians, Chinese and Japanese.

The single area best representing Queens past and present is Flushing, which holds a large Asian population yet retains the Friends Meeting House (137–16 Northern Boulevard) and the nearby Bowne House (32–01 Bowne Street) that both date from the 17th century. In 1939, New York demonstrated its recovery from the Depression with a World's Fair in Flushing Meadows-Corona Park (immediately east of Flushing), its success prompting a second fair in 1964. Among the surviving items are Philip Johnson's New York State Pavilion Building and the 140ft (43m) high Unisphere, depicting the earth and her satellites. Nearby are the USTA National Tennis Center, home of the U.S. Open, and Shea Stadium, home of baseball's Mets.

Across the East River from the Upper East Side, Astoria is one of the world's largest Greek communities and claims countless Greek bakeries, cafés and restaurants. In the days before the industry shifted to Hollywood, the nascent U.S. film industry was based in New York, and in 1919 the company that evolved into Paramount Pictures opened a studio in Astoria. The American Museum of the Moving Image now stands on the studio's site (junction of 35th Avenue and 36th Street). The museum records the era with costumes, props, film-making equipment, and vintage movie posters, and features many more general exhibits on film and television themes.

Staten Island

Totally unlike any other part of New York City, Staten Island is dominated by hills, trees and greenery. Its slow pace and pastoral appearance could be reasons enough to visit, but it also holds interesting historical sites and an excellent collection of Tibetan religious art, and sees regular open-air events throughout the summer.

ALICE AUSTEN HOUSE

Given a camera by her uncle in 1876, Alice Austen went on to take around 8,000 photographs that provide a remarkable documentary of turn-of-the-century American domestic life. Despite the quality of her photos, Austen remained unknown and only shortly before her death in 1952 did her photos find wide attention, following the publication of some of them in *Life* magazine. A short film describes Austen's life and some of her possessions and photos fill this attractive bayside home (a National Historic Landmark, originally built in 1690) into which the Austen family moved in 1868.
www.aliceausten.org

124 D4 ⊠ 2 Hylan Boulevard ☎ 718/816 4506 🕓 Thu–Sun 12–5. Closed Jan and Feb 🖐 Inexpensive 🚌 S51

CONFERENCE HOUSE

The stone-built Conference House, originally known as the Billopp House and built for a retired British naval captain, dates from 1680. It earned its new name as the venue of the only attempt to broker a peace between the Americans and the English after the Declaration of Independence. Held in September 1776, the negotiations proved futile but provided a reason to turn the building, which served for a time as a rat-poison factory, into a museum with period furnishings and an intriguing display on the failed talks.
www.theconferencehouse.org

124 F1 ⊠ 7455 Hylan Boulevard ☎ 718/984 0415 🕓 Fri–Sun 1–4. Closed mid-Dec, Mar 🖐 Inexpensive 🚌 S78

GARIBALDI MEUCCI MUSEUM

Later to become one of the founders of independent, unified Italy,
Giuseppe Garibaldi lived on Staten Island for two years in the
1850s having been forced to flee his homeland. Employed as a
candle-maker, Garibaldi lived in this house that then belonged to
Italian-American inventor Antonio Meucci. Letters, personal items,
and other knick-knacks document Garibaldi's period of occupancy.
A companion exhibit describes Meucci's life and achievements,
not least his inventing of the telephone—an idea he unfortunately
failed to patent.

✠ 124 D3 ✉ 420 Tompkins Avenue ☎ 718/442 1608 🕐 Tue–Sun 1–5
✋ Free 🚌 S78

HISTORIC RICHMOND TOWN

The fruits of 50 years of gathering and restoring 28 17th- to 19th-century buildings on a 100-acre (40ha) site, Richmondtown Village provides a telling peek into bygone days. Period-attired local history enthusiasts lead visitors around the buildings, often furnished with their original occupants' possessions, describing the trials and tribulations of Staten Island life in times past. During summer, the craft workshops are staffed by blacksmiths, shoemakers and carpenters demonstrating the old skills.

The oldest of the many noteworthy buildings is the 1695 Voorlezer's House, a church, school, and home for the lay minister of the Dutch Reform Church. The far grander Greek Revival Third County Courthouse dates from 1837 and functions as a visitor center. Across Center Street, the Historical Museum provides an absorbing overview of the island's changing fortunes and the industries, from brewing to oyster harvesting, that have underpinned its often fragile economy.

www.historicrichmondtown.org

🏠 124 E2 ✉ 441 Clarke Avenue
☎ 718/351 1611 🕐 Jul–Aug Wed–Sat
10–5, Sun 1–5; call for hours for rest of year
✋ Inexpensive 🚌 S74

JACQUES MARCHAIS MUSEUM OF TIBETAN ART

A Wheel of Life, incense burners, ritual objects, and other items from the world's Buddhist cultures (all accompanied by informative explanatory text) are among the collection of curiosities gathered in this stone cottage designed to resemble part of a Tibetan mountain temple. The collection started when Edna Coblentz discovered 12 Tibetan figurines in the family attic, brought home by her seaman grandfather. In the 1930s and 1940s, as a Manhattan gallery owner (married name Jacqueline Klauber), she collected Tibetan art, eventually adopting the professional name of Jacques Marchais.

www.tibetanmuseum.com

✚ 124 E3 ✉ 338 Lighthouse Avenue ☎ 718/987 3500 ⏱ Wed–Sun 1–5 🖐 Inexpensive 🚌 S74

SNUG HARBOR CULTURAL CENTER

While its tree-lined lanes would be enjoyable to stroll in any circumstances, the 83 acres (33ha) of this restored sailor's community are also dotted with preserved 19th-century Greek Revival buildings. The Newhouse Center for Contemporty Art displays works by living American artists in changing exhibitions; and the Veteran's Memorial Hall is a venue of concerts and recitals. In summer, the South Meadow stages outdoor concerts while the attractive Sculpture Park is filled with

interesting works. The Botanic Garden and a small Children's Museum provide more reason to linger in an area originally known as Sailor's Snug Harbor, a hospital and rest home created to provide refuge for "decrepit and worn-out sailors."

www.snug-harbor.org

✚ 124 D3 ✉ 1000 Richmond Terrace ☎ 718/448 2500 ⏱ Dawn–dusk 🖐 Free (grounds) 🚌 S40

Index

Abyssinian Baptist
    Church 68
air travel 12–13
Alice Austen House 108
American Museum of the
    Moving Image 107
American Museum of
    Natural History 58
American Numismatic
    Society 84
Apollo Theater 68
Asia Society 58–59
Astoria 98, 107
Astroland Amusement
    Park 104

banks 17
Battery Park 84
Bowne House 107
Brighton Beach 100
Broadway 45
Bronx 99–100
Bronx Zoo 99
Brooklyn 100–106
Brooklyn Botanic Garden
    102
Brooklyn Bridge 84–85
Brooklyn Museum of Art
    101
Brooklyn Historical
    Society 103
buses 13, 14

car rental 15
Carnegie Hall 46
Castle Clinton National
    Monument 84
Cathedral Church of St.
    John the Divine 60
Central Park 22–23
Chelsea 74
Chelsea Hotel 74
Chinatown 89
Chrysler Building 24–25
City Hall 86
climate 8
the Cloisters 60
clothing sizes 19
Columbia University
    62–63
Coney Island 103–104
Coney Island Museum
    104
Conference House 108
consulates 16

Cooper-Hewitt National
    Design Museum 62
credit cards 18
currency 18
C. V. Starr Bonsai
    Museum 102

Daily News Building 47
the Dairy 22
Dakota Building 23, 57, 64
dental insurance 9
discounts 15
drink driving 15
drinking water 19
driving 8, 15
DUMBO (Down Under
    Manhattan Bridge
    Overpass) 98

East Harlem 65
East Village 75
El Museo del Barrio 65
electricity 18
Ellis Island Immigration
    Museum 86–87
embassies 16
emergency telephone
    numbers 16
Empire State Building
    26–27
excursions 98–111

Federal Hall National
    Monument 87
ferries 14
festivals and events 10–11
Financial District 88
Flatiron Building 76
Flushing 107
Forbes Galleries 76–77
Fraunces Tavern 88
Frick Collection 66
Friends Meeting House
    107
fuel 15

Garibaldi Meucci
    Museum 109
George Gustav Heye
    Center 91
Grace Church 77
Gracie Mansion 67
Gramercy Park 79
Grand Central Terminal
    28–29

Grant's Tomb 66
Greenwich Village 30–31
Guggenheim Museum
    32–33

Harlem 68
Hayden Planetarium 58
health 9
Historic Richmond Town
    110
Historical Museum 110

insurance 8, 9
Intrepid Sea-Air-Space
    Museum 47

Jacques Marchais
    Museum of Tibetan Art
    111
Jewish Museum 68
John F. Kennedy
    International Airport
    12–13

La Guardia Airport 13
La Marqueta 65
Lincoln Center for the
    Performing Arts 69
Lipstick Building 48
Little Bombay 75
Little Church Around The
    Corner 79
Little Italy 89, 92
Little Ukraine 75
Lower East Side 90
Lower East Side
    Tenement Museum 90
Lower Manhattan 83–95

Memorial Arch 31
Met Life Building 48
Metropolitan Museum of
    Art 34–35
Midtown Manhattan
    45–56
money 18
Morgan Library 80
Mulberry Street 89
Museum of Art and
    Design 49
Museum of Chinese in
    the Americas 90
Museum of the City of
    New York 70
Museum of Jewish

Heritage 90
Museum of Modern Art
  (MoMA) 36–37
Museum of Television
  and Radio 50

National Arts Club 79
national holidays 11
National Museum of the
  American Indian 91
New York Aquarium 104
New York City Fire
  Museum 91
New York City Police
  Museum 92
New York Historical
  Society 71
New York Public Library
  50
New York State Pavilion
  Building 107
New York Stock
  Exchange 88
New York Transit
  Museum 104
New York University 31,
  73
Newark International
  Airport 13
Newhouse Center for
  Contemporary Art 111
NoLIta (North of Little
  Italy) 89

Old St. Patrick's Cathedral
  92
opening hours 17
Outer Boroughs 98

passports and visas 8
Peking (historic ship) 93
personal safety 19
pharmacies 17, 18–19
Players Club 79

Plymouth Church of the
  Pilgrims 105
postal services 17–18
Prospect Park 106
public transport 14

Queens 107

Riverside Church 72
Rockefeller Center 51
Roosevelt Island 52
Roosevelt Island
  Tramway 52
Rose Center for Earth
  and Space 58

St. Mark's-in-the-Bowery
  80–81
St. Patrick's Cathedral
  53
St. Paul's Chapel 88, 95
Sculpture Park 111
Seagram Building 54
seatbelts 15
senior citizens 15
Shea Stadium 107
Sheep Meadow 23
Shrine of Elizabeth Ann
  Seton 92
Snug Harbor Cultural
  Center 111
SoHo 93
South Street Seaport
  Historic District 93
Staten Island 108–111
Statue of Liberty 38–39
Steinhart Conservatory
  102
Strawberry Fields 23
students/youths 15

taxis 14–15
telephones 16–17
Thannhauser Tower 33

Theodore Roosevelt
  Birthplace 81
Third County Courthouse
  110
ticket booths 16
time 9
Times Square 40–41
tipping 18
Top of the Rock 51
tourist offices 9, 16
trains 13, 14
travelling to New York
  12–13
TriBeCa 94
Trinity Church 88
Trump Tower 55

Ukrainian Museum 81
Union Square Park 82
Unisphere 107
United Nations
  Headquarters 56
Upper East Side 57
Upper West Side 57
Uptown 57–72
USTA National Tennis
  Center 107

Van Cortlandt Mansion 99
Veteran's Memorial Hall
  111
Voorlezer's House 110

Wall Street 83
Washington Square Park
  31
websites 9
Whitney Museum of
  American Art 72
Woolworth Building 94
World Trade Center Site
  95

Yankee Stadium 99, 100

Acknowledgements

The Automobile Association would like to thank the following photographers, companies and picture libraries for their assistance in the preparation of this book.

Abbreviations for the picture credits are as follows – (t) top; (b) bottom; (c) centre; (l) left; (r) right; (AA) AA World Travel Library.

4l Grand Central terminal, AA/S McBride; **4c** Central Park, AA/S McBride; **4r** Gramercy Park, AA/C Sawyer; **5l** Brooklyn Botanical Garden, AA/P Kenward; **5c** View from the Empire State Building, AA/R Elliot; **5r** American Museum of Natural History, AA/R Elliot; **6/7** Grand Central terminal, AA/S McBride; **10** Polish Day Parade, AA/C Sawyer; **12** JFK International Airport, AA/P Kenward; **13** Coach, AA/C Sawyer; **14** Subway, AA/C Sawyer; **15** Taxis, AA/D Corrance; **16** Telephone, AA/C Sawyer; **17** Mail boxes, AA/C Sawyer; **19** Crowds, AA/C Sawyer; **20/1** Central Park, AA/S McBride; **22t** Central Park, AA/ P Kenward; **22b** Central Park, AA/ P Kenward; **22/3** Central Park, AA/S McBride; **23** Central Park, AA/S McBride; **24** Chrysler building, AA/C Sawyer; **24/5** Chrysler building, AA/C Sawyer; **26t** Empire States Building, AA/S McBride; **26b** View from the Empire State Building, AA/C Sawyer; **27** Empire State Building, AA/D Corrance; **28t** Grand Central, AA/S McBride; **28b** Grand Central, AA/S McBride; **28/9** Grand Central, AA/S McBride; 30 Washington Square, AA/S McBride; **31t** Greenwich Village, AA/R Elliot; **31b** Washington Square, AA/C Sawyer; **32/3** Guggenheim Museum, AA/S McBride; **33** Guggenheim Museum, AA/C Sawyer; **34** Metropolitan Museum of Art, AA/D Corrance; **34/5** Metropolitan Museum of Art, AA/R Elliot; **35** Metropolitan Museum of Art, AA/C Sawyer; **36** Museum of Modern Art, © MOMA/Timothy Hursley 2006; **36/7** Museum of Modern Art, © MOMA/Timothy Hursley 2005; **38** Statue of Liberty, AA/C Sawyer; **39** Statue of Liberty, AA/R Elliot; **40** Times Square, AA/C Sawyer; **40/1** Times Square, AA/C Sawyer; **41** Times Square, AA/C Sawyer; **42/3** Gramercy Park, AA/C Sawyer; **45** Carnegie Hall, AA/P Kenward; **46/7** Carnegie Hall, AA/C Sawyer; **47** Daily News Building, AA/C Sawyer; **48/9** Museum of Art and Design, Museum of Art and Design/Alan Klein; **50** NY Public Library, NY Public Library/Don Pollard; **51t** Rockefeller Center, AA/C Sawyer; **51b** Rockefeller Center, AA/C Sawyer; **52t** Roosevelt Island, AA/C Sawyer; **52b** Roosevelt Island cable car, AA/R Elliot; **53** St Patrick's Cathedral, AA/D Corrance; **54t** St Patrick's Cathedral, AA/C Sawyer; **54b** Seagram Building, AA/C Sawyer; **55** Trump Tower, AA/R Elliot; **56** United Nations, AA/C Sawyer; **58/9** American Museum of Natural History, AA/E Rooney, **60** Cloisters, AA/C Sawyer; **61** Cathedral Church of John the Divine, AA/C Sawyer; **62** Cooper Hewitt Museum, AA/C Sawyer; **62/3** Library at Columbia University, AA/R Elliot; **64/5** Dakota Building, AA/C Sawyer; **66** Frick Collection, AA/R Elliot; **67** Gracie Mansion, AA/C Sawyer; **68/9** East Harlem, AA/C Sawyer; **69** Lincoln Center, AA/C Sawyer; **70** Museum of the City of NY, AA/R Elliot; **70/1** Metropolitan Museum of Art, AA/C Sawyer; **72** Whitney Museum of American Art, AA/P Kenward; **73** Chelsea District, AA/C Sawyer; **74/5** Chelsea Hotel, AA/C Sawyer; **76** Flatiron Building, AA/D Corrance; **77l** Grace Church, AA/N Lancaster; **77r** Grace church, AA/C Sawyer; **78** Gramercy Park, AA/C Sawyer; **80t** Pierpont Morgan Library, AA/R Elliot; **80b** Pierpont Morgan Library, AA/C Sawyer; **82** Union Square, AA, **84** Battery Park, AA/C Sawyer; **85** Chinatown, AA/C Sawyer; **86/7** Federal Hall National Monument, AA/P Kenward; **88** Stock Exchange, AA/C Sawyer; **89t** Little Italy, AA/R Elliot; **89b** Little Italy, AA/C Sawyer; **91** New York City Fire Museum, AA/R Elliot; **93** South Street Seaport, AA/S McBride; **94** The Woolworth Building, AA/R Elliot; **95** Ground Zero, AA/C Sawyer; **96/7** Brooklyn Botanical Garden, AA/P Kenward; **99** Bronx Zoo, AA/R Elliot; **100** Brooklyn, AA/R Elliot; **101t** Brighton Beach, AA/R Elliot; **101b** Brooklyn Museum of Art, AA/C Sawyer; **102/3** Brooklyn Botanic Gardens, AA/C Sawyer; **104/5** Plymouth Church of the Pilgrims, AA/C Sawyer; **106/7** Prospect Park, AA/C Sawyer; **108/9** Staten Island/Conference House, AA/C Sawyer; **110/1** Staten Island/Richmondtown Historic Restoration, AA/C Sawyer; **111** Staten Island/Snug Harbor Cultural Center, AA/C Sawyer; **127** Ice skating at the Rockefeller Centre AA/C Sawyer; **128** Times Square AA/C Sawyer.

Every effort has been made to trace the copyright holders, and we apologise in advance for any accidental errors. We would be happy to apply the corrections in the following edition of this publication.

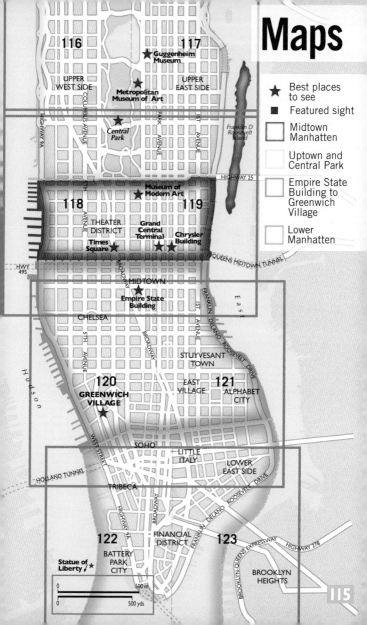

Maps

★	Best places to see
■	Featured sight
☐	Midtown Manhatten
☐	Uptown and Central Park
☐	Empire State Building to Greenwich Village
☐	Lower Manhattan

116

117

UPPER WEST SIDE

UPPER EAST SIDE

★ Guggenheim Museum

★ Metropolitan Museum of Art

★ Central Park

Franklin D Roosevelt Island

HIGHWAY 25

★ Museum of Modern Art

118

119

THEATER DISTRICT

Grand Central Terminal

★ Chrysler Building

Times Square ★

★ ★

Queens Midtown Tunnel

MIDTOWN

★ Empire State Building

CHELSEA

STUYVESANT TOWN

120

GREENWICH VILLAGE

EAST VILLAGE

121

ALPHABET CITY

★

SOHO

LITTLE ITALY

LOWER EAST SIDE

TRIBECA

122

FINANCIAL DISTRICT

123

BATTERY PARK CITY

Statue of Liberty ★

BROOKLYN HEIGHTS

HIGHWAY 278

0	500 m
0	500 yds

COLUMBUS AVENUE

PARK AVENUE

1ST AVENUE

5TH AVENUE

BROADWAY

HIGHWAY 9A

FRANKLIN DELANO ROOSEVELT DRIVE

East River

Hudson

WEST STREET

HOLLAND TUNNEL

HWY 495

BROOKLYN QUEENS EXPRESSWAY

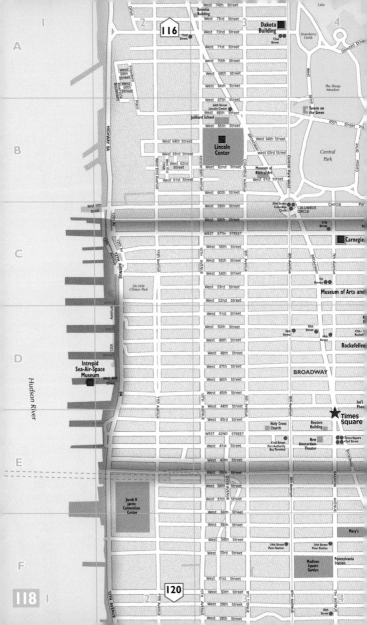

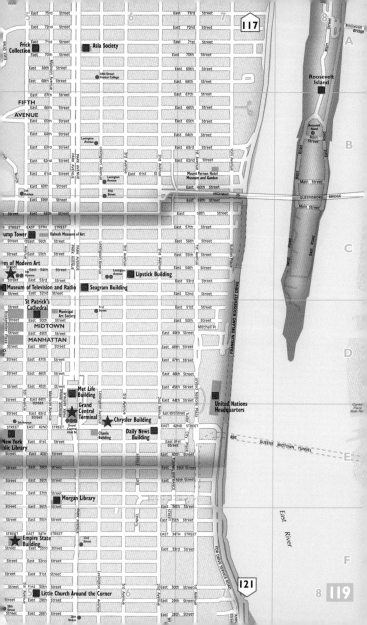

Roosevelt
Bridge

East 75th Street

East 75th Street

East 72nd Street

East 72nd Street

Roosevelt
Island

Frick
Collection

Asia Society

East 71st Street

East 71st Street

East 70th Street

East 70th Street

East 69th Street

East 69th Street

68th Street
Hunter College

East 68th Street

East 68th Street

FIFTH
AVENUE

East 67th Street

East 67th Street

East 66th Street

East 66th Street

East 65th Street

East 65th Street

East 64th Street

East 64th Street

Lexington
Avenue

East 63rd Street

East 63rd Street

59th
Street

Mount Vernon Hotel
Museum and Garden

East 62nd Street

East 61st Street

East 61st Street

East 60th Street Highway

East 60th Street

East 59th Street

East 59th Street

QUEENSBORO BRIDGE

Main Street

Main Street

58th Street

STREET EAST 57TH STREET

East 57th Street

ump Tower

Dahesh Museum of Art

Street East 56th Street

East 56th Street

m of Modern Art

East 55th Street

East 55th Street

East 54th Street

East 54th Street

Lexington
Avenue

Lipstick Building

East 53rd Street

East 53rd Street

Museum of Television and Radio

Seagram Building

East 52nd Street

East 52nd Street

St Patrick's
Cathedral

Municipal
Art Society

51st
Street

East 51st Street

East 51st Street

MIDTOWN

East 50th
Street

East 50th Street

East 50th Street

MANHATTAN

East 49th Street

East 49th Street

Mitchell Pl

East 48th Street

East 48th Street

Street East 47th Street

East 47th Street

East 47th Street

Street East 46th Street

East 46th Street

East 46th Street

Street East 45th Street

East 45th Street

East 45th Street

Met Life
Building

East 44th
Street

East 44th Street

Grand
Central
Terminal

United Nations
Headquarters

East 43rd
Street

Chrysler Building

EAST 43rd Street

Grand
Central
Club St.

EAST 42ND Street

East 42nd Street

New York
blic Library

East 41st Street

Chanin
Building

Daily News
Building

East 41st Street

East 41st
Street

QUEENS MIDTOWN TUNNEL

Street East 40th Street

East 40th Street

49s

Street East 39th Street

East 39th Street

East 39th Street

Street East 38th Street

East 38th Street

Morgan Library

East 37th Street

East 36th Street

East 36th Street

East 35th Street

East 35th Street

East River

Empire State
Building

East 34th Street

EAST 34th STREET

33rd
Street

East 33rd Street

East 32nd Street

East 32nd Street

East 31st Street

East 31st Street

East 30th Street

East 30th Streets

Little Church Around the Corner

East 29th Street

East 29th Street

28th
Street

East 28th Street

A
- New York City Fire Museum
- SOHO
- Haughwout Building
- Tony Shafrazi Gallery

HOLLAND TUNNEL

B
- LOWER MANHATTAN
- TRIBECA
- Washington Market Park

C
- Warren Street
- Park Place West
- Murray Street
- Barclay Street
- BATTERY PARK CITY
- CHAMBERS
- Reade St
- Chambers Street
- Warren Street
- Murray Street
- BARCLAY Place
- Vesey Street
- VESEY STREET
- City Hall Park
- City Hall
- Woolworth Building
- Church of St Peter
- St Paul's Chapel
- Fulton St
- Fulton Street

D
- World Trade Center Site
- Liberty Street
- Cortlandt Street
- Cedar Street
- Albany Street
- Rector Place
- Hudson River
- Trinity Church
- New York Stock Exchange
- Wall Street
- Exchange Place
- American Numismatic Society
- Federal Hall National Monument
- Museum of American Financial History

E
- West Thames Street
- 2nd Place
- Museum of Jewish Heritage
- Robert F Wagner Jr Park
- National Museum of the American Indian
- Battery Park
- Castle Clinton
- Admiral George Dewey Promenade
- Fraunces Tavern Museum
- Shrine of St Elizabeth Ann Seton
- BROOKLYN BATTERY

F
- Ellis Island Immigration Museum, Statue of Liberty ★

I   2   3   4

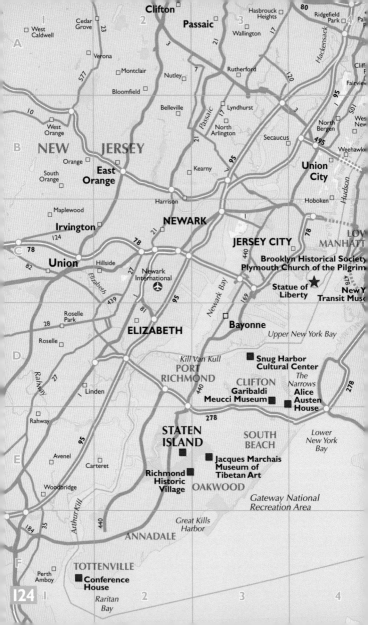

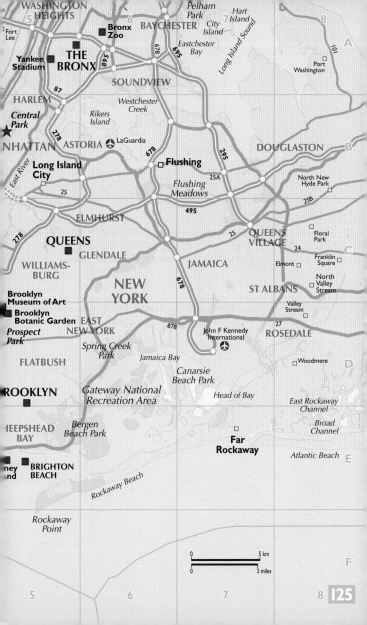

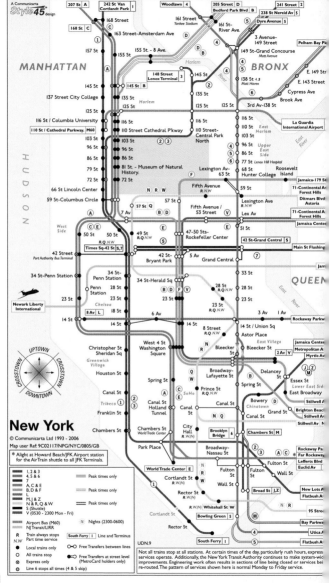

New York

© Communicarta Ltd 1993 - 2006

Map user Ref: 9C02117/NPG/NYC/0805/GB

* Alight at Howard Beach/JFK Airport station for the AirTrain shuttle to all JFK Terminals.

Not all trains stop at all stations. At certain times of the day, particularly rush hours, express services operate. Additionally, the New York Transit Authority continues to make system-wide improvements, making work often results in sections of lines being closed or services being re-routed. The pattern of services shown here is normal Monday to Friday service.

UDN.9